ARE YOU NOW, OR HAVE YOU EVER BEEN?

Praise for Amanda Cockrell's Previous Novels

For *Coyote Weather:*

"A wonderful historical novel, filled with love, doubt, courage, defiance, war and peace, a desire to belong. The characters feel at once familiar and new, ordinary and complex, and so marvelously alive. A treasure of a book."
— Kristina Gorcheva-Newberry, author of *The Orchard*

"The Vietnam War rages through Amanda Cockrell's masterful novel *Coyote Weather,* a story about young love in an impossible, chaotic, fear-driven time. A poignant, compassionate, and suspenseful read, I couldn't put it down."
— Elizabeth Poliner, author of *As Close to Us as Breathing*

"I thought I'd written the best book on the Sixties until a friend sent me this . . . I can't recommend this book more highly."
— Peter Coyote, actor and author of *Sleeping Where I Fall*

For *The Horse Catchers* and *The Deer Dancers*:

"The most satisfying stories about prehistoric peoples that I have ever read." – Ursula LeGuin, author of *Always Coming Home* and *The Left Hand of Darkness*

And for *What We Keep Is Not Always What Will Stay:*

"I loved this story with its deft use of magical realism, its wonderfully quirky yet believable characters, and its honest portrayal of relationships, good and bad."
— Han Nolan, author of *Dancing On The Edge*

ARE YOU NOW, OR HAVE YOU EVER BEEN?

A Novel of the Hollywood Blacklist

Amanda Cockrell

NORTHAMPTON HOUSE PRESS

Jacket art and cover design by Naia Poyer.
ISBN 978-1-950668-36-6 (print edition)
ISBN 978-1-950668-35-9 (ebook edition)
Library of Congress Control Number: 2025906285
Published by Northampton House Press, www.northampton-house.com. Franktown Virginia USA.
Printed in the United States of America
10 9 8 7 6 5 4 3 2

For my parents, who lived through it.

And for Tony, through thick and thin.

"There are some stories that must be told, and told again, in an everlasting rehearsal of love, and betrayal, and regret."

— Jeanne Larsen, *Silk Road*

1953

Liza Jane can barely see Mike's face; he's surrounded by his inquisitors. An array of microphones, one for each news outlet, crowds the table. The pop of flashbulbs from the print press and the floods illuminating him for newsreel and television cameras make him a study in light and shadow. Mike is trapped, bombarded with unanswerable questions, treed by the baying hounds of the Committee on Un-American Activities.

"Mr. Rosen, are you now or have you ever been a member of the Communist Party?"

"I am not a communist."

"Answer the question. If you are not, you have nothing to fear."

"That hasn't been my experience so far," Mike says.

"Just answer the question, Mr. Rosen."

"I have something I want to say. I have a statement I want to read."

"We are not interested in propaganda, Mr. Rosen. Do you refuse to cooperate with this committee?"

"I refuse to discuss my political beliefs, or those of my friends, which is what you're really after."

"And who are your friends?"

Mike is silent. Liza Jane cringes.

"What did you do during the war, Mr. Rosen?"

"I wrote films for the Office of War Information."

"Films filled with Soviet propaganda."

"They were our allies at the time."

"And why were you chosen for that job, Mr. Rosen?"

"Are you a native-born American, Mr. Rosen?"

"Is that your real name?"

"What country are your parents from?"

"Are you a member of the Communist Party?"

"Are you a member of the American Civil Liberties Union?"

"Are you a member of the Writers Guild?"

"Are you now or have you ever been a member of the Communist Party?"

"Have you ever demonstrated against the government?

"You are not on trial here, Mr. Rosen, this is merely a fact-finding board."

"You have been charged with being a communist, Mr. Rosen, aren't you going to answer that charge?"

Mike refuses to testify. Liza Jane knows he has a statement prepared saying his politics are his own business and no one has the right to deny someone his livelihood without more to go on than rumor and innuendo. Liza Jane also knows they aren't going to let him read it. Knows he's sunk. Knows that even if he named people he probably can't even remember now, he'd still be sunk. It was fifteen years ago. He went to three meetings, maybe four. It didn't seem important to count them then.

He sits staring at the microphones, staring at the row of hostile, gelid eyes, eyes with maybe a little panic at the back of them—What if someone names you? Or you? What if someone remembers what you said about the government on your college debate team after your dad lost his job? Eyes full of righteous indignation—*I am the Arm of the Lord*—and eyes too scared to blink.

1988

Liza Jane sets the memory aside. She accomplished nothing then but to witness Mike's ceremony of degradation, the deliberate process that would destroy his career. She is eighty now. She has gone a decade beyond her allotted threescore and ten and survived even the Committee and the blacklist, although she knows she was lucky; she always did know when to leave a party before things went bad.

She still looks pretty good, even if a lot of that is the face lifts, but lately she's felt that some new upheaval is coming, something just on the periphery of her vision, not as awful but fully as unrelenting. Liza Jane isn't ready to go, but she feels the tug as if someone is trying to hand her a ticket and the crowd is pushing her down the platform.

So she's making her will again, because this time she has figured out what she wants to say. There's her niece Liddy off in Virginia with little Zach. Liddy will get most of it. And Bernice downstairs, who lost her job at the same time as Mike. And now Ronald Reagan is president of the country, for God's sake. Reagan was president of the Screen Actors Guild then and it turned on its own people and Liza Jane won't forgive him for that, ever. Mike Rosen has a script he wants to show her and she's pretty sure she knows what it's about and she hopes it shames them all.

Liza Jane crosses that out. If she starts talking about that, she'll just start raving, and, besides, it might invalidate the will. She crumples up the paper, and starts a new sheet. But she has to take care of Bernice, she's always felt she had to take care of Bernice. Liza Jane puts in enough money for Bernice to be comfortable and then enough to make bail on if she gets arrested with

Greenpeace again.

And there is Jeff, who she can see from her upper window, down in the garden weeding the asparagus bed. Or talking to it. Jeff claims that the garden does better if you talk to it, and last year he decided to prove it to her by stretching a rope down the middle and conversing with one half. It seemed to be true. Liza Jane has never heard of anyone else talking to asparagus; music, yes, but not conversation. But maybe Jeff is the only one that asparagus can hear.

They put the bed in just this spring, and asparagus is a long-term commitment at Liza Jane's age. It will be three years before there's anything edible; she wonders if she will ever have a bite of it. If you want to make God laugh, tell him your plans; Mike Rosen said that to her once. From her window she has a good view past the garden to the oak grove at the far end. Up here she's eye to eye with the birds; she can hear them chattering in the live oaks, see a topmost branch bend suddenly with a squirrel's weight. There used to be a tree house in one of the oaks, Liddy's tree house, when she was still Little Liza. It was so sensible of her to have changed her name; no grown woman should be Little anything.

And then there's the kid, not the hypothetical kid she thought once she would have, or even the other one she didn't have, but the real kid who's probably going to upset everyone. She adds another line to the will.

There is still the sense of something slipping up, some journey to be taken. Liza Jane has things she wants to say before she goes. She finishes the will, signs it, and calls the local bank, which has enough of her money in its accounts to be willing to send a notary to the house. After the notary leaves, she goes down to the garden to see how the asparagus is coming along, to ask it to wait for her. But the light is suddenly bright outside, brighter than usual.

I
Prodigal Daughter

1988

HOLLYWOOD. Elizabeth Sidney, whose career spanned more than sixty years, from the silent films of the twenties, through the Golden Age of Hollywood, to a third Oscar at 78 for her performance in *The Raindrop*, died yesterday of natural causes in the palatial home she maintained for 30 years in the small California community of Ayala, north of Los Angeles. She was 80.

Why didn't the house look different? It loomed above Liddy in the dusk, its preposterous bell tower tangled in the live oaks' branches. She had expected the Spanish revival stucco walls and shadowy layers of tile roof to be somehow changed by their owner's absence. The air was full of the fragrance of eucalyptus and the dusty smell of Ayala in summer. A dry breeze carried the scent of oranges from the orchards in the East End. The two huge pomegranates that grew on the west side of the house rustled in the night breeze, scarlet globes ripening in the shadows of their leaves. Seeds of the Underworld—eat them and you'll never leave. Coming home had always been a push-me-pull-you experience, like putting on an old skin, shed determinedly several years ago, too tight in places, achingly familiar in others.

The airport limousine driver wrestled a big suitcase and a smaller one from the trunk and hauled them up the steep front steps to deposit them on Liza Jane's doorstep. Liddy woke up the child sleeping in the back seat and paid the driver, adding a huge tip for having driven them from Los Angeles. He climbed in the limo and swung it around in the circular driveway with an appreciative waggle of his fingers.

There was a light on in the front hall, and one upstairs. Liddy prodded Zach up the steps while he rubbed his eyes, wobbling with sleep. She pressed the bell; a cacophony of yapping dogs answered and the door opened almost immediately.

"Liddy!" Bernice was framed in the doorway, looming and distraught. "Get back!" Her foot shot out expertly, blocking five pugs, who sniffed and peeked at Liddy over her ankle. Bernice hopped away from the door on the other foot, sweeping the pugs backward as she went. Liddy picked up her suitcase in one hand and towed Zach into the hall with the other.

Bernice took the smaller suitcase and closed the door while the pugs swirled around Liddy's feet. She took Liddy's hands in hers. "I'm so relieved you're here."

"I came as quickly as I could."

Bernice peered at her in the light of a wrought-iron chandelier. "You look wan," she said.

"You'd be wan too," Liddy said, "if you'd flown from Richmond with a six-year-old." She sat Zach down on a carved oak bench and he stared around him with sleepy curiosity. The hall was cavernous, floored with terracotta tiles and furnished with Early California antiques. A framed movie poster of Elizabeth Sidney as Queen Elizabeth hung on the wall above a brass urn of pampas grass. Opposite it, a massive staircase curved up to the second story, along a plastered wall lined with posters and signed photographs.

On the table beside the bench was an elaborate fountain pen, and an open guest book. Bernice patted them into place. "You're the first," she said. "Except of course for Harry. Theresa is coming tomorrow, with Sharon. Would you like to see her?"

"I suppose I'll have to see them all." Liddy hadn't slept in thirty-six hours, not since Bernice, and then Harry Lanier, her aunt's manager, had called her to say that Liza Jane had had a stroke and died. Half the population of Hollywood, and nearly everyone in Ayala, would probably come for the funeral. She couldn't expect Bernice to field them all. And in any case, Bernice believed in letting things flow.

"No, dear, I meant Liza Jane. She would want to say goodbye."

Liddy blinked. That sounded mad, even for Bernice. Bernice had been her aunt's companion for twenty-five years, and had not changed appreciably in that time. Her brown hair, now salt and pepper, was cut in bangs across her forehead, and pinned into a knot with hammered silver hairpins. She wore a Guatemalan peasant skirt and sandals, and a Sierra Club t-shirt over her sturdy frame. Her hands were large and covered with Navajo rings.

"Where is she?" Liddy asked.

"Here." Bernice waved her hands vaguely to indicate the back of the house. "There was trouble with the will. She left instructions, you see, and people fail to understand. So we thought it best to keep her here, until you can settle it all."

"Do you mean Liza Jane's body is still in the house?" (After two days?) "For heaven's sakes, where?" (Maybe that was why the house didn't look different.)

"On the veranda," Bernice said. "Night air is soothing to the spirit. And it's cooler there."

"Good God." Liddy looked at Zach, who was staring dreamily at the posters, a parade of faces from long before his time. "He needs to go to bed."

"Wouldn't he like—?"

"No." Liddy took Zach by the hand and pulled him gently to his feet.

"Of course, dear." Bernice picked up Liddy's suitcase and trudged up the stairs with it, the pugs at her heels. "I've put you in your old room," she said over her shoulder, "and dear Zach next door."

Liddy looked at dear Zach, who appeared to be sleepwalking, and oblivious to the conversation. The upstairs hall was long and wide, with bedrooms opening off either side. Bernice opened a door and switched on the light. The little room had an Indian rug on the floor, and a wrought-iron bed with foxes marching across the top. Zach climbed up onto the bed, where he was joined by a pug, and tried to pull the covers over himself, while Liddy tried to wrestle him out of his clothes and into pajamas. She decided to hell with brushing his teeth. They wouldn't rot before tomorrow morning. She bent down and kissed him. "You going to be all right here, kiddo?"

Zach nodded. "You can leave the dog, though," he said sleepily. He curled one arm around it.

"The poor babies haven't anyone to sleep with now," Bernice said. "My allergies won't stand it. I have to close the door."

Liza Jane had always slept with all her pugs. Four trotted out again with Liddy and Bernice, leaving one on the bed. Liddy wondered if they were all going to get one, a pug apiece, like chocolates on the pillow. Harry would hate that.

"Where is Harry?" she asked Bernice.

"He's out talking to Jeff."

"Bernice, what the hell is going on?"

Bernice sniffed. "I'll let Harry explain it. He's been on the telephone talking to lawyers all day. And eating red meat, which is bad for his balance." Downstairs, she pushed open a swinging door at the end of the hall, which led to a flagstone-floored kitchen. The kitchen was enormous, with a pair of armchairs and a reading lamp in one corner. Liza Jane had always liked company while she cooked. And a good spot to get in the hair of anyone else who was cooking. A vase with a dozen wilting red roses sat on the counter and Liddy couldn't help smiling. Roberto Vincente might be a gangster but he'd stayed sweet on Liza Jane his whole life and he sent roses on her birthday; and she always kept them until the petals fell off.

Behind the chairs, a pair of glass doors opened onto the veranda. A wrought-iron railing ran the back length of the house, interrupted by a flight of stone steps leading to the garden, the lower patio, and the grove of live oaks.

On the porch, on top of a sturdy redwood table, was a coffin.

"Here she is, dear." Bernice flipped on the porch light. The coffin was sleek, a gleaming gray like an expensive limousine.

"What was the mortuary thinking of?"

"Well, they did come out," Bernice said. "But she refused to go. You know how she hated those places."

"In the will, I presume," Liddy said. Her aunt had had a horror of mortuaries.

"Oh, yes, she was quite explicit. They were allowed to attend to her here, but if she's taken to the mortuary, it invalidates the whole will. And I'm afraid there are going to be enough difficulties as it is. Some people will not grow and stretch." Bernice lifted the lid of the coffin. "There, dear. I'll just leave you alone for a minute."

The pugs whimpered, puzzled, and Bernice shooed them into the kitchen with her.

Liddy looked down at her aunt. Liza Jane looked much as she always had, still beautiful at eighty, and determinedly still auburn haired, although in the repose of death the softly wrinkled heart-shaped face and famous soaring eyebrows had an uncharacteristic serenity. Liddy felt that she ought to say something to her. "What a trouble you've caused, darling. You'll give Harry an ulcer."

For a moment the painted lips almost seemed to smile. Harry Lanier had been Elizabeth Sidney's business manager for twenty years, and Liza Jane had considered it her function to give him an ulcer.

Liddy set the lid back down on the coffin and slumped into a chair beside it. Coming home to Ayala always made her uneasy, Liza Jane's house too full somehow, even when it was empty. Elizabeth Jane Fox had first appeared on a motion picture set at sixteen, in 1924, as Elizabeth Sidney. By 1966, the year Liddy, orphaned at eight, had come to live with her, Liza Jane had been famous for decades, a movie star of the old studio system, her house always full of people: agents and producers, down-on-their-luck actors, gurus and swamis and friends. She had taken Liddy, her namesake, under her wing in much the same fashion that she had taken all the others, only Liddy was permanent.

Liddy, too, had been Liza Jane, Little Liza Jane, until she had rebelled in junior high, trying to hack some identity for herself out of the glittering and chaotic current in which her aunt swam. While other teenagers dreamed of movie actors and romance, Liddy's idea of heaven had been a quiet tract house in a normal subdivision, a normal husband, and a normal job, if you counted writing mysteries as normal. She had got it too, even if she hadn't been able to hang onto the husband. Nick had died a year ago, just after their last visit to California. When Nick died, Liza Jane had wanted them to come back to Ayala to live, but Liddy had been reluctant to dive back into chaos.

She sat moodily, mourning and torn between sadness and aggravation at being hurled into the maelstrom again. Hordes of people would begin arriving tomorrow from Hollywood, and probably from New York, flickering in and out, flamboyant and quarrelsome, moving from camaraderie to feuds to maudlin sentimentality with the ease of long practice, each on their own private stage.

There would be a steady parade of people from Ayala as well. Ayala was a small town only in the sense of geographic size. Otherwise it had seemed to Liddy rather like living in a Fellini film, into the script of which a few hapless normal people had wandered by accident. Sixty miles from Los Angeles, it was a bedroom community for Hollywood, a colony of screenwriters and actors; a resort town whose Ayala Inn generally had a billionaire or two on the golf course; and a haven since the twenties for religious and philosophical movements whose followers had founded a number of interesting private schools. The one Liddy had attended had felt that competitive sports were injurious to spiritual balance, and had fielded an exhibition folk dance team instead. Ayala was also small enough for Liza Jane to have had a finger in nearly all of its pies.

Liddy watched the moon rising in the darkening sky, a little lopsided behind the spreading, gnarled branches, as if the oaks had a grip on it somehow.

"Hey there! It's Little Liza Jane!"

Two men were coming up the path through the live oaks. She could see the flicker of a flashlight.

"Harry, will you please not call me that. It sounds like Shirley Temple." She smiled in spite of herself, pleased to see him.

Harry Lanier was fifty, round and balding early, in an open-collared shirt and a plaid sport coat, what was left of his brown hair slicked back over his ears. He looked like a kewpie doll who had moved to Beverly Hills. "It's good to see you, honey." He came up the steps to the porch and kissed her cheek. "And thank God, too. You're the executor, you know."

"I didn't," Liddy said, startled. She looked over his shoulder at the man coming up the steps behind Harry. "Hi, Jeff."

Jeff Austin looked back at her, half solemn, his mouth

moving into an uncertain smile. "Hi."

Liddy turned back to Harry. "Harry, what the hell is she doing on the porch?"

"Ah, Christ," Harry said. "She wants to be buried here, in the goddamned back yard."

Liddy noted that everyone still seemed to be speaking of her aunt in the present tense.

"I'll let you read the will in the morning," Harry said. "I'm going to bed, kid. I'm at the end of my rope."

"Close the door," Liddy said, "or you'll have a pug."

When he had gone in, she looked back at Jeff, who was running his fingers lightly along the top of the coffin. He was wearing blue jeans and a leather jacket, and a white shirt that looked as though he had been staining furniture in it. His sandy hair was shorter, just over his collar, but otherwise he didn't appear to have changed any in the last nine years. Whenever she had been home, he hadn't been there. Deliberately, she suspected.

"You look very together," Jeff said.

"I'm not together," Liddy said. "I had to take Zach out of camp, and I called a neighbor to feed the gerbil, and I called my editor to tell her I don't know when she's going to get the revisions now, and I didn't bring any coats because I forget it gets cold here at night, and the refrigerator is going to be full of rotten food when I get home. I'm not together."

"I just meant generally." Jeff eyed her loose gray linen suit and clipped hair. "Dress for success. That's a nice brisk haircut."

"It's a nice simple haircut. I haven't got time to put rollers in it in the morning." She looked at him, half glad to see him, half wishing she could make him dematerialize.

Jeff perched himself on the top rail of the balcony. He was heavier than he had been then, she saw now, more muscular at twenty-eight than at nineteen, with some lines just beginning in his face. Jeff had been her first boyfriend at a time when she had clearly been insane because he was two years younger than she was, and at fifteen and seventeen that had worked out about as well as anyone would expect. The age gap hadn't bothered Jeff, nor apparently his parents, a banker mother who was largely nonexistent and a father who was trying to find himself in a series of human potential movements. When he graduated from high school he began to work for Liza Jane, when she needed the attic stairs fixed or a fish pond dug. Liza Jane adored him, and when Liddy moved out, Jeff moved in. He had the little caretaker's cottage at the end of the oak grove, and dealt with whatever Liza Jane wanted dealt with in exchange for a salary that kept him in food and clay and secondhand books. When Liddy came home to visit, he always managed to vanish. Until now.

"End of an era," he said. "We just put in an asparagus bed, too."

"Jeff, what is going on here?"

Jeff grinned suddenly. "Liza Jane's trick will. It's all invalid if her body leaves the premises. Harry and Arlo Sheppard almost shit when they saw that."

"Who's Arlo Sheppard?"

"He's her lawyer. He inherited her when old Gustafson died."

"And he let her draw up a will like that?"

"Hell, no. It's a holographic will, all handwritten, and she had the sucker notarized." If it struck him as macabre, this moonlit conversation across a coffin, he didn't say so.

"You think it's funny," Liddy said.

"Well, not exactly. I just don't see what's wrong with giving Liza Jane what she wanted." Jeff looked out through the trees. "It would be a nice place to be."

"I don't think it's legal to do that."

"Oh, it's not."

"What happens if the will is invalidated?"

"I guess you get everything, as the next of kin. Didn't think of that, did you?"

Liddy sat down. "No," she said shortly. "I had not."

"And a whole lot of pissed-off beneficiaries. I haven't actually read it, but Harry in his wrath was indiscreet enough to give me the high points. She was really serious about where she wanted to lie."

"She hated cemeteries. She was afraid of them." Liddy wrapped her arms around herself. "Damn, I'd forgotten how cold it gets at night. Charlottesville's always warm all night in summer. So hot you can't sleep sometimes."

Jeff took off his jacket and put it around her.

"You'll freeze," she said.

"I'm tough." Jeff pulled himself back up on the railing. "I'm sorry about your husband."

"He had a heart attack." Liddy paused and stared into the dark oaks. "He wasn't old enough for a heart attack, damn it, but he had one. A birth defect no one knew he had."

Jeff didn't look at her. He swung his feet from the railing and looked at them instead. "You doing okay?"

Liddy nodded. "There was some insurance. And I sell a book every year. I don't know if they're really any good, but they sell."

"Thrillers." Jeff said. "Dark, dashing spies and midnight chases across the Alps. I read them."

Liddy brought her attention back to the veranda and looked at him, annoyed by that accurate description. "Are you working?"

"Sure," Jeff said. "When I don't have anything to read. We put in a koi pond, though, Liza Jane and me. Those big Japanese fish, all kinds of colors. I'll show you. Did you know you can tame them? They'll come up and let you scritch their backs."

"I meant sculpture."

"I know you did. You want to see the fish now? There's a floodlight."

Liddy stood up, pushing her arms into Jeff's jacket. As the

evening was working out, going to make friends with tame fish didn't seem all that peculiar.

Jeff brushed his hand along the coffin again. "We're going to see the koi," he said.

"Will you stop that?"

"If you're going to keep her on the porch, it seems kind of normal to talk to her," Jeff said.

"I'm not keeping her on the porch. That was Bernice's idea. And people are going to talk all right. They'll be here in droves tomorrow. What do you think they're going to say?"

"Probably hold a séance."

"It's disrespectful and ridiculous." Liddy felt her eyes starting to water, and fumbled under the jacket for a handkerchief out of her suit coat pocket.

Jeff put an arm around her. "Come on. Fish are this way." He guided her down the porch steps to the brick path at the bottom.

The koi pond was at the side of the house under a pomegranate tree, fringed with irises and fed by a little waterfall that ran out of a bamboo spout. Jeff switched on a floodlight. There were half a dozen fish, nearly a foot long, red ones, yellow, and orange-and-white.

"We were going to put a bridge over it," Jeff said. "Koi-Viewing Moon Bridge. Very Japanese." He reached into the leather jacket's pocket and pulled out a handful of cat kibble. He tossed it on the water and the koi swam up toward it. "You hand feed 'em," he said. "That's how you get them tame. We've got some highfalutin' koi food, but they like this just as well."

The fish opened their mouths, scooping up the kibble, the floodlight reflecting off their glowing scales. A big fish, speckled black and white, with a big orange dot like a Japanese flag in the middle of its head, loomed up from the bottom. The house rose into the trees above them, the red tile roof shadowy and obscure, a few lighted windows glowing like the fish behind the current of the oak leaves. There was a pug at one of them, on a window seat, his round, flat face pressed against the glass.

"What about the dogs?" Liddy said. They were a complication she could get hold of.

"Bernice took them out for walkies today." Jeff was kneeling by the pool, trying to get a koi to come up to him. "They towed her down Foothill Road like a sled. It was great."

Liddy chuckled. The Arbolada was a neighborhood of narrow, oak-shaded roads winding through the base of the western foothills. There were no sidewalks, but very little traffic, and people walked their dogs and rode horses through there all the time. Still, Bernice must have stopped what traffic there was.

"Is Bernice holding up?" she asked dubiously. "She seemed just like herself, but I couldn't tell."

"I think she's worried about the will," Jeff said quietly. "If it doesn't go through, she doesn't know where she'll end up." He sat back on his heels and looked up at her. "It's all up to you, and you're an unknown quantity these days."

He stood up, still looking at her, as if he were trying to see his way through nine years. A breeze came up and whipped her skirt around her calves, and Liddy shivered.

"Troubled by ghosts, Lid?" he asked quietly.

"No." She looked away from him.

"Sorry to see me? I'd make myself scarce, but it's not in the cards."

"You live here," Liddy said. "I'm the interloper."

"Prodigal daughter," Jeff said. "No fatted calf." He cocked his head at her. "I could give you a glass of wine, though. My place. I'll show you what I've been working on."

Liddy took his jacket off and gave it back to him. "Not tonight. I haven't slept since yesterday morning."

"All right." He shrugged the jacket back on.

Liddy let herself in through the front door. Bernice and Harry seemed to have gone to bed. She checked on Zach and found him asleep, sprawled sideways across the bed. She pulled the covers up around his ears. The pug was snoring beside him.

When she climbed into her own bed, two more joined her, making fat little bumps on the covers. It was the same bed she had slept in as a child, an old rosewood four-poster that had been her mother and father's. Liza Jane had had it shipped from Ohio to give a bereft eight-year-old something to cling to. But Liddy had long ago ceased to associate it with her parents, a dim memory almost forgotten. The bed was part of Liza Jane's house, part of Ayala. Liddy turned over, remembering gloomily that she had once made love to Jeff in it, when no one happened to be around. She could see herself dimly in the mirror across the room, the brisk haircut crowning a heart-shaped face that was very like Liza Jane's, but lacked the eldritch magic with which her aunt had bewitched the camera. A pug came up and breathed at her face, wheezing hopefully. Liddy couldn't tell them apart; Liza Jane always had a herd of them. "Mama's gone," she said, giving its pop-eyed face a pat. "I'm sorry."

Now they were all coming to mourn her.

Sharon Hamilton packed her bag carefully, clothes befitting an agent who had lost her best client. The pink linen suit for interviews, the dark navy for the funeral. She smoothed them with hands she was proud of, still mercifully free of spots and dark veins, long fingers ending in a discreet French manicure. Sharon felt that it was indicative of good character somehow, that her hands still looked nice. She had earned that.

Sharon was picking up Theresa Tate in the morning. Theresa

had sounded weepy and threadbare on the telephone.

"I met her in 1926," Theresa said. "Did you know that? I've known her sixty-two years."

"You told me," Sharon said absently.

"I didn't have any trouble getting away from the set for a few days," Theresa said. Sharon thought she was trying to sound relieved, but there was a forlorn note in her voice.

"Good, good," Sharon said. "They're good about that." She made herself sound reassuring. Theresa was too old to be working. If the producers dumped her character this season, it was going to be hell getting her another job. They probably were going to dump her. The character was already in the hospital, or they wouldn't have been able to shoot around her. "Just don't stay too long," Sharon said.

"No. No, I won't. But sixty-two years. It doesn't seem that long. Do you remember when we all went out together, Liza Jane and Ben, and you and Mike, and me and somebody? And..."

"I don't remember," Sharon said.

"It was when you were still acting, and we took a picnic out Mulholland Drive—"

"I don't remember."

"I'm sorry." Theresa sniffled. "Of course you don't. When you get old, you remember such a long way back. It all comes so clear."

Sharon hung up the phone as gently as she could manage and closed the suitcase. She was only sixty, with ash blond hair and the tight, clear cheekbones and chin line that a good facelift provided. Her petite figure was still good, and so were her hands. She could still be acting, if she had wanted the grief that Theresa had. Her memory was just as good as Theresa's, too. Sharon was just more selective. Things with jagged edges she put away. The time she had been married to Mike fell into that category. Sharon couldn't think about it without being engulfed in a righteous indignation that made her lose practicality. So she put it away, the same way she stored away parts of Liza Jane. It made her competent. Made her a good agent. Sharon had learned not to burn bridges. A coat of paint, the gloss of altered memory, did very well.

Mike Rosen counted pages, making sure the copier hadn't missed any, saying the page numbers aloud while he lined them up on the coffee table in his Santa Monica apartment. Another temporary apartment, just until he decided a few things, got the nerve to buy a house. Apartments had been temporary for years, even since he'd made money again; Mike couldn't seem to lose the habit of traveling light.

He'd made three copies of the script: one for his agent, one for backup, one to take with him. There should have been one for Liza Jane, but he could pitch this without her. She'd told him he should write it, that it was time, and he had, dredged it up out of places he hadn't even known were functional anymore. He wished he could show it to her now. She had a good eye, and she'd been there.

He finished counting and sat back to look at the scripts, at the perfect rectangles of white paper, like loaded bombs. A small ghost popped out of the first script. For a moment Mike thought it was Liza Jane, but it was Sharon, made from the lights in the uncurtained window. She was just a thin thread of white, like wispy smoke, a silent, sulphurous fury.

Mike could see himself too, doubled in the dark windows, a stocky, untidy figure in blue running shorts and a white t-shirt. His gray hair, damp with sweat, framed a square face, punctuated by blue eyes behind steel-framed glasses. He jogged to the copier or the Post Office these days, trying to undo years of neglect and sausage-and-egg breakfasts. He'd made himself learn to leave his curtains open too, to remember there wasn't anyone out there watching him now, no FBI goon tailing him to the barber shop and the post office in a plain dark car. Beneath the windows a long low shelf was stuffed with books, including a string of garish paperbacks, some with his name on them, some with other names. He had kept them in a box in the closet for years, but this morning, in a perverse gesture, Mike had put them in the bookcase.

Mike put a backing on the first script, pushing his hands through Sharon's ghost, and she vanished. She'd be in Ayala, he supposed. He pinned the cover down carefully with brass prongs. It was a good script, probably the best thing he'd done. Frank Hill was half sold on it already, and if Frank starred in it, it would get noticed. Mike stacked the scripts on the table neatly, aligning the edges until they looked solid, one layer beneath the next, a single reverberating phrase.

Frank Hill slumped down in his seat as the night flight from Toronto to Los Angeles lifted off the ground. Only the bridge of his nose showed behind Ben's shoulder. Frank was six-feet-one and broad-shouldered—hard to hide, especially behind Ben Zenovich's slight frame. Ben thought that if Frank could have put a bag on his head, he would have. Nobody recognized directors and pursued them through airports, but Frank Hill was another matter. The flight attendant had nearly fainted when he got on board, and the two women across the first class aisle were nudging each other and whispering. Every so often one of them would stick her head out casually, trying to see around Ben. Ben would look at her and she would flatten back against the seat again.

The women began to argue, sotto voce. "I'm not sure it's him."

"Yes, it is. Ask him."

"He looks too old."

"Christ," Frank muttered.

"Go to sleep," Ben said. "Snore. Break their hearts."

"I'm not sleepy." Frank squirmed and cracked his knuckles. "I'm going to lose the whole character by the time we start shooting again, you know that?"

"No, you're not."

"It's not enough I've got Francie and her lawyers to deal with. Now this."

"Francie's lawyers can talk to your lawyers," Ben said. He ran a hand through his dark hair, salted now with gray. He noted with mild surprise, as always, how far back the hairline had got. You never really thought you were getting old. He looked at Frank. Frank was only forty-five, and he still had all his hair, thick and wavy brown, and the same look of mildly startled swash-buckling that had been his trademark since his first movie, but Ben thought Francie and the divorce had put a few years on Frank, too. "I'll throw Francie off the set if you want."

"I had Francie under control until you shut the picture down for this funeral. She didn't want me to go."

"You got to go," Ben said. "You, me, Mike... we all got to go." He turned the pencil-thin stream of overhead light down to darkness. The jet engines hummed outside the window, wisps of cloud passing, snared in faint moonlight. "Now go to sleep. Maybe Mike will bring that script you're so hot to read." He held it out like a cookie, cajoling a bad child to its duty.

Liddy woke to white sunlight streaming through the window. The bedroom clock said eight, but her watch said eleven, and she staggered out of bed, knowing that Zach would still be on Virginia time. He wasn't in his room. Liddy pulled on a cotton dress respectable enough to meet whoever was likely to show up, and threw the gray suit in the wicker dry-cleaning basket in the hall. Zach's suitcase looked as if he had stirred it with a spade, so she assumed he was dressed.

She found him in the kitchen, eating granola. Bernice was at the stove, frying eggs for Harry with an air of nutrition-conscious disapproval.

Zach tugged at Liddy's skirt. "Mom." He looked up at her apprehensively. "What's that thing outside?"

Oh, lord. "It's a coffin, honey."

"Is there anybody dead in it?" Zach whispered.

Liddy sat down at the kitchen table and poured granola into a bowl. "Liza Jane's in it, sweetie. Harry—"

"Eat your mush," Harry said, "and have a cup of coffee. Arlo Sheppard's coming out, and he's going to let you read the will."

Zach scooted his chair a little closer to Liddy's.

"Sharon called," Bernice said. "She and Theresa will be here for lunch."

"Isn't Theresa shooting?" Harry said.

"No, she's in a coma." Bernice put the eggs in front of Harry. "You're poisoning your body."

"Her character's in a coma," Liddy told Zach. "You remember Theresa, honey. She's Mrs. Talliaferro on Vintage Days."

"You don't let me watch that."

"I showed you her picture."

"And Ben Zenovich and Frank Hill are flying in from Toronto," Bernice said. "And Mike Rosen's coming up."

Harry chuckled. "Sharon'll love that."

"I don't care what Sharon loves," Bernice said.

"Maybe we'll get Roberto Vincente, too," Harry said, eyeing the roses on the counter. "Papers'll have a field day."

"Then it's your business to stop them," Liddy said.

"I can't work miracles. Liza Jane was a publicist's nightmare. She never made any bones about her love affairs. If her old boyfriends want to show up to see her off, we'll just have to try to turn it around. Touching devotion to famous star."

"Notorious mobster attends funeral," Liddy said. "Why don't we just call the National Enquirer?" She put her head in her hands. It was obvious that she wasn't going to be allowed to mourn in private.

"You aren't operating in the real world here, honey," Harry said. "We'll just have to take it as it comes."

"I'm operating in another damn dimension," Liddy said. "My kid's probably going to need a psychiatrist by the time we leave."

Zach pulled at her skirt again. "Do we have to go look at her?"

Liddy put an arm around him. "No, lamb. I don't think you need to."

Zach nodded, but Liddy could tell he was thinking it over. He looked worried.

"Bernice, isn't there a camp or something he could go to for a few days? This is an impossible situation to throw him into."

"I think Apple Valley has one."

Liddy looked at Zach. "Would you like to go to camp at my old school here, just for a little? You know, nature walks and things?"

"Maybe," Zach said.

"Well, we'll try it. If you hate it, you don't have to. I'll run you out there in a little while and we'll look at it."

"Couldn't Jeff take him?" Harry asked.

Liddy put her spoon in her bowl. "No, Jeff could not take him. He's never met Jeff. And I want to see what they're up to out there before I dump him in the middle of it. He may not be braced for Apple Valley. They meditate in a yurt."

The doorbell bonged in the distance, and Harry got up. "There's Arlo. You come talk to him before you worry about camp."

Liddy followed Harry to the front hall. A delivery driver stood in the doorway holding a monumental display of red roses in a basket the size of a laundry hamper.

"What did I tell you?" Harry said.

1934

Liza Jane watches a red sports car coming up the canyon. She's never met Roberto Vincente but Roberto's father, Rosario Vincente, has money in Horizon Pictures. Nobody knows how much money, but Lew Gibbon, who owns the studio, can't handle money at all, and got in trouble. Rosario Vincente made a big investment to get him out again. There's always a price on investments from people like Vincente, who feeds gambling money through Horizon so it comes out legitimate. He's put his boy in to learn the ropes and make sure Lew stays businesslike and doesn't let contract actresses call the shots on him.

Liza Jane is twenty-six and she likes acting better than anything. She's beginning to care what kind of picture they put her in. In the middle of the Depression she's making four hundred dollars a week and feels rich, with a little house up a winding road in Topanga Canyon and a goat. The goat's name is Lullaby and everyone who moves into the canyon buys her, flown with enthusiastic discussion of keeping weeds down and the beneficial effects of goat's milk. No one mentions that goats eat everything, standing on their hind legs to give all the trees a bowl haircut. When someone else moves in, the neighbors will help Liza Jane sell him Lullaby. It's a kind of initiation to the canyon.

The red sports car pulls into her driveway. Liza Jane takes Lullaby by the horns and drags her into the paddock as Roberto Vincente gets out of the car.

He's young, in his twenties, tall and slender, dark hair, dark eyes, handsome in an explosive way. He has on a white summer suit and a striped shirt and he's agile as a cat. He comes up a flight of stone steps tangled with ivy, and says, "Miss Sidney." There's a little Italian in his voice, not much.

"Mr. Vincente." Liza Jane just stands there looking at him. She has on a white skirt and walking shoes, and a white sweater. Her red hair is smooth on top, one careful wave held back with a barrette. She's standing in full sun, her white skirt and sweater a bright flare against the ivy and the dusty hillside.

Roberto says, "It was good of you to let me come talk to you, Miss Sidney."

"Did I have a choice?" Liza Jane says.

Roberto smiles. "Maybe not. We can talk anyway. Mr. Gibbon wants us to talk. About you doing *Heaven's Rest.*"

"I already talked to Mr. Gibbon."

"I know. You got him all upset. Mr. Gibbon doesn't stand up so well to stubborn ladies." Roberto Vincente looks like he thinks he can.

"I won't make trash," she says.

"Now who's asking you to make trash? This is a class picture or we wouldn't be associated with it."

"Horizon's in trouble," Liza Jane says, "or Lew wouldn't have let you get your nose in the door. Now you're trying to make fast money."

Roberto laughs, but he doesn't back off. "We like to be businesslike while we got an investment. That bastard Zenovich brought out two pictures ahead of us last month while Lew's trying to get his sound equipment out of hock."

Liza Jane looks at him, trying to decide how far she can dig her heels in. He's the most alive-looking person she's ever seen, dark and a little reckless, probably dangerous. "Maybe you should have bought Zenovich," she says.

"We don't need Zenovich, on account of Zenovich doesn't need us. Lew needed us, so he's got us. So you got us."

"You come inside, Mr. Vincente," she says. "I want to show you something."

She doesn't wait for him, just goes in the front door. She knows he's not going away. He follows her. Inside there's a ratty looking couch and a couple of armchairs, and a reading lamp with fringe on the shade. A big radio in the corner. She goes in another room off the living room that's got another ratty couch and a portable movie screen on a tripod. There's a table behind the couch with a projector on it. Cans of film all over the place.

"What's this?" he asks her.

"Outtakes, Mr. Vincente. I like to watch my mistakes. It's educational." She opens a can and threads the projector. The interior light shoots up on her face like a candle held under her chin. He thinks she's the most beautiful woman he's ever seen.

"Roberto," he says. He knows he's maybe losing a playing card with that. "You call me Roberto."

"Sit down and watch this, Roberto," Liza Jane says. He sits down.

She's on the screen with David Caldwell, Horizon's biggest male star. There's no sound, it's a silent projector, but anyone watching can tell they're lovers, they're fighting, and they're torn open by it. Even with no words, she practically shoots off the screen. Caldwell grabs her wrist and kisses her. She kisses him back, just with her mouth and body, arms at her sides. Then she pulls away from him and picks up a knife off the table. The camera goes in close on her desperate, driven face, and then the screen goes dark.

"That's not an outtake," Roberto says. Jesus.

"No. That's my test for *Anna Manning*. Did you like it?" The film winds through the projector and she switches off the empty, revolving reel. She watches his hands, wondering what he's done in his life.

"How could I help it?" Roberto says. There's just the white light of the screen in the room now, making a dazzle behind her hair, black and white like the film.

She knows what he's thinking, because she's thinking it too. She sits very still. She hasn't ever slept her way into a part and she isn't going to start with Roberto Vincente.

"That's what I'm capable of," she says. "And you want me to make garbage."

He isn't going to deny that *Heaven's Rest* is crap, not after seeing this. "You're the only actress between pictures," he tells her. "You do it or we'll suspend you."

"Suspend me."

"Then you don't get *Anna Manning*."

"Mexican stand-off," she says.

"I could put a little more pressure on you than that," Roberto says evenly.

She looks him in the eye. "And will you?"

He shakes his head. "No." He grins at her. It lights up his face. "Mexican stand-off."

She rewinds the film and takes the reel off the spindle, while they both think about it. She turns the overhead light back on. "I want *Anna Manning*."

He takes the can of film out of her hand, puts it down on the table. "What if I promise you *Anna Manning*? What if I promise you Lew won't put another actress in it?"

"Will you put that in writing?"

"No." He's not going to budge on that. "We can't let it look like we gotta bribe our people to make 'em behave. It's not good for business." He puts his hand on her arm. "But I'll give you my word. You make *Heaven's Rest*, get Lew on his feet, he can afford to make *Anna Manning*."

"You don't want Lew on his feet."

"We don't want him in the ditch, either. And we don't want to go on putting up dough. You make *Heaven's Rest*, I'll give you my word." He thinks about the film he just saw, and he wonders if she'd like to put a knife in him. Maybe. She's not afraid of him. And she won't have to make crap like *Heaven's Rest* anymore, once the public sees her as Anna. It won't pay them to waste her on it. He tells her that and she actually smiles at him. She's so beautiful he thinks his heart's going to stop.

"One last homer for the farm team?" she says.

"You got it."

"All right," she tells him.

They shake hands on it, and she walks him to the door. He says, "You won't have us in your hair forever."

"Lew's only useful for a while?" The green eyes are shrewd.

"That's right."

"Then he'll go under again," she says. She knows Lew.

"He will," Roberto says. "You won't."

Liza Jane is framed in the doorway, back against the jamb, hands behind her, feet toed in a little. She's thinking. She looks up at him. They both know he's supposed to leave now; he got what he was after. She says, "Do you want to take me to a party?"

"Do you want me to?" He's serious now.

"Yes." Liza Jane thinks about the effect this dark, predatory man is going to have on her hostess. "Yes, tonight." Her eyes are gleeful.

He knows that part of his attraction is shock value, but he doesn't care. There's more to it. He looks past her shoulder and sees Lullaby coming up the porch steps. Lullaby likes company and she can fiddle the paddock gate open. She puts her hard, bony head in Roberto's hand.

Roberto laughs. "Hello, goat."

"Pick me up at eight," Liza Jane tells him.

Roberto Vincente is wearing a tailcoat when he comes to get her, a white carnation in his buttonhole. Liza Jane nods approvingly. He looks like a black panther dressed up for the opera. She slides into the back seat with him; this time he's brought a big dark Packard and a driver. The driver lets them off in front of Marjorie Maly's house in Beverly Hills. Liza Jane wonders how the driver knows when to come back. Maybe he just drives around the block.

She shakes out her dress with an anticipatory grin. She's wearing a long, slinky bias-cut velvet, in panels of emerald and black. She has on long black gloves up to her elbows. Vincente gives her his arm with a look that says he likes the effect. Liza Jane feels like she ought to have him on a leash, something studded with diamonds and a big dark ruby. Marjorie Maly's butler opens the door for them and Marjorie kisses the air politely on either side of Liza Jane's face, her eyes on Vincente.

"This is Roberto," Liza Jane says. "Roberto Vincente."

"Enchanted." Roberto kisses Marjorie's hand.

Marjorie Maly's father owns most of Laurel Studios. Marjorie is a Hollywood princess. She gives parties. Tonight her house is full of people from rival picture companies doing deals. She's invited Liza Jane, but not Lew Gibbon (Marjorie knows who's on their way to where). Maurice Zenovich is there, and David Selznick and Irving Thalberg from MGM. Norma Shearer, Thalberg's wife, kisses the air to either side of Liza Jane too, and chuckles when Liza Jane introduces Vincente.

"And how do you find the picture business, Mr. Vincente?"

"Full of pretty ladies," Vincente says.

Women who ordinarily wouldn't give Liza Jane their time drift over to chat.

"God," Louann Holborn says, back of her hand to her forehead, blue eyes wide. "Another day like this and I'll have a breakdown. Twenty-seven takes on one damn page of dialogue, with a microphone stuffed down my boobs so I couldn't move. I hate this business." She lights a cigarette, exhaling a cloud of blue smoke. "I'm Louann," she adds cozily to Vincente, with a look that says of course he knows that.

"Louann Holborn," Liza Jane supplies helpfully, in case he doesn't.

Louann glares at her. "My dear, wherever did you meet this gorgeous man?"

"He's my brother," Liza Jane says. She pilots him past Louann.

In the next room there are more faces that Roberto has seen on the screen, but with Liza Jane for a guide he's not impressed. She's the one that makes him think maybe he's got heart trouble.

Mixed with the actors are the money men, the short, dumpy ones with the real power—those are the ones Vincente knows about. They eye him with cautious interest. The room is paneled in dark wood and papered with silver. A thick rug compresses under their feet. A slim girl with a sleek waved bob the color of chili powder, three or four shades darker than Liza Jane's, is sitting on top of a piano while the hostess's husband noodles at it. Sheldon Maly doesn't like circulating and glad-handing. He stays in the background and plays the piano.

"Roberto, this is Theresa Tate," Liza Jane says, and the girl leans down from the piano and holds her hand out. Roberto kisses it (they seem to like that) and Liza Jane introduces him to Sheldon Maly, too.

"You're the one got a piece of Lew Gibbon," Maly says. Maly's one of the money men. He knows.

"Just a little piece," Roberto says. Vincentes never have a little piece of anything.

Theresa looks at Liza Jane. She manages to do a little dance step without getting off the piano. "I'll be home early tomorrow. Call me up."

Liza Jane gives her a broad wink. Bringing Roberto Vincente to this party is like escorting a volcano. Everyone's curious. He doesn't look like a tough. He just exudes something. Whatever it is, it's potent. Little ripples whisper behind them as they move through the party, like sharks among expensive fish.

Vincente's driver is waiting outside when they leave. Laughing, they trip down Marjorie's front walk, full of old scotch and brandy. Liza Jane doesn't think Roberto's had as much to drink as he acts like, she was watching him. He's just keeping her company, they're being silly together.

The driver pulls up at the foot of Liza Jane's stone steps and Roberto raises an eyebrow at her. "Maybe I better walk you up."

Liza Jane gives him her hand. Her gloves are stuffed in her bag. They clamber up and she gets out her key. Roberto just stands there and looks at her. She looks back, disappearing into the darkness of her porch, just her face and hair riding on the moonlight. He moves into the shadows, takes her hand again, harder this time, pulls her to him. At the foot of the steps, the driver waits five minutes and cuts his engine.

Liza Jane isn't falling in love. She knows better than that. In the Vincente family, they cultivate subservient women; women who can convincingly claim that they know nothing about their husbands' business affairs. But he's wonderful company; and he's educated, he can quote Shakespeare to her. "You could teach the torches to burn bright," he says, sprawled on top of her on the bed, his tailcoat on the floor, his white tie half untied. Afterwards, they'll locate his shirt studs in the sheets, have to tear the bed apart to find them. Liza Jane's bed is an old brass one with a serape on it for a spread.

"This hasn't got anything to do with *Anna Manning*," Liza Jane says when he takes his mouth off hers.

"Certainly not." But he says, "I could give you more than *Anna Manning* if you'll let me." He's caught by the glow of the bedside lamp on the fan of her hair, an aureole of fire against the sheets.

"Not for this," Liza Jane says. "It's one of my rules." She knows that when you get too old to sleep your way into a part, you're left with nothing, if you started out that way.

"I don't know any ladies like you," Roberto says. Floozies, yes, and good Catholic girls, but not New York Episcopalians who went to boarding school. Not actresses with wings, like those paintings of chaste, sensual angels he's seen in the museum. He can almost feel them flutter around him, giddy and glorious. "You make me laugh," he says. "Make me want to walk around with a big grin."

Liza Jane wriggles around under him so he can get at the long row of little velvet-covered buttons that runs down her back. "Use both hands. Only a Lothario ought to be able to do it with one."

"Is this a test?" Roberto grins, unbuttoning the row with his right hand. "To see how many girls I've had?"

"I don't care how many girls you've had."

Roberto feels a mild twinge that she doesn't. Liza Jane pulls at him in ways he can't even explain, ways no other woman has. He may be falling in love. Men like Roberto don't fall in love with the women they marry, the Vincente family is old-fashioned that way. They fall in love outside where it won't do so much damage. Liza Jane's going to go up like a rocket when people see her in *Anna Manning*. Roberto wants to go with her, stand in that shower of gold glitter, watch it rain down around him. It isn't power; he has that. It's light. Roberto wonders what mark she has laid on him, and whether his father will be able to see it, whether it will be lifelong.

He doesn't go home till morning.

Three years later Rosario Vincente has a stroke, and Roberto, who is more important in the family now, goes back to New York. He knows that Liza Jane won't come with him, he doesn't even ask. But whenever he's in town, he takes her to dinner. The Vincentes keep some money in the picture business; when Maurice Zenovich buys out Lew Gibbon and Horizon, their investment comes along with it. After idealistic Hollywood people start dabbling in communism, joining the Party, he gives her some advice.

"What makes you so convinced it can't work?" she asks him.

On the face of it, the communists are supporting some things that Liza Jane thinks are a good idea, like the unions and opposition to what Hitler is doing in Germany.

"In my business, we understand human nature," he says. "People aren't that altruistic, not when something theoretical gets personal. Trust me, I got first-hand observation on this."

"That doesn't say much for human nature."

"Also the government doesn't like communists." The Vincentes keep up with politics. "Now they got a new committee to investigate who might be one."

Liza Jane knows this because the committee is after the Federal Theater Project for mixing black and white performers and crew; the committee says racial equality is a sign of communism. On the other hand, at the Party meeting she went to, the speaker called homosexuals a bourgeois deviance and passed around flyers supporting Stalin. Bernice believes the more reasonable members will override that faction, but when Roberto tells her she's risking her career, she listens to him.

And every year on her birthday, even after he marries, Roberto Vincente sends roses, a dozen long-stemmed red ones. The last ones come a week before she dies.

II
Testament

1988

Arlo Sheppard arrived with the rose delivery. He looked to be in his thirties, with dark-rimmed glasses and a shock of dark, bushy hair that was the only unruly element about him. He wore a three-piece suit and a tie with a neat regimental stripe, and he carried a briefcase with the air of a man whose briefcase is always organized and not full of spare socks and a sandwich.

"Mrs. Novak, I was awfully sorry to get the news," he said, dodging the roses. "Do you think we could go in the library?"

The library was a sunlit room of wall-to-wall bookcases, with a fireplace and leather armchairs. The three Oscars glinted on the mantel. Arlo Sheppard sat down at the massive table and clicked open his briefcase. Liddy and Harry settled themselves across from him. Sheppard extracted a ten-page sheaf of notepaper covered with a spidery and instantly recognizable hand. He adjusted his glasses with a faint air of despair. "Mrs. Novak, were you aware of this will?"

"No! I know some of the bequests in it, or at least I thought I did, but I had no idea she'd done something like this."

"Well, you seem to be a sensible person. This is all very distressing for you, of course. I really think you'd better read the whole thing."

Liddy took the sheaf of papers. They spoke so clearly in her aunt's voice that she nearly cried.

I, Elizabeth Sidney, formerly known as Elizabeth Jane Fox, wish to state that I am of perfectly sound mind and know what I want. Therefore I am taking steps to see that I get it despite the best intentions of all the people who have only my welfare at heart. I wish my remains to be buried beneath the largest of the three oak trees in the northeast corner of the oak grove at my home in Ayala. Furthermore, I wish my body to be immediately removed from wherever I may chance to have died, and taken straight to my home. If by the grace of God I should have the good fortune to die at home and not in some loathsome hospital, I wish to remain there. For the sake of propriety, I will allow a mortician to visit me, but my body is not to leave the premises, and under no circumstances is it to be taken to a mortuary. In order to be certain that my wishes are adhered to, I hereby state that if my final resting place is not as I have requested, or if my body is removed from my home for any reason, then the rest of this will, and all previous wills, are null and void. Nor is my body to be cremated. You will not get around me in that fashion.

My niece, Elizabeth Jane Fox Novak, is to be my executor. Should this will be negated, this one provision shall stand, and she shall be my sole heir, as I trust her judgment.

All my instructions concerning the disposal of my body having been adhered to, and all debts and taxes having been paid first, I make the following bequests:

To my niece, Elizabeth Jane Fox Novak, I leave my house

at 910 Del Norte Road, Ayala, California, its contents except as specified below, and the lot on which it sits, with the proviso that my companion of many years, Bernice Lewis, shall live there as long as she chooses, and that Jeffrey Austin shall live as long as he chooses in the caretaker's cottage on the premises. To said niece I also leave the sum of $5,000,000.

To Bernice Lewis I leave the sum of $1,000,000.

To Jeffrey Austin, the sum of $250,000.

To Theresa Tate, my jewelry.

To Harry Lanier and Sharon Hamilton, the sum of $250,000 each.

To Ramananda Paradevi, in trust for the Unified Church of Light, the sum of $250,000 and the property in which the church is now housed, commonly known as the Harding Adobe.

To the Ayala Art Center, $300,000 to establish a theater festival in my name.

To Apple Valley School, the Philotheistic Institute, the Ventura County Humane Society, the Adams Home for Children, The Ayala Historic Preservation Committee, St. Anne's Episcopal Church, the Foundation for Holistic Health, and the Ayala Art Center, to be divided equally between them, any rights and royalties as may pertain to or be due from my work, and the residue of my estate when all other bequests have been fulfilled.

And finally, I leave to Alexander B. Murray of 1921 Prospect Avenue, Pittsburgh, Pennsylvania, the sum of $1,000,000.

Liddy looked at Harry Lanier, who was watching her twitchily, as he might someone who was reading the instructions that have come with a bomb.

"Who's Alexander B. Murray?" Liddy demanded.

"Well, he's kind of a complication, too. We've called him. Arlo has."

"And she's left me a house with Jeff and Bernice living in it. I suppose the pugs are 'contents' too."

"Jeff's not living in the main house," Harry said. "Jeff ought to be water a long way under the bridge. So's Murray, for that matter. Don't worry about him."

"You knew about him?"

"I didn't," Arlo Sheppard said hastily.

"I did," Harry said. "Liza Jane told me when I started working for her. I think Theresa knew too."

"Explain," Liddy said grimly.

"Well." Harry got up and took a couple of quick turns across the hearth. He mopped his round head with his handkerchief. "He's kind of an old scandal."

Liddy groaned.

"No, no. He's not Liza Jane's scandal." The doorbell rang and Harry ignored it. "More flowers. The place is a damn hothouse. You been in the living room? Looks like a garden show."

"Harry—"

Harry looked at the Oscars on the mantel. He touched one with his fingertip. "That was for *Across the Bridge*. God, she was good. She had a way of just letting everything out until you'd swear she couldn't do it again, and then she would. If Murray had been her scandal you'd have known about it. Woman never kept a secret in her life. Except this one, I guess, and it wasn't hers. You remember Carolyn Castellano?"

"I've seen her movies."

"Yeah, that's what I meant. She was a friend of Liza Jane's. Not a close friend, just another contract actress. She was younger than Liza Jane, just starting out, but you know how Liza Jane was. She took people under her wing. Carolyn Castellano was kind of a lost kid. Too much fast money, not enough sense. The studio just took her over. Changed her name, capped her teeth, set up fake romances to get her in the gossip columns. She made a couple of B pictures and a couple of good ones. The studio sent out pin-ups of her to the GI's in Korea."

A telephone on an end table between the armchairs rang, and Harry picked it up without lifting the receiver, and turned the bell down. "That's been going on all morning, too. Arlo, did you tell Murray not to talk to the press?"

"I thought maybe I wouldn't give him ideas," Arlo said. "The press don't know about him yet."

"They will, they got noses like beagles. I better waylay him when he gets here." Harry took note of Liddy's outraged expression. "We had to ask him. Just let me finish. Hollywood wasn't like it is now. The studios spent a lot of time getting their stars in the gossip columns, but they clamped down hard if there were any goings-on they didn't approve of. Carolyn got pregnant. The father was an actor, a married one. He wasn't about to ditch his wife for her and take a chance on screwing up his career. This was in the fifties, remember. Carolyn was Catholic and afraid to get an abortion, which wasn't easy to do back then anyway. She poured the whole nasty mess out to Liza Jane, and Liza Jane took charge. Took Carolyn off for a 'vacation' and arranged to have the baby adopted."

"Alexander B. Murray?" Liddy said. "You mean she's kept track of him all this time?" She felt suddenly shut out, and inexplicably angry about it.

"Well, there were extenuating circumstances, you might say. Carolyn had to refuse a picture the studio wanted her to do, and Liza Jane squared it somehow. Ben Zenovich was starting to take over from his old man about then, and Ben was young, ready to worship the ground Liza Jane walked on, same effect she always had on men. And she was box office gold, they were ready to please her. So she squared it. But Carolyn Castellano never got over it, not being dumped by the guy, or giving up the baby. She started drinking, and got unreliable, and then she couldn't get a picture. She had a car wreck a few years later that killed her. So Liza Jane kept track of the kid. Sent money to his parents, made sure he went to college. He never knew about it. She just greased the wheels. Said she felt responsible. The father wasn't much interested. Didn't want to admit knowing Carolyn, much less anything else. He was too worried about his career. That's the funny part. The father was Arthur Symes. Liza Jane finally told me, after he died. All that trouble to save his career, and he was a second banana all his life."

"That's not funny at all," Liddy said.

"You might think it was if you were Carolyn Castellano." Harry said.

Alec Murray's plane banked over the water and settled into a long glide across the city to LAX. Los Angeles looked even murkier and more sprawling than the last time he had seen it. He had just been passing through then. Now it seemed there might be something important hidden below the smog, some startling connection with himself. Jesus. What a way to find out who you were. Assuming he actually did know who he was. And considering how he'd found out about it, he didn't feel he was that much farther along.

The plane touched down with a bump and taxied across endless runways to the Delta terminal. The sun was brilliant, white and dusty outside the windows; a hot wind picked up scraps of trash and curled them over the tarmac. The corridor inched out like a hydraulic caterpillar and attached itself to the plane. Alec closed the book he hadn't been reading anyway, and stuck it in his bag. *Chasing Shadows* by Elizabeth Novak. He had picked it up in the terminal to try to make some kind of connection with the people he was going to meet, but he hadn't really kept his mind on it long enough to tell much, except that she seemed like a good writer. The story moved right along. Some of the police stuff was wrong, but it always was and it didn't matter anyway. Her heroine was a bookstore owner who got embroiled in a spy ring when she found a letter in code in a first edition. Alec wondered if that had ever happened. He also wondered if you could actually tell anything about someone from their book. Or their movies. He'd seen Elizabeth Sidney plenty of times, and had a vague recollection of Carolyn Castellano from the Late Show. He wasn't really sure which one of them it was that he was trying to figure out.

The line inched past the bottleneck at the cabin door, and the flight attendant gave him a practiced smile. "Enjoy Los Angeles, Mr. Murray."

Alec collected his suitcase from the turntable, and a rental car from the Avis desk. The clerk blinked with interest at his government I.D. Alec shoved the case, with I.D. and badge, into his coat pocket. He wondered how these people were going to take to him. No cover here, just Alec Murray. Whoever that was.

He slid into the car and adjusted the mirrors, vaguely surprised to find that he looked just like he had yesterday. Dark hair, brown eyes, a rectangular, solid-looking face that he knew, without really being able to see it himself, was accounted to be good-looking. He wondered if he looked like Arthur Symes, and tried to remember what Arthur Symes looked like. It was pretty strange to have only seen your parents on a movie screen, disguised as someone else.

On the freeway, he had a brief urge to get off on La Cienega and drive through Hollywood, but he didn't. What was he going to do, buy a map to the stars' homes and see where his old man had lived? Probably nobody knew anymore anyway. Or he could just keep going north up over the Santa Susana Mountains and see some old buddies in Fresno, and let this Arlo Sheppard mail him a check, if he was going to. Sheppard had said he thought Alec ought to be there, to protect his interest. Alec didn't know how much he wanted to be rich. But he did want to know about Elizabeth Sidney, and know why she had chosen at her death to remake his life.

He had known he was adopted since he was five, but he had always assumed that his parents didn't know any more than he did. He still didn't think they had known who his biological parents were—his mother had sounded honestly startled on the telephone, but she had admitted to Elizabeth Sidney's part in it.

"We never knew what she was going to do, dear," she had said when Alec had gone over there to see what else no one had told him. "And you never showed any signs of curiosity, so it just seemed easier not to mention it." She was peeling potatoes for dinner, and looked so distressed that he had been contrite.

"I wasn't curious, Mom. I wouldn't ever have gone looking. As far as I can tell, that just messes people's lives up."

His mother put the potato peeler down. "It all just seemed so far removed. Like another planet, really. And your father never thought much of movie people, except to be grateful that we got you."

Alec grinned at her across the worn dinette table. "He never wanted me to be a cop either."

"I had an accountant in mind, or an engineer," his father said from the kitchen door. "Not a movie actor." He shrugged his coat off and put his gun on the end of the counter, beside Alec's. "What the hell is going on? Doris left me a message at the precinct."

"Elizabeth Sidney's left him a million dollars," his mother

said, putting another plate on the table for Alec.

His father whistled. "You take it. Buy your old man a new car. And get out of the DEA."

"I busted my tail to get in the DEA," Alec said.

"You're shoveling sand with a teaspoon," his father said.

"Bill." His mother looked at his father, waited until she had his attention. "Both his birth parents are dead."

Alec thought a quick wave of relief went across his father's face. "They're just people I don't know," Alec said. He was thirty-five, an only child whose one brief marriage had ended in divorce and no grandchildren. They had too much wrapped up in him to put in their minds any fear of losing him.

But it wasn't Carolyn Castellano's ghost he was pursuing up the Ventura Freeway, it was Elizabeth Sidney's.

The coastline ran westward from Los Angeles and the afternoon sun gave the round brown hills a faint golden glow, studded with the stocky spreading shapes of live oaks. Los Angeles appeared to extend solidly all the way to Ventura, an endless city broken only by a few alfalfa fields and orange groves outside of Oxnard. At Ventura he turned inland, and the land grew slightly more countrified. The orange groves came back, and he passed an oil refinery, an aluminum-colored tangle of pipes and tanks with black, bug-shaped drilling rigs moving up and down beside it.

Coming into Ayala, open fields bordered the road, with horses whisking their tails. As he passed the gates of the Country Club stable, a string of riders came out. A teenaged girl was leading them, sitting loosely in a Western saddle and eating an apple. The riders behind her wore expensive jeans and silk shirts and sat stiffly, clutching the reins with both hands.

Following Arlo Sheppard's directions, Alec turned where an enormous live oak, its trunk painted white, sat squarely in the middle of the road. He drove past a school with white board fences ringing its own stable, and turned up into the shady depths of the Arbolada.

The house was high on the hill, behind wrought-iron gates set into stone pillars. He turned into the driveway, and noted with some apprehension that there seemed to be an awful lot of cars ahead of him, parked in the circle in front of the house. Alec cut the ignition and sat in the car, looking at the house.

It was Spanish stucco, three stories at the highest point, with a red tile roof, and a square tower on the left corner with open arched windows at the top. Wrought-iron balconies opened off some of the other windows, and iron railings flanked the double stairs leading to the front door. The house was set at an angle into the hillside, so that the front steps went up ten feet to the door, and the left side of the house rose above a rock retaining wall. Ivy-covered lattice work and a pomegranate tree screened what appeared to be a basement door in front.

While he was trying to decide to get out of the car, the front door opened and a man in blue jeans trotted down the steps toward him.

"If you're the press, go away," he said. "If you're Alexander Murray, you'd better come in."

Alec got out of the car. "I'm Murray."

"I'm Jeff Austin." The man held out his hand and Alec shook it. Jeff opened the rear door and got out Alec's suitcase.

"I'll carry that," Alec said.

"I got it," Jeff said. "I have to earn my keep. I'm the caretaker. Sort of."

Jeff led him up the steps and through the front door. Alec could hear voices from the living room. Jeff put the suitcase down. "Let me go find Liddy. Or Arlo, or Harry. Or somebody." He vanished into the living room, while Alec looked around him at the hall. The framed poster of Elizabeth Sidney as Queen Elizabeth seemed to dominate the room, but Alec's eyes strayed past it to the portraits above the stairs, wondering if Carolyn Castellano or Arthur Symes were among them. His attention was caught, in spite of himself, by a signed photo of Kirk Douglas as a Viking. Before he could look further, Jeff came back, with a brown-haired young woman in a flowered dress.

"This is Liddy Novak," Jeff said.

"I'm Alec Murray," Alec said, while Liddy Novak looked at him apprehensively, and Alec tried to equate her with the author of *Chasing Shadows* and wished he'd read more of it. "I hope I'm not a surprise to you."

"I'm afraid you are," Liddy said with a weak smile. More people spilled out of the living room behind her, giving him the fleeting sensation of having wandered into a studio commissary: a woman in a peasant skirt and a Greenpeace t-shirt, followed by a tall, auburn-haired old woman in a trailing fox-fur boa, a small blond woman in a neat rose-colored suit, a man in what appeared to be a toga accompanied by two women in saris, and a fat, balding man in rolled-up sleeves and suspenders. Behind them was a man Alec was pretty sure was Frank Hill, who was reputed to get five million dollars a picture.

"Let me introduce you," Liddy said. "Bernice Lewis, my aunt's companion." The peasant skirt.

Alec shook hands.

"Theresa Tate."

"Dear boy, at last." The auburn-haired old lady took his hand. The fox-fur boa looked nearly as old as she was. "You don't recognize me, of course."

"Yes, ma'am, I do," Alec said, having done so in the nick of time.

Theresa Tate beamed at him. "Liza Jane would have been so proud. You don't know how she watched over you. At long distance, of course. Dear boy, if she had only seen you. What is it exactly that you do?"

"I'm in law enforcement," Alec said.

"A policeman? Fascinating!"

"Drug Enforcement Administration." Alec wondered how they were going to like that.

Jeff Austin spread his hands out. "Clean, Captain."

"This is Sharon Hamilton," Liddy said with a threatening look at Jeff. "My aunt's agent."

The rose-colored suit. She had a sleek cap of pale blond hair and the tight look that a face lift gave, and was older than she had looked at a distance. Alec shook hands again.

"And Ramananda Paradevi." The man in the toga. He had a benign, beaky face. Liddy ignored the sari-clad followers.

"Our benefactress has made her transition to a higher plane," Ramananda Paradevi said. "There will be a ceremony of passage on the veranda at five o'clock. A healing time for us all."

"Right," Liddy said. "This is Harry Lanier, my aunt's business manager, and Arlo Sheppard, who I think you've talked to." She produced Lanier, the round man in suspenders, and Sheppard, younger, in a very businesslike business suit.

"Frank Hill. And Ben Zenovich." Liddy presented Hill and an older, spare man in argyle socks and a polo shirt. Hill was brown-haired and muscular and slightly self-effacing behind gold-rimmed glasses, and Zenovich was an angular nose and receding hairline, faintly hawklike. Alec shook hands with both of them.

"Great," Harry Lanier said. "And now Mr. Murray needs to talk to Arlo here. You come on with us." He edged Alec out of the crowd.

Arlo Sheppard closed the library door behind them with the air of a Roman bolting the gates against the Visigoths. He had thick bushy hair and a morose expression. He looked at Alec and appeared to find him normal.

"Did you have a good flight, Mr. Murray?"

"Fine." Alec yawned. "Sorry, no sleep."

"Jeff took your bags upstairs," Harry said. "Maybe you can catch a nap."

"Thanks." Alec hadn't been certain that he was supposed to stay here. He looked around the library curiously, noting the Oscars on the mantel. A herd of pug dogs was asleep on the hearth. At the murmur of voices they woke up and snorted at him.

"Are all these people staying here?" Alec asked. "I didn't really get them sorted out too well."

"Theresa Tate and Sharon Hamilton are," Harry said. "I think Ben's going to a hotel. Frank may stay here so he doesn't get mobbed." He looked at Arlo. "I told the Horsehead Ranch to hold ten rooms. There'll be more coming for the funeral."

"Whenever that's going to be," Arlo said. "Look, Mr. Murray."

Alec turned from his contemplation of the Oscars on the mantel.

"Since you're the second largest beneficiary, I'm going to let you read the will. Maybe it will clarify some problems we've got here."

He handed the will to Alec and Alec read it, trying to envision the elusive face behind it. His own name and address leapt at him abruptly from the end. There was no explanation, just the bare name.

"You're as much a surprise to most of us as we are to you," Arlo said. "But you can see we've got problems."

Alec felt almost relieved. There was no way this will was going to hold up, no decisions to make. He'd like to know why they had bothered to drag him out here. His expression must have said so, because Arlo coughed apologetically.

"We're working on a way to invalidate the burial clause only. We thought maybe you could make Mrs. Novak see reason."

"She's the contingent beneficiary," Alec said, startled. "She's the only relative. It's in her interest to invalidate the whole thing."

"If she's willing to take the flak from the rest of the beneficiaries," Harry said. "I'm not sure she is. It could mean a court battle."

"You're a beneficiary," Alec observed.

"I don't mean me," Harry said irritably. "But I'm a professional business manager. I'm reluctant to help invalidate a client's will. Doesn't exactly inspire confidence. The problem is, Liddy won't agree to invalidate the burial clause."

"You mean she wants to bury her in the back yard?"

"She won't say," Harry said gloomily. "She says it's our problem."

"She's got her hands full," Arlo said. In the distance they could hear the doorbell ring again, and then the telephone.

"Well, they won't go away again until Liza Jane does," Harry snapped. "Sorry. But we've already had the press out here. Jeff ran them off, but they're still out there, and we're going to have to deal with them or they'll start making stuff up. I've got a publicist coming up to try to field them, and keep them away from the Ramalama Dingdong and his crew."

Another car crunched in the gravel outside, and Arlo looked out the window. "Harry."

Harry went to the window, and Alec abandoned discretion and looked out behind him.

"Shit," Arlo said. "I hate to say it, but I think the Ramananda's the least of our worries."

A big, black limousine had pulled up in the circle, and a heavy, dark-haired man got out, accompanied by a younger one whose muscular shoulders didn't quite fit his suit.

"Oh, Christ," Harry said.

Alec's eyes widened. "Is that who I think it is?"

"In the flesh," Harry said. "Who'd have thought it?" He gave Alec a harassed look. "You stay away from him, you hear?"

"Honestly, Harry, what do you think he's going to do?"

Theresa Tate had appeared in the doorway. She took Alec's arm. "Dear boy. Pay no attention. Harry's rattled."

"As well he might be," Harry muttered.

"You go talk to Roberto," Theresa said. "Myself, I think it's touching." She sat down on the sofa and patted the seat beside her. "Alec and I will chat."

Alec sat down beside her, almost gratefully. Harry and Arlo had disappeared into the hall. Theresa Tate beamed at Alec maternally, without looking like anyone's mother. Besides the fox fur boa, she wore a green silk Chinese jacket and trousers, and a large carved jade pendant. Her dark auburn hair was cut in a sort of 1920s bob, and she wore green eye shadow and coral lipstick. She might be in her sixties, but he thought she was older.

"You look bewildered," she said. "Are we too much for you? Ask me anything."

"What's Roberto Vincente doing here?"

"You know him," Theresa said cozily. "How nice."

"I've seen pictures," Alec said.

Theresa blinked her lashes at Alec. "Now, I'm not as dizzy as I sound. I know he's a mobster. But he was sweet on Liza Jane, oh, years ago. And even after, he's always sent her roses on her birthday."

"No kidding? Roses every year?" Alec was diverted. A new view of Roberto Vincente, certainly.

"That was one thing about Liza Jane," Theresa said. She sighed wistfully. "I just wish I knew how she did it. All her men went on loving her. I mean, look at Ben Zenovich and Frank Hill. Goodness, she was going with Ben back when she made *Glory Days.*"

"Frank Hill?"

"That was, oh, twenty years ago," Theresa said. "Frank had only had one little part then. He was so young and earnest. Liza Jane introduced him to everyone, to Ben. She was really very good for him. It didn't last long, of course, but she was the one who got him the part in Commando. That was his first big picture."

"Oh."

"Don't you sit there thinking she was immoral," Theresa said. "Oh, yes, you are. I see you doing it."

"I'm trying not to," Alec said. "I didn't know her."

"Of course not." She patted his hand. "I do wish you had. She was my dearest friend. And she was certainly a friend to your mother."

"Tell me about her. I mean Liza Jane. Is that what everyone called her?"

"Absolutely everyone. I met her when we were both in New York, at the old Astoria studio. Such a long time ago, can you imagine? Everyone was trying to learn to talk then, because of sound. Liza Jane and I were lucky. We had good voices. And she had wonderful red hair. Not like mine. A gorgeous clear, golden red. It photographed beautifully later, when color came in, and she never had to dye it. Irving Ohlman used to take her out. He owned a chain of department stores in New York and drove a Bugatti. His mother was afraid he'd marry her. She came to the studio one day and offered Liza Jane a thousand dollars to break off with Irving. Liza Jane offered Mrs. Ohlman two thousand dollars to put it up her ass."

Alec started to laugh. "Did she marry the guy?"

"Oh, no, she never married any of them, not even Donald Wain and he was her real love."

"Donald Wain? Aerospace and military contracting?"

"That's him. But he wanted things she wasn't willing to give. Liza Jane was always smarter than the rest of us. I married," Theresa added. "Four times, and look what came of it. Or rather don't look, because nothing good did, I assure you. Hollywood is just hell on marriage. Or maybe it just makes the wrong people available in the first place. Liza Jane knew better. She lived her life just exactly the way she wanted to."

"That usually involves mowing down a few people who get in the way," Alec said.

"Dear boy, what a cynic you are. I suppose she did, but it was in the gentlest way possible. And she was a very loyal person. You just ask Bernice. They all loved her for it. Except Arthur Symes. He was always scared she'd tell someone about you. I'm afraid she let him think she might. After Carolyn killed herself, Liza Jane never forgave him."

"I thought she died in an accident." That was what Arlo Sheppard had said. Alec leaned back against the leather sofa, a little away from Theresa Tate, beginning to feel battered by so much revelation.

"Carolyn drove her car off a bridge," Theresa said. "Nobody knew whether it was on purpose or not, but everybody knew it was on purpose, if you know what I mean."

"She settled me perfectly reasonably," Alec said. "I have two perfectly good parents. I couldn't ask for better. Why did she haul off and leave me money after all this time? I wasn't even hers." He craned his neck around at the Oscars on the mantel as if to emphasize how little he belonged in this strange house, this glittery world that was like finding himself suddenly in an aquarium full of alien fish. Shifting between whatever skin he put on for his job, and his mother's kitchen, was slippage enough.

"That did surprise me." Theresa cocked her head as if puzzling over Liza Jane's bequest. "I think she just liked to arrange things for people. You could ask her."

"I beg your pardon?"

"At Ramananda's ceremony of passage. There will be a moment for those of us present to ask questions of the departed. If Ramananda feels an answer, he'll tell us."

"Right." Alec looked carefully at Theresa Tate, trying to decide if she was making fun of him or not.

"Well, I don't know if it works," Theresa said. "But I always believe in the possibility. Ramananda has quite a large following."

"Did Liza Jane believe in this stuff?" That didn't square either with the woman who arranged things for people, and did as she pleased. It had been his experience that cults attracted the lost and the bereft.

"She wanted to believe in something," Theresa said. "But she was intelligent, and rather skeptical. It made it hard. She was quite a regular church-goer, and she was involved with the Philotheists and the crystal healing people. She said to me once that she thought they all had hold of different ends of the same rope."

"How many ends has a rope got?" Alec asked, feeling rather as if he were at the end of his. He had been brought up to believe that whatever was on the opposite end of the rope was, by definition, the adversary. "What was she looking for?"

"Reassurance, I expect. The same as the rest of us."

A group of people passed the open door, and Theresa looked up. "Oh dear, Liddy's taking him to see her. I wonder if that's wise." She made an indeterminate movement on the sofa. "People don't look the same. I don't ever want anyone to look at me."

"I want to see her," Alec said abruptly. If he was invading Liza Jane's privacy, she had invaded his.

Theresa got up slowly. "All right. I wasn't going to, but perhaps I'll just steel myself. At my age one develops an aversion to coffins. I suppose one should meet it head on."

Alec followed her down the hall and through the kitchen with a renewed sensation of the world having been jolted into a new focus. He had envisioned the body laid out in a bedroom, like a dead monarch, but Roberto Vincente and his muscle were outside, standing at the head of a coffin, with Liddy Novak beside them, and Jeff Austin in the background. Vincente was patting Liddy's shoulder.

Sharon Hamilton was sitting in the kitchen, tapping her nails jumpily on the breakfast table. "I am not going out there," she said to no one in particular.

Alec opened the glass doors as Vincente took a red rose out of his pocket and laid it in the coffin. Alec had a fleeting glimpse of the famous face, carefully made up, as Liddy put the coffin lid down. It was heavy and it banged closed.

"That's it," she said, and the words came a little too loud. "That's the last time."

"She was always my girl," Vincente said. "You let me know what I can do to help out." He had been a handsome man but now his face sagged beneath his eyes and around his mouth. The eyes were still those of someone accustomed to getting his way.

The sound of footsteps came from below the veranda, and Liddy went down the stone stairs in a hurry, with Jeff behind her, while Alec looked at the closed coffin and at Roberto Vincente and added another question to his mental list.

A quick spatter of angry voices came up from the foot of the stairs.

"Get out! God damn you!"

Alec looked over the wrought-iron railing to see Liddy furiously trying to tug a camera out of a man's hands.

Jeff made a tentative movement toward them, and then threw up his hands in disgust. "Let it go, Lid. You can't stop them."

"He's not going to take pictures!" Liddy lost her grip on the camera, and the photographer stumbled, trying to hold it away from her.

Alec caught a glimpse of Liddy's face, from this angle oddly and briefly like her aunt's. He started after them. This was something he could deal with. Everything else seemed to be shifting planes, but he could bust the son of a bitch's camera.

Alec slithered down the last steps at a run as Liddy dived at the photographer again and he sent her sprawling in the leaves. Alec grabbed him by the collar and the photographer swung at him, the camera tucked under one arm. Alec stuck his feet between the other man's and dumped him professionally on the ground, while more faces appeared above them at the railing. Alec snagged the camera and tossed it at Liddy. A second man came running from the road, leaping Liza Jane's flower bed, skidding in the litter of oak leaves. Alec picked the photographer up and pushed him into his fellow.

"Goodness!" someone on the porch said. "Will you look at that!"

The reporters—presumably that was what they were—disentangled themselves from each other and came after Alec.

"Tony." Roberto Vincente jerked his thumb at the combatants, and his curly-haired muscle headed down the stairs.

Tony pulled the photographer off Alec. Alec flipped the second man and sat on him, until he saw that Tony had the photographer in his grip, one arm bent behind his back. The photographer's face was pallid. "You broke my goddamn arm," he whimpered.

"Nah," Tony said. "Dislocated it maybe."

Alec hauled his own captive to his feet, and they marched them to the road. The reporter twisted in his grip, and Alec said, "Shut up. You're lucky I got you instead of that goon." He felt his heart thudding, the old familiar adrenaline surge. Alec shoved the reporter toward a dark blue Toyota parked by the road, out of sight of the house. "That your car?" He opened the driver's door and pushed him into it. "Beat it."

"I'm gonna sue you," the reporter said venomously.

Tony went around to the other side and slung the photographer in beside him.

"I know who you are!" the photographer shouted. His voice cracked a little when he tried to move his arm. "My paper will sue!"

Tony shrugged. "You got lawyers. We got lawyers."

"That's Roberto Vincente up there. And they got a coffin on the back porch!"

"Well, neither one of 'em wants their picture taken," Tony said. "You gonna take off?" There was real menace in his voice.

The Toyota started to move.

"You're gonna hear from us!"

"The public has a right to know!"

The Toyota lurched onto the road and the photographer shrieked as his arm slammed against the door. "I want a doctor!" The Toyota picked up speed.

"Fuckin' piranha," Tony said. "They ain't legit, they're some supermarket rag."

"How do you know?" Alec leaned against a tree by the road, letting the adrenaline die down.

"Legit papers got all kindsa rules."

"Like don't fuck with Roberto Vincente?" Alec put his hands on his knees and took a couple of deep breaths.

"Not over this kinda crap." Tony straightened his coat. "They like to think they got dignity."

Alec wondered whose dignity he and Tony had been preserving, Elizabeth Sidney's or Vincente's. Now that the edge was off, the world looked slippery again. He started back toward the house.

"Just a minute."

Alec turned. Tony had his hand under his coat.

"While we're alone like, suppose you tell me why you're carrying a piece," Tony said.

Alec wondered if Elizabeth Sidney's friends and relations would display him on the back porch if Tony shot him.

"God damn it, I can see it," Tony said. "You got a shoulder holster on."

"I'm supposed to," Alec said.

"Yeah, why's that?"

Alec reached into his coat. Slowly, in case Tony was inclined to misinterpret him. He held up his badge. "I'm not a hit man, you asshole."

Tony's mouth twitched into the faint indication of a smile. He struggled with it, but he laughed. "Jesus, I guess you aren't." He shook his head. "All right by me. Takes all kinds to make a funeral." He thought some more. "Funny world," he said.

They walked back to the house. Interested faces looked down at them. Liddy had pulled the film out of the camera and thrown it on the ground. She was brushing leaves and dirt off her dress. Jeff leaned against the rock wall beside the steps, his arms folded. Tony picked the film and camera up and took them up the steps to his boss. He was stone-faced now, no sign of amusement.

Liddy looked at Alec. "Thank you."

"Captain Midnight," Jeff said. "And trained retriever."

"Jeff, shut up!" She walked away from him to Alec. "What they'll print will be bad enough without pictures."

Alec thought she looked on the verge of tears, and that it was not her normal state. "You okay?" he asked.

"I guess so," Liddy said. She looked up at the crowd on the porch. Ramananda Paradevi and his chorus line were draping the coffin with gauze scarves and what looked to Alec like the stones out of costume jewelry. He wondered if theatricality was bred in the bone in these people or if death simply accentuated what was already there.

"I have to go pick up my son from camp," she said. "Do you want to come with me? I can show you Ayala."

"Sure." Maybe she could tell him about Liza Jane.

Liddy went up the steps to get her purse, and Alec and Jeff followed her. As Jeff passed the coffin, he brushed his hand along it lightly, below the edge of the scarves.

Roberto Vincente was in the kitchen. The camera was sitting on the counter. He looked at Alec. "Not bad," he murmured appraisingly. "She may have liked you." He looked past Alec at something, maybe just the years. "You should of known her back then. I never cared she had other guys."

1942

Liza Jane is thirty-four. She's been to New York to see her brother Charlie before he ships out and to have dinner with Roberto Vincente. She likes Roberto and their relationship is uncomplicated. The studio doesn't mind. Roberto's several legitimate businesses are assisting the war effort and there is a temporary truce between the government and the mob, who are actually fairly patriotic.

Now she's on her way home to Los Angeles. The train rocks and sways as she tucks herself into her seat in the dining car. The windows are hung with heavy blackout curtains, and the train is crowded with soldiers on their way to the Pacific. Before lunch is over they'll be in Chicago. The white linen cloth is set with silver flatware, a rose in a crystal vase, and a heavy coffee cup turned mouth downward on its saucer.

An imposing steward hands her a menu and ushers a strange man into the seat opposite. Liza Jane raises an eyebrow at him. If it's crowded you can't have a table to yourself, but they don't put men with women traveling alone. And particularly not with her, unless she's asked them to. The steward avoids her eye with expertise.

"I apologize if I'm intruding." The man holds out his hand. "I'm Donald Wain."

Liza Jane blinks. She's sure he knows who she is; and she met Donald Wain last month on the set. Wain has money in the company too, and Morrie Zenovich likes for his backers to meet the actors. It gives them a little something extra, a little glamor for their money. This man doesn't look like an investor, a money man. He looks like a pirate without the eye patch—tall, dark-haired, with a mustache and a glint of the devil in his eye. A pirate in a very expensive suit. He's a bit like Roberto Vincente, the same air of getting what he wants.

He smiles. "You were expecting someone shorter and fatter. That's my father."

Liza Jane inspects him. "Donald Wain, Junior?"

"The Third." He unfolds his napkin and opens the menu. "I gave the steward twenty dollars to put me at your table."

The waiter pours ice water into their glasses from a silver pitcher; the ice chimes against the glass with the sway of the train. The engine ahead gives a mournful hoot, warning away whoever might be along the track.

"How could I miss a chance to have dinner with Anna Manning?" Donald Wain says.

"That was a part," Liza Jane says. He doesn't look like the type to fall in love with an image on the screen.

He's not. "I just joined the Air Corps. I am hoping to play on your sympathy and concern for our boys overseas."

Liza Jane defrosts in spite of herself. She likes a man with nerve and her baby brother Charlie is in the Air Corps. "I suppose it's my duty, then," she says. They grin at each other and a small spark arcs between them, electrically interesting.

They order and by the time the waiter brings their plates he has found out that she has a brother, a father who didn't approve of her acting, and that she is going home to star in a patriotic picture.

She's found out that the Wains have money in airplanes and oil, besides the studio. She wonders if pictures are an amusement for them.

"My father never puts money in anything for amusement," Wain says. "He says as long as you stay with Zenovich-Horizon, it'll make a profit."

"Does he?" Liza Jane wonders how much of an increase in her contract she can translate that into.

The waiter brings coffee and dessert. The train slows and hisses to a stop at Union Station. Liza Jane peers out the window. Soldiers and a few civilians are milling on the platform. A boy, a duffle bag at his feet, is kissing a weeping girl. A baggage cart goes by, loaded with trunks.

"It's like the movies," Wain says. "Little shots of other people's lives."

"You stitch them together and maybe there's a story." Liza Jane points at a heavyset man in an overcoat. "That man out there now— He's a notorious mobster just out of federal prison."

"Are you sure? Maybe he's a blameless family man coming home to the little woman with the evening sausage."

"Nah. Mobster." Liza Jane knows, because he is. The mob still has a piece of Zenovich-Horizon.

"Now that woman there," Wain says, pointing at a blonde in a fox fur, "is a spy for the Germans. She lures helpless flyboys into her web and seduces information from them."

Liza Jane chuckles but she thinks he might be telling the truth, too. Donald Wain looks like a man who knows things and knows how to use the information.

There's a bump as the cars are decoupled and Liza Jane grabs her water glass. After a few minutes they are recoupled to the Santa Fe Chief with another bump and rattle. The engine exhales a sigh of steam and they begin to move again, the rhythm of the driver wheels picking up, faster and faster.

"Can I buy you a drink?"

He takes her to the club car, through the vestibule that floats between the cars. She can see through a crack to the rushing ground below. They sit at a small table and drink whiskey sours. The rails clack and the car swings and rattles. There is something about being on this train, like being encapsulated in a cocoon, that makes her fairly certain something new is going to emerge at the other end. She's almost sure that somewhere along this three-day trip she will take him back to her sleeping compartment, find the bed made by the porter, her luggage, matching red leather cases, neatly stowed, and the rumble of the Pullman car to muffle anything that might be going to happen next.

She knows how it will be. They will wake outside Santa Fe, stretching luxuriously, tangled together in the narrow bed. Rise as the train grinds to a stop along the open platform, past the soldiers waiting to get on, and the Indian women sitting cross-legged in front of blankets full of souvenirs. He will buy her a kachina doll and she will dress hurriedly while he's gone, dab some perfume behind her ears, wink at herself in the mirror.

In Los Angeles she will pretend she doesn't know him because of the photographers who may be waiting, but everything will be forever changed, charged with electricity, and she will feel him in the dark sky overhead, sick with dread when she knows he's flying, living on V-mail and telegrams till the war's end. She will be her own movie.

III
Hollywood Stunned

1988

Liddy backed her aunt's elderly Mercedes out of its stall. Alec looked at the other contents of the garage, impressed. "Is that a Rolls Royce?"

"Yeah," Liddy said. "I'm afraid to drive it."

"I wouldn't be," Alec said. It was beautiful, a gleaming black. He thought it was about thirty years old.

"If we ever settle this damn will," Liddy said grimly, "I'll give it to you."

Alec chuckled. "What would I do with a Rolls?"

Liddy turned the car in the circle in front of the house. Several more cars were parked behind Alec's now. They ran heavily to BMWs, but there was an old Volkswagen bug too, and an elderly Ford.

"You know all these people?" Alec asked.

"Most of them," Liddy said. "I grew up here."

"I didn't know that."

She pulled the car onto Del Norte and headed down the hill. "My father was Liza Jane's younger brother. He sold airplanes. He and my mother were killed in one when I was eight. I lived with Liza Jane after that."

"Charmed life. Sorry, that was awful, you lost your parents. But this—" Alec waved a hand at the tree-shaded road, and the big houses set back under the oak trees. The house next door had a paddock with a pair of horses in it.

Liddy smiled. "It had its moments. There was always something going on. I knew all kinds of interesting people."

"Like Roberto Vincente?"

"Oh, he was always sweet on Liza Jane, even then. We used to see him when we were in New York." The smile flickered reminiscently. The shifting resemblance to her aunt came and winked out again.

She concentrated on the twists of the narrow road, like someone who had driven it a lot, but a long time ago. At the foot of the hill, she turned left into a neighborhood of one-story houses, small but not quite tract houses. They passed a gas station and a grocery store, and she turned twice more, onto Ayala Avenue, and braked at the single stoplight. On their left was a Spanish mission church and a similarly designed hotel with expensive looking cars in the driveway. The post office across the street was an ivy-covered building with a tall bell tower. Beyond the stoplight stretched a tile-roofed adobe arcade with shops beneath it, opposite a park with tennis courts and an amphitheater. There was another tree in the middle of the street. It was all very Spanish, but not self-consciously so. It looked old.

The light changed and they cruised past the Arcade, and then a few more shops and a Tastee Freeze, and then they were out in the country again, a golf course on the right, an open meadow on the left. Beyond the meadow were orange groves.

"The school's in the Upper Valley," Liddy said as the road began to climb.

"You'll miss the Ramananda's ceremony," Alec said.

"That's the idea." The faint smile reappeared. The road began to switchback. They passed a turn-out with a stone bench overlooking the valley floor.

"Good view," Alec said.

"This is where they filmed Lost Horizon," Liddy told him. "Just the opening shots. It's pretty at sunset. And at night when the lights come on. I used to come up here a lot."

He wondered who she had come up here with. It looked like a make-out spot. "You write books," he said after a few more turns. "I've never been able to write more than two decent sentences."

"It's a trick," Liddy said. "It's a controllable world. It's all at second hand." A few more turns. "Tell me what you do. I write about things like that, not very well, probably. I don't really know what it's like to do it."

"It's not very fancy," Alec said. "No spies. Not what people think. It's a job."

Her eyes slid toward him and back to the road. "It's not exactly selling insurance."

"No, I guess not. My dad's a cop. Pittsburgh police. Swore he didn't want me to do it."

"But you did anyway."

"Yeah, I was in the city cops like him. It kept me out of the draft anyway."

"Why did you get in the DEA?"

"More money, in the long run. I took a cut in pay to get in, but the prospects are better."

"Just like a job."

He wondered if after the theatricality of Hollywood, there was something unusual about talking to a person whose job offered the prospect of getting shot for real.

"What's the DEA like?" she asked.

Alec tried to think what to tell her. I lived in a rat hole for six months last year and when I got the guy I wanted, his lawyer stepped in, and he gave me the finger and walked? Let's have some pride here. "I had to finish college," he said. "They won't take you without a degree. Then you go for all kinds of interviews, and the FBI goes around and talks to your friends and your captain and your ex-wife and your third-grade teacher. If they don't find something they don't like, you're in."

"You've got an ex-wife?"

"Just one." He thought of Theresa Tate. "I gather that's small change around here."

"It is in Hollywood," Liddy said. "That's why I went to Virginia and married a contractor."

"Was that just luck?" Alec asked. "Or did you go to Virginia with a contractor in mind?"

"I went to Virginia because I didn't feel as if I was anyone here. Everyone else was about three sizes too large for their skin. I was just Liza Jane's reflection. Or it felt like it then. I met him while I was in college there."

"And you're still married." He made that as noncommittal as he could. He wasn't sure what he thought about Liddy Novak, but there was a dangerous glitter in the few chameleon moments that she looked like her aunt.

"I would be," she said. "But he died."

"Oh, shit, I'm sorry." He half turned to her, but she had her eyes on the road.

"It was a year ago." She eased the Mercedes into a hairpin curve. "Liza Jane liked him. They crawled all over her attic, trying to see if she could make a playroom there for Zach. That's my son. I had a playroom, but Liza Jane was thinking of something fabulously elaborate, like a built-in fort. She kept hoping we'd come back here."

"I found out she paid for my college," Alec said. "Both times. It rattled me."

"It rattled me," Liddy said. She took a turn a little too fast. "I don't resent the money, but why the hell didn't she tell me?"

"Not your business?" Alec suggested.

"You want to tell me what that has to do with it? I just thought I knew everything, but I guess I didn't. I guess I thought I was her kid."

"If it's any comfort," Alec offered, "it hasn't exactly simplified my life, either. What am I going to do if I end up with a million dollars?"

"Start a new religion," Liddy said. She swooped around another curve and then hit the brakes. "I'm sorry. Classic jealous sibling. I apologize."

"I apologize too," Alec said grandly.

Liddy chuckled. "We all apologize. Tell me about the DEA."

Alec felt for familiar turf. "They send you to training camp at the FBI Academy at Quantico. It's a sort of combination of law school and boot camp and the drop-out rate's hellacious. I thought I was gonna die." He wondered if he was showing off.

"From an overdose of law school?"

"From an overdose of exercise. I was the oldest one in my class. When it comes to climbing a 20-foot wall, there's a real advantage in being twenty-five. The only incentive is showing up the FBI cadets."

"They're different?"

"They wear little polo shirts," Alec said. "They're cute as hell." Now he was sure he was showing off. It was too easy. Her interest beckoned him, made him want to be realer for her than the Hollywood people; someone capable, who could do things. Like punch out photographers. He looked out the car window, embarrassed.

The Mercedes climbed the top of the mountain, and the road leveled out into the Upper Valley. Orange groves alternated with apple and apricot orchards, and there was the faint sensation of a hum of bees. The road narrowed as it crossed a gully and then wound through more orchards. The light was whiter than east coast light, dusty and beautiful, everything bordered by unstable auras shimmering against the terracotta roofs and gray-green bushes.

Apple Valley School was a collection of white, poured-concrete buildings that mirrored the white rock face of a mountain in the distance. The yurt was in a meadow, a round, vaguely mushroom like structure with cloth sides. As they got out of the car, a gong sounded from inside it, and a dozen children came out.

"They meditate at the end of the day," Liddy said. "I wasn't very good at it. I'm too distractible."

A lanky teacher in safari shorts, with a peace symbol on a leather cord around his neck, came up with Zach by the hand.

"Hi, Peter," Liddy said. She introduced him to Alec and cocked her head at Zach. "Did you have a good time?"

"I caught a frog," Zach said. "And a water bug. The frog ate it."

"I'm afraid we had an abrupt lesson in the food chain," Peter said.

"We put the frog back," Zach said.

Peter smiled. "We don't tinker with the ecology here, we just borrow a little of it now and then." Shouting drew his attention and he said goodbye and headed for two boys who were rolling in the dirt, ineffectually trying to punch each other.

"This is Mr. Murray," Liddy told Zach.

"Hi," Alec said.

Zach considered Alec warily. "Hi." He had blond hair, and eyes the same gray-green as Liddy's.

"You want to ride in front with your mom?" Alec asked.

Zach nodded, and they climbed in. As Liddy turned the car, they saw that Peter had picked up the two combatants, one under each arm. Peter was stronger than he looked. "If you fight, they make you sit down and talk to each other about it," Zach informed them.

"Sounds reasonable," Alec said.

"You ever try it?" Liddy murmured.

"I don't get much chance."

"Bernice believes in that theory," Liddy said. "She tried to be completely open and honest with Sharon Hamilton one time, about Sharon wearing lizard shoes. There wasn't much space for what you'd call communication."

Zach slid down in the front seat, yawning. Liddy said they had a quiet time at this camp, but that anyone who didn't want to lie down didn't have to; they were supposed to choose. Alec suspected that Zach only lay down when he was too tired to stand up, or when someone forced him to.

Alec looked at the back of Liddy's head. All he could see in the rearview mirror was the arch of her eyebrows. "How many of these people showing up are going to know about me?" he asked her.

"All of them by now," Liddy said. "You're a hot topic."

"I wish you'd sort them out for me. I couldn't keep track."

"They're hard to sort. It's very incestuous and everyone's connected. It'll be like one of those family reunions where half the people hate each other, or used to be married to each other."

She glanced at Zach, who had gone to sleep, no doubt to make sure he still was. In Alec's experience, six-year-olds had some of the capabilities of an intelligent tape recorder, and were prone to repeat conversations best left unreported.

"I'll try," she said. "You met Theresa. Sharon Hamilton is Theresa's agent too. Sharon used to be an actress, and she used to be married to a screenwriter who's coming today. Mike Rosen."

"What's his connection?"

"Mike's another of Liza Jane's beaux. Lovers. Look, she had

a lot, she wasn't a saint."

"And his wife was her agent?"

"I think Liza Jane and Mike happened a few years after the divorce. And way before Sharon was her agent. Sharon's a dynamite agent, and there isn't an agent in Hollywood who wouldn't have killed to get Liza Jane. That was business."

"Okay."

"Well, I told you it was incestuous. Then there's Ben Zenovich. Ben's father bought Horizon Pictures and founded Zenovich-Horizon, but it got sold to a conglomerate in the sixties. Ben's an independent producer-director now. Frank Hill's his protégé. He's made five or six pictures with Ben."

"It sounded like Hill was Liza Jane's protégé, too," Alec murmured.

"Well, he was," Liddy said. "I remember Frank then, it was a couple of years after I came to live with her. He was just starting over again, just out of the Army and Vietnam, waiting tables and things like that when he couldn't get a job. He was very intense about his work, but funny. He really did like Liza Jane, it wasn't just an eye to the main chance. I guess she was about sixty then, but she was a knockout. Frank's an interesting guy. He used to play Scrabble with me, and he knew more weird words than anybody I ever met."

Alec blinked. "This was all going on under your nose?"

"Well, when Liza Jane was at home the house was always full of people. It wasn't just Frank staying there. But I was about ten, and I didn't really have any conception of grown-ups' relative ages. You don't, at ten. So maybe I put two and two together quicker than a lot of people would." She tipped her head and her eyes caught his in the mirror. "If you're going to be disapproving, you'll be doing her an injustice."

"I'm not," Alec said hastily. No one seemed to want him to disapprove of Liza Jane. "Her life just sounds a little larger than life."

"I suppose it was, but she wasn't any worse than the rest of them. It's not their fault really. It's the training. If you spend your life learning to be theatrical, you can't just shut it off. Not everyone's like that. Frank's turning into an absolute hermit. But a pretty high proportion. Liza Jane loved it. It was her element. She never thought a dinner party was interesting if there wasn't at least one fight and one illicit love affair out of it. She was always sweet to me, but it was like growing up in a movie. There had to be plenty of action, and things got rewritten from one day to the next."

They had come to the foot of the mountain. As the Mercedes nosed through the mild afternoon traffic along the Arcade, Alec said, "What about Ayala? The whole town can't be like that. Doesn't somebody have to run things?"

"Make rules that say you can't bury your aunt in the back yard? Sure. But Ayala's too tied to L.A. There's a kind of aftershock that ripples its way in. Well, you saw the school I went to. And the Ramananda's a local product. Hollywood people drive up for dinner at the Horsehead Ranch all the time. The ones who live here direct plays at the Art Center, and work on the Jazz Festival. Bernice is the one who started a petition and made them leave the tree when they redid the Avenue."

"The party in the peasant skirt?"

"Bernice is an Ayala institution by now. She knows everybody. She makes jewelry and has a little shop along here somewhere. She used to be a wardrobe mistress at Zenovich-Horizon. In the sixties she went to Alabama and marched in the civil rights movement. She's working on the homeless and nuclear disarmament now. Every so often she takes a vacation and turns up on the six o'clock news, getting arrested."

"She looked after you? When Liza Jane was gone?"

Liddy chuckled. "Well, she made sure I didn't eat white sugar.

In the sixties, mind you, when doctors were still saying it was food. And that I knew who John L. Lewis was. And Martin Luther King. Things she figured were important. If the house had burned down, I expect she could have managed to get me out."

A few minutes passed in silence. "I was thinking about what you said about jealous siblings," Alec said. "Adopted kids are supposed to be excited as hell when they find their blood relatives. I'm not exactly sure what it is I've got here. It feels like the stateroom scene from A Night at the Opera."

Liddy flicked a glance at him. "Liza Jane had a print of that. There's a wonderful film library at the house. I always loved that picture, but it seemed a little too much like home to really appreciate it." She turned the Mercedes into a side street and pulled up in front of a Chinese restaurant. "Would you mind sitting in the car, in case Zach wakes up? I'm going to get dinner. Bernice can't possibly cook for all these people. And I'm hoping the Ramananda's through with whatever it is he's going to do before we get back. I'm afraid it might scare Zach."

"Sure," Alec said. "It scares me."

Ramananda Paradevi slung his arms toward the setting sun. "Now we're just going to attune ourselves and see what messages come through." An evening breeze whisked the gauze scarves around the coffin, and the amethyst crystal sphere at its center caught the light. Bernice and Theresa Tate and the Ramananda's followers held their hands out toward it. They had been joined by a wispy woman in a straw hat and a man in a turtleneck sweater, who had brought a zucchini casserole and kept saying that Liza Jane had meant the world to them.

"Can't you make them stop that?" Sharon Hamilton glared through the glass doors from the kitchen.

"Not me." Jeff was perched on the kitchen counter. Except for Roberto Vincente, the rest of them had congregated where they always had, in Liza Jane's kitchen. Sharon was still drumming her fingernails on the breakfast table.

Outside, the Ramananda had produced a medium-sized crystal ball and was running his fingers over it, eyes closed.

"Bernice gets worse every year," Sharon snapped. "Where's Liddy?"

"She went off with Captain Midnight." Jeff picked an apple out of a bowl on the counter and bit into it.

"Oh, for— of all the irresponsible—" Sharon gave up on Jeff. "Harry, when does that publicist get here?" She regarded the publicist rather as she might an exterminator, whose function was to arrange interviews with the appropriate people, and to remove the inappropriate of all descriptions. He couldn't remove Bernice, unfortunately, but at least he could get rid of the Ramananda.

"In the morning," Harry said. "I got Steve Bowman."

"He's good," Sharon said approvingly.

"The best. You use him, don't you, Frank?"

"Yeah," Frank Hill said gloomily from the corner. He was watching the ceremony. He hated publicists, but his impending divorce from a rock star wife had necessitated that he hire someone or go mad.

"I'm just as glad he's coming up," Ben Zenovich said. He was standing a little behind Frank. "Francie was in Toronto and she threw a stinking fit when we left. Maybe Steve can divert her off Frank's trail and tone her down some. She was already playing hell with the picture."

Frank shot a glance at Ben over his shoulder. "So does a five-day layoff. Nobody ever toned Francie down," he added moodily.

There was a general murmuring of sympathy. Frank Hill and

Francie Allen had been a show business golden couple when they had married two years ago, with Francie's band playing at the all-night reception, and innumerable Frank-and-Francie stories and the standard quotes from the happy couple about being very much in love. Now that they were splitting, the publications that followed these things had seized upon them with ruthless glee. Francie's temper, volatile at best, was suffering under the onslaught and the aggravations of attempting to part their tangled finances.

"I just want to get back to work," Frank muttered.

"That's the ticket," Harry said. "Work's what matters."

Frank gave Ben Zenovich a baleful glare. "How the hell can I work in the middle of the Goon Show?" He got up, banging his chair against the wall. "If Mike brings that script, I want you to read it."

"Mike Rosen's got some new thing Frank's hot to do," Ben said as Frank disappeared down the hall, his hands in his pockets.

Sharon smacked her fist on the table. "How nice of everyone not to bother to mention to me that Mike's coming."

"Well, you knew he would," Ben said. "Take a deep breath. Mike owes Liza Jane a lot."

"In or out of bed?" Sharon inquired. "And counting or not counting the chance to pitch a script?"

"Most of us owe Liza Jane a hell of a lot more than that." Ben fiddled uncomfortably with his watch. "The script's coincidental."

"Sure. That's why Frank's here. Let's just take a little meeting, as long as we're at a funeral."

"Frank's here because I hauled his ass down here," Ben said.

"I thought you were all grateful to Liza Jane," Sharon snapped. "God damn it, isn't there anything to eat?" She looked at the zucchini casserole with loathing.

"Can it, Sharon," Harry said. "Frank's grateful, he's just embarrassed. She was thirty-five years older than he was, for

Christ's sake. He doesn't want it all dug up again."

"Faint hope," a new voice said. Mike Rosen tossed a tabloid newspaper on the kitchen table, with the air of a man politely implying that he hadn't heard the rest of the conversation. He was in his sixties, his short-cropped gray hair neatly combed now, vaguely professorial looking in a gray tweed jacket over a brown turtleneck. He shook the hands that were offered him, and Sharon's, which wasn't. "Radiant as ever," he said a touch acidly. "Did you know there's a mob boss and his bodyguard in the living room?"

"We noticed," Ben said. "Did you see Frank?"

"He was in there, too, reading a book."

"Good plan."

They inspected the tabloid. There was a color photograph of Liza Jane on the cover, and smaller ones of Frank Hill and Francie Allen.

Francie Furious as Frank Mourns Elizabeth Sidney
Hollywood Stunned by Mystery Heir

"How the hell did they get hold of that so fast?" Harry said. "I'm gonna go into real estate, I swear."

Mike pointed a finger at the darkening glass doors, through which the shadowy forms of the Ramananda Paradevi and his congregation could be seen. They looked vaguely insect like, raising their arms above the coffin, and there was the faint sound of chanting. "They get hold of that yet? Or the mobster?"

"Tomorrow's story," Jeff said from his perch on the counter. "Watch this space. The mystery heir busted the guy's camera, which ought to piss the press off nicely."

Sharon spun around in her chair, her aggravation focusing on Jeff. "And suppose you tell me just what use you are?"

Liddy and Alec came through the door with Zach, their arms

full of sacks, enveloped in the odor of sweet and sour pork. Jeff got down off the counter. "I set the table," he said to Sharon. He disappeared into the dining room while Alec was being introduced to Mike Rosen.

Outside, the insect humming ceased, leaving only a faint chorus of tree frogs. The Ramananda flowed into the kitchen, with his young followers behind him. One clutched an armful of scarves, the other a redwood box, presumably containing the crystal ball. She held it reverently, like an offering.

"The Ramananda has a message for you," she whispered as she glided past Liddy. She looked about seventeen. Her voice was thin and nasal, her hair a dispirited blond. Zach touched a fingertip to her sari.

"A message, yes," the Ramananda said. "The message is peace, and harmony with the vibrations of the Universe. Our benefactress is at peace."

Liddy looked him in the eye. "I'd invite you to stay for dinner, but I don't expect you eat any of this."

"Animal flesh." The Ramananda smiled gently. "No. I tried to convince Liza Jane, but..."

"Well, then, it was good of you to come by. I'm sure your service was... helpful."

"Oh, just immensely helpful." The woman in the hat embraced Liddy. "Don't you look wonderful."

"Thank you, June," Liddy said. Her back to the wall, she added, "Would you like to stay?"

"Well, we shouldn't..." June looked around the room. She had a plain, lined face and an air of wistfulness. "But such fascinating company. Well, just for a little. Don't you think, Stu?"

"Sure," Stu said. He was the man in the turtleneck sweater. "Stu Patterson." He held his hand out to the room. "Glad to meet you folks."

Liza Jane's dining room was enormous, like all of the first floor rooms, and held a table that would seat twenty, in ornate ladder-back chairs, on a red Turkish carpet. A portrait of Liza Jane hung over the sideboard, in no role but her own, wearing an elaborate white lace and cotton dressing gown, her red hair brushed back from her face, and a pug, long since departed, on her lap. She was fifty when it was painted.

They sat down at the table, on which Jeff had provided plates, placemats and napkins, and forks as well as chopsticks. Sharon Hamilton sat as far away as she could get from Mike Rosen, but spoiled the effect by clattering her fork and glaring at him. Alec found himself opposite the portrait, between Theresa Tate and Frank Hill. June and Stu had managed to sit on Frank's other side, and Frank had the strangled look of a man who had somehow contrived to be caught outdoors naked.

"Well! How exciting this all is," June said. "Such an exciting gift to our foundation, too. A sad occasion, of course, but we must all be glad she didn't linger."

There was a muffled snort from Harry Lanier at the other end of the table.

"I rather thought that was the problem," Sharon said acidly, but June wasn't listening to her. She was confiding to Frank Hill, with interpolations from Stu, that she had a wonderful idea for a movie.

Roberto Vincente looked across the corner of the table at Liddy. Tony, beside him, was stolidly wolfing sweet and sour pork. "What plans have you made for the funeral?" Vincente asked.

"Arlo Sheppard is researching the law on private burial grounds," Liddy said.

"Good. You give her what she wants. She was a great lady." Vincente applied himself to his plate without further comment. When he had finished, he stood up and made a motion like a bow at Liddy. "I will be at the Ayala Inn. You tell me when the funeral's set." He glanced at Tony, who put his fork down mid-bite.

As they exited, Frank Hill got up, too. "I've got a script to read," he muttered. "I'll just put my plate in the kitchen."

"He's going to finish his dinner in there," Theresa whispered to Alec. "He hates to talk to people like that."

June looked after him mistily. "Such a nice man, and so interested. Just like I thought he would be. I can always tell. Well, we must be running, too. The foundation's in such an uproar. Looking for guidance in the crisis, you know."

"Foundation for Holistic Health," Stu said. "You folks come and see our work. Open invitation. Any time." They departed with a wave.

"Bolt the doors," Harry suggested.

Bernice put her chopsticks down. "A little more love and sharing would be becoming in you, Harry. Those are Liza Jane's friends."

"So am I," Harry said. "I'm not required to like the rest of 'em."

"We aren't required to like you either," Theresa said. "We're just polite."

"I don't like any of you," Ben said. "Give me another egg roll."

Harry grinned at him and passed the paper carton down the table. "I'm sorry to hear Mrs. Talliaferro's still in a coma," he said to Theresa.

"Well, it's restful that way," Theresa said, "All I have to do is lie down."

"The makeup must be unpleasant," Liddy said.

"Oh, that's the irony, dear. They hardly use any. Makes me

look dreadful." Theresa sighed. "I remember the days when it took four hours in makeup to make me look that bad. I'm afraid there's a rumor in the wind that it's fatal, too. I don't suppose any of you have heard any scuttlebutt?"

"Not out my way," Ben said.

"Well, you wouldn't," Theresa said. "Cinema snob. Ben doesn't do television," she said to Alec.

"Aggravation factor's too high," Ben said.

Harry lifted his bottle of beer. "To a speedy recovery for Mrs. Talliaferro."

"I hope she makes it," Alec said. "I like her."

"Dear boy. It's a terrible grind, though. I get up at five, and I'm afraid my bones do feel it."

"Why don't you retire?"

"Oh, dear." Theresa laughed gently. "No money."

Alec looked embarrassed.

"Oh, don't blush. Everyone knows. My last husband was into creative finance. I'm afraid the IRS discovered it before I did. Liza Jane offered to help out, but of course I couldn't do that." Theresa snatched up her napkin and wiped her eyes. "Damn, I'm crying again. Oh, God, she was so good to me."

To Theresa Tate, my jewelry. The bequest clicked into Alec's mind. Not money, but jewelry, which could be sold quietly, and with unscarred pride.

Theresa blew her nose.

Alec looked up at the portrait above the sideboard. The green eyes looked back at him serenely, but the expression in the curving lips was less placid than it had seemed before. He thought he saw pity and a certain bewilderment in it. For whom, he couldn't say.

"She was good to all of us," Mike Rosen said. "Possibly more than some of us deserve." Under his tweedy demeanor, there was some raw, unscabbed nerve, Alec thought.

"What's that supposed to mean?" Sharon abandoned the

pretense that he wasn't there.

"I just meant me," Mike said. "She got me an assignment when no one would hire me." He looked a little belligerent.

"Oh, dear, the bad old days." Theresa translated for Alec again, although this time a lot of them looked as if they wished she wouldn't. "There was a blacklist in Hollywood after the war and through the fifties, during all the communist-hunting and the McCarthy hearings. A lot of people got in trouble who were perfectly innocent."

Sharon pushed her chair back. "A lot of people got in trouble who were stupid, too. I'm going to bed."

"Maybe we should just meditate or something," Harry said, "and not try to carry on a conversation."

Liddy was picking pieces of chicken out of the moo goo gai pan for Zach. She stopped when she noticed that he was yawning and feeding them to a pug under the table. "I'm going to put him to bed," she said.

"I'll help you." Jeff picked Zach up and slung him over his shoulder. "He's dead on his feet."

"Godalmighty, what a day." Liddy said as Jeff dumped Zach on the bed with the foxes. She began tugging Zach's jeans off.

"That's a nice kid," Jeff said. He poked in the chest of drawers into which Liddy had finally managed to sort Zach's clothes, and pulled out a pair of G.I. Joe pajamas. "These do?"

"Fine."

Jeff sat Zach up while Liddy unbuttoned his shirt. "We met this morning. I took him to see the fish."

"Thanks." Liddy hauled Zach to his feet. "Come on. Two

nights in a row without brushing your teeth is against the Mommy Rules."

"I can do it," Zach said. He went in the adjoining bathroom and turned the water on.

Liddy sat down on the bed. "I think he liked camp, thank God. There isn't anything for him to do here but listen to grown-ups fight about stuff he doesn't understand."

Jeff sat down beside her. "Sharon was in a snit."

"Wasn't she just? But I don't feel I can take it on myself to make her behave. You wouldn't think a divorce that old would rankle that much."

"Mike was prodding her," Jeff said. "He's got something under his hat. Didn't you notice a certain sense of great dark clouds of history rolling over the table?"

"I haven't got time for history."

"Yeah," Jeff said. "How was your outing with Captain Midnight?"

"Will you not call him that? It wasn't an outing. I showed him the town while we were picking Zach up. I asked him about his job."

"Man of action. Derring-do."

Liddy gave him an exasperated look. "If you must know, I'm not happy with my books. I can write to the genre. They sell. But I'm not always sure why the people I write about do the things they do. I thought maybe he could tell me."

"Did he?"

"Not exactly. I think maybe he could."

"Maybe you could, if you got a little deeper into 'em. I think you're scared to quit hanging around the edges of what you already know and jump in, afraid you'll drown in whatever's in there."

"You know what I think?" Liddy said. "I think the pot's calling the kettle black."

Jeff got up as Zach turned the water off and padded into the bedroom. "The pot has a passing acquaintance with the kettle," he said, "and I offered to show you what I've been doing." He stood in the doorway a moment. "It's not easy to leave off the simple thing and make what scares you. Art's a bitch that way."

"Maybe I'll write the definitive You-can't-go-home-again novel," Liddy said. She started tucking Zach in. "God knows there's material."

The dinner party had broken up. Sharon had gone to bed, and Frank was shut in the library with the script. Ben and Mike went out together, more by chance than design, to drive their separate cars to separate cabins at the Horsehead Ranch. Theresa announced her intention of going to bed as well, and Harry headed down to a little paneled study in the basement to make phone calls. They seemed to spend an inordinate amount of time on the telephone, Alec had noted, with nearly as many calls outgoing as incoming. He wondered who paid the phone bill, or whether there was so much money floating around that nobody cared.

Bernice was clearing the table, and Alec picked up a stack of plates and a bucket half full of fried rice. A flood of pugs surged around his feet. Bernice fed them the scraps off a fork. Alec was still aware, although he had ceased to be actively unnerved by it, of Liza Jane's body outside the darkened glass doors.

"I expect this has made a lot of trouble for you," he ventured, trying to reconcile this plain woman in a bun, feeding pugs, with the activist of Liddy's description.

"It's all part of the flow," Bernice said, but he thought there was an edge in her voice that she might not have noticed.

He brought the rest of the cartons from the table. Bernice put the empty ones down for the pugs to lick. "Just put the others in the refrigerator. Someone will eat them tomorrow."

There seemed to be a lot of other stuff in the refrigerator already: the zucchini casserole and home-baked bread and other funeral offerings, and a glass dish of some kind of sprouts. Alec wedged the cartons into the corners.

Bernice stacked the plates in the dishwasher, and put the pugs' cartons in the trash. "Breakfast," she murmured, inspecting cupboards.

"Does wonton keep?" Alec asked, looking into the last carton.

"Not very well." Bernice dried her hands on her apron with decision. "We can't go on like this. Tomorrow I cook."

"For all these people?"

She smiled at him. It changed her face immensely, gave it a look of things being very nearly right with her world. "Oh, we've always had a lot here. It didn't seem right until they all started coming."

Alec thought that he had begun to see the layers of Liza Jane's life around the dinner table. Bernice and Liddy as the nucleus, or maybe just the base. Her business manager and her agent as one layer of the Hollywood contingent; old friends and lovers as another. Friends from Ayala as another, the people who had trooped in and out all day bringing fruit baskets and bread. Maybe the Ramananda was another, a toga-clad spirit guide for whatever strange soul search Liza Jane had embarked on. Not to mention Roberto Vincente. He wasn't sure where Jeff Austin fit in, and even less sure where he himself did. He seemed to have been a thread running unmentioned through her life somewhere. A peripheral one, he would have said, but did you leave a million dollars to periphery?

"I've put you in Liza Jane's room," Bernice said.

Alec looked at her and made some startled, indeterminate noise, like a comic book character saying, Huh? Wha-?

"We're out of bedrooms, you see." Bernice's voice was matter-of-fact, as if it was logical that he should rest in a dead actress's bed. "It's a big house, but there are seven people staying here, besides me, and I hate to make Liddy sleep with Zach. Children thrash around so. I slept with Liddy once, in a hotel, when she was nine. She wrapped up in all the covers, like a cocoon, and had dreams. I got up and read a book."

"I wouldn't want to put her out," Alec said hastily.

Bernice was untying her apron now, hanging it up. "I could have put Liddy in there, of course, but I thought—" She looked at him directly, with sad eyes. There was a splotch of something on the Greenpeace t-shirt. "I thought you might attune yourself. I thought there might be something left."

"Oh, sure, it's fine," he said hastily. "Anything."

Bernice took him upstairs, and he followed her into a bedroom with a Chinese carpet and a Victorian mahogany bed with a hand-pieced quilt on it. He wasn't sure what he had been expecting (a round bed, satin sheets?) but it didn't look like it. It looked like his grandmother's room, with overtones of glamour. His suitcase was on the chest at the foot of the bed.

"Goodnight," Bernice said. "I'm glad you've come."

"Bernice—"

She looked back at him from the door.

"Did you know about me?"

"No," Bernice said. "But I'm not surprised."

She vanished into the hall and he saw the hall light go off. Alec looked around, wondering if there was anything left. How did you know? He had always felt like a dead battery as far as any spiritual revelations were concerned, but Liza Jane so thoroughly permeated her own house that it might be hard to tell. This room seemed as close as he might get to the heart of her. There were no movie stills or signed photographs here, only a collection of what looked like family pictures on the walls. Alec looked at them, wondering if he was prying, or whether he was supposed to.

Liza Jane with a man in a World War II flying jacket, who looked vaguely like her. Liza Jane and Theresa Tate, young, in twenties bobs and Cupid's-bow mouths, sitting on the horses on a carousel, giggling and waving. Liddy in a garishly striped minidress, her hair hanging over her shoulders, not quite a teenager. Liddy in a white dress, solemnly clutching a diploma. Liddy and Jeff Austin (young, long hair, faces not defined yet) standing on the front porch, his arms around her waist, leaning back from each other, mugging for the camera.

Alec got into bed. A pug nosed the door open and joined him. It licked his nose and snorted, and curled up on his feet. Oak leaves rattled against the window like a splatter of rain, but the sky was clear and moonshot; a ghostly luminescence drifted through the trees. Alec lay on his back, eyes open, trying to see if anything was drifting in it; Liza Jane, walking the perimeter of her kingdom. What had brought her to settle so deeply into this house that she couldn't leave it now?

He turned to switch off the light. Another picture, in a silver frame, sat on the nightstand: Liza Jane and a man Alec didn't recognize, arm in arm under a tree. Liza Jane had on a suit with big shoulders and a narrow skirt, and a little hat with a veil. The man was in uniform, tall, ruggedly good-looking. A billboard in the background said: Buy War Bonds. The man looked out confidently at the camera. Whoever he was, Liza Jane would have seen his face every night before she slept.

1943

Liza Jane is thirty-five, and she's dancing with Donald Wain at his mother's USO benefit. Mrs. Wain doesn't approve of actresses, but a tame celebrity draws everyone else in. Mrs. Wain is doing her bit for the war that's making her husband rich.

Clothes are skimpy now. There's a government regulation for everything, including how much material you can put in a dress. Liza Jane's gown is slinky black velvet, slit to the knee, with little cap sleeves and shoulder pads. Her hair hangs in waves from a low side part. She knows that her fame and face are a valuable commodity. She's been on a USO tour to Burma, posed for a pin-up in shorts and a halter top, joined the Red Cross.

Don's home on leave, the second celebrity at his mother's party, in an Air Corps captain's uniform, with a store of exciting stories to tell about the air war. He also has nightmares, which his mother doesn't know, although Liza Jane does.

His mother has hired Tommy Dorsey and his orchestra for the occasion. Liza Jane and Don are doing a fast, fancy foxtrot to "The G.I. Jive."

"You're a brick to do this, you know that?" Don says.

"All for the war effort." Liza Jane grins. She came to see him, and he knows it. Don is thirty-six, dark-haired, with a debonair mustache. He's a businessman, too old to be flying planes, but he had a private pilot's license before the war, and he's good at it, and determined, despite the dreams he has of circling slowly, spinning down to a black ocean in a plane he can't get out of. Liza Jane doesn't know why Don's so determined to keep flying, and she doesn't think he knows either, and suspects it's because he's afraid. Her brother's in the Air Corps, too, God knows where. She gets V-mail from both of them, censored half the time.

The war is both terrifying and exhilarating to Liza Jane. She is more comfortable now in the company of women, ordinary women, than she has ever been before. Women are flying transport planes, welding armor plating in shipyards, leading their lives, so many of them, without men to lean on, that Liza Jane feels they have come alive. Even Mrs. Wain heads a Civilian Defense unit, knows the silhouettes of enemy planes and scans the skies from a lookout post on Mulholland Drive, a Helen Hokison cartoon matron with binoculars and a steel hat. No one has seen a Japanese plane yet, but in New York Liza Jane has seen tankers burning on the sea, hit by German subs; she's watched drowned and oil-begrimed bodies come in on the tide.

The orchestra swings the song to a fast close and Mrs. Wain takes the microphone. The party has a red-white-and-blue theme, with bunting over the blackout curtains. She introduces Maurice Zenovich, whose actors and actresses, she says, have done so much to lift our boys' morale. Zenovich-Horizon is making a fat contribution, in the hope that the other guests will be induced to pony up, in addition to the fifty-dollar tab for their tickets.

Liza Jane, terminally irreverent, thinks of another Helen Hokison cartoon. A hatchet-faced woman in uniform is sitting by a lectern in somebody's drawing room. Beside her, the hostess is informing an audience of assembled Mrs. Wains that "Miss Whitehead has come to tell us how to amuse sailors."

Now Mrs. Wain introduces Liza Jane: "A special treat." Liza Jane fiddles with the microphone (she's taller than Morrie Zenovich) and sings "I'll See You Again" and then "When the Lights Go On Again." She's not a trained singer, but she can hold her own. She has a husky alto voice that's just right for the mood.

Morrie Zenovich says, "Atta girl," and when the orchestra tunes up again she dances this one with him, revolving solemnly, looking down at the top of his bald head.

Morrie says, "So how's the millionaire flyboy?"

"He's fine." Liza Jane can see Don waiting to dance with her again, sitting smoking at one of the little ice cream tables his mother has rented to put around the edges of the ballroom.

"Well, don't do anything stupid," Morrie says.

"What's stupid?"

"Don't get married and pack in your career," Morrie says.

Liza Jane gives Don a sideways glance. "He hasn't asked me."

"Well, when he does, don't."

"Morrie—"

"You listen to me, kid. I haven't steered you wrong yet. You aren't cut out for pushing a perambulator and going to the goddamned garden club."

"Heaven forfend," Liza Jane says. "The garden club anyway."

"All of it," Morrie says. "You take the perambulator, you'll get the rest. This guy's gonna run his old man's business after the war. His wife he's gonna want home in a cute little apron, not up there on a movie screen kissing in her underwear some other guy. You stick with the damn gangster if you gotta chase men. He doesn't want to marry you."

"I'm not seeing him," Liza Jane says. "Don doesn't like it. And I have no intention of quitting work."

"You will if you marry him," Morrie says gloomily.

The next day Don picks Liza Jane up at the studio and takes her to lunch. Morrie Zenovich watches her get in the car, and he shakes his head. She hasn't listened to him, he can tell by looking at her. She's got on a little gray gabardine suit and a big cartwheel hat with cabbage roses and a gray veil, and she looks breathless. Actresses, Morrie thinks. They haven't got any more sense than the rest of the women in this war, all getting married en masse, like sheep.

The subject of marriage doesn't quite come up at lunch, but Liza Jane and Don are working around the edges of it. They're both in their thirties, never married, and excited and unsettled to find themselves thinking about it.

"You want a drink?" Don says.

"Not till dinner. I'll fluff my lines."

"I've only got three more days," Don says. "Can't you get time off till I go?"

"Not in the middle of a picture." She tries to explain it to him again. Don already has money in Zenovich-Horizon, but it's an investment. He doesn't really understand how making a picture works. "I can't ask to shut down a whole set." A movie simply eats money even when it's not shooting.

"Can't they shoot around you?"

"The production schedule's all set. They'd have to cancel extras, try to bring in people who're tied up somewhere else this week, mess up the contracts for everything that's rented. The next set's not even built yet. You can't just whip up a jungle." The movie is set in the Philippines, and locations now are created entirely within a sound stage. An encapsulated world. Liza Jane sticks a fork in her salad. "It's just not feasible."

"The studio might as well own you," Don says.

"It's my job."

Don looks at her thoughtfully. "How important is it to you? All the hoopla and the magazine covers?"

"The acting's important to me," Liza Jane says. "It's what I do."

"What about me?"

"You're important, too. More than anybody. But you're not a job."

Don grins. "Maybe I could be."

Liza Jane thinks about what Morrie said while Don drives her back to the studio. She knows that's how Don looks at marriage. But she's too happy just to be with him to argue about it now. She's never been in love before. He walks her back to the sound stage as if he's seeing her home from a date, and she beckons him inside with her. She can't bear to turn him loose, and maybe if he sees how things work...

From the outside, Sound Stage 23 looks like a warehouse; it reads ZENOVICH-HORIZON in big black letters on the side. Over the door it reads DO NOT ENTER WHEN LIGHT IS ON. Just now everyone is streaming back from lunch, from the actors' lunch room and the crew commissary. A short, bald man with a paunch pushes past them, muttering irritably to himself.

"Who the hell is that?" Don asks, offended.

Liza Jane snickers. "That's Laurence Hotchkiss."

Don opens his eyes wide. He puts his hand about three feet off the ground. "That's Hotchkiss? I thought it was a Munchkin."

"It takes him a while to get dressed," Liza Jane says. "Come on." She takes him into her temporary dressing room inside the sound stage and pulls off the cartwheel hat. She puts a finger to her lips. "He wears lifts," she whispers. "And a wig." Don is starting to laugh. "Shush! And a corset. One day it popped." She's starting to giggle again. "It pulled the buttons off his shirt!" By this time they are both dissolved in laughter. Liza Jane puts her finger back up to her lips. "Larry's very sensitive," she manages to hoot before she breaks up again. She's been taking off the gabardine suit while she talks and pulling on an Army nurse's fatigues. Don looks a little embarrassed. Everyone on the set knows he's in there while she's dressing.

Someone knocks on the door. "Ready, Miss Sidney?"

Liza Jane tucks her arm through Don's, and tells him, "Come on."

A single work light illuminates the set. Ford Waring, the director, is blocking the scene with Liza Jane and Larry Hotchkiss. Larry is taller now, with dark hair and a muscular physique. Don Wain finds himself a seat in the shadows and watches, bemused. He sure as hell wouldn't have known Hotchkiss on the street. It makes him wonder how much of all the other people he sees on the screen comes out of a box from Western Costume. Liza Jane is standing toes in, the way she does when she's concentrating, listening to Ford Waring. All of her is real anyway. It doesn't matter that there've been other men, Don thinks, not now that she's his. He wishes there hadn't been so many, but Hollywood is like that; it's hard to blame Liza Jane.

She paces out the scene with Hotchkiss, moving around a desk with a battered typewriter, a swivel chair, a cot, a radio set against the rough-hewn wall. They run through it again with dialog to be sure Ford has what he wants. Larry Hotchkiss goes to a calendar on the wall and flips it to the next month while Liza Jane is telling him she can't see him again, she has a fiancé at home.

"That calendar business isn't in the script," Liza Jane says as soon as they finish the run-through.

"It's July 31st," Larry says. "I'd turn the calendar. It's in character."

"We'll see how it looks on the take," Ford says.

"He does that all the time," Liza Jane mutters, patting her foot while the set is being lit. Her lighting stand-in turns this way and that, like a mannequin pivoting, chosen for the resemblance of her height and coloring to Liza Jane's. The stand-in walks through the scene again and again under the hot lights, while her marks are laid down and the camera angles set up to Ford's satisfaction. Tracks are laid for the camera, a cumbersome apparatus on rollers, with a seat behind it.

Until now Don has had no idea how much time actors spend standing around waiting for this kind of thing. Liza Jane has a knitting basket full of socks for soldiers. She stops patting her foot with a sudden shrug of her shoulders, pulls up a chair next to Don's, and starts to knit.

"Ford's being nice," she says, weighing that against letting Larry get away with murder. "Some directors won't let outsiders on the set."

The hell they won't, Don thinks. Nobody's going to tell him he can't keep his girl company. But he's restless; he's used to being the one doing things. He'll slip out, he thinks, once they start, come back and get Liza for dinner.

A bell rings. The assistant director shouts, "Quiet!" A perfect silence descends. It's almost suffocating. Ford Waring nods at the cameraman.

"Roll 'em!"

"Speed," says the cameraman. The slate man clicks his board.

Guns Over the Pacific: Scene seven, Take one. Scene seven, Take eight. By Take ten, Larry Hotchkiss has added five distinct bits of business, each fussier than the next. Liza Jane is fuming. She rounds on him as soon as Ford yells, "Cut!"

"Goddamn it, if you pick up another pencil or twiddle another knob on that goddamn radio, I'll stuff your head through it!"

Larry sniffs. "I am merely attempting to give my character verisimilitude."

"You're attempting to hog as much as possible, and you're ruining the whole scene with your stupid tricks."

"I'm not the one who's screaming."

They glower at each other. Ford Waring is trying not to hear them. He hates squabbling actors.

Liza Jane is furiously aware that Larry Hotchkiss is getting paid more than she is. Male stars always are. "I have a date tonight," she says acidly. "I don't have time to wait around while you play childish games and cost us more takes. And I'm not taking a back seat to a vaudeville ham!"

Hotchkiss regards her mournfully from his famous dark eyes. With the wig and makeup, he's wonderfully handsome, his face the heart-throb of a million housewives. "You aren't the director, sweetie," he points out. "Perhaps if your character could step beyond the cardboard outlines with which you have so far delineated her, you wouldn't suffer in comparison to my ability to round out a role."

"That does it," Liza Jane snarls. She taps her foot until Ford has to notice her, Don Wain forgotten, all her focus on Larry Hotchkiss.

"Take it easy," Ford says. "You'll bust a gut." He pats her backside. "Let's try it again," he says lazily. "Larry, go easy on the business."

Take twelve. Larry has abandoned two of his five shticks. Liza Jane is boiling, but she has it well on the back burner, a little simmer hissing inaudibly. The next shot is a love scene, passion in the radio shack. Larry can't take his fatigue shirt off because his corset will show but the Hays Office censors wouldn't let him anyway, fortunately for him. The trick here is to signal to Joe Breen and the Hays Office that he gave her a chaste kiss goodnight while implying an unbridled coupling to any member of the audience smarter than Breen.

The set is lit to give a misty glow to Liza Jane's red hair, pinned in a knot on top of her head, and accentuate the slender body under the baggy fatigues. Larry's hairpiece is tousled in artful disarray, one dark lock draped over his forehead like Superman. It is a night scene, the only ostensible light coming from a lantern on the radioman's desk. Even here, Larry can't leave the business alone. He touches Liza Jane gently on the chin, brushes her hair with an odd gesture with just the palm of his hand, not the fingers, plays with the dog tags around her neck until they jingle. He kisses her, manly, overpowering, rising just taller than she is in his lifts. Liza Jane wriggles against him in a good screen clinch, one hand splayed on his shoulder, the other on the back of his head, long fingers tangled in his hair. She waits until he's into the kiss before she gives his hair a good yank. The wig comes free and she waves it like a flag behind his back, while he tries to pull away from her. Ford Waring is collapsed laughing and there are shrieks from the crew.

Larry yanks himself back from her while Liza Jane dances across the set, his wig just out of reach in her hand. "Verisimilitude!" she says, making a chant out of it. "Veri-si-mil-i-tude!"

Larry abandons the wig, cheeks flaming, and slams the door to his on-set dressing room. Liza Jane tosses the wig in the air, catches it on the end of a broom that leans in the corner of the set, and plants it in a metal wastebasket. She gives Ford a look, imperious and delighted with herself, that says, You'd better let me win this one.

"What in hell was that all about?" Don Wain says. He's standing in the shadows by her dressing room, a sheaf of pink roses under one arm. "Is it dinner time yet?"

"Go home!" Ford shouts, trying to quit laughing. "You rotten bitch!" He's going to have to soothe Larry.

"Didn't you see what he was doing?" Liza Jane says to Don. "All that shtick with the radio and the calendar and the cigarettes?"

"I just got here," Don says. "I ducked out to take care of a few things." He hands her the roses.

"Oh." Liza Jane stares at them as if wondering where they came from. She wonders how long he's been gone. She hasn't the faintest idea. Don notices that, puzzled. He thought she'd be annoyed he hasn't paid more attention to things that are obviously important to her.

Liza Jane cradles the roses and beams at him lovingly, Larry Hotchkiss forgotten in his turn now. They have the whole evening to spend. She doesn't have to be on the set tomorrow until five. She can sleep later, she thinks. Next week.

She takes Don down to the Hollywood Canteen, where she's due to put in a shift. She could have begged off, but she wants Don to see that Hollywood people really are doing something for the war. The canteen is full of soldiers on their way to Guadalcanal, Midway, Corregidor. Basil Rathbone is behind a counter, serving coffee and sandwiches, and Hedy Lamarr has a tray of dirty dishes balanced on one hand. Harry James's band is playing, and on the dance floor, Marlene Dietrich is dancing with a sailor. Three others are trying to cut in.

Liza Jane holds her arms out to Don, proud of the way he looks in his uniform. Theresa Tate is there, too, dancing with the boy who's going to be her second husband, a cute blond in a Marine lieutenant's uniform. There's a sense of urgency in the air, all these boys about to ship out. Theresa's lieutenant has a flask, and they all take a nip from it (nothing is served at the canteen but coffee) and Theresa and Liza Jane compare notes in the ladies' room. When they part at midnight, Theresa's lieutenant is amorously drunk and talking about Las Vegas.

"Not again," Liza Jane says. "She's got to have more sense than that."

"Nobody has any sense right now," Don says as they get in the car. He slides an arm along the seat, hugs her. "No time for sense." He grins. "I hate it when you girls get sensible, and start talking about joining the WACs. Do me a favor and don't join the WACs, okay? I don't want to come back and find my girl in khaki underwear."

"I don't think you're in much danger," Liza Jane says lazily. She can't think of anything worse than joining the Army. She doesn't know how the men stand it.

Don takes his arm back and puts the car in gear. They skirt Griffith Park and turn up Olive Avenue into Burbank. At the end of Olive, Country Club Drive winds up into a canyon. Liza Jane likes the canyon. She had a big new house in Topanga, but it was too far out for gas rationing. Everything is rationed now, steak and sugar and butter. Everyone saves scrap: old tires and tin cans, bacon grease for explosives, newspapers and empty toothpaste tubes. There are bins of them on Liza Jane's back porch. She lets in a cat that's been sleeping in a nest of old stockings (for powder bags for naval guns) and fixes Don a late snack of eggs with hoarded ham and butter, and a martini. Liquor isn't rationed but it's hard to find and expensive.

Don beams at her. "I met a guy who saw you in Burma. He couldn't believe you were really my girl. I had to pull out your picture."

"He'd better believe it," Liza Jane says. They stare at each other for a while. They only have two more nights, counting tonight.

"When the war's over," Don says, "no more tours. I'm going to want to know where to find you every single night." He holds her hands on the kitchen table.

Liza Jane thinks that when the war is over, pictures will be made on location again, but she doesn't say it. Don will understand better when the war's over, when they have more than three nights together at a time. Then he'll change his mind. Don doesn't know it, but the world's going to change, has changed. Women are doing things they never dreamed of. They won't be content to go back in a candy box afterward. None of them will. It won't be just Liza Jane who thinks that anymore. Don is intelligent, loving, sympathetic. He'll see what's happening and he'll change his mind.

Don is oblivious to what she's thinking. He says, "I brought you something," and takes a little velvet box out of his pocket.

It's a ring, a huge, square diamond in a white gold setting. "I don't want you to put it on your left hand yet," he says. "Until we make sure I come back in one piece. But I want you to have it now. Just a present." He puts it on her right hand, and she smiles at him, misty eyed. "God, I love you," Don says.

Liza Jane has made a terrible miscalculation. When the men come home, the women, desperately grateful to have them back, tired of holding jobs and doing without and coping alone, want only to retrieve a normal life. They disappear from the work force in what seems to Liza Jane an almost instantaneous flurry of ruffled curtains and nursery furniture. The studio begins to make a series of domestic comedies in which marriage is always the prize, and the women's magazines are full of advice on how to make life comfortable again for the returning veteran. "Has Your Husband Come Home to the Right Woman?" the *Ladies' Home Journal* asks.

There is no new order, no changed world. They have all gone back in the candy box again, leaving Liza Jane rebelliously outside.

Don comes home and starts to make money hand over fist in a booming economy, and he wants the kind of wife everyone else has, the kind of wife Liza Jane is miserably unsuited to be. She tries to tell him that she can be his wife and her own woman both, but she can't. Don has fought a war, and she knows he still has the dreams, and now he wants his pipe and slippers to chase them away. The war against the Nazis and the Japanese has turned into a cold war against Russia and Don paints a nightmare scenario for her of the Soviet Union having nuclear bombs, the capability of doing to America what America did to Japan. The hunt for communists has put the movie industry under suspicion now and he wants his wife out of it, and away from people who are being investigated. He is not, by his lights and most other people's, unreasonable. It is Liza Jane, he says, looking baffled and hurt, who is unreasonable.

"I thought you loved me. We were supposed to start a

family." He looks honestly bewildered. Every other woman in America is picking out a wedding dress for the man they were afraid might not come back.

"I can do that and still work," she says.

"Dump our kids on nannies? Is playacting on a movie set more important to you than I am? Than our children are?"

"Playacting? This is my career, it's not playacting. It's what I do."

"What about our kids?"

"Plenty of mothers work."

"Only because they have to. My wife doesn't have to."

She says, "I love you. More than I ever have anyone. But I have to work. I'm not a person if I don't work."

"My wife wouldn't be a person?"

"Not my own person. I'll drown."

"The investigations are going to get ugly," he says. "Some of the people you associate with are going to be dangerous to know."

"Are you threatening me?" she asks levelly. His father, Donald Wain Sr., has a finger in a lot of political pies.

"Of course not." He backs away from that. "I'm not asking you to quit right now, in the middle of a picture. Take some time to wind up your obligations." He holds his hand out, takes hers, taps the ring gently. "I'll be here. I'm not going anywhere. We can work this out, you'll see."

Liza Jane spends so many sleepless nights thinking about how they can possibly work it out that she shows up to the set looking like hell and fluffs her lines. It's no good. There is no answer. Finally, in the most desperate, howling misery she has ever known, she gives him back his ring and goes to make a movie in New York. A photographer snaps her having dinner with Roberto Vincente. After that, Don doesn't call her anymore.

IV
Spin Control

1988

Steve Bowman, the publicist, arrived in the morning with a briefcase and a plan. He shook Liddy's hand, congratulated her on her choice of dress for the occasion—a demure slate gray with a white collar and sensible pumps—and talked about spin control.

He was young, blond hair combed back from his forehead and cowed with styling gel. He took a look at the tabloid and dismissed it. "Forget it. Those are the 'Elvis is alive' people. They aren't worth suing. What we've got to contend with here are the serious press. The best we can do with the tabs is just not talk to 'em. Now I want a list of everyone who's involved."

Liddy gave it to him. They were sitting in the basement office, where Harry was on the phone again, at a battered old desk that Liza Jane had used to keep notes on her garden. The walls were pine-paneled, but the concrete floor had been painted and left bare, making the room cool and faintly cave-like even in July.

Steve went down the list with a professional eye. "Frank. Frank's got to talk to them, to counter whatever Francie's going to say. That woman's a loose cannon. And they'll want Ben. We can use Theresa Tate, but I'll give her some guidelines first. Keep them away from Bernice Lewis. And Roberto Vincente, for God's sake. And this caretaker person. They'll think he's a live-in boyfriend. I want him out of the picture. Where is he now?"

"He's gone to take my son to camp," Liddy said. "And he lives here."

"Jesus, that's not good. We want to preserve her dignity."

"You aren't doing it," Liddy said. "And I don't like your implications." Harry was making soothing gestures at her from the telephone. Liddy ignored him. "Look here, Mr. Bowman—"

"Steve. Steve."

"All right, Steve. If you can keep this situation from turning into a circus, we'll all be grateful. But I'm not going to inform anyone that they are a non-person, especially Jeff. And your insinuations about him are off the mark and disgusting." So far she was maintaining her own dignity, but it was getting iffy.

"Hey, whoa," Steve said. "Don't get me wrong. I'm just out-thinking the press here. And while it's all between us, she had quite a track record."

"Well, it didn't include Jeff!"

Steve was making notes. "How would you describe their relationship? Miss Sidney had some reason to be pretty fond of him. Harry's basically told me about the will. Two hundred-fifty thou, isn't it, and a life interest in a house?"

Harry got off the phone in a hurry. "We all want to work together here, Steve, but Little Liza's just not used to looking at things from a PR standpoint."

"Don't call me that."

"Hey, that's great. You're named for her, aren't you? We can use that." Steve made a note of it.

"I haven't been called that in years," Liddy said, "and I don't like it. There was only one Liza Jane, and that was my aunt."

"The press'll love it," Steve said. "She never had kids, did she?"

"Well, I don't love it. So don't use it." Liddy compressed her lips and gave him a baleful stare.

"Liza Jane raised Liddy." Harry felt through the swamp for safer ground. "You might say she raised Jeff Austin, too. Jeff's an old friend of Liddy's. As you say, Liza Jane never had kids, so she kind of took on Jeff. And I've told you about Alec Murray."

"Absolutely," Steve said. "Absolutely." He turned his attention to Harry with relief. "Now there's our key story. Absolutely key. It'll impact very well on the situation. I think we might get him on Oprah, maybe Phil Donahue."

"Oprah's people already called," Harry said.

"Piece of cake." Steve glanced at Liddy. "You want to go get him, we'll see what his schedule is, call them back."

"I think you've lost your marbles," Liddy said to Harry, "but I'll get him."

They heard a snort of laughter as she went out. "I'll come with you," Steve said and went after her. "I thought you said she was going to cooperate," he said over his shoulder.

"She is," Harry said. If you considered what she was capable of. Liddy had never been malleable, any more than her aunt. He sighed and picked up the telephone. The City Council had agreed to send someone out to look at the oak grove and "assess the situation," but they weren't going to like what they saw and Ayala zoning laws were revered slightly above the word of God.

The living room and hall were full of people again, their numbers doubled since yesterday. Liddy saw Stu and June Patterson, the Ramananda, the headmaster of Apple Valley School, and a milling crowd of others whom she took to be representatives of Liza Jane's other beneficiaries, here to waylay the City Council and make known their interest in the situation. They'd make it known to the press, too, if the press gave them half a chance. If Steve Bowman was worried about loose cannons, he'd better duck.

"Dear Liddy," they said as she passed. "Such a strong soul... Liza Jane would be proud... oh, yes, our complete support..."

"Is there some reason," Steve Bowman inquired as he caught up with her, "why you have refused to invalidate the will and find a nice place in Forest Lawn for Christ's sake?" There was a suggestion of teeth on edge in his voice. He had Frank Hill to think about too, and this situation would draw reporters like flies.

"Sure," Liddy said. "That's not what Liza Jane wanted."

"And just how important is that?" Steve asked. "Being as she happens to be dead?"

"Important," Liddy said. She doubted that Liza Jane would consider being dead a disqualification.

Alec Murray was in the library, reading the Ayala Valley News and watching the parade in the hall.

"Steve Bowman," Liddy said. "Alexander Murray."

They shook hands.

"Steve wants to chat with you."

"Down in the study," Steve said. "Do a little brainstorming, look over our situation."

Alec got up warily, with a glance at Liddy. Liddy returned an innocent stare, with only a brief qualm that she was throwing him to the sharks. If Alec hadn't expired from culture shock by now, he could deal with Steve Bowman.

"Great," Steve said. "Great. Now what do they call you? Al?"

"No," Alec said.

"Great. Now here's the scoop, Al..."

Liddy watched them go, supposing that the victor would eventually emerge with the scalp of the loser.

"So good to have you home." Margaret Collins, president of

the Art Center, made pecking sounds at the air on either side of Liddy's face. She was tall, with thick, dark hair permed and held back with pearl clips. Her voice was deep, not quite masculine, but almost. "That's a fearfully handsome young man," she said. She lowered her voice to a dull boom. "Is there any truth to the rumor that he was Liza Jane's?"

"None." Liddy thought that she'd have to put a stop to that one. "Just look at him," she suggested to Margaret, "and then look at a picture of Carolyn Castellano."

"Well, I didn't think so." Margaret fluffed her hair and looked unconvinced. "But you know how people like to embroider. We'll have to take some steps."

"Not if people don't keep mentioning it."

"My dear, I won't breathe a word." Margaret went away looking conspiratorial.

Liddy went in the kitchen and buttonholed Bernice, who was rolling out calzones on the kitchen table. Liddy took a deep breath. The kitchen was a haven of familiar smells.

"Margaret Collins just asked me if Alec was Liza Jane's."

Bernice cut a circle of dough and started putting filling in it. "Margaret has very few original ideas."

"Well, is he?"

"He is not." Bernice looked up from her dough. "Trust me, he is not." Liddy started to ask her how she knew, but Bernice didn't look as if she was going to tell her that. There was something closed about her expression, unlike Bernice enough for Liddy to back off.

"I'm going to go hide," Liddy said. "Harry's flack is in the basement with Alec. If you absolutely have to have me, I'll be upstairs."

Bernice relented. "History has a lot of convoluted folds," she said, rolling up a calzone. "Some of them really aren't important now." The briefest flicker of a glance at the porch. Then back to the calzones. "If he'd been hers, she'd have kept him."

"Okay," Liddy said. She went into the hall and up the stairs fast enough to ignore anyone else who might be lying in wait. As she passed Frank's room, she noted that Frank was in there with the script, oblivious to the chaos below, or maybe just barricaded against it. He looked up as she went by and she gave him a little wave. At the end of the hall, another flight of stairs went up to the third floor and the attic. There was finished space there where Bernice had her workroom, and Liddy had had her playroom. She went in the playroom and found it full of furniture under sheets, and miscellaneous bric-a-brac. Whatever wouldn't fit in the attic, she supposed. Liza Jane was a keeper.

There were two old wardrobes from somewhere, one of them with the door ajar, the sleeve of an elaborate gown hanging out. Costumes with *Zenovich-Horizon, Elizabeth Sidney,* and the name of the film neatly lettered inside in indelible ink. Liza Jane had always tried to keep one from each role. Liddy closed the wardrobe door gently. The room was dusty. There was a toy box in the corner and she knelt in front of it. Liza Jane, who had had no idea of what eight-year-olds played with, had bought her an unsuitable series of stuffed animals before she had discovered that Liddy was too old for them. They were still here. Liddy took out a pink rabbit, an expensive Beverly Hills rabbit, with an embroidered scarf that said, "I belong to Liza Jane Fox" on it. His plush fur was still soft, and Liddy rubbed it against her cheek before she put him away. Zach was probably too old for him now too.

When she got to the door, she saw that her shoes had made footprints on the dusty floor, and for some reason it made her want to cry. She closed the door and went up one more flight, bare terracotta steps inside a narrow crescent stairwell, and came out in the bell tower high above the valley.

There was actually a bell in the bell tower. If she tipped her head back, she could look up into its wide bowed mouth. The tower floor was the red clay color of the roof tiles and a white plastered stucco bench ran around three sides, under open arches. The inner curve of the arches had been painted pale blue. Liddy sat on the bench and leaned her arms on the sill, looking out. You could see across the whole valley from here, out over other houses down to the roof of the Arcade and the tower of the post office in the distance. To the left was Topa Topa Mountain with the ocher line of a fire road cutting across its midsection. Liddy and Bernice and Liza Jane had walked the pugs up there, Liza Jane in a leather flight jacket that she kept for dog walks. Occasionally Jeff came with them. Once two of the pugs had found a dead chicken and carried it back proudly between them all the way to the car, despite protests. Jeff had finally wrested it loose from them and sailed it out over the valley to keep them from retrieving it. Liddy had been worried that it would hit someone, but Jeff had said that statistically the probability of nailing someone with a chicken from an altitude of five hundred feet was practically zero.

Liddy could see the circle of the driveway from the tower. Two more people she couldn't identify from above went up the steps and she thought wistfully of dropping a chicken on them. Once, she had lain in wait for Jeff up here, armed with a water balloon.

As if summoned by memory, Jeff came up the stairs and sat down beside her. "Boiling oil," he said. "That's what we need."

"I was thinking of that," Liddy said.

Jeff leaned out of the arch. "You got a good clear angle to the front porch. You want me to boil some?"

Liddy tucked her feet under her and leaned her elbow in the arch, facing him. "I hate to admit it, but you're a comfort to me. How did Zach seem when you dropped him off?"

"Chipper," Jeff said. "Said they were going to study mud today. Earthworms and so forth, I expect. Things that live under rocks. The world's subfloor."

"I see you met Harry's flack."

"Not so far. You didn't take to him?"

"I don't like his hair," Liddy said moodily.

"Oh. You know, Lid, you could get rid of all these people if you broke that will."

"Oh, God, don't I know it." She twisted a fold of her skirt in her fingers. "I just can't do it."

"Figure you'll be mobbed by the heirs?"

Liddy shook her head. "I could give them what she specified. I just can't bring myself to put her in the ground in a place she hated. You know how she felt about cemeteries."

"Cremation?"

"No, she hated the idea of that, too. I don't know why."

"A little too close to the flames of hell," Jeff said. "I feel that way myself, but I wonder why she was so afraid."

"I'm not sure it was fear," Liddy said. "I think maybe it was just this house. She lived here so long, storing up her life here. I think she wanted to be physically part of it. Ashes just blow away."

Jeff cocked his head at her thoughtfully. "Going to live in the house, Lid?"

"Oh, I haven't got that far."

"Yes, you have," Jeff said. "You aren't sure if you want Bernice growing sprouts in the refrigerator, and me at the bottom of the garden like Thurber's unicorn."

"The unicorn is a mythical beast," Liddy said. "Have you given any consideration to the thought that you may be as crazy as a jaybird?"

"Don't count your boobies before they're hatched."

There was something companionable about sitting up here quoting familiar stuff at each other. "You're a mythical beast," she said. "I won't be seduced by you."

"Never crossed my mind."

The hell it didn't, Liddy thought. She could feel the old

remembered spark between them, had felt it the first night, wasn't going to admit it, knew he felt it, too. "I was speaking figuratively," she said.

"No talking to unicorns. Stick to the straight and narrow." He leaned forward, solid-seeming enough even at this height. His hand brushed her arm.

She started to cry and he pulled her against him, let her weep on his chest. Liddy sobbed, shaking in his arms. "You haven't cried for her yet, have you?" he said gently. He stroked her clipped hair. "Ah, hell, where'd all your hair go?" Liddy sobbed harder. "She was old, babe. And she had a stroke. You know she'd have hated to be stuck in a wheelchair, talking out one side of her mouth or something."

Liddy said something unintelligible between sobs. After a few minutes the sobs faded, and she sat quietly, sniffling. "Your shirt's wet," she said.

"It's a hot day."

She sat up and wiped her eyes with her hands. "You found her, didn't you?" She wasn't sure how she knew that. Something in the way he had talked about it.

"Yeah. I was there. We were in the garden, kind of checking out the asparagus bed. You haven't seen the garden yet. All organic. Lady bugs and praying mantises. She just said, 'Oh, Jeff,' and then she keeled over. We called the paramedics but she didn't wake up."

"I'm glad she wasn't alone." Liddy wiped her face with her fingers again, trying to take the mascara smudges off, probably smearing them all over. There were black streaks on Jeff's shirt.

Jeff looked out over the valley, watching miniature cars pass miniature orange groves. "I felt like I should have been able do something."

"You couldn't," Liddy said.

"No." A moment passed. "Christ, I feel old."

"I just turned thirty," Liddy said.

"Did it ever occur to you," Jeff said, "that we were awfully young?"

"Jesus, yes. You were. It's a wonder I wasn't arrested."

He laughed. "You used to worry about that."

"Because you teased me about it."

"Too young to have any sense."

Liddy didn't feel as if she had any now, just a hollow feeling in her stomach from tears and no breakfast. Maybe from Jeff. Whatever it was, it was making her dizzy.

Jeff looked a little off balance too, and suddenly the bell above them began to hum. It took her a moment to realize it wasn't inside her head.

Jeff jumped up as the floor began to sway under them. "Jesus! Come on!" He grabbed her hand and pulled her toward the stairs.

They slithered down them at a run, feeling the tower lurch around them. The tremor stopped by the time they got to the second floor, but they could still hear the faint distant humming of the bell.

They stood still, waiting to see if it was going to do it again. The lower stories didn't seem to be as shaken as the tower. There were pictures askew, but nothing on the floor.

"Is anybody else upstairs?" Jeff asked.

"Just Frank."

"Frank's going downstairs," Frank said, coming out of his room. "God, I hate California."

"Welcome home." Jeff made a little bow to each of them. "The elements rejoice to see you."

"I've got to call the school." Liddy looked at Jeff uneasily. "Will you... go look at Liza Jane?"

"Sure, babe." Jeff trotted down the stairs and Liddy picked up the hall telephone.

Peter answered and assured her cheerfully that there was

nothing amiss but a broken beaker in the science lab. "We're going to have a geology lesson this afternoon. We use what's at hand. You can come get him if you want to, but it's really better to stay put until we're sure it won't do it again."

Liddy thought about the road to the Upper Valley. "No, let him stay. Is he scared?"

"Doesn't seem to be. The California kids are all pretty blasé about earthquakes, and it seems to rub off."

"Okay. Tell him I called, though." Liddy put the phone down. It was funny what you could get to be blasé about, until adulthood shoved you into a sense of mortality. The hall downstairs was full of agitated voices.

In the basement, Alec looked at the cup of pencils rocking on the desk. "What the hell was that?"

"Earthquake," Harry said. "A little one. Jeez, what a morning. Where were we?"

"Shouldn't we make sure everyone's all right?" They could hear the pugs yapping hysterically outside. Alec looked uncomfortably at the ceiling beams, made of the first-story flooring joists.

"That wasn't enough to rattle the windows," Harry said. "Anyway, the basement's the best place to be."

Steve Bowman smoothed his hair, as if the quake might have rearranged it. "Let's just brainstorm a little more."

Alec began to feel like a political prisoner being interrogated by a maniacally cheerful reeducation committee. He leaned gingerly back in his chair and folded his arms. "I am not going on some talk show." He looked accusingly at Harry. "You don't want me to talk to the press."

"Not without some briefing," Steve said. "Just a few guidelines."

"Right. And after that I broadcast my face to every dope dealer in the country." He had discovered that that was his best defense. They refused to take seriously a disinclination to discuss his private life on national TV—most of their clients were burning to—but the perceived theatricality of his job appealed to them.

"I've got it!" Steve said. "Now don't tell me I'm a genius, just listen. This is high concept. We put you on Oprah, back to the camera, lots of shadows. Oprah tells them about your job—we give her some life-and-death situation stories. She tells them about your real parents. We put Carolyn Castellano and Arthur Symes up on a screen behind her. We talk about how you were crazy to find your birth parents, how you searched for them. How just out of the blue Liza Jane makes it happen for you—"

"I don't know about Arthur Symes," Harry said. "That's just hearsay. His estate could sue."

"Half the women in the country are claiming to have had Presley's kid. We aren't making any claim on Symes's estate." Steve turned back to Alec. "Then you talk about how you could quit your job now, but you're going to stick with it because you're needed out there on the firing line, fighting for a drug-free America." He looked at Harry again, struck with inspiration. "Jeez, I think we've got a series here."

"I think you're a moron," Alec said.

"Well, that's just the house number," Steve said. "We can put it in development. Look, you do Oprah, then we'll talk. Geraldo Rivera." He grabbed his notepad again. "Geraldo would kill to get you, he loves crime stuff. But a class act all the way. It's got to be a class act. I'll talk to Geraldo."

"I think we may be going a little fast for him here," Harry said.

"I know some people at Lorimar," Steve said. "You get a good agent, you can write your own ticket. Not Sharon, Sharon's out of touch with the whole multimedia thing. I love Sharon, though. I'll make some calls."

Alec felt as if he were talking to an android that had run suddenly amok. "Suppose I can't act?" He was beginning to wonder if that mattered.

"Not to worry. You do a few talk shows, have some fun with it. If you lay in the back story, I think the audience'll make the buy."

Alec resisted the impulse to take him by the throat. "Let me get your attention here," he said. "I'm not going to 'do' Oprah, or Geraldo Rivera for God's sake. I am not going to capitalize on a couple of actors I never met just because they happen to be my birth parents. I am not going to put my mom—that's Mrs. Murray to you—through that. And I am not going to turn my job into the Sunday morning comics, for which, incidentally, I would get canned. You got that?"

"Hey, whoa. We're just trying to beat out the concept here. If something bumps you, we can talk. So far we just got the notion." Steve spread his hands, indicative of his willingness to negotiate, be reasonable. He was a good guy. "We're just trying to put the right spin on this for Liza Jane's sake. Now, you owe her, Al."

"Alec."

"Alec. Sorry."

Alec looked at Harry. "I'm going upstairs. Aren't either one of you two assholes worried about somebody being hurt?"

"I'm worried," Harry said. "Steve, we're interested in damage control here, not career moves."

They realized that the faint sonorous humming of the tower bell had been overlaid with the voice of a woman screaming. Or at least a woman being loud.

"I don't like the sound of that," Harry said.

"Shit." Steve was out the door before either of them could move.

Harry looked at Alec. "He gets carried away," he said. "But he knows his job." They followed Steve from the office, past the projection room across the hall, to the outer door, which emerged from an ivy-entwined lattice screen into the driveway circle. It was quicker than the stairs. There was a pale blue Mercedes, sleeker and newer than Liza Jane's, parked slantwise in the circle, the driver's door open. A big tapestry-woven bag spilled its contents from the driver's seat onto the gravel. The front door of the house was ajar and the screaming had coalesced into the sound of combat inside.

Francie Allen was in the hall—tight black leather pants, black boots, a big turquoise shirt, her crimped blond hair standing out from her face as if it had been electrified. She was in the act of throwing a pair of black wraparound sunglasses at Frank. The pugs were yipping back and forth across the floor like marbles. Frank caught the sunglasses and Alec heard them snap in his hand.

Everyone else was in the hall, too, wild-eyed between fear and fascination, heads swiveling between Francie and the television that someone had turned on.

"I could have been killed!" Francie screamed. She was shrill, giving it the trained projection she used on stage. "The car was slewing all over the road, I nearly hit a tree, I could have been fucking killed because of you!" She looked for something else to throw.

"Francie—" Steve Bowman took a step forward, warily, like a patrolman approaching a possibly rabid mastiff.

"Fuck you!" Francie screamed at him. "I don't like you!" She glared at them, swinging her heavy hair. "Get out of here! I'm going to get you for this, Frank! I'm going to—"

Frank took two steps forward and grabbed her by the wrist. He dragged her behind him into the library and slammed the door.

"...place the epicenter near Piru," the television said. A calm, earnest voice, implying that the announcer had not two minutes ago been under his desk. "...5.4 on the Richter scale. No reports of any significant damage."

"Just Francie," Steve said. He looked at the closed door. "I swear that woman brought it with her."

Frank was inaudible behind the door but Francie wasn't. "I know why you came down here, Frank, and it's just so disgusting I want to puke. Reporters have been calling me up. I'll give interviews, Frank!"

"I thought she was publicity-shy," Harry murmured.

"Not when she's mad," Steve said. "She's got a temper like a Molotov cocktail."

"I'll tell them you sleep in my underwear, Frank! I'll tell them you're queer! I'll them you've got AIDS!"

Alec listened to the shrieking in the library and wondered, because he couldn't help it, if it would take the heat off him. He felt sorry for Frank Hill.

Liddy, a little rumpled, hair over one eye, sat down on the hall sofa and leaned her head back.

"Possibility of aftershocks," the television said. "Or another major temblor."

Jeff leaned over her shoulder. "Liza Jane's okay," he said.

A pug got in Liddy's lap, whimpering, and she stroked it. She looked at Alec with the flicker of a weary grin. "Aren't you glad you came?"

Francie's voice rose to a crescendo. "When I get through with you, you'll be poison! If there's one more story about you and that senile old hag, I'll fix you, Frank!" She banged the door open and emerged in a cloud of sulphurous fury, rubbing her wrist.

Frank, abandoning reserve, shouted, "You're small change. You couldn't influence a PTA election! If you weren't stoned all the time, you'd have enough sense to shut up and let it blow over!"

The door whammed shut again, quivering against the jamb.

Francie spun around, gave the closed door the finger, and glared at Liddy. "You're her niece, aren't you? Well, I'm not leaving until he does."

"Suit yourself," Liddy said. "I'm afraid we don't have room for you unless you want to sleep with Frank, but the Horsehead Ranch is nice." A pause. "They love celebrities."

Francie clenched her fists and unclenched them. "I'm not leaving," she said again. She went and sat in a corner on a hassock, arms folded.

"Christ," Steve muttered. He managed a public relations smile. "I'll get your purse, sweetheart."

"You get Frank out of here," Francie spat. "I can't believe he was fucking that hag! She was old even then!" Her eye lit on Alec. "You! You're her bastard from somebody else she was fucking. I saw your picture in the paper."

Steve, Jeff, and Liddy converged on Francie and Alec retreated to the kitchen. Bernice was putting calzones in the oven. A pot of sauce bubbled on the stove. "Is that harpy still here?"

"I'm afraid so," Alec said. "She seems to think I was Liza Jane's," he added. "A lot of people seem to think that."

"You aren't," Bernice said. "I told Liddy that this morning. I'm telling you that now."

1951

Liza Jane is forty-three and she still has time left, she thinks as Bernice drives her down Ventura Boulevard. Plenty of time. You just have to think of it that way and get it over with. It's not in the cards right now.

It's raining and the traffic on Ventura Boulevard is bumper to bumper because some moron who doesn't know what to do when it's wet has skidded into a lamp post up ahead. Liza Jane is still enough of a New Yorker to feel scornful about that, but she wonders if she'd know how to drive in the rain now, either. She sits, gloved fingers laced across her midsection, a stupid, prim little hat on her head. She's not very far along. The doctor made her swear to that, told her if she was lying, he'd quit in the middle. He's not impressed by actresses, but he's supposed to be good. Bernice knows two other people who've been to him. If he's so good, why is he doing this? "A gal gets in a little trouble, I just want to help her out," he said. But he made her pay up front.

She could turn around and go back, she thinks. Bernice has edged the car around the wreck and the rain is still coming down, dirty and cold. They are in Bernice's car, not Liza Jane's. The doctor told her that, too. "Now don't you come in some fancy car. You just dress like a little housewife, and you come in this lady's auto. I take a lot of chances for you gals. You do what I say."

Almost there, Bernice says. She has on an old skirt and a sweater, the kind of thing she wears to work. Bernice never cares much what she looks like, even at thirty-three. Maybe she makes it a point to dress like a Russian tractor-driver. Bernice has never got pregnant either. But she's willing to do this for Liza Jane. Liza Jane feels a surge of gratitude. If ever there was a woman with the courage of her convictions, it's Bernice. Bernice knows you can't go back and change things. Can't go to bed praying you'll wake up yesterday. Or two months ago with a diaphragm that doesn't have a hole in it.

The thought of going back splashes away with the rain, and Bernice pulls the car up outside a motel. "They won't let me come in. When you're ready, just wait out front. Not by the office."

"I know," Liza Jane says. She manages a smile. "Low profile." It's not much of a smile.

"You'll be all right," Bernice says. "This man's all we've got."

Liza Jane thinks that 'we' means women in general.

Liza Jane gets out and goes to the door. Room 23. Her high-heeled shoes make squelching tracks in the dirty yard and the rain splashes them out again. She knocks and a curtain twitches in the window beside her. The door doesn't open until Bernice's car pulls onto Ventura Boulevard again. Liza Jane is shivering with the cold, and with the morning sickness that she's beginning to get every day, when the chain rattles and the door swings in. "God damn it, get in here," the nurse says as if she's kept them waiting.

The nurse has on an old brown dress the color of the carpet on the floor. "Take your underthings off," she says. The doctor is over by the bed, but he doesn't bother to look up.

Liza Jane goes in the bathroom and puts her purse on the rickety sink that's full of rust stains. She peels her underwear off—stockings and girdle and underpants—and rolls them up and puts them in her purse with her gloves. She comes back in with her purse and hat and shoes in her hand. No one tells her where to put them, so she sets them on a chair.

The nurse looks at her watch and points at the bed, and the doctor finally looks up at her. "Now you just relax," he says. It's a bedside voice, professionally soothing, it might be recorded. When Liza Jane doesn't move, he snaps, "Lie down, damn it!"

There's a plastic sheet on the bed, with a towel over it. Liza Jane says, "Shouldn't I take my skirt off?"

"No. You stay dressed." The nurse hands her another sheet to put over her with a look that tells her she has no right to be prissy.

Liza Jane lies down on the towel, and hikes her skirt up, trying to keep the sheet over her, but she feels despairing, dwindling into terror in this grubby room. The nurse looks at her icily, and she knows what the woman's thinking: that she thought she was hot stuff, picture in the movie magazines, didn't have to play by the rules. The nurse's eyes are almost pleased.

Liza Jane feels a stabbing pain that nearly knots her up. She wails and the nurse puts a hand over her mouth. They won't give her an anesthetic; they want her out of there fast.

"Hang on there, honey," the doctor mutters. "But you gotta be quiet."

Liza Jane nods and stares at the ceiling, gritting her teeth. The nurse takes her hand away, but she's ready to put it back if there's any more noise. The doctor drops something and swears and the nurse looks at him with a quick, heavy snap of her head. She snatches the instrument up and washes it in the sink, and Liza Jane feels blood pooling under her. She moans and stifles it when the nurse comes back. The nurse is younger than Liza Jane, but she looks as if no one has ever taken care of her or pampered her, and there is a permanent bitter line around her mouth.

Liza Jane is sick, nauseated, and the room starts to swim around her like dirty water. The doctor stands up and takes a drink out of a bottle in his bag, and the nurse puts a towel between Liza Jane's legs.

"Get up and get dressed as soon as the cramping stops," the nurse says. She stands there, waiting.

"You'll bleed for a couple of days," the doctor says. "But don't worry about it. You're supposed to."

The nurse looks at her watch again and hands Liza Jane a Kotex, and Liza Jane slides her legs off the bed. She's shaking now, and everything looks blurry, as if the rain has come inside.

By the time Bernice picks her up, she can see blood dripping into the rainwater, little pink splotches. There's blood all over the car by the time she gets home.

Finally she has to call her regular doctor, the one who doesn't do abortions. When he's through with her, when he's packing his bag with quick, tidy movements, he says, "I could lose my license for not reporting this."

Tears are running down her face, and he mutters, "I ought to, and put that son of a bitch out of business. You dumb moron, if you had to do this, why didn't you go some place you could have it done properly? It's not as if you don't have the money." He throws an exasperated look around the bedroom of her big, expensive house.

He's given her a sedative. Liza Jane shakes her head; it's almost the only thing she can move. "I couldn't," she whispers. "I'm working. This is all the time I can take away from the set."

The doctor lets out a long breath. He's middle-aged, scrubbed, and sober, with four children and a wife who takes care of them. Liza Jane knows he likes her, but he's not sympathetic, not over this. "I hope this movie's worth it." His voice is brusque. "You aren't going to have another one."

V

The Eddystone Light

1988

The representative of the Ayala City Council pursed his lips to stress the importance of zoning. "I do not think there is any way in which Miss Sidney's request can be honored."

Francie Allen dug the toe of her boot in the oak leaves. "And you're hanging around for this?" It was hot. Hot, dry Southern California summer, with the earth and its inhabitants just recently shaken, so that they looked askew to her, splintered and prismatic the way the audience looked, through coke and adrenaline, in the middle of a concert, lights flashing off-on-off-on on hungry faces. They weren't looking at her this time though, except covertly. They trailed after the councilman, a soft doughy man in a white shirt, like some weird religious procession. Francie hung back. "My lawyers gave me the fucking newspapers to read, but I didn't believe it."

"Isn't there any other adjective in your vocabulary?" Frank asked. He had on an old plaid shirt, buttoned at the collar, and Francie wondered how anyone who looked like a Bible Belt hayseed could make women practically come when they saw him on the screen.

"I'm not a fucking high society bitch out of the last century," she said.

"No, you're an uneducated slut with the vocabulary of a hooker."

She stuck her hands in her back pockets, malevolent but making a pose. "You didn't used to think so."

"I always thought so." Frank took a pair of gold-rimmed glasses out of his shirt pocket, polished them and put them on. He knew the glasses annoyed her, too. "I just thought there was something else."

"Well, you don't know from shit. I can't believe you'd make such an asshole of yourself over Elizabeth Sidney. Goddamn, Frank, she had one foot in the grave when you were screwing her."

"I had an eye on my career," Frank snapped. "Just like you. But I liked her. She was something else."

"Piss on her," Francie said. "Now everyone's laughing at me, because you're making a spectacle of yourself."

"Yeah, right. You got a list of hotels as long as my arm that you can't go back to because you and the band trashed the place. You're like a bunch of kindergarten kids nobody ever taught manners to. Half the time you're so stoned you can't see straight, but I'm a spectacle."

"I hate you."

"Yeah, I know. Why don't you go away?"

"I won't," Francie said. "You know why? Because you want me to."

"Well, isn't that a coincidence?"

"You aren't staying to piss me off," Francie said scornfully. "You haven't got that much blood in your veins. You can't even stand to have people look at you, unless you're on the screen. Unless they can't get at you." She advanced on him venomously. "God knows I ought to know that. You know what I think? I think you're staying for Mike Rosen's script. You're like some goddamn hermit crab. You've got to have a new shell to back into."

"I don't have to read the script here," Frank said.

"Yes, you do! Ben put the picture on hold, and you feel naked, so you're reading scripts!" Her hand shot out and closed around his shirt front. Enraged, she beat furiously on his chest with her fist. "You're afraid one of these days someone's gonna see you naked!"

He grabbed her wrists and pushed her away from him. "Enough! I spent two years of my life trying to live with you. I'm through listening to hysterics."

"You didn't live with me! You lived in the same house." She backed off, eyes narrowed. "Am I embarrassing you, Frank? I hope so. Maybe they'll all see you naked."

I hate him, she thought, stalking away from him. What did I want with him? Fuck it, it was an experience. The crowd was still milling around the councilman, a bunch of damn dumb old people. What did it matter where you got buried? They looked like sparrows to her now, hopping and quarreling. She saw herself as a tall, black-legged, turquoise bird with a vicious beak, and she joined them, thinking vindictively that she'd give them something to write home about. I saw Francie Allen and she was such a bitch.

"Cremation, now," the councilman was saying. "Cremation would solve all your problems."

"Fire is so cleansing," June Patterson said. "Ramananda, don't you think it is?"

"She didn't want to be cleansed!" Liddy snapped. "She

wanted to be buried. Mr. Abbott, we've been through all that. I just told you, she specifically—"

"I didn't hear that part," Mr. Abbott said. "Sorry."

"Maybe if we could all be a little quieter." June gave Francie Allen a toss of her head, lips pursed.

Mr. Abbott said, "You people have got to understand that the law only allows a certain amount of influence from beyond the grave."

They all glanced at the veranda.

"Sorry," Mr. Abbott said again. "What you have to understand here is that you can't just haul off and put a dead body any place you feel like it."

"Anarchy would result," Jeff said solemnly.

Mr. Abbott ignored Jeff. "Mrs. Novak, as I understand it, it has been, er—" he looked at his watch— "four days now. You really must come to some decision."

"I have," Liddy said. "I want her buried here."

She looked just like her aunt, Mr. Abbott decided with a certain amount of horror. He had encountered Miss Sidney alive on several occasions, notably the hell that she and everyone else had raised about that tree in the middle of Ayala Avenue. Bernice Lewis had got up a petition about the tree, but Elizabeth Sidney had led a parade that had chained themselves to it. In Mr. Abbott's opinion, she was just as much trouble dead, but this time she wasn't going to get away with it.

He straightened his glasses. "Mrs. Novak, there are laws regarding how long an individual is permitted to keep a corpse on their premises. If you don't offer us some viable alternative, we will really have to invoke those laws."

The Ayala heirs surged around him. Except for Alec Murray, they comprised the rest of the entourage.

"We at the school feel that there must be some way to accommodate Miss Sidney," the headmaster of Apple Valley said.

He wore khaki slacks and a t-shirt with a whale on it, but his expression let the councilman know exactly how much money Apple Valley School brought into Ayala.

"The harmony of our lives together is to be taken into consideration," the Ramananda said.

"Wellness," Stu Patterson said. "We must think of the wellness of the valley."

"The land on which our temple sits," the Ramananda added solemnly, "is part of our communal heritage. The temple itself is adobe, and ancient of its kind. There has been a developer interested in it. A Mr. Benshoof, who builds condominiums."

"Fake Tudor," Jeff said. "With turrets. You like turrets, Mr. Abbott?"

"The Art Center has planned the Elizabeth Sidney Modern Drama Festival," Margaret Collins said. "We assumed," she added darkly, "that it had City Council's support."

"Do you have any idea how many cats and dogs go unspayed each year, producing litters that have to be destroyed?" The representative of the Humane Society fixed Mr. Abbott with an awful eye, indicating that he personally would be responsible for future depredations.

"The children, Mr. Abbott! Have you any idea how many abused children—"

"Our work for the homeless—" Noel Ballinger, the rector of St. Anne's Episcopal Church, looked only faintly uncomfortable at allying himself with the Ramananda. The Ramananda's given name was George Simmons and the rector had assisted at his confirmation.

"The Philotheistic Institute—"

Mr. Abbott counted up the number of people talking to him at once and multiplied it by the average income and influence of their backers, which was surprisingly high for any other town, if not for Ayala. But he dug his heels in. You had a city council to keep the nuts from running things. They already had a tree in the middle of the street where it was a wonder no one had run into it.

Mr. Abbott made a gesture of putting on his hat, if he had had one. "Mrs. Novak—" He nearly said, "Little lady," but he had done that once to the director of the Humane Society with awful results. "Mrs. Novak, if you cannot come to some agreement with the other beneficiaries by—" Mr. Abbott consulted his watch again— "within the next three days—" Mr. Abbott attempted to look benevolent— "we will really be forced to Take Some Steps. I'm sure you'll understand that we're busy just now. Quite worried about this earthquake." Mr. Abbott surveyed the oak grove as if expecting it to lurch again. "Perhaps this has been a warning to us all. Settle upon a suitable burial place, Mrs. Novak."

He marched off to his car, back straight, while they glared after him.

"That is an impossible little man," Margaret Collins announced, in tones that must have reached Mr. Abbott, if not Saturn.

"Dear Liddy. You are so strong." June Patterson clasped her hand.

"I'm just pigheaded," Liddy said.

"Pigheadedness can be an excellent thing." The Rev. Mr. Ballinger was blond and slight but with a certain stubbornness to his chin.

"We have just begun to fight," Margaret announced.

Liddy thought they all looked pigheaded. And much too interested in the situation to go away. She wondered if Mr. Abbott had actually considered the ramifications of trying to remove Liza

Jane by force.

"Heavens! What is that?" Margaret shaded her eyes. A florist's van had drawn up, inching around Mr. Abbott's departing car. Two men were unloading a monstrous arrangement of flowers.

"A tribute for our dear lady," the Ramananda said.

"Who do you suppose it's from?" June Patterson dropped Liddy's hand. Diverted, they all set off across the garden to see.

It had been Liddy's decision not to break the will, but now she felt swept along on their tide. Curiosity and excitement, as well as cupidity for their causes, gleamed in their eyes. Jeff had gone to help wrestle the floral arrangement into the house, and Liddy found herself walking after them with Alec. Francie Allen stood alone, watching the receding tide. She looked subdued, as if the explosion had blown itself out temporarily, but Liddy didn't know what to do with her, so she left her there. Everyone else was clustered around the florist's van.

"Don't they ever keep their noses out of anything?" Liddy muttered.

"They're all caught up in it," Alec said. "Exciting times." He sounded like someone used to seeing people caught up in things. Used to standing a little away, maybe. Outside. She'd bet he wasn't used to this.

"Bully for them," she said. "I wish they'd get out of my hair."

Alec looked at her sympathetically. "Am I in your hair?"

"No, you're an oasis of normality. I rather suspect we're in yours."

"Nothing I can't handle." They ducked past the fishpond and the pomegranate trees and stepped across a low hedge of lavender into the driveway. "Oprah Winfrey proposed marriage, but I turned her down."

"Good move. Show business marriages are hell." Liddy smiled at him, just the corners of her mouth, but he smiled back.

"I'm sorry I sicced Steve Bowman on you."

Alec shook his head in bewildered amusement. "He wants to star me in a series. The new Don Johnson."

"Oh, for God's sake."

"It's high concept," Alec said solemnly.

Liddy chuckled. "You know what's awful? You could probably do it."

"Harry Lanier seems to think so," Alec said. "At least I think he does."

"Harry's hungry. Liza Jane was his biggest client."

"He'd have to be starving. I'm not sure what universe we're inhabiting here."

"Plan 9 From Outer Space?" Liddy suggested. He looked perplexed, so she explained. "Worst science fiction movie ever made."

Alec seemed to give that some thought. "I don't know. I thought Frankenstein Meets the Space Monster was worse."

"You saw that?"

"Sure. Class-A rotten. I'd put it right up there with Santa Claus Conquers the Martians. Maybe with The Horror at Party Beach."

Liddy looked him in the eye. "Where do you see this stuff?"

Alec ducked his head. "Well, I didn't want to admit it around here, but I'm a movie freak. I watch everything. Nothing is too horrible."

Escapism? Maybe. Maybe he needed that. Liddy was pretty sure it wasn't a fascination with Hollywood. Or hadn't been. "I'll show you how to run the projector in the film library," she told him. "We've got practically the entire history of cinema down there."

"Great."

They went up the front steps. The flowers were being admired in the living room, a naturalistic arrangement of varicolored lilies and heaven knew what in a four-foot basket, fighting for space with Roberto Vincente's roses.

Theresa was reading the card. "Oh, dear me." She handed it to Liddy. Alec looked over her shoulder.

"'The saddest words of tongue or pen.' Donald Wain." Liddy stuck the card in her pocket.

"Are these, it might have been," Theresa said sadly. She tucked one arm through Liddy's. "You come with me. That old fool could have made it come out differently." She scooped up Alec with the other arm. "You too."

"Where are we going?" Liddy inquired.

"Out." Theresa marched them through the kitchen and onto the veranda. "Poor Liza Jane," she murmured as they passed the coffin.

She died on the train. That idiotic old song had been going through Liddy's head all morning. Liza Jane had always loved it. Now Liddy had begun to visualize her aunt's life as a series of cars swaying into some eternal night, windows vaguely lit, strange people passing behind them. She stumbled a little going down the steps, trying to negotiate those moving cars.

"If you keep on like this, you'll pass out." Theresa led them around to the back of the house where there was a patch of patio with an old chaise longue and two deep canvas chairs. "Sit down. They won't have the crust to come looking for you back here." She prodded Alec toward the other chair. "You, too. You look done in."

Alec sank into the cradle of the chair. From there they could see the oak grove, branches tangled against the sky. "Why the hell would she wanted to be buried there?"

"Just because you don't know why doesn't mean she didn't have a reason," Theresa said.

Liddy took the card out of her pocket and balanced it in her hand, peering at it as if it were tea leaves.

"That woman—I can't remember her name—the one with the deep voice," Alec said. "She thinks I was Liza Jane's too."

"I'm going to kill Margaret," Liddy said.

"You were, dear," Theresa said. "But not in the way Margaret has in mind."

Liddy wondered if Theresa knew what Bernice knew, and if she was going to spill it. She let Donald Wain's card fall, watching it flutter to her lap. "What about Donald Wain?" She had always pictured him as passing from Liza Jane's life in the forties, reappearing later as an octogenarian on the cover of *Forbes,* with no solid existence in between.

"I'll tell you the parts I can," Theresa said. "You may have to ask Bernice for the rest."

"Bernice is a clam," Liddy said.

"History's strange stuff," Theresa commented. "Bernice has made a pretty uneasy peace with parts of it. I can only give you my version." They watched her settle herself more comfortably in the chaise longue, young faces, troubled and curious, intent on her movements. "Goodness, I feel like Mother Goose."

"That's Donald Wain in the picture in her bedroom," Alec said suddenly, recognition sliding the young face across the older, famous one.

"You have a good eye," Theresa said. "He had a piece of Zenovich-Horizon. And one of his corporations bought it up when it was about to fold. But he wasn't a movie man. Just money. I suppose one shouldn't ever want money, one might get it, and it seems to have fearful limitations. Still," she added briskly, "at my time of life, one might be willing to try the experiment."

Liddy wanted to prod her. Theresa always got sidetracked. She opened her mouth, saw Alec shake his head.

Theresa looked back into some invisible distance. "It was during the war. Donald was making a mint in various things. He fell in love with Liza Jane, like everyone always did. He wanted to marry her."

"And she wouldn't?" Alec asked.

"Oh, that was the tragedy. He was the only man she ever did want to marry. But the price was just so high. Donald wanted her to give up acting. He wanted her to be an executive's wife. I don't think she ever really considered doing that—she wasn't like me, I always ought acting was just a job. I would have ditched it in a minute. But Liza Jane couldn't. She kept hoping he'd come around. He didn't come around. Fini. Well, almost. She might have waited longer if he hadn't thrown his weight behind the Un-American Activities Committee investigations. She was furious about that. Don bought into the idea that the movie industry was a hotbed of communist propaganda, another reason he wanted her to quit."

Liddy tried to imagine what Liza Jane had loved about Donald Wain and couldn't. She supposed it didn't matter, since she had loved him. She felt irrationally angry not to have known that. Wrong again. Another shift in the ground. Another lurch. Not even a piece of the puzzle. A new puzzle, the old one collapsing into it.

"What about me?" Alec asked.

"You were an accident," Theresa said. "Not that sort. I don't know why," she added irritably, "no one seems to think there is any way to create a child except by climbing into bed. You were...a ghost maybe."

Liddy made a movement with her hand. Alec's hand shot out and closed over hers, stilling it.

"You were Carolyn's." Theresa said. "There wasn't any doubt about that. But Liza Jane had just been through two bad affairs, one with Donald and then one with Ben. I don't know what went wrong with Ben. They stayed fond of each other, but something fell apart. Maybe she just didn't love him the way she had Donald. And of course he was a lot younger. And she wanted a child and couldn't have one. She had some kind of complications and had to have a hysterectomy. And in those days, not if you weren't married, either—look what happened to Ingrid Bergman. When Carolyn had you, I think Liza Jane just transferred all of that to you."

Alec raised his eyebrows.

"She kept such close track of you, closer than your adoptive parents realized." She smiled at him; he nodded, attentive. "She didn't want to disturb the balance. But she wanted to know everything you did. A really expensive private detective is practically invisible."

"A detective!" Alec's face flashed into an instantaneous explosion of fury, and Theresa flinched. Liddy put her hand out as if to protect her.

"You must have had some sense of it," Theresa protested. "I thought you seemed so much more interested in Liza Jane than in Carolyn."

"Carolyn didn't leave me a million dollars and screw up my life," Alec said. "Jesus!" He narrowed his eyes at Theresa. "Nobody asked me if I wanted to be somebody's obsession."

"I suppose not." Theresa pulled herself up out of the chaise longue. "I don't think I'd better stay now. I think I've been stupid."

"This doesn't exactly jibe with what you told me yesterday," Alec said.

"It's the expanded version." Theresa rubbed her hands together. Long-fingered hands, an old lady's hands, with a big jade ring. She fidgeted unhappily with the stone. "I wasn't going to tell you that, but then you get started, and then you tell a little more, and then a little more." She looked as if she were about to cry.

"And what's the little more you still haven't told me?" Alec's voice was flat now, the words clipped off as if he was trying to get it under control.

"I don't know." Theresa said. "Maybe there's always more, but I don't know what it is. I'm sorry. Don't be angry with her." She hurried away around the side of the house, leaving a thin, furious silence.

"Right," Alec said.

A spider let itself down from the eaves of the house and Liddy watched it start a web in an azalea bush against a sunny wall. A good spot for flies. Everything ate something. Frogs ate water beetles. People ate people. She felt for Theresa.

"She didn't mean to tell you that," she said to Alec.

"No. I pushed it."

"You're very good." She watched the spider some more.

"I'm supposed to be good! It's my fucking job! I make my living figuring out who's lying. Telling them lies. Sometimes we're all lying." He glared at the grass.

She watched his face. It looked under a very tight rein now, but flooded with an outraged sense of being invaded. Watched. She looked away carefully. Was it the job that made the fact of the detective so terrible? Frightening possibly, and dangerous? Or was it the invasion itself, deceit in a sphere of his life that should have been free of it? Having experienced neither, she couldn't know. Or was he ashamed of having used the job, his own knack for lying low, to prod Theresa into indiscretion?

The spider started another leg of its web, balancing carefully, scuttling along it. When she looked back at Alec he looked ready to howl at the sky. She felt sorry for him, too, for herself, for Liza Jane. "Love's a horrible force," she said. "I'm sorry you got caught in it."

Some of the fury ebbed from his face. "It's all right."

He sounded stiff but abruptly under control again, so that she felt she might be able to walk along the unsticky spokes of the web, before the cross-hatching went up. "Tell me about the job," she said. "Why do you do it?"

He looked at her suspiciously. "Why do you want to know why I do it?"

She cast about her for some plausible reason and could only come up with the truth. "I think I want to know why you aren't afraid to do what you do."

"I do it because I'm good at it, probably the same reason you write. Because it feeds something in me that I need. I can balance the chance of getting killed one of these days against that and still come up wanting to do it."

"Does belief come into it?" What did the spider want besides lunch?

"Idealism? I think narcotics ruin lives, if that's what you mean."

"That seems pretty clear cut." Pat, but a relief. The spider as Spiderman.

"Don't bet on it," Alec said. "The road to hell is paved with idealists. You can't live with someone for six months, shoot pool with him, go to his daughter's wedding, and not have some reaction when you turn around and nail him. Especially if he's only a mid-level fish and in so deep he couldn't get out if he wanted to, and you helped get him that deep. And you've done some of the same things he's done to keep your cover. It gets slippery. And idealism tends to get skewed when your own government's dancing a tango with someone like Noriega for politics' sake. It's a wonder more agents don't fall down that well than do."

"What does it look like?" Liddy asked. "The well."

"Black as the pit," Alec said, "and lined with money."

She tried to look into it, caught only a brief glimpse of seduction and chaos. Not so pat.

"So far it hasn't been a problem," Alec said. "I'm pretty good at holding onto my own identity."

And what happened, she wondered, if somebody from

outside your life took your identity and tossed it around in a can for a while, the way they'd all been doing with Alec's. "No wonder you got mad," she said.

Alec looked at her speculatively. "This is the first time I have ever tried to explain the job. Most people just want to know did I ever kill anybody."

"Did you?" She wanted to know that, too.

"No." He didn't seem to mind the question now. "I tried to once. I thought I had. It turned out the shot went about two millimeters past his head and the son of a bitch fainted."

"What would have happened if you had?"

"If you want reality, a lot more than you put in your books," he said. "Investigations, counseling, endless crap."

"Counseling." She hadn't thought of that.

"You can't blow somebody away and not have some kind of psychological complications," Alec said. "Not unless you're a psycho. We had two guys last year, ended up in a street shoot-out two weeks out of the academy. It shook them up good. It would shake me. And if you stay shook, the next time out, you won't shoot, and the guy will get you."

Liddy wrapped her arms around her knees. What would happen if you weren't sure if you were still shook?

"I'll tell you a funny story," Alec said suddenly.

"All right."

"Vincente's torpedo thought I was here to hit his boss. He almost pulled a gun on me after we tossed that reporter out."

"That's your idea of a funny story?"

"Well, I thought it was. Tony the torpedo did, too. He laughed like hell when I showed him my badge."

"Where did he get an idea like that?"

"He saw my shoulder holster through my jacket. Tony's good." Alec lifted the edge of a lightweight linen jacket and Liddy could just glimpse it, a blunt dark shape under one arm.

"You're in a houseful of lunatics and a small child and you're carrying a loaded gun?"

"I'm carrying it, not the lunatics."

Liddy stared at the smooth outline of the jacket, the gun invisible to her again, but known now. Tony had seen it without being shown while everyone else was arguing about PR. She wondered how much of the same world Alec Murray and Tony inhabited.

"I don't leave it lying around," Alec said, "and I take the clip out when I take it off. Don't worry about Zach."

"I just didn't know you had it. I guess I should have. I mean, I'm not a moron."

"Does it bother you?"

"I'm just...aware of it now." Not so much of the gun itself, but of the gun as an obscure symbol for Alec Murray. She thought a psychologist could probably make rather a lot out of that that she wouldn't like.

"I can't get rid of it," Alec said quietly.

"No. I know you can't."

She looked at him solemnly. Why hadn't she thought that he was carrying a gun? That it wasn't some remote and dangerous object that came into being when he wanted it, but part of his everyday life. Something that he was careful to keep from children. And that might kill someone, or kill him. His very normality seemed both solid and capable of crumbling at the touch.

They sat there a long time. Alec watched her curiously. She sat perfectly still, sunk in the canvas chair, but seemed restless, something flickering behind her eyes. He wasn't sure if she was rattled by the gun, or by something else. Or if she was rattled. He put out his hand, on impulse, took hers, and felt the quick jerk of her fingers within his curled palm. Gray-green eyes flicked up to his. He knew that there was a certain amount of intimacy attendant upon losing your temper in front of someone, and spilling your guts to them, and that he had done both. He bent forward, half out of his chair, leaned toward her. He wondered how much of this was the electrified moment, how much not.

Another car crunched in the gravel drive beyond the house, a distant sound of eggshells breaking. Liddy slipped her hand out of his.

Jeff came around the side of the house with a pug at his heels. He looked at them both consideringly and stuck his hands in his pockets. "More company," he said. "High winds with a spattering of rock stars and a ninety percent chance of tycoons."

"He's here?" Liddy closed her eyes briefly, opened them again, and got up. "Donald Wain," she explained to Alec. She glanced at Jeff. "I presume."

"Why not? We have all other life forms represented." Jeff caught Liddy's arm as she started past him. "Hold on, babe. Theresa says you need to blast out of here for a while. I'm dancing tonight. Do you want to come?"

Liddy stopped, balanced on one foot, and her mouth rippled into a smile. "At the Art Center? Yes!" She headed purposefully down the path around the house.

Jeff looked at Alec. "You can come, too, if you want to. It's folk dancing. I teach, sort of. Probably not your cup of tea, though."

Folk dancing? "Sure," Alec said, mostly because he suspected that Jeff would prefer he fell off a cliff. "Sounds interesting." He could still feel his heart pounding and he felt argumentative.

Jeff rocked back on his heels, hands in his pockets again. "She doesn't need another complication right now."

Alec thought, You may have auld lang syne going for you, dude, but she doesn't need you either. He tried to equate the woman who had sat in the garden with him just now with the long-haired girl who had stood on the front porch with her arms around Jeff. "You look sort of like a complication yourself," he said.

"I'm an old complication. New complications have to get in line."

They inspected each other warily.

Jeff grinned. "We could bark at each other."

"We could ask Liddy what she wants."

"Neither of us, I expect. And you could go apologize to Theresa. She was crying into her scarf over spilled beans."

"Yeah, I could." Alec started around Jeff.

"Attaboy, Captain."

Alec turned around. "If you are by any chance hoping I'll deck you, I won't."

Jeff shook his head admiringly. "That's restraint. You're a credit to the force."

Alec contemplated decking him anyway. He thought he probably could. "Tell me something. Did Theresa tell you what it was she told me?"

Jeff looked reasonably serious for a minute. "Yeah. You look like it really wigged you out, too."

"Wonderful. The whole goddamn world probably knows by now."

Jeff held his hands up. "Not from me, Captain."

"Thanks."

They looked at each other, still wary.

"Don't let it go to your head," Jeff suggested.

"I'll try not to." Alec went to find Theresa while he still felt contrite enough to admit he'd been a jerk. Jeff didn't follow him.

He stayed on the patio, whistling. When he was almost out of earshot, Alec recognized the tune: "The Eddystone Light." *Me father was the keeper of the Eddystone Light, and he slept with a mermaid one fine night.*

Christ.

Alec went up the veranda steps and stopped abruptly at Liza Jane's coffin. It had begun to seem almost normal to have it there. He touched it with a fingertip as if it might be red hot. It wasn't. It was warm with the sun. Alec resisted the temptation to open the lid, knowing there would be nothing now that could speak to him. He would have liked to have known her, he thought. Instead she had popped up at him out of nowhere, money in one hand and a dubious pedigree in the other. *A voice from the starboard cried Ahoy, and there was me mother a-settin' on a buoy.*

Arthur Symes and Carolyn Castellano seemed to have drifted from sight, except genetically. If there was any other mother in competition with his mom, it wasn't the miserable drunken figure of Carolyn, it was Liza Jane. Maybe it was a good thing his mother hadn't known that, and Alec wasn't going to enlighten her, but he knew it had something to do with why he hadn't called home since he had been here. He went in the house, looking for Theresa and a telephone, in that order.

Theresa was in the living room, with Liddy and a large older man whose beetle-browed gaze had apparently banished Steve Bowman to a corner, where he lurked among the baskets of flowers. Theresa looked shaken, makeup repaired but just slightly off, as if the printing had slipped.

Alec brushed her hand. "I'm sorry."

Theresa's hand closed on his gratefully. "I'm a garrulous old lady," she whispered. "Sometimes I don't have any sense."

"Sometimes I have a tendency to shoot the messenger," Alec said. "So quit worrying about it."

"Mr. Wain, this is Alec Murray," Liddy said.

"How do you do, sir?" Alec said.

Wain inspected him. "I heard about you. What's this nonsense about wanting to be buried in her back yard?"

Steve Bowman tried to pop out from among the flowers. "We think it was just kind of a whim."

"I didn't ask you." Wain gave Alec the once-over again. "You look like you have some sense."

"It wasn't a whim," Alec said.

"Well, you take care of it," Wain told him. He had a rumpled face and eyes like ball bearings. "She was as stubborn as a pig. Got away with everything."

"It's not my decision," Alec said.

"Might as well be. Everyone else is running around like a bunch of wet hens." Donald Wain looked at Theresa with exasperation, and at Steve Bowman with loathing. "Hollywood."

"You'll have to let it work itself out, Donald," Theresa told him with unexpected firmness. "You're as stubborn as she was. We aren't your corporation."

"Damn good thing. I'd be broke." Wain looked at his watch, took a pill out of a case in his vest pocket. "I'm not as young as I was and neither are you." He gave Theresa an appraising look. "You've held up pretty well, I'll say that. But you let Murray here take charge."

Alec wondered how Liddy was taking to the tenor of this conversation, but she seemed to have mentally thrown up her hands. The phone rang and she dived for it before Steve Bowman could get it.

"You can't just pop back in forty years later and start appointing committees," Theresa said to Donald Wain.

"That's kind of you, Mr. Vincente," Liddy said into the telephone, "but I don't think it's necessary."

Wain snapped his head around to Liddy, diverted. "Is that son of a bitch here?"

Roberto Vincente's voice was a low growl audible through the receiver, heavy with authority, as determined as Donald Wain's.

"All right, Mr. Vincente. Thank you. But I think I can handle it." Liddy put the phone down. "He says," she informed them, with a malicious grin at Steve Bowman, "to let him know if I want anybody leaned on."

Steve glared at her and stalked out. Theresa giggled. "He sounds just like you, Donald."

"I wouldn't give that gangster the time of day," Wain snapped, "but he knows how to get things done. You tell him I'll handle it."

"I won't," Theresa said. She handed Wain the cane that he had propped against a table. "You come in the kitchen and I'll get you a drink before you have a stroke."

She escorted him out, winking over her shoulder at Alec. "They're jealous of each other," she whispered.

Alec looked at Liddy. "A pair of eighty-year-olds?"

"I don't think age makes much difference," Liddy murmured.

Or the passage of time either, or even the fact of one of the principals being dead. Love really was a hellishly powerful force. Everyone in the house seemed to be tangled in it, either battering their heads against it like Francie Allen, or trying to pull their feet free like Frank Hill. Or both, like Sharon and Mike Rosen. And what about the blacklist? It seemed somehow entwined in everything.

1951

Liza Jane is forty-three and she still takes Ben's breath away. It makes him hungry just to look at her skin. He's twenty-four, a hotshot who emanates power that has the pretty girls in

Hollywood hoping he'll discover them, but Liza Jane has something they can't give Ben. It's a kind of power, too, something in the soul that radiates. It warms him.

Hollywood power feels precarious now, with HUAC and the communist-hunters breathing down everyone's neck. Jews are suspect anyway. In response, Ben's old man has become the most upright of the upright. He's got his Aunt Miriam and her daughter Elise living with him, and now a cousin who was in the camps. Maurice Zenovich isn't going to do anything that will let people point a finger at him and say he's not American. That's why he changed his name from Moritz. He calls Ben this morning on location.

"We got now to shut it down."

"In the middle?" Ben looks around uneasily at the fancy Santa Barbara hotel room, at last night's bottle of champagne. At all the money this location shoot for *Richard Plantagenet* is costing. His father knows what it costs to build a goddamn castle. They could have gone to England for the same price, used a real one.

"Shut it down," Morrie Zenovich says, his accent coming out the way it does when he gets upset. "The director, or the star even—him we could replace. But the writer—we got now a whole script we can't use."

"Are you sure?" Ben knows it's a stupid question before it's out of his mouth. Nobody's sure, it's all innuendo. But if you're on a list, you're dead; that's sure. And Mike Rosen is on a list, there's no other explanation.

"The backers are calling me all morning, I don't know how they found out so fast, they got noses like bloodhounds. Do it!" Morrie Zenovich slams the phone down, scared and angry that his hotshot son is arguing with him about this.

Ben gets dressed. Liza Jane is long gone, out to the location. Ben has stayed behind, working on the books in his pajamas. At least now she can get some rest, he thinks. Some time off from getting up at four a.m. Not that she'll thank him for it. But maybe the two of them can go somewhere, go down to Mexico, loll in bed, sleep late in the morning, send for room service. Liza Jane drove back to L.A. partway into the shoot, three days when they didn't need her, and came back with some kind of bug; she hasn't looked really well since. Not healthy. Beautiful, yes. Ben sighs and picks up his keys. Beautiful has a temper, and it's likely to get the upper hand when she hears this news.

Ben thinks about what to say on the drive from Santa Barbara out to the country near Solvang where they've built a castle. It's a hot, blue day, perfect weather. He can see the castle's battlements as he comes up the hill. There are trailers and trucks, cameras and lighting booms all around it. It looks as though it's being besieged by the twentieth century. The infidels have come. Ben parks the car and stalks up the hill with the ultimatum from the Crusaders.

Liza Jane is in a mobile dressing room being pinned and sewn into a medieval gown with a trailing skirt that has to be gathered up and carried in her hand. Bernice has brought an illustrated fifteenth century Book of Hours to show the actresses how to do it. Liza Jane has got the walk right, slightly swaybacked, hand resting on her abdomen, but Charlotte Lawton keeps trying to kick the skirt out of her way as she walks.

"You sway, you don't goosestep," Bernice says irritably, while an assistant knots Charlotte's headdress into her hair so it won't fall off. It's a stuffed, heart-shaped affair that frames her face. Charlotte swivels her eyes impatiently and shrieks.

Liza Jane's headdress is lying on a sofa where they rest between takes. Charlotte snatches it up, her heart-shaped roll of brocade askew across one eye. "Don't do that!" she yelps.

"Give it a rest!" Liza Jane says. Charlotte is more superstitious than anyone Liza Jane has ever met, even on a movie set. New rituals are added constantly to her repertoire. Whistling sends her into hysterics and she patrols the set looking for green socks and open umbrellas.

"Never put a hat on a bed!" Charlotte says, clutching it to her.

"It's hardly a hat," Bernice says. "And it's not a bed."

"I nap on it," Charlotte says. "That makes it a bed. This picture has just been a nightmare from start to finish." She looks at them accusingly.

"It's barely started," Liza Jane mutters.

"Do you know where they've put me?" Charlotte demands. "In the hotel? You won't believe it! Right next to a garbage chute! It's simply unbearable."

"Miss Lawton, I got to do your headdress," the assistant says.

Charlotte takes a deep breath and makes a visible effort to calm down. Bernice takes a quick look at Liza Jane, whose hand over her abdomen may mean more than holding up her skirt. Liza Jane nods that she's okay.

Bernice starts putting glue inside the deep V-neck of the dress, which almost meets the high waist. Liza Jane grits her teeth. The glue makes her itch.

"When this is over," Charlotte says chattily, relaxed now, "do you know what I'm going to do? I'm going to go home and just lie by the pool all day. I feel secure at home, don't you? I have my pool, and Angelina and Manuel. And Howard when he's home, of course. And there's the shelter. What will we do if the Russians attack while we're on location? I mean, are there any bomb shelters out here? Does the studio think of that? At home I have forty-seven hundred cans of food in the shelter and six months' worth of water."

"Forty-seven hundred?" Liza Jane is startled out of her

private thoughts.

"Meat and beans and fruits and vegetables, and powdered milk." Charlotte ticks them off on her fingers proudly. "Everything for a balanced diet. It's very important to think of nutrition when you're thinking of survival."

"How many people does the shelter hold?"

"Just Howard and me," Charlotte says.

"What if he's not home?" Liza Jane whistles "Taps," barely audible, under her breath.

"You quit that! Charlotte screeches. "You don't believe in anything! You just quit that!"

When Ben gets to the set, Sid Halley, the director, is talking to Liza Jane and Charlotte and Thomas Axton, the star who's playing Richard the Third.

"I want a stand-in," Charlotte says stubbornly.

"I can't shoot a stand-in, I want both your faces," Sid says.

"I'm not going to let anyone slap me in the face," Charlotte says. She looks warily at Liza Jane, who is the one who is supposed to do the slapping.

"I'll be careful, all right?" Liza Jane says.

"You'd enjoy it too much," Charlotte says astutely. "I don't want my face marked."

"Just get her a stand-in," Axton says under his breath. "Maybe we'll get something done."

Sid Halley looks around to see how he might get by with a stand-in, and sees Ben coming up the hill. "No money men allowed," he says jovially, hoping he can shoo Ben away. This discussion doesn't need anybody else in it. "We're spending your dough like water out here, you aren't supposed to see it."

"We got a problem," Ben says.

"It'll have to wait," Liza Jane snaps. "This costume is hotter than a fur coat. Either we shoot now, or I'm going to undress." Bernice Lewis is still fiddling with the heavy yellow brocade train as they talk. Liza Jane's hair is pinned up under a fat overstuffed headdress that means she has to hold her neck perfectly straight. It looks like some kind of pearl-studded sea urchin.

"You might as well take it off," Ben says. "By a problem, I mean a problem."

They all turn to stare at him. He has their attention now. Bernice has gone pale.

"We're shutting the picture down," he says flatly. Might as well drop the ax. "I hate like hell to do it, but I haven't got a choice. The company accountants have been going over the books, and they don't like what they see. You're right about spending money like water. We just haven't got the cash flow for a historical right now."

"We already spent most of it!" Sid Halley snaps. He squints his eyes at Ben. "I don't buy it."

"You don't have to," Ben says. "We'll pay off your contract. For God's sake, man, back off." He looks at Bernice as if he expects her to back off, too, literally. Bernice's name has come up before and he was half expecting it to be her his old man wanted canned. But Bernice doesn't back off. She gets up and puts an arm around Liza Jane.

The silence is thick, like the silence that hangs around someone who has cancer, with the same queasy sense that it's contagious. They even know who has it. People have been dropping like flies for months, but there's only one person whose name could shut the picture down. Funny, really, Ben thinks. Writers don't have much clout in Hollywood or much respect. But it was Mike Rosen's script that got Halley and Axton and Liza Jane in. It was literary, they said. Now it's supposedly full of communist propaganda and so now it can't be used. Writers have no power in Hollywood until they go down in flames. Then, only then, can they take people with them.

"The world's going to hell on a stick," Halley says. He turns away, yelling for an assistant director to get the cast and crew together. "You tell them," he says to Ben. "You bloody tell them."

Ben waits until everything has been packed up and shut down. It's like a funeral that you have to go to. He assures everyone that they'll be paid. He expects Liza Jane to yell at him, but she doesn't. To wait until they can be private and then yell at him, but she goes back to the hotel with Bernice, in Bernice's car, and just leaves her own car sitting on the lot for Ben to deal with.

When he gets to the hotel, Liza Jane's in her own room. The sea urchin hat and the make-up are gone and she looks so sad it turns his heart over. He thinks she's sick.

"You really wanted this part, didn't you, honey?" He sits down next to her. The hotel room has a Polynesian theme. The sofa is upholstered in a pattern of tropical leaves and parrots with huge, efficient-looking beaks. They joked last night about being afraid to sit on it.

"I always want what I can't have," Liza Jane says wistfully.

Ben is baffled. He's never seen her sad. Furious, yes, biting back at whatever it was, just spiking her beak in it like the parrots, but not sad. He doesn't know what to do with sad.

"You want some dinner?"

Liza Jane shakes her head.

"You want to drive back tonight? Shake the dust off our

shoes. We could go down to Mexico, see some real parrots."

"No." She pats his cheek, affectionate and distant. "Ben, go away and leave me alone, just for tonight, okay?"

Ben goes, because he can't think of anything else to do. Later when he goes down the hall to the hotel bar, he stops outside her door and hears her crying. He knocks, not really wanting to, out of his depth. Bernice Lewis sticks her head out. "Go away," she says. "Go get a drink. You aren't going to help."

"Neither are you," Ben snaps. But he goes.

Ben drives back to L.A. the next day. Liza Jane doesn't come home for three days. He doesn't know what she's been doing all that time, maybe just sitting in that room and crying.

In a month they start to shoot *Glory Days* instead. Liza Jane is fine by then. She looks good, like her old self. Relieved, Ben figures she's happy with the new part.

They've gone to Samoa to shoot, everything's opened up since the war, everyone's in competition for the most exotic location. Liza Jane's making a fuss about that; she hates location, hates the tropics, bugs as long as her arm in the bed. Ben has flown over with the company to get them settled, plans on staying as long as he can. Until his old man wires him to come home. Ben likes Samoa. The air is riven with the bright flash of birds, whirring past him on little eggbeater motors. It's hot and sticky and no one wears any more clothes than they have to.

At midday, it's too hot to do anything but lie around on cushions in their hotel at Pago Pago. The island of Tutuila is only fifteen degrees south of the equator. Liza Jane says the hotel gives new meaning to the term tourist trap. The shower pours water out of a canister that has to be filled by hand. A large number of interesting bugs come out with it, and Liza Jane and Angela Simone have taken to bathing in shower caps and washing their hair in a bucket. Angela, cast as a native beauty, wears a sarong most of the time, unlike the Samoan native beauties, who wear Mother Hubbards supplied by the mission school. Liza Jane is wearing white shorts and a thin Mexican blouse embroidered with red poppies. She fans herself and drinks iced tea, stretched across the bed in a puddle, while Ben tilts the bamboo shades and stares at the crystalline ocean. What would it be like to live out here, he thinks. Shed your skin down to some older, darker layer, put out to sea in a pahi.

"Come with me in my canoe," he says to Liza Jane, eyes gleaming. His hair is dark and wavy, brushed down with brilliantine above a face that has a golf course tan. His nose and brows are bony and intense, intelligent. "And I will take you to the Tolelaus, the Tuamotu, the Tongatapu." He's found a map of the South Pacific on the bedroom wall, hand-painted by some previous tenant, and reads them off: "Tonga, Apia, Suwarrow. Pukapuka, the Danger Islands. The Iles du Vent and the Iles du Desappointement. Rangiroa and Bora Bora. Huahine. The Ile Surprise."

Liza Jane hangs her head over the edge of the bed, propped in her hands, listening. Her elbows are braced against the side of the thin mattress. Ben comes and sits on the floor, facing her. He kisses her lips. "Never the Iles du Desappointement. Always the Ile Surprise."

She kisses him back and he's flooded with love—and relief. There's no reason to wonder about the other thing, any more than there is to talk about that other picture, or Mike Rosen. Publicly, the studio has "budget trouble," but *Glory Days* will pull them out. At twenty-four it is easy to assume that the truth will stay where you put it.

VI
Figure, With Repeats

1988

Alec wondered what you wore to go folk dancing. He wasn't really sure he knew what folk dancing was—he had a vague image of Zorba the Greek—but he had turned up a picture among the collection in Liza Jane's bedroom, of Liddy in black boots and a red skirt with ribbons sewn around it, and a multicolored vest. She wore a headdress of flowers and trailing streamers. He was fairly sure she wasn't wearing that tonight, so he opted for blue jeans and a black t-shirt and boots, not so much for effect as because he could fit a little revolver in an ankle holster in the boot. He took the clip out of his automatic and stuck the automatic on the top shelf of the closet with the shoulder holster, in among a stack of hatboxes. He put the clip in the chest at the foot of the bed.

He caught a glimpse of himself in the dressing table mirror, dark and surly looking, and tried a smile. He looked as if he'd been stuffed. "You know why I'm doing this?" he asked the reflection, but the reflection didn't.

In the downstairs hall he encountered Francie Allen, pacing

up and down with an erratic and restless energy. She brightened when she saw him. "Hey, you going out?"

"Yeah."

"Is there any place good to go in this town?" She grinned at him, turquoise shirt bunched up, thumbs hooked in her black leather pants. "You want some company? I never went out with a cop."

"Makes us even," Alec said. "I never went out with a rock star."

Francie eyed him appraisingly. "Might be an experience."

"I'll bet," Alec said. "But I'm booked. I'm going folk dancing."

Francie rolled her eyes, "Jesus."

"It's an experience," Alec said.

He found Liddy and Jeff in the kitchen with Bernice and Zach. Zach had his pajamas on.

"Eight o'clock," Liddy told Bernice. "Not a minute later. And thanks."

"We'll be fine," Bernice said.

Zach smiled. "We're going to play Scrabble."

"Get Frank to play," Liddy said. "He'll come out if Francie goes away."

"Francie will have to go away," Bernice said. "I'm delighted to say there's no place to put her."

"She suggested she stay with me," Jeff said. "I declined. I'd sooner shack up with a hyena."

They heard tires spin in the driveway. Strike two, Alec thought. He wondered whether Francie was trying to make Frank jealous, or was just so wound up that she had to work it off some way. There wasn't any sign of anyone else in the hall. They all worked, he had discovered, wherever they were, reading scripts, learning lines, making telephone calls, making deals. The death rate for deals, Theresa had told him, was about ninety percent. It paid to keep fishing. Even Francie had had three phone calls from her manager, although she had been too mad to call him back.

They went down the steps into lingering sunlight. The blue Mercedes was gone, leaving furious tire tracks in the gravel.

"She split," Jeff said.

Liddy laughed. "Up over Blue Mountain on a broomstick."

"Bereft of gentleman callers," Jeff said. "Poor Francie."

It took Alec a minute to pin down the quote, but not to know that they were reaching back into some shared past. He wondered again why the hell he was tagging along, and decided that it was to piss off Jeff, which seemed as good a reason as any.

"Afraid you'll have to take your own car," Jeff said. "Mine only holds two."

"Right."

Jeff's car was an ancient Triumph, rust-spotted and topless, with a dismantled stereo system entangled like octopi behind the seats. Jeff got behind the wheel. Liddy tossed a book and an empty bread sack into the back with the stereo, and got in beside him. "You can follow us," she said to Alec. "You go down Ayala Avenue along the Arcade and hang a right past the park." She scrabbled around for a seat belt, found it, and wrestled the catches together.

Alec got in his rented Ford and followed them down the twisting road, taking the same route that he and Liddy had taken yesterday. On the surface, Ayala looked like paradise to him. The *Ayala Valley News* reported small-change crime—a 7-Eleven held up—in the same tone that the Pittsburgh paper would have given a quadruple shooting. The rest of the news consisted of the program for an upcoming blues festival, and what appeared to be a vocal but well-bred brawl over whether the city park ought to be fenced. Alec had told his mother as much on the telephone that afternoon, when she wanted to know if he was all right. She had heard about the earthquake. She had sounded enthralled and a little star struck at his description of Liza Jane's household, especially by the presence of Frank Hill, who was her favorite movie actor. Alec hadn't the heart to tell her that he looked like an accountant off-screen.

She had asked him when he was coming home, and who had been at the funeral, and he had bogged down trying to explain that there hadn't been one yet.

"She always seemed so sensible," Doris Murray said. "Of course, I suppose in Hollywood... Dear, what about your job?"

"I've got a lot of vacation stacked up. It's all right, Mom."

"Dear, if you do get this money..."

"Yeah?"

"Please think about quitting. I know how badly you wanted it, but it would just kill your father and me if anything happened to you."

"I know," Alec said. They had been through this before. "What about Dad? He's due to retire, if he wasn't so stubborn."

"You father's too old to change," she said. "You just got started. Practically. You don't know how young you are. And the odds are worse." Two agents shot to death in Los Angeles. One tortured to death in Mexico. He knew she wouldn't name them; she was afraid to. "Not that I mean you should stay in California..."

Was she afraid of that, too? He wasn't sure.

"Just think about it. Please."

"I'll think about it, Mom."

He realized that he had been deliberately not thinking about it, and tonight didn't seem a particularly good time to start, so he followed Jeff's Triumph through town and down a side street to the Art Center, and thought instead about how he could annoy Jeff further. Live for the moment.

Jeff parked under a row of eucalyptus trees, one of them with a dangling branch. It hung just above the ground, baring a strip of raw wood above it. Jeff pointed to it as Alec pulled in beside him and got out. "Earthquake. Eucalyptus are real unstable. Sometimes the whole tree comes down."

No one seemed particularly worried about it. The parking lot was full of cars and they could hear music through the open windows. The Art Center was a squat and attractive example of California Bungalow architecture, with a shingled roof. A poster outside the door advertised a production of *Crimes of the Heart* directed by a name Alec recognized.

"Everyone who lives here gets into the act," Liddy said. "We're very arty."

Alec wondered if she noticed she'd said 'we.'

Inside, a long room opened off the lobby, its walls hung with the current art exhibit, its wood floor bare for dancing. A tall, thin man in slacks and ballet shoes was fiddling with the tape recorder at the far end. There were folding chairs around the walls, and Alec discovered that folk dancers looked very much like his mother's square dance group except that more of them were young. He recognized Margaret Collins, the Art Center president, in a white silk shirt and jade skirt, and Peter, the teacher from Apple Valley. Jeff took his shoes off and wandered down toward the man in the ballet slippers.

The tape recorder gave a squeal and a whistle and Jeff knelt down to fiddle with it while the instructor balanced on one foot and waved his arms, storklike. The tape spun out a few notes and everyone jumped up and joined hands.

"I remember this." Liddy grabbed Alec and pulled him into the line. "This is a hora. This is easy." Jeff got in front of the line, with his back to them, and went through the steps slowly for the newcomers, while Liddy swayed, moving her feet just inches, remembering the dance.

"I'll fall down," Alec said.

"No, you won't." She flashed him a smile. She had on a long

gray-green cotton skirt and a white embroidered blouse and canvas shoes. Silver earrings with little bells on them swung in her ears. The instructor punched the tape recorder; Jeff took the lead end of the line, while Alec staggered after Liddy. The music was a lot faster than the demonstration, but about halfway through he began to get the hang of it. The line snaked around the room, exuberant, moving faster. When it was over, Liddy was laughing, gasping for breath. "Oh, my," she said. "That takes me back."

"You do this a lot?"

"Not in years, and I'm out of shape. But I used to be on an exhibition dance team."

"I saw a picture. In Liza Jane's room."

"That's me."

"What now?"

The instructor and Margaret Collins were pacing sedately up and down the floor, arms entwined in a kind of crisscross pattern, while another couple attempted to follow suit. Margaret and the instructor revolved and somehow switched places without letting go their hands. The other couple became hopelessly ensnarled and came to a standstill. Jeff untangled them, took the woman and wove her successfully in and out of the pattern. He gave her back to the man and started toward Liddy.

"Can you teach me that?" Alec asked Liddy.

"Sure." Liddy tucked her left hand behind her back, took his left hand with it, and reached across him for his right. Jeff kept going with what Alec thought with satisfaction was a faintly annoyed look.

The instructor started the music and Alec stumbled.

"You're okay," Liddy said. "That twist is the only hard part." They turned and somehow came up right. They turned again, face to face, entwined. The music was light with the suggestion of a fiddle in it. In front of them, Jeff moved with an irritatingly easy grace, paired with a woman with long black hair.

Alec found he had the hang of this dance, too, and was scooped up for the next one by Margaret Collins, and after that by the woman Jeff had danced with. Even men who were unhandy on their feet were at a premium for couples' dances. About two-thirds of the dancers were women, ranging from a teenager in a blond punk haircut, whom he recognized as one of the Ramananda's devotees, to an elderly woman with white hair and tennis shoes. He had to admit that he was having a good time, tempered perhaps by a mild aggravation that Jeff danced so well. Alec's previous impression of Jeff had been that he was a layabout, but the bastard wasn't even out of breath. Even though Liddy was not among the women who were trying dance with Jeff, she was watching him. And Jeff knew she was watching him. Alec grinned, at himself and at them. There was a certain element of the quintessential high school dance being enacted within their trio.

The music stopped and he took a deep breath, glad that at least he was in shape. The instructor in the ballet shoes galloped to the center of the room. "'Hopak,'" he announced. "By request."

Alec looked at Liddy, and she shook her head, laughing. "Nobody learns this one in one night." Jeff came up and took her hand, and she ran out into the middle of the floor with him. She kicked off her shoes and sent them spinning under a chair.

The music reeled the dancers out across the room. It was a dance of multiple figures, none of them repeated. Liddy whirled in and out of the pattern, all the steps coming back to her, danced now alone, now with Jeff's hands around her waist, moving in the pattern, a spiral that progressed but never came back on itself. She capered, hands above her head, while he spun in circles around her, arms outstretched. His hand caught hers, pulled her to him, and they spun together, parted, came together again, ended in a theatrical tango dip that wasn't in the dance.

"You haven't lost it, Lid." His hand steadied her as she got her breath back.

It was unnerving how easily the pattern of the dance had come back and a moment of irrational panic washed over her. She fled to the ladies' room, locked herself in a stall, and found herself trapped with Margaret Collins, on the other side of the partition.

"Liddy, is that you?"

"Yes." There wasn't much use saying it wasn't.

"I just think you're brave to come. But it's so good for you. We all need release." Margaret's further words were drowned by the flushing of the toilet. "...and so nice of you to bring Alec. I know the poor boy's at sea."

Liddy thought of saying that he wouldn't be at sea if Margaret would just shut up about her theories concerning his ancestry, but she had never succeeded in squelching Margaret yet.

"Liza Jane used to come all the time, you know, even after you left. She was just a watchword to us all." Margaret was washing her hands at the sink, but plainly not going away, and could probably have been heard in Ventura. Liddy emerged from her stall reluctantly.

In the mirror over the sink, her head looked odd to her, her hair damp around the forehead and beginning to curl in wispy tendrils. Her eyes were round and apprehensive. I don't know what I'm doing, she thought.

"We have the most wonderful festival planned for Liza Jane," Margaret said. "All completely experimental works. So important for a community theater. One mustn't stagnate." She put her lipstick on and inspected it.

"Mmmm." Liddy was still staring at herself. Liza Jane's

mouth and eyebrows looked back at her.

"You do see that. You're so intelligent." Margaret looked at her with a beady, appraising eye. "You come back and stay here. We need people like you. Someone with their feet on the ground."

Someone with Liza Jane's money, Liddy thought. But it wasn't just money Margaret was looking for. Everyone seemed to have an ill-conceived need for continuity. "I'm not Liza Jane," she told Margaret desperately. "I don't live here." She fled back out the door.

Jeff and Alec were waiting for her.

"We're going to do 'Black Nag,'" Jeff said. "Come on."

"You're supposed to be teaching," Liddy said. "Get someone who doesn't know it. I'll teach it to Alec."

Jeff didn't say anything but after Liddy had tugged Alec into the set he came back with the white-haired woman in tennis shoes. They were joined by Peter and the woman with the long black hair.

The dance was fast and complicated, nine figures danced in sets of three couples. Liddy felt those steps coming back to her too, moving down the figure, spinning from Alec to Jeff to Peter. Jeff's partner and Peter were breathless and cheerful. The black-haired woman danced with energetic grace, hair flying. Alec was concentrating on the steps, not light on his feet but creditable. He bumped into Liddy, going the wrong way in the reel, and laughed. Jeff's partner took him by the hand and pulled him into the right spot.

"That was great," Alec said when the music ended.

"You're in better shape than I am," she said.

"You want to sit the next one out?"

Liddy nodded.

Alec sat down beside her. "I never paid much attention to dancing. There's more to it than there looks like, isn't there?"

"Lots more."

"Do you want to go somewhere and have a drink afterward? Jeff, too. Of course."

Liddy looked sideways at Alec. "You don't like him, do you?"

"No, but he doesn't like me." Alec sounded cheerful about it.

"Something in common," Liddy murmured.

"I'm afraid so." He gave her a long look, companionable but watchful, as if he knew where they might be going here.

Liddy hadn't been in love with anybody since Nick died. She wondered if she was going to fall in love with Alec Murray on two days' acquaintance. That sounded stupid enough to be right. She saw he wasn't wearing the gun. Maybe it wasn't as much a part of him as she had thought.

At the end of the last dance there was a general gathering of coats and shoes. Liddy leaned on Alec's shoulder, putting her shoes on. She looked around for Jeff and discovered that he wasn't there. She headed for the parking lot. The Triumph was gone.

"Oh, damn!" Liddy stared uncertainly up the street.

"Looks like he took off," Alec said. He didn't sound unhappy about it. "In which case, how about that drink?"

"I can't," Liddy said. She got in Alec's car. "Just take me home. I've got to talk to him."

Alec shrugged and got in. When they got to Liza Jane's house, the Triumph wasn't there, either.

"Shit!" Liddy fumbled in her purse for her car keys.

"What the hell are you doing?"

"I'm going to find him," Liddy said.

"What do you think he's going to do, throw himself in the river?"

"No, but it's my fault. I pushed him away and I hurt his feelings."

"Jesus." Alec looked exasperated.

"He's one of my oldest friends, Alec, and I was crappy to him because I'm terrified of getting sucked back into this place."

"Get back in the car. I'll take you."

"I don't think that's a hot idea."

"You can't drive around by yourself all night, looking for that moron."

"This isn't L.A. And I know where to look."

"Then I'll drop you off if we find him," Alec said. "Come on."

Liddy gave up and got in the car. "Everything's gone haywire," she said. "I'm sorry."

"Tell me where to go."

"The park."

The park was empty, black as a pool of ink.

"Drive up the grade toward the Upper Valley."

Alec muttered something and backed out of the park. They drove in silence. Finally Alec said, "Just how important is this guy to you?"

"I've known him a long time," Liddy said. "And it's not—"

"Not my business? I'll grant you I'm not exactly a sound relationship counselor."

"Your divorce?"

"It wasn't fun."

"What happened?" she asked. "Was it your job?"

"In a way. I promised her I'd get out of the cops, and then I wouldn't. I should have known I wouldn't."

The car started up the grade, switchbacked around the first turn. "What are we looking for here?" Alec asked.

"His car. At the turn-out."

It was there, parked beside the stone bench. Alec pulled up on the shoulder, twenty feet away. "Dramatic," he said.

"We used to come up here," Liddy said. "Don't snipe at me, Alec."

"All right." He grinned at her, relenting a little. "It's been a fun date. Unusual." There was some bite in the words.

"Oh, we're that." She lifted a hand and he turned the car, headlights slashing into the blackness, illuminating a strip of sagebrush and manzanita across the road. He headed down the mountain, brake lights flowering briefly at the bend.

Jeff was sitting on the bench. Liddy sat down beside him.

"You get it on with the Captain?"

"Yes, we made love in the ladies' room."

"You could have brought him up here, if it wasn't so crowded."

"Oh, stuff it, Jeff."

Jeff shrugged. "It's a good place."

"I wasn't looking for a good place." Particularly not this good place.

Jeff leaned back, stared across the valley.

"Why did you take off?" Liddy asked.

"Why did you? I thought something was happening."

"I don't want something to happen."

"Then why are you here?"

"Because I don't want you to sit up here all night and get pneumonia. You haven't even got a coat on."

"You aren't my mother. Whatever you used to think."

"I never thought I was your goddamn mother."

"You were two years ahead of me. It used to matter a lot. Didn't it occur to you I hadn't grown up yet?"

"All the time." She glared at him. "It occurs to me that you still haven't. Will you just come home?"

"No," he said. "I'll sulk if I want to."

"Well, I'm glad you have a plan."

"It's more than you've got. You're obsessed with this Murray guy, you know?"

"I'm not. I just met him."

"You think he's got some kind of key to life on the edge.

Guns and heroics."

"That's a cheap shot."

"Shall I punch a photographer for you? Ragnar the Viking, bring you a severed head now and then, let you polish my shield?"

"Stop it!"

"All right," he said grimly, "I'm jealous."

They looked over the valley floor, spangled with lights, and the silvered orange groves. The summer bug chorus was tuning up, insistent, reproduction on their minds.

After a while Jeff said, "Let's go home."

She got up and they walked to the car. A cloud rolled across the moon again, slid past it, trailing streamers of light, insubstantial as ghosts. Jeff dug an old blanket out of the back and put it around her. When he pulled out onto the road, the wind whipped her hair into her eyes. The Triumph was noisy, and she had to shout to talk to him. "I wasn't coming on to Alec. I just panicked. It's like putting my foot in glue, coming back here."

"It always made you crazy, didn't it?" That was the difference between them. Jeff had loved the chaos of Liza Jane's house and happily rode along on whatever wave was coming in.

"It still does."

"Maybe that's good." Jeff braked at the stop light by the Arcade. "Maybe what you need is an un-rest cure."

"I'm fine," Liddy said.

"Sure. You've got writer's block and your sex life's a mess."

"My sex life is practically nonexistent, and I haven't got writer's block."

"You're afraid to get out of your formula. I've read your books. You're good, but you could do more. You know it. That's why you're trying to soak up some emotion out of Murray. You're afraid to work with your own past. I don't mean me, just this place. You grew up here and then you ran like hell."

"I just wanted something normal. Not all the drama and

upheaval, it all felt like theater, not real, you know?"

"No. They were way too real. You really should write that you-can't-go-home-again novel."

"You don't know anything about it."

"I told you I've been working," Jeff said.

"I want to see it."

"I don't feel like proving it to you. I invited you the other night and you wouldn't come."

"I don't want you to prove it to me. I just want to see if you've put your money where your mouth is."

"Think you'd know?"

"Yes."

"Okay." The light changed and he gunned the car, whipping the wind around them. He turned in at Liza Jane's gates and down a side road that ran behind the house and skirted the oak trees. The caretaker's cottage was really a guest house, stucco like the main house, with a flat tile roof, and a porch with a Chinese lantern vine growing up it.

Inside, it was a jumble. Like Liza Jane, Jeff was a keeper. There were stacks of *Southwest Art* and *Organic Gardening, Whole Earth Review* and *Mother Jones* spilling off a collection of dilapidated tables onto the floor.

"You ever think about bookcases?" Liddy asked.

"They're full," Jeff said. "You want some wine?"

"Yes."

He went into the kitchen and she followed him, stepping carefully. A marmalade cat twined around her ankles.

Jeff scooped the cat up and put her on the kitchen counter. He poured Liddy a glass of wine and opened a can of cat food. The cat inspected Liddy.

"This is a she," Jeff said, filling a stoneware bowl. "Name of Elizabeth."

He poured himself some wine, and took the glass back in the

living room. "In here," he said, and she followed him through it into what had been a sun porch. It had windows on three sides, louvered glass panes that were all open. "Cold?" Jeff closed the panes. "This is mostly where I work. There's more, at galleries."

"Galleries?"

"Not many. Some." Jeff looked embarrassed. "There's a place in Beverly Hills."

"You better watch out," Liddy said. "You might get successful by accident."

Shoulder high shelves lined the fourth wall, overflowing with clay and casting equipment, odd blocks of wood and stone, and rolled-up sheaves of pen and ink studies. Jeff leaned against the shelves waiting with an uncharacteristic uncertainty for her reaction.

She stared at the clay figure on the work table. It was a man, motionless in the middle of a dancer's leap. Bare arms outflung, hands and feet minutely detailed, face almost a blank, with the restless energy of a compacted spring. More dancing figures, bronze and clay, leapt along a shelf behind Jeff's head. A spinning woman; a prancing one, outstretched fingers clasping invisible hands; an old man solemnly capering. At the end was a little bronze of a cat hunting something, caught in the same dance.

"How long have you been working like this?" Liddy demanded.

"Three years maybe. Not all dancers. But I like the movement."

Another piece caught her eye, tucked into a middle shelf in a jumble of clay tools. She picked it up. It was a little elfin bronze, with a gamin face and dragonfly wings.

"That's potboiling." Jeff took it away from her and put it back. "I sell a bunch of those to the fantasy art people at Ren Faire every year.

"She's cute," Liddy said.

"She's too easy. Those are simple buttons to push. Everyone wants to be the fairy queen, go around with magic crystals."

Liddy thought the little sprite had a slightly malevolent grin. "Then why do you do them?"

"It pays the bills. Bronze is expensive."

"Not so pure, then."

"I'm pure enough. I put my guts in the rest of it."

Liddy looked back at the dancers. Some of them were almost faceless, identity transposed into the dance. Others had faces that she recognized from the Art Center. One woman, a clay study still wet, was frozen in midstride, one foot held high. She looked as if she didn't want to be dancing, driven instead by some force beyond her control. The face was sketchy and half hidden by her hair, but Liddy knew who it was. There was something too intimate about it; the artist had known the subject too well.

"I want that."

"Not for sale." Jeff shook his head. "You can't have it, Lid. Those are my memories. Here, I'll give you something else." He pulled a rubber band off an old cigar box, and took out a pair of earrings, little bronze pomegranates on thin wires. He balanced them in his hand. "Souvenir of the Underworld. Six seeds is all it takes. Afraid to wear them?"

"No."

"Don't believe in ghosts?"

"I believe in a good flashlight."

Jeff chuckled and took the silver earrings out of her ears, and put the pomegranates in. He closed her fingers over the silver ones. "You can cast these into bullets."

"The werewolves are bad this year," she said.

"You think this Murray can keep 'em off for you?"

She shook her head. "I think they're after him, too."

"Werewolves are like that. Bite anybody. Even the woman who's pure of heart."

"And says her prayers at night," Liddy said. "I used to think there were werewolves under my bed. If I hung my toes over the edge, they'd get me."

"They will, Jeff said. "They love toes.."

Liddy started to laugh. "I'm not going to listen to you. You'll have me afraid to walk home."

"Then don't," Jeff said quietly.

It would be so easy. So easy to forget about Mr. Abbott and the will and this houseful of people, half of them at each other's throats, and just get into bed with Jeff. And try to tell herself in the morning that it didn't count. It would count. Liddy picked up her purse, held it in front of her with both hands, a shield against lunacy.

Jeff opened the front door for her. The moon was still up, almost full, and the clouds had vanished so that it vibrated in the sky, potent as everyone always thought it was. Liddy started off up the path, ignoring it.

"Remember, you could have stayed," Jeff shouted after her. "Don't blame me if they get you."

The lights of Liza Jane's house swam in the oak trees ahead of her like reflections in a pond. They had looked a lot like that the first time she had seen them, a fish bewildered in new water. She wondered how they looked to Alec, whether he would flounder or swim in this new skin he hadn't asked for. It still stung that she hadn't known about him, and still didn't understand why any more than he did.

1952

Liza Jane is forty-four. She is on the cover of *Life*, red hair clipped into an elegant fluff around her ears, one lock dropping down gamine-like over the famous eyebrows. The eyebrows are arched, winged, and they give her a mercurial look, chancy and maybe a little dangerous, that the studio makeup artist cultivates. She is a star and beautiful. Even in the poisoned air emanating from the House Un-American Activities Committee hearings in Washington, Liza Jane is untouchable, almost; she's the studio's darling.

Carolyn Castellano, whose real name is Luisa Ruiz, is crying in her lap in her dressing room on the Zenovich-Horizon lot, and the willful, mercurial face is somber now. Carolyn is beautiful too, but nobody's darling. Not smart enough, not quite talented enough. Just twenty-five and beautiful. Liza Jane can cry and just let the tears run down her cheeks, but Carolyn cries with her whole body, howling, sniffling, terrified. Her black hair is a wet tangle across her face.

Liza Jane drags her up by the shoulders and sits her against the back of the couch. "Quit it. Somebody's going to hear you."

"It doesn't matter!" Carolyn wails. Her face is red, slick with tears, and puffy. She looks at Liza Jane as if she has just been sentenced to death, as if there is no worse thing that can come. She is pregnant. The studio will can her when they find out. Her Catholic family will never take her back. She puts her knuckles to her mouth, trying to be quiet.

"How far along are you?" Liza Jane asks her.

"I don't know." Carolyn is too scared to count. But she is starting to show. Someone is going to find out.

"Four months? Five?"

"Five," Carolyn whispers.

"It's too late to do anything about it, now."

"I couldn't." Carolyn puts both hands to her face. Catholic Carolyn has a very real fear of hell. "I thought maybe it— would go away— by itself—" Carolyn is hiccupping with tears "—but it didn't."

"They don't as a rule," Liza Jane says grimly. "I know." She pulls Carolyn's hands away from her face, exasperated. "I told you not to go with Art. It is Art's, isn't it?"

"He said we'd get married," Carolyn wails.

"Art's already married," Liza Jane says. "What does he say now?" But she knows that too. She knows Arthur Symes.

"He says it's not his! But it is his. How could he leave me?"

He left you because he's a lightweight. He left you for the same reason he went out with you in the first place, because he's a bastard. Liza Jane doesn't say any of that. Carolyn doesn't need home truths. Home truths have no power to pierce fear. Later, when Carolyn isn't flattened by fear, maybe she can learn about men. If she's smart enough, and Liza Jane isn't sure she is. Liza Jane isn't sure, either, why Carolyn has come to her. They aren't close friends. Carolyn was the ingénue in Liza Jane's last picture, accorded her a kind of schoolgirl admiration, confided her infatuation for Arthur Symes to her, got some advice she didn't take. But now she's here, and Liza Jane knows she's hers, the way any lame thing that gives itself to you is yours. Damn it, she thinks.

She gets a tissue off the makeup table and does what she can with Carolyn's face. She says, "Look, I'll come up with something."

It's dark outside, but that doesn't matter on a sound stage. Liza Jane stands in the middle of a tropical air field now, with palm trees and bunting-draped bleachers, and a single-engine plane looming in the shadows, while the makeup man powders her face again. She has an aviator's helmet over her red hair and it's hotter than hell under the lights. They're finishing up *Glory Days*, adding some interiors, and exteriors that don't require location footage.

"One more time," the director says. Liza Jane groans.

"Maybe this time you can keep from blocking me," Angela Simone snaps. She wears a sarong and a cascade of black hair that looks to Liza Jane's eye far too much like a wig. Why does Hollywood always want to cast white actresses as South Seas beauties? Sultry is Angela's stock in trade.

Liza Jane looks her up and down. "Nobody could block you. Your tits stick out like the Queen Mary." She says to the director, "Maybe you could get her to keep her bosoms the same size for the whole picture."

Len Freed, the director, looks at them warily. Angela has a rep for wanting to be the only sexy one on the set and Liza Jane doesn't take that kind of thing well.

"She's got three different sizes," Liza Jane says. "They've grown two inches since yesterday."

"That's a lie!" Angela says. She looks ready to pull off her sarong to prove it.

"What about the beach scene?" Liza Jane says. "I don't care how tight your tits are, they don't stick straight up when you're on your back!"

"Helen!" Len shouts. An assistant wardrobe girl scoots up. "Go ask Helen to look at this sarong. Honest to Jesus," Len mutters. He doesn't want Angela's tits changing size on screen either. The audience will howl.

Helen appears, looking exasperated, and takes Angela off to re-adjust her sarong.

"That last take was fine," Liza Jane says. "I probably did block her tits. With any luck."

"I want to do it again," Len says. "We can smooth out that business with the wheel chocks. And I want you to look more uncertain. Your guy's falling for someone else."

Liza Jane chuckles. "Never happened to me. Angela has a new musician. Shall I put the make on him and prove it?"

"Goddammit, Liza—"

"Yeah, yeah." She knows they ought to do the take again, she's just tired and she's got Carolyn on her mind. It's a long, fussy take, six pages without a cut. The new Cinemascope camera that Maurice Zenovich has leased from Fox makes a long, narrow screen. You have to keep the actors moving around a lot, and not too close together. Liza Jane and Angela have to cross and re-cross each other while Liza Jane checks the chocks behind her plane's wheels and they argue about the man. Liza Jane's androgynous aviator's clothes make a counterpoint to Angela's sarong, and the thick, verdant world of the tropical set. The plane looks like a huge dragonfly, something that might grow out of this hot, wet landscape. The lights make everyone break a sweat in two minutes. Even the air feels sultry from all the plants, growing in boxes set below the level of the floor, and disguised with dirt and leaves.

Angela comes back and gives Liza Jane a black look. Her tits look smaller. She switches her bottom from side to side as she walks past to make up for it. At least Angela Simone knows how to take care of herself, she won't get eaten by the system. Not yet anyway.

"Lights!" Len yells.

They come on, blazing, pulling the set into some dimension of its own. Beyond the flats that edge the set, it is dark; the murmur of the crew settles into silence. The extras take their places on the air field. Beyond the soundstage walls, out where the world is real, Carolyn is doing God knows what, probably crying in her car.

By the time they finish, it's ten o'clock. No one quits work at five in this world; you quit work when the work's finished. This is the last scene on the air field. The crew has to pull this set down tonight, uproot surprised palm trees, build a Buddhist shrine by morning.

A crowd of bit players in 1920s costume file past Liza Jane, smiling at her, telling her goodnight, while the soundstage lights go off again, one by one, with the brilliance of tropical suns winking out. Liza Jane stands on the darkening stage and waits for Ben. She knows he's there, has been there, in the darkness beyond the set. He hugs her, his eyes lighting up just to hold her. When the last extra leaves, he kisses her.

"You were good," Ben says. "You're always good, but you were extra good today. You want dinner?"

"I want to talk to you."

"I won't fire Angela."

Liza Jane makes a derisive noise indicating her general superiority to Angela.

"Then anything." Ben sweeps his hand extravagantly. "A new limousine, roses in your dressing room?" He takes her left hand, eyes hopeful. "A diamond ring?"

"A favor," Liza Jane says. "For someone else."

Ben is a producer now, a studio man, wary. "Maybe you ought to tell Someone Else's agent to talk to me."

"It's not that kind of thing," Liza Jane says.

Outside on the lot there is a small-town street, with trolley tracks and a row of buildings behind which there is only air. Liza Jane heads down the street, a shortcut to her dressing room. Ben follows her.

"All right. Get that idiotic rig off and you can tell me at dinner."

He watches, snapping the silver strap of his watch, while she strips off a flight jacket and khaki slacks. She is still wearing the aviator's helmet, goggles resting on the top. She poses for him, grinning, in the helmet and her underwear.

Ben yanks it off and tosses it on the sofa. "I don't know how you can wear that thing and still look good. It made every other woman we tested look like a turtle."

"Age and experience," she says grimly. She wriggles into gray tweed slacks and a silk shirt before he can try to take anything else off. Ben is twenty-five and hungry.

They walk through the Zenovich-Horizon lot, through a shifting and illusory landscape. Lit only by security lights now, the small town street gives way to a Pacific battlefield, barbed wire entangled in black sand. Beyond it is a cobblestoned alley with narrow houses leaning over it. The houses have balconies and pots of flowers in the front and doors that open onto rooms abruptly sliced off beyond the camera's eye. They pass through a graveyard and a country fair before they reach the parking lot.

The studio offices surround it, a low-slung stucco sprawl with red roofs. There are still lights on in some of them, especially the story department. Poor things, Liza Jane thinks; no status, no dinner. Ben has a big black Chrysler. They get in and he lifts a hand to the man at the gate as they pass. Liza Jane leans her head back against the upholstery.

"Where do you want to go?"

Liza Jane doesn't care, so he takes her to Chasen's, and they settle into a booth. She orders a martini and a steak. For some reason she's starving, as hungry as if she were Carolyn.

"You better watch it," Ben says, grinning. "You won't be able to fit into your little aviatrix pants." He's only half joking. An actress in the middle of a picture can't afford five pounds between scenes.

"I'll starve tomorrow," Liza Jane says.

Ben wonders what she wants with him. Is he an appetite as abrupt and fleeting as the urge for a steak? Admittedly, he pursued her to start with, and the atmosphere on a movie set is electric and conducive to flash fires. Ben spends more time on the set than his old man knows about.

The martinis come and Liza Jane waits until Ben has had half of his. Then she says, "It's Carolyn. She needs some time away."

Ben says, "Carolyn's supposed to start a picture next week."

"She can't. She's a nervous wreck."

"It's in her contract," Ben says. "If she doesn't do it, I can suspend her."

"She's got to have six months. Put somebody else in the picture. Put Angela in it." Liza Jane smiles sweetly. "It would be a break for her."

Ben wonders why Liza Jane is going to bat for Carolyn. "Tell Carolyn to talk to me."

"She can't. You've got to do this through me, Ben. When was the last time I asked you for a favor?"

"Never," Ben says. "New development." He knows she could have asked him in bed, when his brains are in his trousers, but she won't. He's not sure she looks so good herself. "You okay? You don't have to take on the world for this woman."

"I might as well save somebody," Liza Jane says, and Ben flinches. The blacklist got her last picture killed, sunk Bernice Lewis and Mike Rosen with it, and she's still pissed.

On the surface, everyone is pretending it doesn't exist. *Modern Screen* and *Photoplay* run long silly spreads: Liza Jane and Marilyn Monroe giggling at the Academy Awards, although no one who admits to being a communist or won't testify before a Congressional committee is allowed to win an award; Liza Jane dancing with Kirk Douglas; Rock Hudson dancing with the girl of the week; Betty Bacall and Bogie; Elizabeth Taylor with an old husband, a new husband; columnists like Louella Parsons and Hedda Hopper, dragons in hats and pearls, enjoying their clout, enjoying terrorizing all those pretty girls.

Under the surface, everyone is dancing very carefully. Only the reckless or those too famous to touch—maybe—are willing to argue the question in public. In private, a lot of people are arguing, troubled by conscience, but the forces of reason keep winning: We have to work. We've struck a balance. We've got it organized now. Don't tamper with it. We have to work.

"I told you I tried," Ben says.

"I'm fine," Liza Jane says, relenting. "I picked up some damn bug in Samoa. I hate location. I want a picture that's shot entirely at the Beverly Hilton."

Ben chuckles. "Your life story?"

"Yeah." She crinkles her eyes at him, friendly, but not about to be sidetracked. "What about Carolyn, Ben?"

Ben throws his hands up. "All right. All right. Against my better judgment. But she better act her butt off in whatever we put her in after that. I don't care if it's *Lassie's Revenge.*"

"Thank you." He can see the relief.

If he has any idea what's up, he doesn't voice it. You don't have to lie about what you didn't ask. "I'll tell the old man she didn't test right for it."

Their steaks come and he watches her eat, wondering if she's going to let him come home with her. Six months ago, it would have been a foregone conclusion, but lately he never knows. He wonders if there's somebody else or if it's just burning itself out with the picture. He says, "Can I take you home?"

She looks like she's about to say no, but instead she says, "Is that a condition?"

"No."

"Then you can take me home." She rests her chin on her hand and smiles at him. And he's lost. She has sunset hair and gray-green eyes the color of sage. There's a song, by Frankie Laine, "The Girl in the Wood," about a kid who meets a woman who looks like Liza Jane in the woods one day and never quite makes it back to reality. That's him, Ben thinks. He knows they aren't going to last much longer, but he's going to remember it.

Liza Jane finishes her steak and he pays the check. The parking attendant brings Ben's car up. Ben backs it out around a woman with apricot hair and three matching poodles. He reaches to take Liza Jane's hand, but Liza Jane is watching the woman with the poodles and the rest of the people on the street. She always does that. Once she made him stop and buy a map to the stars' homes, so she could see how many people who were dead were still on it.

Liza Jane has a house up in Laurel Canyon now, but Ben thinks she's getting restless. She never seems to stay in a house long, as if once she's made her nest there, there's always something lacking in it. Or maybe she just wants to keep the maps outdated.

She says, "Let's go down along the beach," which is the opposite direction from Laurel Canyon, but Ben heads down toward Santa Monica and they cruise along Venice Beach and then up along the Pacific Coast Highway as far as Malibu. It's cold and wet and the salt spray makes everything damp. Ben thinks that living out here would be like an endless grunion hunt on cold wet sand.

"It's romantic," Liza Jane says with a chuckle.

"Making love on the wet sand is vastly overrated," Ben says.

"You bring a towel, stupid."

Ben shakes his head. "Nope. Hays Office would never go for it." He knows Liza Jane is trying to entice him down on the beach—it's practically deserted here. He's not sure why, probably just sheer devilment. He slides a hand across the seat onto her knee. "I had in mind a bottle of champagne, maybe a fire."

"Okay," Liza Jane says, suddenly amenable. He has the feeling she's trying to make their affair last, maybe as bewildered as he about what's gone wrong.

Ben turns the Chrysler up Coldwater Canyon and then along Mulholland through the dark knolls of the Santa Monica Mountains. A fox stares at them from the side of the road, crystal eyes caught in the sweep of the Chrysler's headlights, and then vanishes in the chaparral, tail tip a plume of smoke.

Liza Jane says, "It's an omen."

She sounds delighted, as if she means it. Ben remembers that her last name used to be Fox. Her old man, a straight-laced mill-owner from upstate New York, didn't like having a daughter on the stage. But what it might be an omen of, he can't say.

Ben heads up Laurel Canyon where Mulholland crosses it, and then turns again, farther up on a side road that winds like a corkscrew. There's a tiny palette of parking space at the top of a steep driveway, and Liza Jane's house sits just above it, almost hidden by a huge bougainvillea that hangs off the roof. Liza Jane lets them in. The living room is a mess of scripts, stacked on chairs, spilling off the coffee table, three open on the sofa.

Liza Jane kicks one out of her way with her foot. "I don't want to talk about scripts," she says before Ben can open his mouth. "What's happened to decent parts for women anyway? You could star Angela Simone in any of these."

"You said you didn't want to talk about scripts," Ben says.

Liza Jane makes a big show of biting her tongue. She sticks it out and wiggles it at him between her teeth.

Ben produces the bottle of champagne he had in an ice bucket in the car—he likes to do things like that—and gets two glasses out of Liza Jane's kitchen. Except for the jumbled scripts, the house is immaculate, three levels of soft, thick Chinese rugs going down to a thumbnail-sized patio at the back, a little jewel with hibiscus and night-blooming jasmine planted around it. There's a pond with fat goldfish, and peepers among the water hyacinths. The night's warm here, thick with the jasmine smell. Liza Jane opens the French doors from her bedroom onto the patio to let the jasmine in.

Ben chuckles suddenly. The bed reminds him. He wants to grab her and pull her down on it, but the bed has something else to say. "We got another communiqué from Breen today," he tells her.

Liza Jane turns from the doors, leaning in the frame. "He wants to put Angela in a Mother Hubbard," she says hopefully.

Breen is Joe Breen, head of the Hays Office, enforcers of the Motion Picture Production Code. Thanks to Breen, everyone in Europe thinks all American couples sleep in twin beds.

"No," Ben says. He pulls the letter from his pocket. "Page 65," he reads: "'The fade-out between Lillian and Jack on this page unmistakably indicates a sex affair. Some means will have to be found to correct this basically unacceptable situation.'" Ben peruses the letter further. "He also thinks Jack drinks too much."

"Ask him if he'd like to find us a new plot," Liza Jane says.

Ben sits down on the bed. He downs his champagne. He says, "No wonder Jack drinks too much," and fills his glass again. "I think we have to re-shoot the fade-out. I haven't talked to Len yet. Breen says if you have your coat on..."

"Tell Breen I always do it with my coat on,"

Liza Jane doesn't seem as mad as he thought she was going to be. Tonight she seems wavy, like a distorting mirror, shifting from one form to another with every movement. A little manic, perhaps, or maybe that's just the picture winding up.

Ben sets his champagne glass down and puts his arms around her, pulling her back onto the bed with him. He kisses the back of her neck, wrinkling his nose when her hair tickles him. Just to hold her sends a jolt through him, a mild electric charge burning something invisible into his skin.

Liza Jane thinks maybe she ought to marry Ben. He has the kind of bony face, hawk nose and deep-set eyes, that's going to age fast; she wouldn't look ridiculous with him. His old man would split a gut. Maurice Zenovich didn't raise his boy to marry a shiksa actress nineteen years older. Ben kisses her neck, bites her collarbone. He's been in love with her for two years now and it's the longest she's stayed with anybody in a long time. Liza Jane doesn't sleep around, she only has one man at a time, but they don't last, there's always a reason why it won't work. Ben might be okay if she could just go back and change history a little. Liza Jane thinks about Carolyn Castellano wanting to do that, and now she wants to cry and not make love. Ben's hands feel futile on her skin, as if nothing they do will make much difference.

Ben may not have noticed. He's young and powerful, a hotshot, a Boy Genius in the business; and a young erection doesn't wilt easily. Liza Jane thinks about Carolyn Castellano, and this baby that nobody wants. She wraps her arms around Ben's back, holds on, as if she might fall away from him through the bed if she doesn't.

VII
Werewolf Weather

1988

The earth was still restive. It creaked and sighed, and nearly all of Liza Jane's mourners and houseguests—she seemed somehow to still be the hostess—woke at least once.

Liddy dreamed about werewolves and sat up with a lurch to find one foot hanging off the edge of the bed, and a pug licking her toes. "Christ!" She batted at it with her foot. "Go away." The pug whimpered at her. "Oh, never mind." She scooped it up and put it on the bed. "Go to sleep." In the morning, all the rest of them were there.

Jeff poured another glass of wine and said to the cat, "I was too young," despite what he had thought then. Girls matured faster than boys—that seemed to be generally accepted parental wisdom now, according to his friends who had kids. Maybe their two years' difference had been more like five. Jeff found he didn't care much for the notion of himself as a pre-pubescent brain in a sexually functioning body.

Probably Liddy hadn't either. He knew for certain that she had never told any of her college friends how young he was. He wondered what would have happened if they had met for the first time now, when two years didn't matter. He hadn't been sure what it was that Liddy had seen in him, despite the cocky pride that came from getting it on with a girl two years older. Liddy had strained against what had seemed to Jeff an ideal existence: a house in which something was always going on, an aunt who loved her, gave her pretty much a free rein, but always knew what she was up to. If there was anything of Liddy's that Jeff envied, it wasn't the money but Liza Jane. He had loved the house, an embodiment of its owner, with interesting, flamboyant people in and out of it all the time, the same ones who had driven Liddy nuts, but the connection of the heart had been to Liza Jane as much as Liddy. He had needed a mother and Liza Jane had needed a son although neither one of them ever said so. Once the will was settled, the house would empty out, all that energy flowing away, probably to Liddy's relief, if she stayed. And what was his place here now, without Liza Jane to take care of?

Ben Zenovich finished Mike's script at dawn, carried it from his Horsehead Ranch cabin to Mike's, and stood, fist raised outside the door, for almost a minute before he dropped his arm and went away again without knocking. He got in the car instead and sat with his arms folded on the wheel and his forehead on his arms.

Frank was too young, Ben thought. The script was called Inquisition, and it was Mike's catharsis, but Frank just saw a good part, full of intellectual angst and heroics, not a creature from the black lagoon, dripping swamp water. Ben looked at his watch. Six o'clock. He couldn't go over there yet. He turned the key in the ignition anyway. He could sit and wait until Frank got up, and then he could tell him he wasn't going to make this picture. Ben wanted to kill the thing quickly, as if it were some monstrous mutant child, fathered by all of them.

When he got to Liza Jane's house, there were some lights on, so Ben rang the bell and it was answered by the pugs and Alec Murray, in shorts and a sweatshirt. Alec had a book in his hand.

"You always get up this early?" Ben asked.

"No," Alec said. "Do you?"

"Never, when I can help it." Ben tossed the script on the coffee table in the living room. "Trying times. What are you reading?"

Alec held up the book: *Liza Jane: A Biography of Elizabeth Sidney.*

"That's a piece of shit," Ben said. "Liza Jane hated it."

"Is it inaccurate?"

"No, she just thought it was glossy. She didn't try to stop it, though. If you fight them, they do something worse."

"It's flattering," Alec said.

"Hell, yes. And about as deep as an inch of bath water. If you're trying to figure Liza Jane out, it won't help much."

The book was mainly a list of her movies and her lovers, neither with much further explanation. Alec put it down. "You tell me about her," he suggested.

"Why are you so hot to know?"

"I want to know where I fit in, for Christ sake. So far what I've heard makes about as much sense as this book. Woman comes along, leaves me a whole lot of money, probably makes me totally unfit for my job, and you want to know why I want to know? I've got some jerk trying to get me to be on Oprah. I've got reporters calling me up, I'm associating with a known mob

figure, and my boss wants to know that the hell I think I'm doing."
He looked disgusted.

Ben smiled. "Yeah, you're a cop, aren't you? I forgot."

"DEA," Alec said. "It's a federal agency, and we like a low profile. Vincente knows who I am. His boy Tony spotted my weapon about two minutes after we met. It's embarrassing."

"You wear a gun around?"

Ben didn't appear to have thought of that. Nobody thought of that. Characters in movies carried totally improbable arsenals of weapons and blasted each other into bits with them. But nobody ever expected people to have real ones. "Look," Alec said, exasperated, "I've explained this to Liddy already. I'm supposed to wear it."

Ben grinned. "Under your sweatshirt?"

"Under my sweatshirt."

"Makes it kind of hard to get at."

"I'm not expecting to shoot anybody."

"You could shoot Francie Allen," Ben suggested. "Public service."

Alec tried to figure out what the guy was doing here at six in the morning. Ben had an uneasy air of waiting about him. His receding hairline and the angle of his nose, straight down the bridge with no lumps to it, gave him the look of someone with his face thrust forward, watching. His polo shirt and gray slacks looked as if he had slept in them.

"You dodged my question," Alec said after a minute.

"What question's that?"

"About Liza Jane."

"Oh, hell. I can tell you about Liza Jane," Ben said. "It won't get you much farther, but I can give you some facts. I was vice president of production at Zenovich-Horizon when your mom— I mean Carolyn here—got pregnant. I didn't know she was pregnant, but when someone wants to take a six months' vacation for her nerves, the thought crosses your mind. I wouldn't have been too surprised to hear about you, if you know what I mean. Except that Liza Jane kept track of you, I can't figure that. At the time I didn't ask. Carolyn was supposed to start a picture for us, and I let Liza Jane talk me into letting her off the hook. Having done that, I didn't want to know any more about it in case my old man asked. He wanted his stars to be pure as choir girls, and he might have canned her. Carolyn, I mean."

"That's not exactly the impression I get of Liza Jane," Alec said.

"Liza Jane was different. She was a major star, and nobody could do anything with her, including my old man. He put up with Liza Jane. Not Carolyn."

"Why did you?"

"For Liza Jane," Ben said. "You had to have known her. That woman could charm the birds off the trees. I would have done anything for her then."

"Uh huh."

"Well, I would." Ben grinned reminiscently. "We were in the middle of one of those hundred-mile-an-hour passionate affairs that are half champagne and good lighting, and half the excitement of making a picture. You have to be in the business to understand that part. It fizzled out right after that. I never was quite sure why, but things had been rocky for a while. Anyway, I did what she wanted me to for Carolyn, and didn't regret it. She paid me back."

"Liza Jane?"

"Oh, yeah. Carolyn never was much use after that. She was unstable to start with, and she got to be a real lush. Sorry to talk about your mom like that, but frankly I don't think it was so much giving up the kid—I mean, you—as it was the guy who walked out on her. Now I find out it was Arthur Symes. Poor Carolyn, what a schmuck to waste your life on."

Alec tried to summon up more than a mild sympathy for Carolyn, but it wouldn't come. Liza Jane was the one who had arranged his birth, arranged his adoption. Arranged and then dismantled his life. "How did she pay you back?"

"I wanted to direct," Ben said. "My old man never let me. He said we weren't creative types, we were money types, the guys with the big picture. You get pegged as one thing in Hollywood, it's hard to change. When the studio broke up, I couldn't get anyone to give me a shot at it."

"Don't you produce your own pictures?" Alec asked. "The ones you direct?"

"I do now," Ben said. "That takes a bankable name. And anyway, I didn't want to then."

"Why not?"

"I just went sour on it," Ben said. "Never mind. It's history. Anyway, Liza Jane was about to sign to do *Across the Bridge* and she wouldn't commit until they signed me to direct. She was taking a chance—for all she knew, I could have screwed it up royally. Fortunately the critics loved it and it made money. After that I didn't have any trouble."

"Didn't she do sort of the same thing for Mike Rosen?" Alec asked. "I gathered, from what he said at dinner—"

"Yeah," Ben said abruptly. "Yeah." He got up, picked up the script. "Maybe she should have let the son of a bitch sink."

Alec heard him going upstairs where various footsteps and stirrings were going on. After a while people began to filter down. Bernice headed for the kitchen, followed by Sharon Hamilton in her bathrobe. Liddy came down with Zach. Alec saw her and stood up.

"Good morning," he said.

"Good morning." Liddy looked a little embarrassed. "I'm sorry about last night."

"It's okay." He thought she looked on edge, too. Everyone in the house was as ornery as a bunch of tarantulas. "You look like you could use coffee," he said. "I started a pot in the kitchen."

"I could use a drink," Liddy muttered.

Bernice was at the stove in the kitchen, and Sharon was reading the *Los Angeles Times* in an armchair, her back to the glass doors.

"Does anybody have any idea why Ben is upstairs yelling at Frank?" Liddy inquired. She sat Zach down at the table and reached for the cereal.

"Something about a script?" Alec said.

Bernice smacked her spatula on the skillet. "Dammit, not this morning."

Frank came in, buttoning his shirt, with Ben behind him. Frank had his glasses on and he looked stiff-necked and stubborn. "It needs to get made, Ben." He reached in the refrigerator for a carton of milk. "It's part of our common culture."

Ben stopped in the doorway. "I'm not going to dig our guts out and brood over them." He glared at Sharon. "Mike's written a script about the blacklist," he informed her.

"Whose guts?" Frank said.

Sharon put the newspaper down and walked out. "God damn him," she said.

Frank looked at Ben. "Whose guts?"

"Our common culture's, since you put it so niftily," Ben said.

"It's part of collective memory," Frank said. "You can't pretend it didn't happen. If I can make a picture about Vietnam, which happens to be my collective memory, you can do this. You ought to jump at it. It's a director's movie."

"It's a crucifixion movie. Starring Mike Rosen as Jesus. A hundred-fifty pages of ego."

"Maybe Mike's entitled. It's a good script." Frank looked at the rest of them. "You folks excuse us." He picked up a bagel and went out again, past Ben. "I want to make it," he told Ben.

"You're too young!" Ben yelled after him. "You don't know from shit!"

"Ben—" Bernice said.

"You go to hell," Ben said. He went down the hall and out the front door.

Liddy looked at Alec. She ruffled Zach's hair. "Just your average story conference."

"Really?" Alec was unsure whether they carried on like that all the time, or she was being sarcastic. Normal assumptions held water like a sieve with these people.

"Godalmighty." Harry Lanier came in and sat down. "Sharon's up in her room, walking around in circles and growling," he announced. "Do I want to know why?"

"Mike's written a screenplay about the blacklist," Liddy said. "It seems to have touched a few nerves."

Harry whistled. "Is that what it was? He showed Liza Jane a treatment a few months ago, but I thought it was something he wanted her to do."

"He wanted to know what she thought would happen if he wrote it," Bernice said. "She told him it would shake people up, but to write it if he needed to." Bernice wiped her hands on her apron. "She knew he needed to. Maybe we all needed him to."

"Tell that to Sharon," Harry said. He caught Alec's bewildered expression. "That was what Mike and Sharon got divorced over."

"I don't know much about the blacklist," Alec said. "That was the McCarthy hearings, wasn't it?"

Bernice flipped the coffee grinder on, effectively blocking any answer while the beans sank into the whirling blade. When she turned it off, she asked Alec, "Do you remember a while back, when Ronald Reagan gave Mikhail Gorbachev a copy of *Friendly Persuasion?*"

"No," Alec said. "Not really. I've seen it, of course."

Bernice poured the ground coffee into a new filter. "You probably never noticed it doesn't have a screenplay credit. Written by nobody." She looked at Alec, her expression tight-lipped. "'Nobody' was Michael Wilson, who was a wonderful writer. He was blacklisted because he didn't think his politics, or his friends' politics, were any of the committee's business, and he wouldn't give any names. He and Carl Foreman wrote the screenplay for *The Bridge on the River Kwai*, did you know? Well, of course you didn't. You won't see their names on those credits either, and the Academy refused to give them the Oscar it won. Ronald Reagan was president of the Screen Actors Guild during some of the worst of it, and he turned on his own, turned into a dedicated communist-hunter, because it was expedient. They destroyed people. Now he presents *Friendly Persuasion* to the Soviet premier and calls it an American classic. People have extremely convenient memories."

"Most people do." Harry looked at Alec. "That's why you don't know about it, kid. There've been a few things done on it, not much. Nobody talks about it. Even I don't. And I was too young to be involved. But it was there. You worked with it, or you didn't work. Now everyone's ashamed of themselves. Collective bad conscience."

"What about Mike Rosen?" Alec asked.

"The same thing happened to Mike," Bernice said sadly. "But Mike was young. He was just starting out. He'd only sold two scripts, a comedy and a wonderful historical about Richard III, before they got hold of the fact that he'd been to a couple of Communist Party meetings in the late thirties, when he wasn't even quite twenty. The House Un-American Activities Committee wanted him to name everybody he'd ever seen at those meetings, and he wouldn't do it. It was brutal. After that no one would give him a job. No one would ever say why—no one would admit that there was a blacklist, you understand. There were people on a kind of graylist, who had never been called to testify, who were on it because they were liberals, or sympathetic to the blacklisted people, or just because someone had heard some unsubstantiated thing, or had their name mixed up with someone else's. There was no way to tell if you were on it." Bernice paused. "And you couldn't trust anyone," she said heavily. "People who'd been friends for years. That was the worst part. Your friends might give them your name to save themselves. And they didn't trust you either. You might be about to turn them in, or you might be blacklisted yourself and the guilt would be catching. You felt hunted all the time. Every time someone turned you down for a job, you started to wonder if you were blacklisted. You couldn't tell. It nearly destroyed Mike."

"What happened afterward?"

"He couldn't work. He couldn't sell a screenplay or a book either. His name was poison. He got by with writing potboilers and soft-core pornography under another name, and finally Liza Jane got him an assignment, although they wouldn't give him screen credit. When it died down in the early sixties, he gradually started working again, but it was hard. He was too old to be just starting out. He's sold some screenplays, but he's never sold a serious book, and he tried, after he got back into Hollywood. Writers don't get much recognition here, and Mike wanted to be one of the literati. I think he felt the world owed it to him. But it never happened. Maybe he was just too old by the time he started. The blacklist waylaid him all those years. We lost the best years of a lot of good people. And in the meantime, it cost him his marriage."

"That'll be why Sharon's up there chewing nails," Harry said. "She's afraid she's in the script."

"She may be," Bernice said. "She wanted him to testify and get off the hook, and he wouldn't do it, so she left him, before he dragged her down, too." Bernice poured hot water through the coffee. She seemed to be striving gamely if unsuccessfully to be charitable. "Sharon was an actress in those days, and she was scared silly. The Screen Actors Guild was eating its young."

Alec thought the whole industry had a tendency in that direction, but he was fascinated in spite of himself. This was the history that had overlapped his birth. He couldn't quite make the connection with Liza Jane, but it was there somewhere. He looked at Liddy, a bowl of untouched granola in front of her, green eyes studying Bernice. Had Liddy grown up knowing about the blacklist, or was all this new to her, too? And what about Bernice? Bernice had been more than just there. Bernice was a woman who had marched in Selma, had chained herself to the White House fence for nuclear disarmament. Bernice had been a wardrobe woman at Zenovich-Horizon in what Theresa Tate had called the bad old days. What had Bernice been doing in the bad old days?

Bernice poured him a cup of coffee. "It was all a long time ago. History does have a way of coming around again, but it's never quite the same on the second pass."

"Hell, it's never the same on the first pass," Harry said. "Just ask Mike and Sharon."

Jeff came through the glass doors. "Today's metaphysical thought. The class will write an essay on that." He flicked the top of Liddy's head with his finger.

Jeff and Alec looked at each other without comment. Alec saw that Jeff had left a water glass of flowers on top of Liza Jane's coffin.

"Then what version will this movie be?" Alec inquired.

"Going to be a star, Captain?" Jeff asked.

"Shut up," Liddy said, not irritably. "Mike's written a screenplay about the blacklist and everyone's having hysterics."

"Some of us are having them more quietly than others," Bernice said. "I expect it will be its own version. Truth as Mike sees it, filtered through Frank Hill, and a director and a cameraman."

"Not the real truth then?"

"I doubt there is a universal one. Memory is too pliable."

"Inconvenient as hell," Jeff said. "But pliable." He made a faint motion with his hands, as if twisting something into shape.

"I doubt one could get along otherwise," Bernice said.

Alec had the impression they were all talking about something else besides Mike's screenplay. Several things else. The undercurrents appeared to be meeting head on. "So why write it?" he asked. "Why spill your guts to the world if it's not even going to be true? Or at least not definitive?"

"Because your best work comes out of your guts," Liddy said. She flicked an eye at Jeff. "It's just that some people don't like the looks of other people's guts."

"A revolting metaphor," Harry Lanier said. "Taken literally."

"Creation's revolting," Jeff said. He poured himself a cup of coffee. "I say Huzzah for old Mike."

"Mike may be sorry," Liddy told him. "He may find out he rearranged his guts when he spilled them, and they won't go back in."

"Would you two get off the subject of guts?" Harry said. "I haven't eaten."

"Have some granola," Liddy said. "No nasty associations."

"I want bacon," Harry said. "Associations and all."

"How about tripe?" Jeff asked. "Lots of that floating around."

"Fundamental structure of the universe," Liddy said. "Entrails. We're trying to see the past in them."

"I thought you read the future in them," Alec said, feeling goaded. He had the sensation of having his nose pressed against a glass.

"Time is circular," Jeff said. "That's the Ramananda's theory anyway."

"The Ramananda thinks he can conjure spirits from the vasty deep," Alec muttered.

"Bravo, Captain." Jeff grinned at him.

"Mom." Zach tugged at Liddy's sleeve. "I'm going to be late."

Jeff put his coffee cup down. "Come on, kiddo. I'll take you. We can discuss the meaning of life." Jeff put him on his shoulders. "You can tell me what we've all been talking about."

"I don't know," Zach said. "It sounded dumb."

"That's a perceptive kid," Harry said.

"He's smart enough to eat granola," Bernice said. "Since we're out of bacon. Do you want me to cook you some tofu?"

"I want an Egg McMuffin," Harry said and got up. "Tofu does not prepare a man for the L.A. Times. They will be here at ten. I may come back, or I may go to Mexico."

"I'll have a bagel," Alec said, and got one. He wondered why Bernice had run Harry off with tofu. He thought it had been on purpose. "What does this script have to do with Liza Jane?" he asked abruptly. Might as well ask what you wanted to know. Sometimes you startled people into telling you.

Bernice didn't look startled, but she sat down across from Liddy and Alec and made a gesture as if to take their hands. "You're a government man, aren't you? I expect you have some very firm convictions."

"On some things," Alec said.

"On right and wrong and loyalty."

"Doesn't everyone?"

"That's just the trouble," Bernice said. "They never match. In 1953, no one could look at what Stalin had done and not be repulsed. In 1938, we were still in the middle of a depression. People were living in hobo jungles because of capitalism. We thought communism could save the world. Something had to."

"We?" Liddy said.

Alec tried to picture Liza Jane in a Worker's Paradise.

Bernice laughed. "Not Liza Jane. Her causes were always closer to home. No, I meant Mike and me. You see, I was the one who got him in."

Alec blinked. "Into the Communist Party?"

"I'm afraid so. Ben knows, that's why he told me to go to hell. And because Liza Jane went with me once. Really just for a lark, I think. The studio was terrified someone would find out. I had to quit my job before they threw me out on my ear. I was no loss, but she was valuable."

"So she kept quiet about it." Liddy looked uncomfortable.

"She would have testified for the pleasure of telling the Committee to eat its hat," Bernice said. "But she couldn't without putting other people at risk. It was too late to save Mike. That's what I mean about loyalty being complicated." She went back to the stove, interview clearly ended.

There was more, Alec thought. She wasn't telling it, but there was more. This was the easy confession, her own. Whatever else there was, or had been, was Liza Jane's.

1953

Liza Jane is forty-five. She doesn't know what the world is coming to, and doesn't know whether that is middle age or because the world really is going to hell in a handbasket. The blacklist is a like a disease, like something you catch that doesn't show symptoms for fifteen years, so there's no way to tell how you got it. She thought it had all died down after the Hollywood Ten, screenwriters who refused to testify, went to prison, but now it's up and kicking again, this time with Joe McCarthy in the Senate to shove it along. Even the government is scared of McCarthy. The hearings have become a public show, real-life blood and guts to be viewed, real-life spies to be unmasked. How did the communists get the bomb? How did they take over Czechoslovakia and Hungary? How did they get China? "Traitors in the high councils in our own government," says Richard Nixon, Congressman, then Senator, from California. Traitors in the government, traitors in the Army, in the Voice of America. Traitors in Hollywood, slipping communist propaganda into movie and television scripts.

Somehow they are all making it seem legitimate, and Liza Jane feels as though people with some clout, what dubious clout movie stars possess, need to speak their convictions. Everyone else seems to have the convictions of a weasel.

She says that to Ben before she leaves for Washington, and Ben says, "Liza, for God's sake, stay home."

She says, "I won't, damn it."

Ben says, "If anyone digs up—if anyone opens their mouth, I can't save you. Shit, why did you have to tell me that?"

"I thought I'd better. Forewarned is forearmed."

"I don't want to be forewarned! I don't want to know that! If anyone finds out I knew that—"

"Who are you worried about, Ben? Me or you?"

"I'm worried about the whole damn studio," Ben says. He's good and mad. He hates the whole thing. He's got the American Legion and the DAR sending him petitions, circulating crazy lists. One of them is called Red Channels and has half the Democrats in the country on it. The red baiters have the Screen Actors Guild baying on the trail: the Crusade for Freedom, "A counterattack against communist lies and treachery." Everyone's seeing communists under the bed like bogeymen, and everyone's trying to shout louder than everyone else for fear someone will say they're communists. All Ben wants to do is work, and he can't work in this mess, he feels like he's got his feet in tar, like the mammoths in the La Brea Tar Pits, which are a big attraction in Los Angeles.

"You're gonna sink me," he tells Liza Jane. "They're gonna find my goddamn skeleton six feet under."

"You'll have company," Liza Jane says.

"Look, Liza—" Ben takes her hand. "Don't go to Washington. I'm asking you."

"I'm going." Liza Jane pulls her hand away, but she pats his arm with it. They haven't been lovers in nearly a year, but there's something still there, always will be. More than she'll tell him. Maybe her confession about her quick fling with the communists is a sop to her conscience. "I've got to go, Ben. Somebody's got to speak up."

"Well, why you?" Ben says. "The Committee for the First Amendment tried that six years ago. All they got was bad publicity."

"Because they've subpoenaed Mike Rosen, that's why," she says, and watches Ben flinch.

Ben sinks down in a chair and puts his head in his hands. Liza Jane feels a little sorry for him, but she walks out anyway. Ben's got to fight his own battle. She's got all she can do to fight hers. She's known this was coming for over a year, ever since the studio stopped a film in mid-production and no one knew why and everyone knew why. She's carried the fallout from that around with her ever since.

Mike's wife has left him. Sharon saw a lawyer even before the subpoena came. When they found out the studio had killed his picture he could see the terror in her eyes, and the instinct for self-preservation, and knew it was just a matter of time.

Sharon knows which side her bread's buttered on, but she

gives it one more try. "Mike, please. Just tell them. Who do you owe anything to?" She's blond and ethereal, pretty as a butterfly. That used to work.

"Me," Mike says. "I owe it to me." He's not pretty, never has been, isn't now at thirty-three. His face is a little lopsided, his ears stick out, he looks like someone's nice English teacher. English teachers are suspect too.

"Just tell them who was there," Sharon says. "What's wrong with that? Just tell them the truth."

"They don't want the truth." He's packing his suitcase, a clean shirt and a change of underwear. "They want scapegoats, someone to take the blame because the government fucked up."

"You fucked up!" Sharon is so scared she's shaking. She's up for a good part, and they haven't any money; they've lived hand to mouth since they got married. The business is like that; she knows writers whose children think that going to the Unemployment Office with Daddy every other Monday is something everyone does. But this is different, this is permanent. There are writers and directors living in Europe, self-exiled because they can't work here; her agent is nervous, has told her that if Mike's out, she'll be out. An FBI agent has been sitting in his car across the street for weeks. Every time she comes out of the house he tries to get her to talk to him.

"You and your damn communist friends!" Her voice rises higher while Mike stands there, trying to fold his shirt. "If they mean so much to you, go live with them!"

"My friends aren't communists," Mike says. Most of them anyway. Not now.

"Then why don't you say so? If they aren't communists, they don't have anything to be scared of."

"You're so goddamn stupid it's a wonder you've got enough sense to get out of bed in the morning." Mike keeps his voice level, and Sharon's screaming bounces off him like ping-pong balls. He feels detached, nearly dazed, the inevitability of everything that's going to happen to him solidifying around him like amber. He folds the shirt into a lump and sticks it in the suitcase. Sharon picks up an ashtray off the nightstand and throws it at him, hits him in the chest. He watches her walk out, with the big glass ashtray spilling down the front of his shirt, cigarette butts everywhere.

Liza Jane gets on the plane and watches the ground disappear under her. Her ears feel stuffed up and when she reaches into her purse for chewing gum she finds the little envelope of pictures from Mrs. Doris Murray. Carolyn's back at work, but Carolyn didn't want to see them. Carolyn's drinking too much, and trying to pretend she doesn't care that Arthur Symes has written her off. Arthur Symes is throwing his weight around in the Screen Actors Guild, waving the flag and cursing communists. Arthur Symes is very upstanding.

Liza Jane looks at the pictures. The kid is three months old. His eyes look like they're going to be brown and he has a tuft of hair that sticks straight up like the top of a carrot. For some reason, he makes her think of Mike's script, *Richard Plantagenet*, the movie that won't ever get made now. It's about Richard the Third and the princes in the tower, poor little murdered babies, but in Mike's script Richard didn't do it. Mike's never believed in the obvious villain. Now all the unobvious villains are getting off scot-free.

But when she lands in Washington no one will let her speak and she has to watch from the visitors' gallery. She's used to her fame getting her what she wants but not today. These people don't trust art, they never have, and a film is art, collaborative art. A lot of people's individual truth, making up one big one. Maybe they're right to be afraid of it. No one wants to hear actors' unpopular opinions right now unless they're guilty as hell and on the witness stand, so she watches with her gut twisting while the Committee hammers at Mike.

"Are you a native-born American, Mr. Rosen?

"Are you a member of the American Civil Liberties Union?"

"Are you a member of the Writers Guild?"

"Are you now or have you ever been a member of the Communist Party?"

Ben meets her at the airport in Los Angeles, detaches her from the Hollywood beat reporters who want to ask about her trip, whether she spoke to the Committee, what her opinion is on communists in the industry, and whether she knows any.

"It was educational, they didn't find me important enough to speak to, no opinion at all, and no." She needs to throw them some kind of bone or they'll print God knows that. She gives them a smile, pauses long enough for a few photos and then lets Ben hustle her across the tarmac to the terminal and a waiting car.

"What's the hurry?"

"Larry Hotchkiss," Ben says, putting the car in gear. "He's agreed to give testimony in executive session."

Liza Jane makes a disgusted face. "Of course he has." Larry is a fine upstanding anti-communist and they no doubt want to know who he suggests they accuse. Executive session testimony is supposed to be secret, for favored friendly witnesses who would just as soon not be on the news. Then the committee leaks anything they think would be useful to make them look good or to scare people.

"There's speculation he might name you," Ben says grimly. "I told you not to make yourself conspicuous."

Liza Jane doesn't ask him how he knows. Hollywood is a constantly churning rumor mill and she's well aware that Larry Hotchkiss holds grudges. "If he does, he's making it up."

"Are you sure?" Ben asks.

"There is no way Larry knows anything." Liza Jane hopes she's right. "Nobody does but Mike and Bernice. And you."

"Which I wish I didn't. And does that matter? You made a fool of him and he has a long memory. He wants to give them somebody, and he'll look extra patriotic naming you, naming a big star. He'll do it more in sorrow than in anger, you know Larry. Plus you got higher billing than him last time."

Liza Jane feels sick to her stomach. The business with Larry's wig doesn't look quite so funny now. They've been in two pictures together since then and he hasn't forgotten. She takes a deep breath. "You tell Larry," she says evenly, "that if he names anybody, I will say what I saw when I opened the wrong dressing room door."

Ben looks wary. "Which was?"

"Larry and Eddie Morrison." Ed Morrison is the new blond teenage heartthrob, twenty-five playing seventeen.

"Jesus," Ben says. Homosexuality is a career killer in Hollywood only if it becomes public. Then it's toxic.

Liza Jane likes Eddie; the exposure would bring him down with Larry. She feels slimy even for threatening it.

"Jesus," Ben says again. He's quiet for a minute. "I'll make sure he knows."

"Don't mention Eddie. There are bound to have been more."

"Not if I don't have to."

"Just take me home," Liza Jane says. She wants to throw up.

The idea of actually making good on her threat feels as shameful as the people naming names for the Committee, someone who would sacrifice anybody else just to get the hounds off her own trail. She hopes she has Mike's courage if it comes to it.

Larry Hotchkiss backs down and doesn't name anyone at all, unsure of exactly how vengeful Liza Jane may be, but it's years before she stops feeling like she's looking over her shoulder. Mike writes detective stories, romances, pornography, anything he can sell. Liza Jane keeps track of him, almost the way she's begun to keep track of the kid. Lends him money, asks him to dinner, takes him to bed. Finally she gets him a job writing a movie again: *Elizabeth Regina* for Zenovich-Horizon. Mike's good at history, Zenovich-Horizon is having some troubles, and Liza Jane offers some big salary concessions if they'll agree to give Mike the assignment. The assignment, not the credit. Morrie Zenovich likes the script, but not that much. Like *Friendly Persuasion*, this movie is written by Nobody. It will be 1969 before Mike sees his name on a screen credit again.

VIII
Taking A Meeting

1988

The reporter for the *Los Angeles Times*, a fortyish man with a country boy face and a look of being rarely astonished, had been cornered in the living room by the Ayala heirs; they had all reappeared somehow.

He was listening solemnly to the Ramananda expounding upon the Unified Church of Light, with interjections from Margaret Collins about the proposed Elizabeth Sidney Modern Drama Festival, and from Stu and June Patterson in chorus, on wellness. Steve Bowman was trying to extricate him.

"Mr. Chapman's got limited time here," Steve said.

"Well, we realize that," Margaret snapped. "And, of course, that there are more important people than we. However—"

"It's so important that the public know what dear Liza Jane intended," June Patterson said.

"That's right," Stu said. "Tell the truth and shame the City Council."

Chapman smiled. "I understand that she wanted to be buried here—on this property? And that there's some difficulty about that?" He held a little tape recorder out to Stu.

"She felt the vibrations here in the valley," Stu said.

"It was just kind of a whim," Steve said. "A lady's entitled to that." He winked at Chapman. June glared at him and Margaret snapped her teeth. "We're getting it all settled," Steve said. "As soon as Harry's had his chat with you, he's going to take a meeting with the council, work it all out. She was quite a gal, you know. Didn't like Hollywood glitz, Forest Lawn, nothing phony. I love that. We think maybe there's a local cemetery."

"Does Liddy know about this?" Margaret demanded.

Steve smiled at Will Chapman again, trying to shove Margaret back by sheer willpower. "Little Liza Jane. You've got to meet her, Will, she's something. Grew up here with her aunt. She's literally devastated right now."

"Uh huh. When do you expect to announce the funeral?"

"This afternoon. Tomorrow, max."

"I understand Roberto Vincente's in town."

"I wouldn't know about that. He's not really a player here."

"We had dinner with him," June said. "He came for the Ramananda's service."

The Ramananda smiled blissfully. "There is spiritual potential in all of us."

"I heard he put a rose in the coffin and broke a photographer's camera," Margaret Collins said.

Steve clenched his hands. "We're getting off the story here, folks. Listen, Mr. Chapman doesn't have a whole lot of time and he wants to have a chat with Frank Hill, so I'm going to have to ask you to excuse us."

June looked around expectantly. "Such a nice man. He had dinner with us, too. We have a movie idea that he's interested in."

"Mr. Hill is a very private person. Now if you don't mind—"

Will Chapman, who had developed an almost maniacal gleam in his eye, said, "I'll be around for a while. You folks can catch me at the Horsehead Ranch if you want to."

"Well... I'll just pop in the kitchen then, and say good morning to Liddy," June said.

They surged around Steve and Will Chapman for another few moments, like waves lapping at some shoreline. When they were gone, Steve put his back to the door. He grinned conspiratorially (it took some effort) at Chapman. "Forget them. This town's cuckoo, you know that."

The door thumped behind them. He peered around it, and let Harry Lanier in.

"You look like the Alamo," Harry said. "Relax. They're all in the kitchen. Good morning, Will."

"Going to have a funeral, Harry?"

"Any day now. What can we do to make you happy, Will? To keep some of the irrelevant stuff out of this?"

"You mean like the party in the bed sheet, or like Roberto Vincente?"

"We just want to keep it dignified."

"Maybe you ought to get the coffin off the porch."

"We're working on that," Steve muttered. He brightened. "Hey, look, Miss Sidney was a real pal to her friends. Frank Hill and Ben Zenovich have got some damn good things to say."

Harry grabbed him by the shoulder. "Not in the same interview," he hissed.

"I want to talk to this Alexander Murray," Chapman said. "He's the real mystery man, isn't he?"

"I'll line him up for you," Steve said. "You chat with Harry and Frank first. We're here to help out." He departed in search of Alec, wondering what carrot he could offer for cooperation. As he passed through the hall, he gave an uneasy glance at the front door. Francie Allen never got up before noon, but once she was conscious, she'd be over here after Frank again. And now Frank and Ben Zenovich were pissed at each other. At least that was what Harry had sounded like. Steve felt that they were getting away from him, unmanageable as a flock of starlings. I've got to beat out a positioning statement. Hand it out, tell them to stick to it, he thought, quailing a little at the prospect of presenting a positioning statement to Donald Wain or Roberto Vincente. That was what came of having a dead person for a client. You couldn't talk to a dead person, and they couldn't knock anyone else into line. No more dead people, he thought.

"Look, I liked Liza Jane," Will Chapman was telling Harry. "I was sorry as hell to see her go. But the tabs have got this anyway. You might as well give me the straight dope, let me put it in perspective."

Harry groaned. "Why the hell do you think you got invited? Just see if you can't leave out the weird religions, and anything Francie Allen may want to say about Frank Hill. That woman's got a mouth on her like a garbage can, and she never heard of the word 'libel.' Just a word to the wise there."

"I know Francie," Chapman said. It wasn't exactly a promise not to talk to her, but Harry knew he wasn't going to get one. You could suggest to the press, but you couldn't give orders unless you wanted to make them stubborn. When Will Chapman got stubborn, somebody got flayed alive in his column.

"All right. Here's the story on the funeral." Harry handed Chapman a typed sheet of paper. "That's the straight story, as far as it goes. When it goes any farther, we'll give it to you. Here's a list of people who're in town for the funeral."

"Can I see the will?"

"I'm still talking to Arlo about that. It's touchy, but I think so. I'd rather you got it straight. There're rumors all over."

Chapman chuckled. He had heard most of them already. "It's a pity you're on the wrong side of the fence, Harry. I haven't had so much fun in years. I could write a book."

"God knows, so could I," Harry said. "Don't."

"We'll see. Who else are you letting in on this press conference?"

"Nobody. Not even *Variety.* They'll have to pick it up from you. That ought to get me some points, damn it. Except for the local paper. That's a courtesy call. But they're a weekly."

"Dust beneath my feet." Chapman leaned back in his chair and grinned. "Bring 'em on."

Alec was hiding in the projection room down the hall from the basement office. He knew Steve Bowman was looking for him, but he wasn't going to talk to Will Chapman, whose writing he rather liked, but he wasn't going to talk to him anyway. He was still too uncertain of what his relationship with Liza Jane had been to try to define it for the press. And that would just upset his mother, who was upset enough to find his high school senior picture staring at her from the Kroger check-out stand. God knew where they had got that. He looked about fifteen, and the headline read, *Carolyn Castellano Secret: Long Lost Son Discovered. Drug Agent Finds Real-Life Mom Beyond the Grave in Wacky California Channeling Session.* Harry Lanier had said there wasn't much point in trying to straighten them out, they didn't care if they were straight.

There had been a picture of Liza Jane's coffin, too, taken with a telephoto lens, with the Ramananda and Theresa and Bernice around it. And a picture of the oak grove, in which "top scientists" had detected unexplainable vibrations. The story alerted readers to possible psychic causes of the recent earthquake, and said the distraught family was consulting Shirley MacLaine.

The projection room was dim. The light was on a rheostat and Alec had it barely turned on, so that the room was murky, thick with the shades that might come spilling out of cans of film or reels of tape. Maybe the top scientists weren't so far off. Psychic vibrations or not, all the penned-up electricity generated by recent revelations was enough to move any amount of earth. On impulse Alec took down *Friendly Persuasion,* and then *Elizabeth Regina,* and ran the credits past. Both written by Nobody.

Alec had some professional experience at being Nobody. It was disorienting and unpleasant when you did it by choice. What if someone did it to you, simply erased your existence? Alec thought it was a wonder that Mike Rosen had turned the experience into a screenplay instead of just cracking up.

Alec put *Friendly Persuasion* away and left *Elizabeth Regina* out. One of Zenovich-Horizon's last big spectaculars. Produced by Ben Zenovich. The room had adjustable, upholstered seats, the kind movie theaters didn't have anymore, and a big screen adapted for film or tape. There was even a popcorn machine at the back. There was still popcorn in it so Alec got some. He settled in to watch Elizabeth Sidney as Elizabeth the First.

On the screen Liza Jane, very young, younger than she had really been certainly, stood in a muddy road watching William Cecil fling himself down on his knees and kiss her hand.

CECIL
Your Majesty.

ELIZABETH
(to the maid)
The Queen is dead.

MAID
(curtsies)
God save the Queen!

Elizabeth turns to the camera for an instant and flashes a wide, triumphant smile.

"God, that was Liza Jane all right." A crack of light from the doorway split the screen for a moment, and Donald Wain sat down beside Alec. "I know that look," he said. "Meant she'd got her own way. And what are you doing in here? What about the funeral?"

"Watching a movie," Alec said. "And I'm not in charge of the funeral."

"Somebody's got to be. That damn studio flack's no use. Wanted me to talk to some reporter. I told him to stuff it."

"So did I." Alec was beginning to like Wain, to have some idea of why Liza Jane had liked him. He said, "Harry Lanier and the lawyer are going to make some special plea to the city, but the decision is Liddy Novak's, not mine."

"You watch your ass," Wain said. "She looks a damn sight too much like Liza Jane."

"I just met her," Alec said.

"Doesn't matter." Wain settled himself in his seat and put his cane across the seats in front of them. "You take my word for it, son."

On the screen, Elizabeth's face was framed in a stiff ruff, imperious, demanding, slightly amused. Robin Dudley, in a velvet doublet, sat on a footstool at her feet. Alec wondered how much of the edge in the old man's voice was regret and how much an unextinguished frustration that Liza Jane wouldn't bend her life to his.

"Maybe you should have married her," Alec said, slightly amused at his own temerity.

"When you're eighty-one," Wain informed him, "there may be a lot of things you should have done. And you'll remember what an asshole you were at thirty-five."

"Sorry."

"I got married," Wain said. "My wife died a couple of years ago, rest her. Raised three kids and was always home for them. Home for me. Didn't farm them out to housekeepers while she was off acting in Pago Pago or some goddamn place."

"Bernice Lewis doesn't strike me as a typical housekeeper," Alec murmured.

"Woman's a lunatic. Wants to save some two-inch toad out in the desert where we're trying to test a booster rocket. Doesn't care if the space program goes tits up as long as we've got enough toads."

"Maybe toads are important." Alec hadn't actually given toads much thought, but he felt like prodding Donald Wain for marrying someone else, having the kids that Liza Jane had wanted. "How do you know toads aren't an unknown link in the cosmos? Maybe the whole ecology goes tits up without toads."

"Take my advice, son, Wain said. "You get out of here while you can."

Alec looked at him thoughtfully. "Then why did you come back?"

Wain didn't answer. He was looking at the screen. Liza Jane, in a green brocade gown, was dancing a stately minuet with Robin Dudley.

Theresa Tate came in and sat down beside Wain. "Is this where everyone's hiding?" she inquired. "I've given Will Chapman my two cents' worth and been dismissed."

"Why did you talk to him?" Wain said.

"Donald, you simply do not understand our business, and

you never have," Theresa said. "I can't afford to be difficult. He's talking to Frank now. I must say," she added thoughtfully, "I thought Frank looked difficult. But he can afford it. I suppose it's the row with Ben." She seemed to know all about it. "I don't think they've ever really butted heads before. And of course Frank's got that hellcat on his trail."

"That's an appalling young woman," Wain said.

"Oh, she's dreadful," Theresa said. "And vulgar. None of us were ever vulgar."

Wain smiled, turned away from the fleeting image on the screen. "I saw you dance a rumba on a bar one night."

"So you did. Oh, wasn't that a long time ago?" She glanced across him at Alec. "Dear boy, is that popcorn?"

"It is."

"Would you fetch me some?"

Alec got up and filled a sack. Theresa offered some to Wain, and they sat in the odd companionship of shared memory, watching the movie.

Alec tilted his head back and propped his feet on the seat in front of him. It was still a good movie. Alec had seen it two or three times on the Late Show or a rented tape. He watched a lot of movies in the middle of the night. It was a good way to unwind, shake off whatever demons might have attached themselves to him in the course of the day. Funny how he'd never noticed there was no screen credit.

When it was over, Theresa and Donald Wain stood up. Theresa was blowing her nose. "Now you've seen her at her best. My dearest friend. I'm not ready to join her, mind you, but I do miss her so." She dabbed carefully at her eyes with another handkerchief, but there were black smudges of mascara in the green eye shadow.

"I've seen it before," Alec said. "But I didn't know Mike Rosen wrote it."

"Dear boy, don't go taking sides in that," Theresa said. "Ben and Mike will just have to slug it out."

She didn't seem to care particularly who won, but when Wain said, "Any idiot could have predicted communism wouldn't work, the blacklist wouldn't have happened if people weren't so stupid," she glared at him.

"You don't know anything about it, Donald. Those people weren't wicked, they were just trying to make a better world."

"I didn't say they were wicked. I just said they wouldn't have been in trouble in the first place if people had enough brains to see that, given human nature, communism isn't going to be a successful system."

"This is supposed to be a free country. That includes the right to be wrongheaded if you feel like it. The government had no right—"

"I didn't say it had a right, although if you thought the reds were harmless, you're naive. I just said that, historically and philosophically speaking—"

"You can't be philosophical about your friends!"

"For God's sake, Theresa, I'm not speaking personally." Wain looked exasperated. He picked up his cane. "I'm talking about the overview."

"What overview?"

"Common sense. The ability to be farsighted. Think things through."

"Maybe the right wing should have thought things through!" Theresa snapped.

"That's my point," Wain said. "Nobody thinks things through."

They departed, still arguing, with the peculiar ease of people renewing old acquaintance. Alec, in the darkened projection room, added up Liza Jane's hidden fling with the communists, her love affairs with Donald Wain, Mike Rosen, and Ben Zenovich, her championing of Carolyn Castellano, her forays into curious religions, and her reluctance to leave this house, even dead, and came up with an aberrant and unsolvable equation that seemed to shift its signs and figures while he looked at it.

He prowled along the shelves at the back of the room. All Liza Jane's films were there, beginning with the silents, and hundreds of others, from Alain Resnais to the Keystone Kops, Kurosawa to Ford. Liza Jane had liked movies, the fanciful tricks you could do with a camera, Liddy had told him. She had hardly ever done stage work. Alec wondered if there might still be some key here, some film in which Liza Jane would unexpectedly turn to the camera—to him—and tell him what the hell.

He took down her first and her last: the silent *Love in Bloom*, a prairie saga about a mail-order bride who defiantly plants flowers between the rows of a Nebraska wheat field; and *The Raindrop*, about an aging archaeologist who falls in love with a young treasure hunter. Liddy said that Liza Jane had described it as "Sweet Bird of Youth meets Indiana Jones," but she had won an Oscar for it.

He put on *The Raindrop*, a good film copy, not on tape, and watched it all the way through. It didn't explain anything, except why she'd won the Oscar.

He was putting it away when the door slammed open and Frank and Francie Allen exploded into the room. They stopped short when they saw Alec. Frank said, "Christ!" and stalked out again.

Francie stood on the tips of her toes, uncertain whether to pursue Frank or scream at Alec for having been in the room.

"I'll leave," Alec suggested.

Francie slumped suddenly. "Oh, fuck it. It's too late. We weren't getting anywhere anyway." She eyed him speculatively. "What are you doing?"

"Watching movies," Alec said cautiously.

"Oh, yeah? Which ones?"

Alec held out *The Raindrop* before it occurred to him that under the circumstances, the premise was unfortunate.

Francie's eyes narrowed into galvanic blue slits. "That's not a fucking joke!"

"I wasn't making one," Alec said. In the interests of peacekeeping, he didn't add that he hadn't seen much parallel. Liza Jane's Clare Winter had been drab and scholarly; at least until the end, when she chased her fleeing lover and his stolen artifacts across the desert with a gun in her hand. The avenger on Frank's heels was his wife. Her eyes snapped with an electrified fury, and he thought she was high. "If you don't tone it down some, you're going to self-destruct," he suggested.

"What do you know about it?"

Alec put the can away. "A whole lot, as it happens, professionally speaking. How would you like to have a heart attack?"

Francie put her hands on her hips. She threw her head back. She was wearing a leather miniskirt and shoes with spike heels, and a couple of blouses layered over each other, but neither one buttoned up much. "Why don't you bust me?" she said. "Get some publicity."

"I don't want any publicity," Alec said.

"You're an asshole, you know that?"

"And you're a junkie. One of these days they're going to find your stoned butt dead in some bathroom with puke all over the place. You'll be glamorous as hell."

Francie glared at him. Her expression wavered, changed in a flicker to a look of predatory interest. "I could show you some things," she said.

"I've seen most of them," Alec said.

"You don't know anything about me. You don't know anything about being an act. I have to work. I can't work with

Frank pulling this shit. I'm gonna fix him," she added vengefully.

"Not with me," Alec said.

"I think you're a hunk. I bet you're not as straight as you look." Francie took a couple of steps toward him, put her hand on his chest, and dropped it down a couple of inches suggestively.

Alec pushed her away. He had a low tolerance for sexual temptation, and maybe for danger, but he wasn't nuts. Francie Allen was as unstable as nitro.

She looked at him furiously, arms stiff at her sides, fists clenched. Then she wavered into a pout and suddenly burst into tears. "Don't shut me out! I can't stand being shut out."

Alec looked around helplessly, embarrassed. Finally he put a hand on her shoulder, made her sit down. "Quit that. You'll jack yourself up till you get sick."

"I don't care!" Francie wailed. "Fucking stupid asshole world, I hate it." She began to pound her fists on her knees, hard enough to leave bruises. Finally he took hold of them.

"Quit it!" He put her head on his chest, let her cry into his sweatshirt. The mood spent itself, finally, left her gasping for breath, and then, slowly, settling in against his chest. He couldn't figure out how to detach himself, and in a minute it got trickier yet as her hand crept into his lap. Alec swiveled his eyes around desperately, hoping for reinforcements, for Frank Hill to come back in, or Theresa, or Steve Bowman who was on the payroll to deal with this. Or even Jeff, who, he felt irritably, would have figured out how to keep this from starting in the first place. Francie's fingers fiddled with the button on his shorts.

"Cut it out," he hissed. "Or I'm gonna dump you on the floor."

"Loosen up," Francie whispered. "You'll have something to tell the other narcs." She got the button undone, and practiced fingers slid down inside his shorts.

Abruptly the earth lurched under them. Alec flung himself

backward in the seat. Francie stared at him, eyes wide, breath coming in gasps again.

Alec pulled her out of her seat. "That wasn't passion, you cokehead, that's another earthquake. Come on!"

She stumbled after him, half scared, half single-minded. He pushed her against the doorjamb because he had read somewhere that that was the place to stand. The floor swelled and sank, an unstable elevator reversing abruptly. Francie screamed and buried her face in his shirt.

This was worse than the first tremor, he thought. It was like standing on the deck of a ship, a highly unnerving sensation on dry land, and he wondered if everyone upstairs was as unconcerned about this one as they had been yesterday. The cans of film were rattling in their shelves and the light fixtures began to sway precariously.

Francie jerked her head away from his chest and looked around, eyes beginning to widen into hysteria.

"Get me out of here!" she shrieked. She tried to plunge past him through the door and Alec yanked her back.

"Hold on. Stay put till it stops." The floor kept heaving and Francie began to fight him. Alec got a better grip on her. The prospect of being trapped in a projection room with a hysterical rock star was only marginally better than being trapped upstairs with Steve Bowman, but she was higher than a kite and there wasn't any telling what she'd do. Her eyes were as glazed and bright as marbles and her mouth was a magenta loop of terror. She tried to bite his hands.

"Quit it or I'll smack you."

The floor heaved one more time and they lurched against the frame, Francie plastered against him. She began to whimper, and not knowing what else to do, he wrapped his arms around her and just held on.

The floor stilled itself, and finally the only movement left was the vibration of the film cans, residual motion clacking and clattering into silence.

"All right." Alec willed the lurching in his chest to die down, too. "I think it's over."

Francie shuddered and tilted her head back, eyes heavy now. "Wow," she said.

Her hips were still pressed against his. She moved a little from side to side, suggestive if not subtle. Her arms were around his waist and she licked her lips. Upstairs he could hear yelling and consternation. Not so unconcerned maybe.

"Would you really have hit me?" Francie asked him. Alec could feel her fingernails in his back.

"Of course not, Alec said. "What do you think I am?"

"Frank wouldn't hit me, either," Francie said. "But he wanted to." She pushed her hips against him hard.

Alec was beginning to feel a certain sympathy for old Frank. "There are better ways to get your jollies," he suggested and pushed her away. "I think I've had all the excitement I can stand."

Francie stared at him, bewildered and quivering, hair tousled around blue marble eyes that were hunting hungrily for something. Alec wasn't sure whether it was reassurance and human contact, or just lunch.

"Come on," he said uneasily. "Let's go see what gives upstairs."

Francie's hands balled into fists. "You're just afraid little goody fucking two-shoes is going to come in and catch you."

"And you're hoping Frank will," Alec said.

"I hate this goddamn house!" Francie shrieked. She rocketed around him into the hall and crashed into Steve Bowman.

"Hey, Francie! You all right, sweetheart?"

"Get fucked!" Francie said.

"I think the earthquake shook her up," Alec said. Her spike heels disappeared up the stairs at the end of the hall. "Everything all right upstairs?"

"Yeah, yeah. Didn't even break a dish." Steve's professional bonhomie had slipped a little and a strand of his moussed hair was sticking out sideways. "I've had Will Chapman up there for nearly four hours talking to every dingdong in the house, and I find you down here screwing around with Cocaine Lil."

Alec buttoned his shorts and leaned in the doorway. It felt comfortably solid now. "I'm a white knight," he said. "I was saving her from the earthquake."

"Look, Al, be a pal. Don't stir up Francie. I've got enough to deal with."

"My name's not Al," Alec said. "Not your pal, either."

"Alec." Steve snapped his fingers. "Sure—Alec. My brain's just gone to mush today. You'll love Chapman, Alec, he's a real sweetheart. Just try not to piss him off, though," he added thoughtfully.

Alec folded his arms across his chest. "I'm not going to talk to him. I've got what you might call religious convictions about talking to reporters."

Steve spread his hands out, a practiced gesture indicating that he was warm and sincere and might be going to hug whoever he was talking to. "You don't need to worry about Chapman. He's a sweetheart."

"No."

Steve gave up on warmth and sincerity. "Look, goddamnit, I can't keep the situation under control here if you people won't cooperate."

Alec unfolded himself from the doorway and advanced on Steve. There might be some percentage in keeping his temper but he couldn't put his finger on it at the moment. He grabbed Steve by the shirtfront and pushed him backwards down the hall. "I've had reporters crawling up my ass for three days, and if you think I'm uncooperative now, you try bringing another one around." He gave Steve a little extra push for momentum, and let go.

Steve backed up and fell over a pug that came skittering through the hall. He shoved the pug away and glared at Alec, rubbing his collarbone. "You're a psycho, you know that?"

"So I've been told." Alec went back in the projection room and shut the door, mentally daring Steve Bowman to open it again.

"Stay away from Francie!" Steve yelled through the door.

Alec ran his hands through his hair and sat hunched forward in his seat, trying to figure out exactly what it was that he was taking out on Bowman. He had come here looking for the thing that Bernice had not been telling him about Liza Jane, and he still had a sense that it was here, wrapped up in something so disturbingly mundane that he couldn't see it. The film cans stared down at him, round and enigmatic as giant nickels. All he had got for his pains was to be warned away from Liddy Novak by Donald Wain. And from Francie Allen by Steve Bowman, who no longer looked so much like a man with a plan as he did a man in a missile silo in which someone had just punched the wrong button.

Alec dismissed Francie Allen. He wasn't crazy yet. There was a certain flattery attached to being pursued by her, but he knew he'd feel flattered only as long as he evaded her. The image of Liddy was harder to shake off. And even there Alec was unsure how much it was Liddy who drew him and how much the restless spirit of her aunt, calling down earthquakes on them, flickering magically just out of reach. He was beginning to feel like the Eddystone lightkeeper's son. If he continued to pursue that iridescent, scaly tail through unknown waters, what bizarre siblings might he find that he had?

The second tremor moved like a quiver of unease through the valley, so that everything stood askew the brink of things that only geologists might contemplate with confidence. Theresa and Donald Wain, having a drink together in the kitchen and arguing chattily, ignored it through sheer willpower, but Ben Zenovich found himself staring queasily as it rocked a table and slid Mike Rosen's script to the floor. In her bedroom, Sharon Hamilton watched it smash a water glass, and she snatched up the carafe to smash it against the wall for good measure. Liddy and Jeff stared at each other, unnerved, across Liza Jane's rocking coffin, and held it down with their hands. Bernice, who had been feeding the koi, bent down and tried to push the sloshing water back into the pond with her fingers.

Downtown, it interrupted electric service and brought Harry Lanier and Arlo Sheppard's meeting with the City Council to the unsatisfactory conclusion it had been headed for anyway.

The City Council resided in an elegant rambling cluster of Spanish style bungalows behind the Arcade. Inside, the mayor and the rest of the five-person council, including Mr. Abbott, were mopping up a pool of water from an overturned pitcher and dispatching a herd of minions to take stock of possible damage to the Arcade. Their collective expressions gave Harry and Arlo to understand that significant history was at risk here, and dead actresses who wanted to be buried in the back yard would have to wait. Or better yet, take themselves off to be buried elsewhere.

Convenient for them, Harry thought grumpily. Liza Jane had loved Ayala, loved the Arcade. If it was falling down, they presumed she would want to do her bit.

Roberto Vincente, who hadn't been invited and was there anyway, looked unmoved. Harry was almost grateful for the old devil's presence. Godawful publicity, of course, but there was something about Vincente that made even the stout of heart and the most opinionated reluctant to make final statements.

The mayor mopped his brow with the towel he'd been using on the table. With the power out, it was dim and rapidly getting hotter in the council chamber. "Well, I think we've heard all the arguments," he said. "Now the Council will have to take this up at a closed session—"

"Why is that?" Roberto Vincente said. "You got something to hide?"

"We don't make all our deliberations public," the mayor said. "As I am sure a man in your position can appreciate—"

"I got no worries over my position," Vincente said. "Let's talk about yours."

"Mr. Vincente," Arlo murmured, "I don't think you're helping."

"You're outta your league, kid. She was a great lady. She wants to start her own cemetery, pipsqueaks aren't gonna stop her."

"Now see here—" Mr. Abbott attempted to get a grip on the meeting again.

"I got a man outside, Vincente said. "I want you to talk to him."

"We've heard all—"

Vincente opened the door anyway and the Ramananda wafted in.

"Oh, Jesus," Arlo said.

"We've already talked to the supposed beneficiaries," the mayor said. They had been at him all morning, shuttling between the reporter from the *Times* and City Hall, giving him their latest self-conducted opinion poll and beetling off again to tell it to the press.

The Ramananda raised his arms in benediction. "Enlightenment works in many ways," he said.

The mayor glowered at him. "That's fine. We're all pretty enlightened here. I don't think you folks realize that that's the council's whole point. Zoning restrictions keep Ayala unique. Throw them out, and we'll look like San Fernando Valley."

Ramananda Paradevi bowed his head, apparently inviting prayer. None was forthcoming. "Light is all around us. The eternal simultaneous I AM. It comes from many sources. I am humbled."

"Thank God for something," Harry said.

The Ramananda fixed bright eyes on the mayor. "God's plan to transmute the energy of the planet Earth has begun. Our benefactress saw that, and wished to ensure the way."

"Get to the point," Vincente muttered.

"Ah, yes." The Ramananda gathered his robes around him and smiled beatifically, but Harry thought he saw a nasty gleam in his eye. "My temple—our temple—left to us by our benefactress. The Harding Adobe."

"Old," Vincente said. "Historic. You boys should have put it on the Historic Register. How fast do you think you can do that now?"

"I received a communication this morning," the Ramananda said. "From Mr. Benshoof. A developer. You perhaps have heard of him."

Abbott snorted. "We heard that yesterday. We are not going to be threatened with fake Tudor towers, Mr. Vincente. That is the precise point of our zoning laws."

"Yeah, well, you boys got it all wrong. And ladies." Vincente bowed to the female members of the council. "If Mrs. Novak sells off that adobe, you can maybe keep Benshoof from putting up anything you don't like, but you can't keep him from tearing down what's there."

"Are you threatening us?"

"I'm hoping you got deep pockets," Vincente said. "You're gonna need 'em. I know about Benshoof. He's got a herd of tame lawyers; long arm too. But I got a longer arm than you ever dreamed."

The mayor tidied up his papers, took off his glasses and laid them on the stack. His mouth was a thin line. "If you are under the impression that you are helping matters along, Mr. Vincente, you are mistaken."

Vincente shrugged. "She was my girl. You give her what she wants. Now, excuse me, I got business to take care of."

"A man of confused karma," the Ramananda informed them politely when Vincente had left. "And quite possessive."

"Ramananda," Arlo said wearily, "why don't you go home, too? I don't think you ought to be hanging out with him."

The Ramananda's expression of good will was wilting. Possibly it was the heat, although he was the only one of them who was really dressed for it. He looked vaguely like someone on his way to a sauna. "I am an unworldly man," he began, and Harry rolled his eyes. The Ramananda was probably as unworldly as a cobra when it came to something he really wanted. His temple, for instance, which experienced considerable competition from Ayala's other centers of enlightenment. To give the Ramananda credit, he led the simple life he preached and did not suggest that his followers present him with expensive cars, but Harry imagined that humility had its limits.

"You aren't keeping very good company, George," the mayor snapped. He had gone to school with George Simmons before George had transmuted himself onto a higher plane. "Maybe you ought to stick to flowers and incense."

Ramananda Paradevi leveled a finger at the mayor's nose. "Roberto Vicente is a troubled soul, not unlike some of the rest of us. Even a troubled soul may serve the Light. You ought to try it yourself."

Arlo picked up his briefcase with one hand and made a similar gesture at the Ramananda with the other. "Let's let these folks talk it over, okay? I think we've said our piece."

Between them Harry and Arlo edged the Ramananda out of

the chamber. Harry mopped his brow. "You think we did any good in there?"

"No. They don't want to force the issue with some kind of court order and piss off all these people but they aren't going to give in," Arlo said. "They'll just hang on and hope Mrs. Novak will get sick of having her aunt's body on the porch. Or hope the house falls in. And frankly, Ramananda, you and Vincente weren't helping. If you'll just lay off, Mrs. Novak may give you the temple when she ends up with it."

"Of course she will." The Ramananda gazed dreamily at a flower bed full of blue lilies of the Nile. "She is a young spirit, and much confused, a seeker like all of us. But her instincts are excellent. There is an aura of cosmic harmony."

"Then what the hell were you doing in there?"

The Ramananda detached his gaze from the lilies and bent it in mild surprise on Arlo Sheppard and Harry. "Seeking a soul's peace. I have never quite believed that one could pray another into heaven, but Liza Jane chose her path for her own reasons. If possible, I should like to help her along it." He blinked blandly and sauntered off down the walkway, nodding left and right as if to invisible followers.

Arlo looked at Harry. "What is that moronic dingbat talking about? Just off the top of your head?"

"You got to quit hanging around with us," Harry said. "You've stopped talking like a lawyer. She thinks being buried where she wants has something to do with where she goes from there, I suppose. Ramananda thinks so anyway. So does Mike Rosen."

"How does he know?"

"It's what he told me while Frank and Ben were yelling at each other about his script. Liza Jane told him the script was his ticket and the oak trees were hers."

"Ticket to where?"

"To the next stop. For Mike, I'd say she meant back to the land of the living."

1956

The year after Mike and Sharon's divorce is final, Liza Jane is forty-eight and she lives on the beach at Malibu. It isn't as fashionable as it will be later, and it still has a lot of ratty little cabins strung out along the sand, in between the old beach palaces. Liza Jane likes the sound of the water, and watching the boys on their surfboards bobbing like seals out there, waiting for a big wave. When it comes, they stand up on the boards, balancing, soaring; they make her think of the figureheads on ships. When she walks on the beach, sometimes they whistle at her, and she thinks, Not bad for an old broad. She's been letting her hair grow this year, which is driving her hairdresser crazy, but what's the good of being a redhead playing Queen Elizabeth if you have to wear a wig? Liza Jane hates wigs, they make her head itch.

Elizabeth Regina is going to be a blockbuster, a Technicolor historical with lavish sets and costumes, that will open at Christmas and make everyone pots of money. And Liza Jane has Zenovich-Horizon over a barrel about the script because it is unthinkable that anybody but Elizabeth Sidney should play Elizabeth Tudor. That's how Maurice Zenovich put it to her. "You got us over a barrel. I don't like it, but Ben says the script is good, it's right for you, so okay, but no credit. That I've got to be clear on. No credit."

Mike understands that. He's grateful just to get the job right now. Liza Jane has kept track of him since *Richard Plantagenet* got shut down; he's been her lover the last few months. He's good company, funny and literate, when he isn't trying to drink himself out of his misery. Mike's been beaten, he's got a softer, vulnerable edge to him that's different from the men with power, men like Roberto Vincente and Don Wain and Ben. The older she gets, the less Liza Jane likes bending to that power.

The Malibu house is a stucco Spanish-revival from the twenties with a bougainvillea-covered archway. The Pacific Coast Highway goes right by the door. On the other side, the house looks down to the beach through big glass windows with wrought-iron curlicues across the top and bottom, and a patio with steps down the gentle slope to the sand. The kitchen is big and plastered white, with wrought-iron pot racks full of copper pans. Liza Jane has a woman who cooks and cleans for her, but she likes to do the cooking herself when it's for a man. It's sensual, a kind of aphrodisiac. She hardly ever cooks for anyone she doesn't want to go to bed with.

Liza Jane hears Mike's car scrunch on the sand by the highway as she comes up the patio steps from the beach, her pockets full of shells. She lets him in and he hands her a paper cone of calla lilies and chuckles at her outfit. She's wearing a peasant blouse and green sandals, and a painted Mexican skirt, covered with huge flowers, that she bought on Olvera Street. She spins around so that he can see how the skirt spreads out in a circle, as she goes in the kitchen to put the lilies in a vase. Mike almost always brings her flowers. It's the only present he can afford, but he's regular about it. Tonight they're celebrating. *Elizabeth Regina* starts shooting next month and the final script's been accepted. If it's a success, Mike may get other jobs, word will get around. He'll be somebody worth taking a chance on as long as he's docile and doesn't want too much. Like screen credit.

Liza Jane gets a bottle of wine out of the cupboard and hands Mike the corkscrew, and then she gets her pots and pans down off the rack, and a bowl of scallops out of the refrigerator, and starts to make Coquilles St. Jacques.

Mike lifts his wine glass in her direction. "To Elizabeth."

She grins. It's a nice double meaning. She knows he's grateful, but she doesn't like him to tell her.

Mike's face is still boyish, with deep lines cut across it. The combination is painful. "Ben called me," Mike says abruptly. "To say he liked the script."

Liza Jane nods. That's a good sign. Ben didn't need to do that. He could have done it through Mike's agent. Liza Jane's been careful with Mike, kept him from burning any bridges. She's convinced things will get better. She's an optimist. If Mike's bitter, who can blame him? He's been writing smut to buy groceries.

"It's a good script," she says.

"Of course it is. Nobody writes better than old Mr. Anonymous."

Liza Jane gives him the cheese to grate.

"And Sharon called me."

Liza Jane stops whisking sauce, looks at him over her shoulder, eyebrows raised.

"She wants more money," Mike says. "She found out about the script and she wants more alimony."

Liza Jane lets out a hoot of laughter that settles down into a chortle while she refills their glasses. "Sharon's businesslike," she says. "You have to give her credit." Neither of them asks how she found out. Hollywood scuttlebutt is notorious, completely unstoppable. Everybody in the industry knows Mike wrote *Elizabeth Regina*. These days there won't be any fuss as long as it's not overt, as long as he can't have any credit. Sharon's willing to take a piece of the action.

"She's a goddamn piranha," Mike says.

Liza Jane shakes her head, still laughing. "This is the piranha pool. Everyone's got their teeth in some poor cow that's just trying to get across the river."

"Except you, maybe," Mike says seriously. "I don't think I've ever seen you chew the flesh off anyone."

"Don't bet on it." Liza Jane puts her hands on his shoulders, so that she can look up at him, standing there in her flat shoes, her face solemn now. "Sharon and I are just sisters under the skin," she tells him.

"Ha," Mike says.

"Oh, trust me on it."

Liza Jane gives him the shallots to peel and chop. She snuggles her head against his shoulder and he bends down and kisses her, mouth heavy with wine. Liza Jane likes the fact that he'll get in the kitchen and cook with her. She gets a can of mixed nuts out and opens it, and they pick through it for the pecans while the sauce cooks.

Mike watches her and thinks she'll make a hell of a good Queen Elizabeth. She has a kind of imperious shimmer to her and a way of getting into a historical part that seems natural. He's almost stopped wincing every time he thinks about *Richard Plantagenet.* But it still wells up sometimes, a cold, furious rush of despair that makes him want to howl. If *Richard* had been made, Liza Jane might have got her Oscar for that instead of for *Glory Days.* Mike might have won for the script; *Richard* was the best script he's ever done. Neither one will get an award for *Elizabeth.* It's too soon for Liza Jane, too late for Mike. The Oscar for *Glory Days* sits on the coffee table in Liza Jane's living room. Mike eyes it with an envy that's nearly suffocating. You aren't supposed to care about things like that, you're supposed to be above all that, to know that it's all political anyway, to slap the winners on the back and tell them that they deserve it more than anyone. But Mike wants it. He wants to be known, he wants not to have disappeared, not to have slid nameless into the quicksand from which no one will take his calls.

Even his agent was edgy about keeping him on, until this deal. "I'll tell you, I can't sell you," he said. "I can't sell you anywhere in the industry in this country. You might do better going to Europe."

But Mike doesn't want to go to Europe, hasn't got the connections to do him much good. He was just getting started in the business, and he doesn't speak anything but English. So he holds on here, sells some pornographic detective novels under a pseudonym to the kind of publisher who doesn't care where his stuff comes from, and his agent negotiates him a marginally better deal for them than he could have got on his own. And he looks at Liza Jane's Oscar and wants to cry.

Liza Jane knows this. And she has enough sense to let him do it and pretend not to notice. She's not going to put the Oscar away, apologize for it, apologize for winning it. She feeds him scallops and new peas from the Farmer's Market, and coffee, and a kind of grainy half bitter Mexican chocolate for dessert, and more wine, and they go to bed in the west bedroom upstairs, where they can hear the surf running up the sand, sliding away again, running up, mysteriously unending.

The sun is just going down, a big burning marble being extinguished in that cold gray pool, bits of flame floating on the water. Liza Jane feels cool to Mike too, on the surface, like a mermaid dragged from the kelp. But the legs that twine around his are solid, substantial. Her red hair floats around her face like the sunset outside, her eyes on his. She is in his arms; she knows he is here. Without speaking, she names him, and her cool naked body lies along his like a bandage.

IX
Exhumation

1988

Bernice made beans and salad and garlic bread for dinner. She set the beans on a hot plate in the dining room, and pointed at them and said, "Dinner," whenever anyone wandered by. There didn't seem much point in trying to get them all to sit down and eat with one another. They were as skittish as antelope, ears swiveling for danger. Those who were still speaking to each other had gathered around the television in the library to see if IT was going to happen again. No one on television seemed to know either, not even the guest seismologist, but an evangelist in Detroit had proclaimed the Second Coming, and someone from the Unarius Society in Los Angeles said that superior beings from space were even now descending to explain matters.

"Well, that would be tidy," Liddy said. Zach, flown with the excitement of watching the yurt fall down at camp, had been put in bed, and she felt uncertain as the fault lines under the earth. Harry Lanier had said that the City Council probably wasn't going to cooperate, and Steve Bowman kept showing her cemetery prospectuses.

Ben had gone back to the Horsehead Ranch, but Sharon, who was staying in the house, cast vitriolic looks at Frank whenever she passed him, which she contrived to do several times.

Liddy tried to remember what she had heard about the blacklist. It had been over before she came to live with Liza Jane. She had known Bernice hadn't been able to work in Hollywood, but Bernice hadn't seemed to want to, once things had blown over and she might have. As a child, Liddy had never contemplated the idea that it must have touched her aunt personally. Now she thought, how could it not? What would it have been like to see your friends become non-people, disappeared persons, a blank space in the air where they had been? How often would you wonder if it was going to happen to you? Half-heard conversations came back to her:

"They lived in France for five years, you know."

"He was a front for a lot of people. He'd pitch a script for you, they'd pretend he'd written it as long as you stayed out of sight."

"He's teaching math in some high school, such a shame."

"There was an FBI man across the street in my neighbor's driveway for a month."

Grown-up snatches of talk that some piece of her brain had snared and imprinted. She wondered how Zach was taking all this, all the grown-up histrionics. He seemed more worried about the coffin, and kept asking Liddy when they were going to bury it. She couldn't tell if he was relieved that they hadn't, or afraid of it. She had sat with him until he went to sleep.

Alec picked his plate up and drifted toward Liddy when he saw her come in and stand staring vaguely at the food. "You look beat," he said.

"I wish someone would bury me," Liddy said wistfully. "It sounds so peaceful."

Alec looked at her hesitantly. "You want to take a walk?" he asked.

"Yes, let's."

They went out through the kitchen, edging past Frank, who was writing notes in the margins of the script, his glasses on the end of his nose. Sharon was hovering at the counter now, making a martini. Her eyes darted toward the script and back again and vermouth splashed down the side of the glass.

Liddy pulled the French doors closed behind them. "I don't know which is worse, the earthquakes or that script. If Sharon doesn't quit that..." They went down the steps, skirting the presence in the coffin.

"I never thought of a piece of writing as being capable of raising such a stink," Alec said. "I guess I thought it was all made up."

"Not this," Liddy said. "That's the trouble. Writing feeds on emotions. The writer's mainly. When it feeds on somebody else's too, look out."

Alec looked thoughtful. "I tossed your publicist down the hall earlier," he said.

"Oh, bravo." They walked on companionably, along the brick walk that went past Liza Jane's organic garden, bordered with marigolds. A redwood bench sat beside the path under the oaks. Alec dropped down on it and patted the seat beside him. "We could wait out here until they all coil up and eat each other." He gestured at the lighted windows suspended beyond the trees.

Liddy sat down. "You're a very enterprising sort of person."

"Because I tossed old Steve on his can?"

"Liza Jane would have loved it."

"Donald Wain says you're a great deal too much like your aunt," Alec said, "and I ought to watch out."

"Mmmm." Liddy wondered if that was advice for her, too.

"What did you think I was going to be like?"

"I don't know," Liddy said. "When I found out about you, I just thought, oh, shit, how could she do that? She didn't even know you."

"Except with a telephoto lens."

"Yes, there's that." His face was flecked with spots of moonlight coming through the leaf shadow. It was like trying to see through a keyhole. "How much is this money really bothering you? Most people would jump at it."

"Well I'm not going to give it to charity. Maybe it'll smooth the path. There's so much money in drugs, you have no idea. It's like working at the mint. You can't think about it as real money or you go crazy. Or you cross over the line, start figuring you're entitled to some of it."

"Do you think about that?" This from Captain Midnight?

"I don't think about it seriously," Alec said, "but it's still a hell of a lot of bills. On the other hand, if you've got your own money, maybe you aren't willing to go out and get shot at for a salary. Then what do I do?"

"Have you ever been...hurt, on the job?" Again that sensation of looking through a keyhole. You knew you shouldn't, found reasons to keep doing it anyway. Jeff had accused her of eating it up, feeding on the kick of danger at one remove. He was probably right.

"Once. Put me in the hospital. When I got out, I was single again."

"What happened?"

"She figured the next time something went bad, I might be worse off. She wasn't going to stick around and see."

"No, I meant...how did you get hurt?"

"I know you did." She thought for a minute he wasn't going to tell her. Finally, he said, "I went after a guy for about a year— got in his organization." Alec's mouth twisted. "I'm good at that. It's one thing to tell yourself the guy's a gila monster, don't make friends, but sometimes it happens anyway. He liked movies, too. He grew up in a street gang, saw all the dealers with their limos. We'd watch the Late Show together, drink beer. You pretend something long enough, it gets real. When we busted him, he called me a goddamned Judas, and shot me. He got killed in what happened afterward."

Liddy found herself unwilling to look at Alec full on. The dark edge to Alec's stories was seductive to a person with a well-swept life.

"You taking notes?" Alec asked quietly.

"Sort of. Do you mind? I thought it might make my books more real." The writer as vampire.

"No, I don't mind." He swung around a little on the bench, looked up at a drift of something smoky in the oaks that might have been an owl. The eyes came back and rested on hers. "I don't usually tell people stuff like that."

"Why did you?"

"You asked."

"Would you tell me anything I wanted to know?"

"If I knew it. I don't know much more. I don't even know what you're doing out here with me." There was a trace of a question in that.

"Cannibalizing you," Liddy said darkly. "Just like Liza Jane."

Alec chuckled. "It's all right. I never knew a writer before."

"You won't feel that way if you end up in a book."

"You do that?"

"Not so far."

"But you feel it coming on?" He put an arm around her shoulders. "Go for it. I'll buy twenty copies for my friends."

She leaned her head against his shoulder, pretending not to notice she was doing it. "I'm almost afraid to. If you write about people, I think you change them. Or you change your perception of them. The fiction gets more real to you than the truth. Or you raise untold hell, like Mike."

"Mike's just the trigger. He's the pin in the grenade. Nobody's singlehandedly responsible for anything. You get to thinking you are, you'll cut your throat."

Liddy screwed her head around and looked at him. She thought he probably knew a lot about that. Was that how he lived with it? At a certain point you just chalked it up to inevitability, a tangle of forces you couldn't direct? His face was very close to hers, moon washed now over dark brows and the sharp plane of cheekbones, as if she had somehow slipped through the keyhole, or been invited in. His lips moved, and he put the other arm around her, not protectively but with a necessity that might come half of whatever loose ends had been dangling between them since yesterday, and half of the frustration of the last two days—grasping at the only solid thing he could touch in Liza Jane's house.

And what was she grasping at? A sense of reality? Or that dark edge of excitement? Stuff it, she told the half of her mind that was doing the asking. She seemed to hear Jeff asking the same thing, and she told him to stuff it, too. She was half in Alec's lap, his mouth against her throat, his hands beginning to travel over the thin silk shirt, when her own hands bumped against the hard, blunt outline of the gun. Liddy flinched into immobility for an instant and then her hand slid past the holster, down his ribcage to the center of his back, where her fingers could feel nothing but the coiled muscle under the skin.

Alec's hands moved on, feeling her breasts hungrily, sliding up bare legs beneath the jersey skirt.

"Yoo hoo! Anybody home?" The crunch of footsteps in the driveway turned into a click of heels on the brick walk, and they lurched apart. Liddy tugged at her skirt and wished she could get at Alec's gun.

"I rang the bell," Margaret Collins boomed at them, "but nobody answered."

"They're all listening to the news," Liddy said with difficulty. "We think there's going to be another quake."

"Possibly tonight," Alec said.

Margaret peered at them. "Alec. So nice to see you. I hope you're enjoying your stay here. So trying for you."

"Parts of it are excellent," he said.

Liddy shot Margaret a baleful glare that was fortunately masked by the shadows. "It's awfully late," she said pointedly.

"Well, I'm here for a council of war," Margaret said. "I just talked to Fred Abbott, the old stuffed shirt, and I don't think we're getting anywhere."

Liddy stood up. Margaret wasn't going to go away. Going away was never one of Margaret's scenarios. "Just go on in," she said. "They're all in the library. We'll be right along."

Margaret gave them a thoughtful glance, and said, "Oh, dear." She headed back up the walk. After a few steps, she turned and waved coyly over her shoulder.

Liddy looked at Alec uncertainly. He laughed and put an arm around her, companionable again, although she thought he was breathing a little hard. "Come on, I'll walk you home," he said. "Maybe she was providential."

When they got to the house, Margaret was holding forth in the library, but she stopped long enough to give Liddy and Alec her best smile. "There they are!" she said brightly.

Jeff looked up from his spot on the floor and started, damn him, to laugh. Liddy raised one clenched fist from her side just high enough for him to see an extended middle finger. She abandoned Alec and stalked upstairs.

Three pugs were on her bed. She scooted them off. By the time she had her nightgown on, they were back. They wheezed at her hopefully and she put the pillow over her head.

This time no werewolves entered her dreams, just a parade of everyone infesting the house.

Jeff's little bronze sprite was conjuring people out of the air, two by two: Francie Allen and Frank Hill; another Frank and Ben; Mike and Sharon; improbably, Donald Wain and Bernice. There was music to the dance, something she knew, just on the edge of memory. The pugs trotted hopefully at the end of the line. They were on a riverbank and a boat was rocking on the water, waiting for Liza Jane. Liddy ransacked her purse for silver for the boatman. He would leave in a minute if she couldn't find it. Harry Lanier and Arlo Sheppard were snatching the will back and forth between them like Tweedledum and Tweedledee. She pulled her coins out triumphantly and the ground opened to swallow her.

Liddy sat up in bed, staring blankly into faint sunlight, and discovered that the bed was still rocking. The pugs were scratching frantically at the closed door.

She rocketed out of bed and through the connecting bathroom into Zach's room while the floor slipped under her. The bathroom medicine cabinet came down with a crash, showering glass across the tiles. This was worse than the last two, this was the real thing.

Liddy snatched Zach out of bed just as he woke, and dragged him through the door into the hall. The iron bed vibrated behind them like the low notes on a bass and there was another splintering of broken glass as a picture came off the wall.

The hall was full of people stumbling out of their bedrooms. Frank was in his underwear, clutching his glasses in one hand.

Sharon was trying to put on her robe. Bernice propelled her down the stairs. "Get in the closet!"

The broom closet was set into the angle in the kitchen beneath the first floor stairs, and they herded obediently into it, dodging in sheer terror past the wrought-iron chandelier in the hall. They could hear breaking glass everywhere, and above it the sonorous humming of the bell in the tower.

"Get down on your elbows and knees," Bernice said. "Put your hands over your head."

Alec pulled Liddy into the closet, and they got Zach down on the floor and braced themselves over him. The house rocked around them while everyone huddled together, crouched like turtles.

"I can't see anything!" Sharon wailed. "What's happening?"

Liddy tried to look around, couldn't see anything but odd angles of chins and elbows, and the rocking legs of the heavy kitchen table.

"Mama!" Zach whimpered.

"It's okay, kid," Alec said. "You hang in there."

"Just be still, baby." Liddy wrapped her arms around him. If she twisted her neck, she could manage to see a piece of the glass doors to the veranda. The wrought-iron railing bulged and began to swing. In the oak grove one of the ancient trees leaned and then toppled groaning across her field of vision. The floor heaved under them in crazy swells, and a terrified pug slid across the kitchen floor.

The bell in the tower was ringing now, slinging itself from side to side, bawling iron-mouthed. Liddy tried to envision from which part of the lower house the tower rose, and wondered what would happen if the bell came down.

"We should have gone down to the basement," Sharon moaned. "It's below ground."

"We may be heading there," Frank muttered as the floor

tilted.

"Where's Theresa?" Harry said suddenly.

They all counted noses.

"Oh, Jesus."

"Look!" Sharon screamed.

They all lifted their heads and saw the veranda railing pop. The redwood table with the coffin began to sail majestically down the sloping flagstones.

Bernice began to struggle to her feet.

"Get down, damn it!" Frank hauled her back with one hand, and she fell on him, her long salt-and-pepper braid flying over one shoulder.

The redwood table's legs bumped against the stone lip of the veranda and they watched queasily as the coffin slid like a launching ship down the table's length and through the railing. As they heard it thud, the ground shivered into solidity again, and the bell notes slowed from their frantic clangor to a low tolling.

Down the hill a siren started up.

"Am I alive? Harry said. "Jesus, that was something."

Alec pushed himself off Zach and stood up. "We've got to find Theresa."

"I'll come with you," Frank said.

Slowly they began to disentangle themselves from one another, slightly embarrassed now to have been huddled together in their underwear.

"I want you to stay with Sharon, baby," Liddy told Zach. Sharon didn't look like she was going anywhere.

"I want to go with you." Zach's lip trembled. The other earthquakes had been fun, like carnival rides. This one was frightening.

"You can't, baby." Liddy kissed him, her hands shaking. "It won't do anything else now, but I've got to check on things and it may be rickety."

"Stay with me, kid," Harry said. "We'll go check on Theresa. I don't see any cracks in the ceiling," he told Liddy. "If the house hasn't fallen in by now, it's not going to."

Alec scooped Zach onto his shoulders. "Yeah, you come with us." Zach clung to his neck.

Sharon didn't say anything at all. She was very carefully not looking at the veranda. Liddy kissed Zach's knee and picked her way through the wreckage of the kitchen floor after Bernice. Bernice was already outside.

The slope of the veranda floor was abrupt and the hole in the railing was a twist of jagged iron. Bernice looked past it, very still in her blue cotton pajamas and her long braid. Below the retaining wall, the coffin lay on its side with the fallen oak arching above it. None of the other trees were down, and the coffin was still latched, but beyond, at the end of the grove, a chasm had opened in the earth, as if some fearful thing had come up through it.

Alec and his search party found Theresa still in her room, sitting on the floor. One leg was tucked under her and the other stuck straight out at an angle that made it obvious why she hadn't gone anywhere.

"I fell," she murmured, wincing as Alec lifted her carefully onto an upholstered chaise longue. "Just getting out of bed. Actually, I think I was more tossed out of bed. I'm awfully afraid it's broken. I just couldn't steel myself to crawl through all of that." She gestured at the broken picture glass on the floor. "So I just tucked my head down and prayed."

Frank peered at her leg. "You need a doctor. I'll see if we can get anyone out here."

"You might put some pants on first," Theresa said gently. She clutched Alec's hand. "It hurts like hell," she whispered. "I don't suppose you could get me a drink."

Liddy found Jeff kneeling in the oak grove, cradling a dead pug in his arms.

"Oh, no." She knelt beside him sorrowfully.

"The tree hit him," Jeff said. He was wearing jeans and no shirt or shoes, as if he had grabbed the first thing that came to hand. "It almost got me. Who would have thought one of those things would fall?"

"What were you doing outside?" Liddy demanded. "I was afraid the cottage had come down on you."

"It was still there when I left." Jeff laid the little body down in the oak leaves and stood up.

Liddy brushed a hand against the pop-eyed face. "Poor baby." She looked at Jeff again. "What did you go outside for?"

"None of your business."

Liddy sat back on her heels, feeling the prickly leaves digging into her bare feet. "Did you think you could catch the damn coffin if it fell?"

"Maybe," Jeff muttered. "Just shut up, Lid, will you?"

Liddy slumped forward with her head on her knees, her forehead against the thin nightgown, crying. When she looked up, scrubbing her eyes with her fist, she saw that Jeff was trying to right the coffin. She picked her way gingerly across the leaves and helped him. The coffin was heavy, expensive and lead-lined. The limbs of the fallen oak scratched her face as they heaved at it. The oak was horrifying, its roots clawing at thin air.

"I'm not sure we can do it," Liddy said.

"The hell we can't," Jeff said.

He pushed again, and they got it to rocking, and finally it went over with a heavy bang. Jeff walked around it, inspecting it. His chest was laced with scratches from the oak.

Liddy folded her own scratched arms across the front of her nightgown. Jeff was staring at the coffin as if trying to make up his mind to do something.

"Do you think we ought to—?" Liddy motioned at the coffin.

Jeff sighed. "I think we have to." He looked at her, pulling leaves out of his hair. "You can go in the house if you want."

Liddy shook her head.

"All right, let's do it." Jeff lifted the latch. He hesitated a moment, and then Liddy came to him and together they raised the lid all the way up.

Liza Jane lay askew in the coffin, one hand outflung as if to stop its flight. But her skin was cold and the face was already not quite Liza Jane's. Jeff lifted her gently and repositioned her, and Liddy folded the still arms back where they belonged and put Roberto Vincente's rose in them.

"Just a minute," Jeff said when Liddy started to close the lid. She knew what he was going to do before he moved, and she waited while he picked up the little pug and brought him over.

"Jeff, I don't think they'll let you do that." Liddy didn't intend to stop him, she just felt doleful and pessimistic, convinced of the general injustice of authority.

"Who won't?" Jeff stood cradling the dog in both hands.

"The mortuary. She can't stay here. Jeff, this has gone too far."

"Backing down, Lid?"

"Oh, I don't know!" Liddy was furious to find her face running with tears again.

Jeff knelt and curled the dog at Liza Jane's feet.

The leaves crunched behind them, and Alec came out, dressed. He eyed Jeff with respect and didn't say anything about the dog. "I left Zach with Bernice," he said to Liddy. "We saw you out here. I told her I didn't think she needed to come. She looked like hell. Zach was actually taking care of her."

"Good. He'll be all right then. What about Theresa?"

"Busted leg. She fell out of bed, but she's okay. Frank threw a movie star tantrum on the telephone and got a doctor to come out. Must be nice." He looked at Jeff. "You better put the lid down," he said gently.

Jeff lowered it. "She's not going to a mortuary," he said stubbornly.

"Nobody's going anywhere for a while," Alec said. "The house is a mess."

"Did anyone call the Horsehead Ranch?" Liddy asked.

"Harry did. They're all right. Or anyway about like they were yesterday. We couldn't get anything on the news yet."

"I think it's shaken itself out," Jeff said. "This was what it was working up to."

"How do you know?"

"Native California instinct. Sometimes the aftershocks get worse instead of better. And the birds are back. Haven't you noticed how quiet they've been the last couple of days?"

They cocked their heads to listen, and a sparrow lit on the fallen oak, chirruping at them. "*Old Farmers Almanac*," Alec said.

"That's me. Walking Foxfire book."

"What do your instincts tell you about that sinkhole or whatever it is?" Alec asked.

They looked past the fallen tree and the coffin to the cleft in the earth.

"It looks grisly," Liddy said. "Will it get bigger?"

"Swallow you whole," Jeff said. He looked at it thoughtfully, as if he were measuring it, and him. "The thing opened up nearly under my feet. It scared me shitless."

They began to walk toward it anyway, to prove to themselves it wasn't going to grab them, Liddy thought. She envisioned Jeff, panic-driven, sliding past the hole and the fallen tree while the earth heaved. If the coffin fell, what had he planned to do, catch it?

They stood warily on the edge, looking down. Liddy balanced on one foot and then the other, a hand on Jeff's shoulder, picking oak leaves off her feet. The hole was a split in the earth, three feet across at the top, and narrowing as it went down. A tangle of little roots crawled across it near the bottom and the sides were lumpy with rocks, dirty quartz and a tumble of red sandstone. The newly sheared earth was rapidly drying, but Liddy felt queasily that it was waiting, if not for something to go in, then for something to come out, some subterranean Thing lurking just under the debris at the bottom.

"Serpents," Jeff said. "Ground worms. What was that thing in *Dune?*"

"Oh, God, Jeff, don't."

"Something's down there," Alec said suddenly. They stared at him, as if half expecting him to slay the serpent of their imagining, but he climbed down into the hole instead. It was almost shoulder-high.

"Hey, man, I wouldn't do that. Maybe it's not through."

Alec tugged at what Liddy thought was a rock, jutting from the dirt near the bottom. His hands slipped off it and he fell backward, a little shower of dirt raining down on him. "Shit!"

"Here, damn it, I'll help." Jeff climbed down, too. They wrestled with it in the narrow crevice, getting in each other's way. It was wedged in by a big rock above, that must have been put there on purpose, and Jeff pounded at it with another rock until it shifted. Whatever it was, it was made of gray metal, the color of the coffin; it clanked as the rock hit it.

"Okay, quit." The thing stuck out from the earth enough to get hold of now, a flat curved edge like a wheel. Alec latched on with both hands and seesawed it back and forth until he could pull it out. Liddy knelt on the edge of the cleft and the three of them stared at the thing. It was a film can.

Alec handed it to her and climbed out. "You tell me," he said.

Liddy hefted the can, bemused. There was a reel inside. Who would bury a can of film?

Jeff slithered out of the crevice while Liddy brushed the dirt away. It was rusty and there wasn't any label. "Liza Jane?" he said.

"It has to be. Jeff, do you think she could have been..." Liddy left the sentence unfinished, words dangling unhappily.

"Senile?" Jeff snorted. "Never." He looked at the can. "I don't know."

"Give me that." Alec took the can and began to pry at the rusted lid with his pocket knife.

"Pandora's box, friend," Jeff said. "You sure you want to open that?"

The knife slid along the rim and stabbed him in the thumb. Alec stood up. He stuck the thumb in his mouth and the knife back in his pocket, the can under one arm. "I need a screwdriver."

"In the toolshed," Jeff said, giving up.

They weren't going to stop him, probably shouldn't. It would all shake out, Liddy thought. Like the earthquake. The morning had that sort of inevitability about it. She said, "We'd better look at the cottage." Whatever had fallen down or fallen in, it would be her responsibility now.

Jeff nodded and she followed him across the yard. Inside they found most of the shelves toppled and the orange cat prowling angrily among overturned books. In the studio all the bronze dancers were on the floor, and the clay figures broken.

"Oh Jeff. I'm so sorry."

He shrugged. "Do you want breakfast? Bernice will have

enough to contend with."

Liddy righted a kitchen chair and sat on it. She rubbed her feet. "I feel like I've been walking on nails."

"You don't go barefoot enough." Jeff opened the refrigerator and half its contents slid out. He picked up a carton of eggs and started picking shells out of the broken ones while she shoved everything else back in. "Pre-scrambled." He dumped them in a pan and looked thoughtfully at the stove. "Smell any gas?"

Liddy shook her head.

Jeff put his hand on the knob and then changed his mind. He got a hot plate out of the cupboard instead and plugged it in. "I'd hate to blow a new oven to hell, much less us. Liza Jane just bought me that. We were learning to bake bread."

"Bernice bakes bread, doesn't she?"

"I think baking with Bernice intimidated her. We had fun practicing together. Some of it was edible."

A quick flash of jealousy rocked her. You left, she reminded herself. If Jeff had taken her place she ought to be grateful.

Jeff surveyed the fallen spice rack. "Where's the rosemary?"

"I'll find it." Liddy began picking up the little bottles. "Here it is."

"Good. Take a guess at half a teaspoon. I don't know where those are either." The utensil drawer was on the floor in a jumble of spatulas and forks.

Liddy shook some rosemary into her palm and dusted it off into the eggs. Jeff got a loaf of bread from under the kitchen table, fortunately encased in a plastic bag. "This was our most recent effort. I haven't had the heart to cut into it. Slice us some."

A pot of aloes had fallen off the windowsill onto the cutting board. Liddy washed the board in the sink and dried it. Apparently they still had water. The aloes lay on the counter, uprooted, their fat green spikes oozing gel. When she had found a knife and sliced the bread, she tucked them back in their pot and broke off a piece.

"Here. Turn around."

Jeff turned sideways, stirring the eggs with one hand, while Liddy rubbed aloe on his chest. Bernice had always kept a pot of aloe, she remembered; this was probably the offspring of hers. When she had finished with Jeff, she started on her arms; the scratches were already beginning to redden. The cool gel brought back tactile memory of a series of skinned knees and sunburn, and Bernice's hands smoothing the gel over her skin. She ought to take some back to Charlottesville. When she went back to Charlottesville. And what if she didn't, and how would Jeff feel about that?

Jeff put the eggs and toast on the table, and a bottle of scarlet juice with a familiar masking-tape label. Pom/Appl. Bernice's mixture. Mercifully unbroken, it looked like liquid rubies in the shaft of light from the kitchen window. Jeff sat opposite her and they ate in silence, with the cat twining around their toes.

When they had finished, they added the dishes to the pile that had been in the sink to start with, and Jeff said, "I need to check on something else. I made some masks for a mummer's troupe and they're out in the shed. I'm going to be pissed if they're wrecked. Do you want to see them?"

"Sure."

The masks, made to sit over the wearer's head, were strung on a clothesline in the little shed behind the cottage, mostly undamaged. Jeff took one down with obvious relief, a heavy cardboard ram's head, painted black and white, with curving horns made from uncoiled toilet paper rolls. Oblong pupils peered at Liddy from each side of the head, and a coiling red tongue lolled from the open mouth. Jeff settled it on his shoulders and did a little dance step.

"How do you see?"

"Through the mouth," he said, still capering.

The rest included a hobby horse, a knight, and an old woman

with broom straw hair. On the end were a damsel and a dragon. The dragon had a crest of green and orange feathers down its back. The damsel was white-faced, like a geisha, with round pink spots on her cheeks and hair braided from yellow gingham. The dragon had an almost roguish look, more jester than dragon, and the damsel had a long pointed nose. Liddy took her down and put her on. Through the damsel's eyes she had no peripheral vision, just bright, overlapping circles, across which the ram danced solemnly, chanting.

With a host of furious fancies,
Whereof I am commander,
With a burning spear and a horse of air,
To the wilderness I wander.

His voice was hollow, muffled by the ram's head.

Still I sing bonnie boys, bonnie mad boys
Bedlam boys are bonnie
For they all go bare and they live by the air
And they want no drink nor money

Jeff halted where she could see him. "She wanted me to make her a sign for the front door," he said. "BEDLAM. Something elegant in bronze. I wish I had gotten around to it. I kept thinking I would. She always said the house should have a name."

1962

Liza Jane is fifty-four. She has come up to Ayala with Theresa for the Tennis Tournament, and they're staying at the Horsehead Ranch with a lot of other people. The Tennis Tournament is very chic. The hotels are always so full of people from Los Angeles that the tournament committee parcels out the players to residents who have guest houses.

Liza Jane and Theresa have driven up in Liza Jane's convertible, with the top down and their hair blowing like mad, and giggling as if they were twenty again. Now they're walking through the park toward the tennis courts, seeing who else is here, feeling let off the leash and happy. Liza Jane is between pictures, and Theresa is between husbands. Liza Jane has a thermos bottle full of martinis, and they sit in the bleachers and drink it, watching the tennis players smacking the ball in their bright, white shorts.

"He's cute," Theresa says, and they start to rate them, laughing like fiends.

"That one's my favorite," Theresa says. "The blond with the nice legs."

"You have a weakness for legs," Liza Jane says.

"So does Art Symes. Look."

Symes has divorced his wife, the wife he wouldn't divorce for Carolyn, and he has a new cookie on his arm. They are sitting in the bleachers opposite Theresa and Liza Jane. The cookie has a high, teased hairdo like a beehive and bright pink lipstick.

"Has that son of a bitch ever once asked you about his kid?" Theresa is the only one Liza Jane has told.

"Nope," Liza Jane says. She pours some more martini in her cup. "You want to see him?"

"Who?"

"The kid." Liza Jane takes her wallet out of her purse. It's a white purse to match her white pique dress. Liza Jane has always worn a lot of white, and white's what you wear to a tennis match anyway. She's still a knockout. Her hair is long now, halfway down her back, and she wears it pinned up in a loose knot with a wave over one eyebrow. She looks easily young enough to be the kid's mother. She hands Theresa a picture, like anybody showing off their child.

It's a school picture, a nine-year-old in a coat and tie, dark hair slicked down, a pious expression and just a little bit of mischief in his eye.

"Cute," Theresa says. She looks at Liza Jane. "Where'd you get this?"

"His mother sent it to me," Liza Jane says. "I keep in touch."

"She doesn't mind that?"

"I don't ask her if she minds. He doesn't know. I make sure he's going to a good school. Send some money at Christmas."

Theresa sighs. "You feel responsible for the whole goddamn world, you know that?"

"Will if I want to," Liza Jane says. "I don't do any harm."

Theresa thinks she's had a little too much martini. She probably has herself. Her last divorce wasn't any fun, and it's a release to come up here and get tipsy with her best girlfriend in this pretty little valley. Neither one of them ever had any children, and they're too old now. They went through menopause together, kind of like a team, the way they always used to get their periods at the same time. And Liza Jane had to have a hysterectomy. That gave Liza Jane the blues for weeks, even though it just kind of set the cap on the inevitable.

Liza Jane puts the picture away and Theresa brightens. "We could go pick up a tennis player," she says. "Or we could go say 'Boo' at Art Symes. He's scared to death of you."

Liza Jane laughs. This place is too pretty to get down in the dumps. "Or we could pretend we think that tootsie's his daughter."

"Who is she, anyway?"

"God, I don't know. Some script girl. I'll tell you what I want to do. I want to go see real estate agents." Theresa thinks Ayala is pretty, but Liza Jane's in love. She's been in love since they got here, driving up a little two-lane road through all those oak trees.

"Are you crazy? It's a two-hour drive to the studio."

"Screw the studio. I'll tell you something, if you promise not to tell."

"Honor bright," Theresa says. That's their password. They've never told on each other, not since they met. When Theresa was seventeen and Liza Jane nineteen, in New York, they cut their thumbs with a paring knife and swore they were blood sisters.

"Zenovich is going to sell. Ben told me."

"I heard scuttlebutt," Theresa says. "You're sure?"

"I'm sure." Maurice Zenovich, who bought Horizon Pictures when Lew Gibbon went under, is going under himself. "I've stayed too long at the fair," Liza Jane says. "I don't really know why."

"You stayed for Ben," Theresa says. Ben Zenovich and Liza Jane haven't been lovers in years, but the friendship is there. That's endured.

"Maybe," Liza Jane says. "Anyway the studio system is dead. I'm going to jump. Be my own woman. Live here." She grins. "New frontiers." She's not going to work for the corporation that's buying out Maurice Zenovich. She wonders if the Vincentes still have money in the studio. Roberto wouldn't tell her, but they probably do. They'll work that out with the corporation, business is business.

"You still have to work in L.A.," Theresa says. "For whomever."

"I don't care." She's pigheaded. She's been here twenty-four hours, knows she's going to settle in. She feels as if she can breathe here, figuratively and literally. L.A. smog damn near requires a gas mask on a bad day. She gets up. "Come on. You can watch tennis players' butts all week."

Theresa gives up and goes with her. They find a real estate agent in an office in the Arcade, next to a health food store. The agent is at the loose end of a slow afternoon, doodling on her desk calendar.

"I want a house," Liza Jane says.

"What sort of house?" The real estate agent wonders if she's serious. She's met enough movie people to know they get whims. Like children. They forget the next day.

"I'll know it when I see it." Liza Jane pours the rest of the martini into the thermos cap and drinks it while the real estate agent scrambles for the multiple listings book. "Start at the top end."

Liza Jane is serious. The third house they look at is the house on Del Norte. Liza Jane stands in the circular driveway, staring up at it.

"Mission San Ostentacion," Theresa says. "You could have peons. They could call you Doña. Is that a bell tower?"

Liza Jane grins.

"It's empty right now," the real estate agent says. She unlocks the front door.

Outside there are a couple of pomegranate trees by the west side of the house, blazing balls of magenta-colored flowers that echo the terracotta of the steps. Liza Jane likes their looks. But the oaks amaze her. There is a huge grove of them, ancient trees with heavy trunks and low, contorted branches. The real estate agent is still standing by the massive front door, but Liza Jane goes around through the overgrown yard to the back and stands under the oak trees. There is a nest of something, possums maybe, in a big hole in the tallest one. The branches are interlocked, crossing over and under each other, a living web, heavy and permanent. Underfoot there is a carpet of brown, prickly leaves and shiny, pointed acorns. A chipmunk scoots out from the weeds and dashes for a hole near the roots. Overhead she can see a hawk circling, riding the updraft over the bowl of the valley.

The real estate agent gives up and comes after them, getting her stockings full of foxtails. "The lot is three acres," she tells Liza

Jane. "You could put in a swimming pool, if you took some of the trees out." Movie stars always want swimming pools.

Liza Jane looks at her as if she's lost her mind. "Not a branch. Not an acorn." She tilts her head up to the trees again. "What it needs is a tree house."

"Right," Theresa says. "You can live in it when you find out the plumbing doesn't work."

The real estate agent looks worried and confesses to the existence of a septic tank. The house isn't on the city sewer line.

Liza Jane isn't interested in plumbing. She thinks about having house parties here. Not the people she has to invite; at this distance, only the people she wants. Of her brother Charlie coming, with Susan and little Liza Jane. She and Charlie can build the tree house for Little Liza. She thinks wistfully of inviting Mr. and Mrs. Murray of Pittsburgh, knows she can't do that. But she envisions him in the tree house anyway, dark eyes peering through the leaves like the chipmunk.

"Do you want to see the inside?" the real estate agent asks.

"I want to see it all!" Liza Jane turns, running through the foxtails, stopping at a pomegranate tree to break off a sprig and stick it in the buttonhole of her white pique dress. She knows her mythology.

She swoops through the inside, opening doors, climbing up to the tower, already thinking about what to do with the kitchen. There is some furniture still there, including a wrought iron bed with foxes running along the headboard. Liza Jane pounces on it, declaring it a sign. The house looks a little run down, but not much. Theresa is the one who flushes the toilets, pokes at the plastered walls, demands to see the furnace. After all these years, Theresa is still a New Yorker and has discovered that Californians are casual about furnaces. When she has pronounced this one solid, no holes exuding deadly carbon monoxide, she finds Liza Jane in the bell tower, arms braced in the arch, looking across the valley.

Ayala is still rural. There are a few tracts going up in the East End, but it's mostly orange groves from the end of the Arcade as far as the foothills. The afternoon sun gives it the glossy look of a model village, and a toy train chugs past the Ayala Inn golf course and the park, on its way to a packing house in the East End.

The real estate agent is telling her about the guest cottage, about the zoning—one horse per acre—about the absence of water in the basement. Liza Jane isn't listening. She's looking out over the valley, thinking about the oak trees; about the pugs—she has two of them now, Lew and Phoo—who've never really had a place to run before; of Bernice Lewis, who's had trouble finding a job even now, and how Liza Jane will need someone to hold the fort while she's shooting; of coming home to this house, to the oak trees, solid and eternal with some kind of answer hung in their branches like the tree house, a little door through which she may go some day and know, if she has asked the question right, what the hell things mean.

X
Revisionist History

1988

Th telephone was ringing in the cottage. Jeff hung up the tram's head and sprinted for the door. "That was Murray," he said when Liddy caught up to him. "He got the film open and ran it. He doesn't know what it is, but it upset Bernice. She said she'd tell him about it, but not until you're there because she only wants to go into it once."

"Jesus."

"Brace up, Oatsu-san," Jeff said. It was a subtitle from a samurai movie they'd once seen together, funny for being totally inadequate to the situation, theirs or Oatsu's. They walked back to the house with an escort of worried pugs.

"They know someone's missing," Liddy said. "Poor little babies."

Harry met them at the door. "I'm getting concerned about our situation here," he said.

"Brace up," Liddy said. She went inside and found Bernice and Frank sweeping up glass, and Theresa with her foot on a hassock. Alec was on the telephone, the can of film under one arm as if he was unwilling to turn his back on it.

"I'm not making any decisions right now," he told whoever was on the other end. He slammed the receiver down, affronted. "I've got idiots calling me up asking for money I haven't even got yet," he announced. "So far I've heard from three charities, a stockbroker, and my cousin in Detroit who wants to invest in ultralight planes."

"Tell them you're leaving it all up to your business manager," Liddy said. "Give them Harry's number. That's what I'm doing."

"Give them Arlo's," Harry said. "That's what I'm doing."

"Vultures," Theresa said. "Don says we ought to have a temporary secretary to screen those calls."

"We probably ought to," Harry agreed, "if we could find an icicle who won't talk to the press. I haven't got time."

"Where's Zach?" Liddy asked.

Bernice shook a dustpan full of china shards into a big wastebasket. "He's taking out trash for me."

"I'll find him," Jeff said. "And I'll finish that." He took the broom and dustpan out of Bernice's hands. "Go have your powwow."

"I have to dress." Liddy bolted up the stairs. In the hall she nearly collided with Sharon, who was pacing up and down in a penned fury.

"Is he down there?" Sharon demanded.

"Who?"

"Mike. When he gets here, I want to know."

"Then go down there and lie in wait for him," Liddy told her. She ducked into her room and shut the door. The house seemed to seethe beneath her, all its inhabitants with fangs bared and fur puffed up like Kilkenny cats ready to claw each other into subatomic particles. If she didn't have a funeral and send them all home, there wouldn't be anything left but footprints.

Liddy leaned against the door with the urge to lock it and let them self-destruct. In the dressing table mirror, her hair hung in her eyes and over her ears, and she thought, depressed, about letting it grow out again. Most women cut their hair when they wanted to reorder their lives, but she didn't have enough left.

She went in the bathroom and took a shower. In the closet she found an old pair of jeans and a t-shirt that had been hers. She put them on and went downstairs barefoot, hair dripping down her neck. The hell with Steve Bowman and his wardrobe suggestions. She wanted mightily to tell him so, but deprived of that pleasure since he wasn't there—probably at the Horsehead Ranch handing out positioning statements—she went down to the projection room. Through a window, she saw Jeff and Zach stacking up stones that had come out of the retaining wall, keeping a good distance from it. The iron railing hung like a skeleton over the rubble. Item number one: Call a mason. Item number two: Call a blacksmith.

Bernice and Alec were waiting in the screening room. Alec didn't say anything but Bernice made a worn gesture with one hand, motioning to her to sit. Bernice had dark circles under her eyes, and Liddy realized with a kind of lurch that Bernice was getting old, too.

"Are you sure you're up to this?" Liddy said.

"I can't re-bury it," Bernice said. "I have to be."

"I think you do too," Alec said. He looked dogged.

Whatever it was had surfaced almost of its own volition, so maybe it had something to say. But what had it said to Liza Jane that had made her dig a hole and weight it down with a rock?

"What about the rest of them?" Liddy asked. "Does Harry know?"

"You tell Harry," Bernice said shortly.

Liddy looked at Alec. He just shook his head and flicked the lights off and the projector on.

A hiss of garbled sound and numbers flashing backward on a white screen. A clapper wavering in somebody's hands: *ZENOVICH/Richard Plantagenet/Dir: Halley/Cam: Franklin.* A woman walking on a castle battlement with two little boys by the hands. Her face was framed in a round medieval headdress like a pillow, and she carried her trailing skirt bunched up in one hand in front of her. It took a minute for them to realize that it was Liza Jane. Another clapper. Another scene: A dark man turning a crown in his hands. A battle scene, armored knights on armored horses. The boys again, looking over the battlements. They dropped a ball, and the dark man laughed and threw it back to them. Liza Jane again, in a garden, bending over a needlework frame, with another woman beside her.

The scenes were in no particular order, only that in which they had been shot. Location footage; the expensive stuff. Some were repeated several times. Rushes; or outtakes, maybe. The tail end of the film slipped through the projector, whipping on the take-up reel, and Alec shut it off.

"There's a little more," he said, "but the splice has gone bad." He poked a finger at the strip still dangling from the projection reel. "It's just more of the same."

Liddy looked at Bernice. "I never saw this. I never heard of it."

"It doesn't exist," Bernice said.

"I met a man upon the stair." Alec flicked his finger at the loose film again. "A little man who wasn't there." He looked at Bernice, too, waiting. "He wasn't there again today," he suggested.

"My God, I wish he'd go away." Jeff had come in and was leaning, arms folded, against the back wall. "No offense intended, Captain. I got the same sort of feeling myself. Revisionist history and time warp. I passed Zach on to Theresa," he added to Liddy. "He's drawing spaceships on her cast. Bernice, what the hell? Ben is here, incidentally, undergoing some sort of angst in the parlor. Mike came with him."

"Oh, good God." Liddy tilted her head as if listening for sounds of strife, or possibly gunshots, but none came.

"Sharon's in the kitchen, poisoning their tea."

"This was Zenovich's film, wasn't it?" Alec said.

"This is the one the blacklist killed." Bernice said. "Mike had written the screenplay and when he got listed, the studio yanked us all back from location. Budget cuts, they said, but we all knew. It was my last film, too. They put *Glory Days* in the shooting schedule instead, but by then the word on me was out."

"Oh, Bernice." Liddy looked at her sympathetically, put her hand on Bernice's shoulder.

"Well, I'd seen the handwriting on the wall," Bernice said. "Everyone was terrified. Funny how that sort of thing lasts. When it turned up today, I honestly thought I was going to be sick."

"You didn't know?" Alec leaned on the seat in front of her, bent over above Bernice, his hands clutching the seat back, knuckles tight. Prosecutor confronting recalcitrant witness. But he was going to find out. They were going to know. What in that film had Liza Jane seen fit to hide but not destroy? Where had she spoken some answer that she wanted no one to hear?

Jeff and Liddy backed off almost imperceptibly, withdrew without moving, watching Alec and Bernice in the faint dusty light that spilled from inside the projector. Whatever there was to know was Alec's.

"No," Bernice said finally. "I didn't know. I've always believed in going on. But Liza Jane always took things with her. I don't know whether they were a comfort or a torment, but she took them."

"Why was this movie so important to her?"

"I don't think it was, until it got killed," Bernice said.

Killed. To kill a picture. Alec had been around Liza Jane's household long enough to have heard the expression. Now it was apt, an act of murder. "She didn't hide this, did she?" he said. "She dug it a grave."

"I think so," Bernice said.

"And put a rock on it so its ghost wouldn't walk," Liddy said. Alec saw again the fleeting resemblance to Liza Jane. Saw Jeff put his arm around her lightly, oldest of protective gestures.

"I suppose you've noticed," Jeff said, "that she buried that film where she wanted us to bury her."

"The exact spot?"

"On the mark. I thought it was a bit pat for the ground to open in the right spot. It must have been because it had been dug once already."

"All right, why?" Alec said. "For Mike Rosen's sake?"

"No, I don't think so." Bernice hesitated. "She didn't...well, they didn't go together until years later. She felt bad about it, of course, everyone's conscience was very precarious then. But communal guilt wasn't her style. Liza Jane's motives were always very personal."

"For you?" Alec suggested gently. He tried to see Bernice as she had been then. In her thirties, head of wardrobe, successful in her field, full of convictions, out on her ear for being a communist.

Bernice reached out and flicked off the projector light. "That's bad for it. Jeff, dear, turn the lights on."

The darkness that encased them drew back suddenly, opening up wide-angle, framing them in long-shot: Bernice in her seat, Liddy half turned toward her, Jeff with his hand on the switch; Alec looming over them, demanding and uncertain; Liza Jane in her can of film.

Bernice folded her hands, heavy with turquoise and carnelian rings, bare nails trimmed off square, laid them carefully on her skirt, amid green denim folds. She could have worn the same outfit in 1953, Alec thought; probably had. This year it just happened to be in style.

"I think," Bernice said, seeming to gauge some formula in her mind—how much upheaval could be added to the air?—"that it was simply the fact that it died, and really for nothing, for stupidity and fear." She too sounded as if it had been alive. "It would have been a good movie. It was about Richard the Third, you know. The Shakespearean monster who was supposed to have murdered his nephews. Mike liked Richard, even though he got bad press. He said if Shakespeare could write his own version, then so could he. I gathered that it was one of those things that medievalists nit-pick over. It didn't matter."

Alec felt argumentative. "Why didn't it matter?"

"Because it was so long ago, we'll probably never know the actual truth. This was Mike's until they took it away from him. After that, I suppose it was Liza Jane's." She looked Alec in the eye. "God knows she paid for it."

Now he was going to find out. Now he was going to know, and once he knew, he would always know. There wouldn't be any undoing it. "I'm not hers, am I?" Alec said. Odd how the thought that he might be had stayed at the back of his mind, not quite dislodged.

"My poor Liza Jane," Bernice said. "She must have wanted you to be, quite desperately. That's why this film mattered, you see. It was what she was supposed to keep afterward, what she did it for, because her work was important, art was important. And then they killed the damned project."

Bernice's voice was agonized, and Alec's face went taut. Whose ghost was he? "She had an abortion, didn't she?" he said with an unexpected flash of insight.

"She was pregnant," Bernice said. "While they were shooting *Richard.* She didn't want to marry the man—I think she was still pining for Donald Wain—and she thought—my God, at her age!—that there was still time.

"I set it up for her. There were a few days they didn't need her on location and I knew someone. You had to know someone. You have no idea what it was like back then. It was in a sleazy motel in Van Nuys. It was raining. I took her out there, but they wouldn't let me stay. I drove around the block, over and over, until I saw her standing on the sidewalk. She had to pay them double, once for the abortion, and once because they knew who she was. She was a movie star, they said. There was too much chance of someone snooping."

Liddy leaned forward, arms wrapped around her waist, protectively.

Alec put his head in his hands. Whose ghost? Nobody's ghost—the little man who wasn't there. Like Mike Rosen. But Mike had been alive, if anonymous. Could you be your own ghost? Alec felt vaguely sick.

"I have never been pregnant," Bernice said carefully. "I am in no position to pass judgment on anyone, except the doctor, who was a drunken butcher. And all the pious sober doctors who wouldn't have lifted a finger to help her. He damaged her badly. She had to have a hysterectomy later."

"She had an abortion to make a movie that got scrapped," Alec said slowly.

"If you look closely," Bernice said, "if you can bear to, you can see that she's just starting to show. There's one piece of the balcony scene..."

Alec threaded the film again furiously. Liza Jane walked along the parapet again, turned her profile to the low sun, let the bunched gown slip from her hand.

"There." Bernice pointed her finger at the image, already slipping past them. "Does it surprise you now that she helped Carolyn?"

"Helped her?" Alec's voice grated past his teeth, jagged with anger. "What she did was, she buried a goddamned film instead of a baby. And then she stole another one out of someone else's cradle."

"In a way," Jeff said. "From another perspective, she gave Carolyn's cuckoo to your mom to raise. Your mom seemed appreciative."

Take three, alternate ending. The first kid didn't play; call Casting for another one. Alec glared at them all. "Have you people got any idea what it's like to grow up wondering where you came from, to decide you're better off not knowing, and then to have someone come along and shove it down your throat? And then to find out that not only were you not wanted in the first place, you're somebody's goddamn replacement? I'm not even sure whose. The dead kid? The kid she couldn't have with Wain? Some fucking fantasy? I've got more goddamned parents than you can shake a stick at. I was sired by a fucking committee!"

"Take it easy, man," Jeff said.

"Alec—"

"Go to hell." The film flipped through the projector again and spun on the take-up reel. Alec snatched the reel off and made a motion as if to throw it. Then he stalked out with it under his arm.

Steve Bowman passed Alec in the hall, dodged instinctively, and simultaneously achieved an ingratiating smile. "Crazy day." He shook his head wonderingly. "Don't get lost now. Donahue's people may be coming over."

The other three came out of the projection room, and Liddy

and Jeff took Steve by the arms and turned him around.

"This way, man," Jeff said. "We want you to brief the pugs."

"Mama!" Zach scooted down the stairs, met them halfway up. "There's a lady on the phone for you."

"Honey, can you tell her I'm not here?"

"Theresa told her you're not here," Zach said. "But she didn't hang up."

"Oh, all right." Liddy looked at Steve. "Do me a favor and stay away from Alec Murray, all right?"

"Sure," Steve said, eyeing her jeans and t-shirt. "Sure, babe. Say, why don't you let me look through your suitcase, help you make some choices?"

Liddy let go of his arm. If Alec hadn't escaped by now, he was on his own. "I'm clean and I'm not naked," she said. "That's the best you'll get this morning."

"Sure, sure," Steve said. He cast a wary eye up the stairs. "Maybe I'll just leave Murray on the back burner for a while," he added.

Liddy surveyed the group in the living room. Francie Allen was there too, and even Donald Wain and Roberto Vincente. No one was actually speaking to anyone else. It was more as if the final earthquake had bunched them together into a restless herd. Fire on the veldt. The pugs snorted when they saw her and arranged themselves around her feet. Liddy picked up the telephone, and Zach sat down by Theresa's hassock again with his markers. "Blam," he said, drawing a starburst.

"Liddy!" Margaret Collins' voice boomed at her from the telephone. "We have a tragedy!"

Liddy tried to pay attention to Margaret, to stop seeing Liza Jane standing on a Van Nuys street corner in the rain. "What is it, Margaret?"

"The Post Office tower! There is terrible damage. A dreadful crack halfway down the side. We're simply distraught."

"Oh. Well, I'm sorry to hear that."

"We must all rally around. Immediately. There must be funding."

"Margaret, this isn't the time—"

"Oh, no!" Margaret was shocked. "I wouldn't dream of asking for a donation now. I do know that's impossible. But the community must be involved, right away. We're going to have a street fair!"

"Uh huh," Liddy said. Margaret seemed to be waiting for some comment. "Good idea."

"Tonight! While emotions are still high. A gathering of the community. To bind our wounds. I'm in charge."

"Of course you are."

"Well, Stu and June Patterson offered, but they're simply impossible—I won't have them snatching cigarettes out of people's hands. Anyway, we'll have a parade of solidarity for the tower, and a street band. I know some marvelous musicians who've agreed to play. And celebrities to take pledges. 'Button, Button' has agreed to make us some buttons for donors—'Tower Power'—and the Ramananda will lead us all in meditation. And of course I thought that with that wonderful bunch of people you have up at the house now, you'd want to help. Bernice has always been so involved, and your guests would really be an asset." Margaret lowered her voice conspiratorially. "I know women who'd pledge their back teeth just to have Frank Hill pin a button on them. Now do say you'll see what you can do."

Liddy had a vision of Francie Allen loose among the denizens of Ayala. But she felt rocked by earthquake and revelation into a state of plasticity wherein Margaret could probably mow down any argument she offered. And the feeling took hold that they might be distracted from impending mayhem by public service. "I'll see what I can do," she told Margaret.

She put the phone down. "That was Margaret Collins," she

said. "She wants me to put you all on a leash and bring you to a street fair."

To Liddy's surprise, they agreed to go, although she suspected that it was less altruism than a kind of carnival spirit—a lark. As a tribe they moved easily between despair and elation.

Theresa settled herself in a wheelchair produced by Donald Wain from heaven knew what source. "I feel like Cleopatra in a sedan chair. Are you sure you know how it works?"

"It's not a flying saucer," Wain said. "You push it and it goes." He handed Theresa her purse. "And have you been to the bathroom? Because they'll probably have those portable things, and I'm not going to take you."

Theresa chuckled and arranged a fringed Chinese shawl around her shoulders. "Heaven forbid."

Steve Bowman was in a fine mood, and had had a long serious conversation with Margaret Collins about press coverage. Even Frank had agreed to pin buttons on palpitating female bosoms for the cause. Francie was coming too, for motives unknown—and, Liddy hoped uneasily, unobjectionable—but it ought to make the street band's day.

Roberto Vincente, too, although Vincente seemed to see himself in the guise of a prospective patron. He patted his pocket. "I want to see her town. Maybe do something for it. Do you know she never, not once in all those years, asked me for a favor?" Vincente peered at Liddy. "You look like her. It's funny, all these years I'm getting old and fat, I never think of Liza old." He sighed heavily. "I send her roses every year, I always get a note back. Who am I going to send roses to now?"

"Send 'em to your wife," Donald Wain snapped over his shoulder.

Vincente snorted and made a stately progress to the door.

Bernice appeared and started scooping the pugs into the library. They had begun to trail Liddy everywhere, a pug motorcade wherever she went.

"Help her with those, Don," Theresa said. "If they get out, they'll try to follow the car."

Liddy began to feel as if the expedition was a large animal grown beyond her control. She went to look for Alec. She had seen him come in, but had no idea whether he was hiding or dressing.

He was dressing, tucking his shirt into dark slacks. His face was tight though. He had shoved the reel of film on the top of a wardrobe. "This all right for a street fair?"

"You're coming?"

"I'm not staying here."

"Look, I didn't get a chance to talk to you—"

Alec buckled his belt. "It's not your fault. And I'm aware I'm being an asshole."

"There's a lot of that going around." Liddy looked at the collection of pictures that decorated the room, stopped, aching, at Liza Jane and the old man who was downstairs now pushing Theresa's wheelchair. "Don't be so hard on her. She didn't want anything people aren't entitled to."

"When I was five the sisters at my kindergarten told me I should pray for my real mother's soul. I hadn't even known I was adopted. My mom thought I wasn't old enough. I feel like I'm five now and my whole life just got rewritten."

"I was eight when my parents died," Liddy said. "Did you ever read *Eloise* when you were a kid?"

"Little rich girl who lives at a hotel with her nanny? Yeah."

"I felt like all of a sudden I was Eloise at the Plaza. I didn't know what to do with it. It's possible I understand."

Alec picked up his jacket. "Barely." He softened. "Come on, let's go to the damn fair."

1966

Liza Jane is fifty-six, too old now to be somebody's mother. Her brother Charlie has flown his plane into a mountain, vanishing in a crescendo of fire and leaving an eight-year-old child behind. Now the child is sitting on the cedar chest at the foot of Liza Jane's bed, wrapped in a serape, and looking too tired to cry. This is not the baby of Liza Jane's imagining, or the child in the hoarded stack of pictures, and Liza Jane is not sure what she ought to be doing with this real child, suddenly acquired.

What should she be saying? Don't cry? She's past crying now. They loved you? Then why did they die? It will be all right? It won't be all right. Little Liza has long reddish brown braids with pink ponies on the ends. Liza Jane sits down beside her and pulls her into her lap, serape and all. She bends down, her own hair coming out of its hairpins, and she can just see them both in the mirror on the bathroom door. She says, "We'll just have to muddle through together, lamb."

Little Liza doesn't say anything, but a hand comes out of the serape and grabs the first thing it feels, the sleeve of Liza Jane's blouse, and a strand of her hair, red as fire. Little Liza doesn't know about the fire, hasn't asked about the crash, won't for weeks. Her aunt's hair seems warm to her, and comforting. She's cold because she's so tired. They've flown from Cincinnati to Los Angeles, driven up to Ayala with Bernice in Liza Jane's car. Left in snowfall, touched down in a blaze of December sun, as if the world has suddenly tilted the other way. All her things, her toys and so forth, will follow. Tonight she has only a Barbie doll in an old red dress and a suitcase full of winter clothes too heavy for California.

She says, "Will I go to school?"

Liza Jane says, "Yes, but not tomorrow." Bernice has been talking to the headmaster at Apple Valley, which Bernice approves of. Liza Jane doesn't know much about schools. The headmaster said to give her until after Christmas to touch ground.

Little Liza nods, relieved that she will be going to school, and that she won't be going tomorrow. Everything has been too all-at-once.

"Are you hungry?" Liza Jane doesn't tell her she has to eat something, is perfectly prepared to let Little Liza skip dinner if she wants to. Neither Liza Jane nor Bernice knows how to talk to children, so they talk to her as if she were grown up.

"I think so."

"All right. Let's see what Bernice can find us." Liza Jane unwraps her from the serape and looks at the suitcase. "Nightgown first?"

When she has on a flannel nightgown and bedroom slippers, they go downstairs. The house looks enormous to Little Liza. She's been here before, with her parents. It was almost like being in a hotel. Now she lives here.

The kitchen is full of pugs. Little Liza sits down on the floor and hugs them and they lick her face. She has never had a dog before because her mother was allergic to them. Now she feels almost guilty to want these so much. She looks up at Liza Jane and Bernice. "They would have bought me a dog," she says. "If they could."

"Of course they would. I'm glad you like mine."

Bernice gives her a sandwich and a glass of red juice that has a sweet-tart taste. Bernice pours it from a milk jug that has a masking tape label: Pom/Appl. "That's from our trees," Bernice says.

When she has eaten, they put her in bed, in the little iron bed with the foxes on it. "I bought this bed when I bought the house," Liza Jane says. "Because of the foxes. It's so heavy they didn't want to move it. It can be yours until your own comes." They have agreed that Little Liza can pick whatever she wants to ship here from the house in Cincinnati. She has picked her parents' bed instead of her own, which makes Liza Jane want to cry every time she thinks about it. What am I going to do with her? she thinks helplessly as she tucks her in. Her own words come back to her—muddle through.

Little Liza scrunches up in the bed. It has a crinkly old-fashioned horsehair mattress that makes a nice sound.

"Goodnight, Liza Jane."

The child looks up, almost startled by the name. It seems odd that they both have the same one. She says, "Goodnight, Liza Jane," trying the sound of it, almost like speaking to herself. "Goodnight, Bernice." She studies them sleepily. She hasn't really bothered before, just on a visit, but now they are important. Now they are hers, and she's theirs. She wants desperately to be theirs, to go on being somebody's. Liza Jane is beautiful, like a miniature version of the face she's seen on the movie screen, almost magical to a child's eye, with a necklace of pearls and a faint aura of fairy dust. Liza Jane is magic, but Bernice fixes breakfast.

They kiss her and leave her alone, leaving the door open so that she can just see a slanted rectangle of the hallway. She tries to remember the name of that shape, they learned it in school, but it won't come. She concentrates on the shape, because she doesn't want to remember that her mother won't kiss her anymore. She tries to imagine her mother in heaven with white angel's wings, and bright feet. There's a song her father liked, about "Shall we gather at the river, where bright angel feet have trod?" So she has always imagined angels with glowing feet, making sparks like stardust.

They aren't coming back. It hits her all at once, and she knots herself into a ball under the covers.

Grief fades—slowly. But living with Liza Jane is an adventure, and Little Liza is young, with the mercifully short memory of childhood. Liza Jane buys her a horse that they can keep in a corral by the guest house, and Little Liza can even ride it downtown. There's a hitching rail beside the library. In the summer sometimes Liza Jane takes her on location with her, or to the studio, with lunch at the Farmer's Market for a treat. Liza Jane doesn't mind people asking for her autograph while Little Liza tries to make up her mind at the pastry stall.

Little Liza gets to know an odd collection of famous people. It isn't until she is much older that she discovers that people think it odd that she has played Scrabble with Frank Hill and several unsuccessful candidates for President. It isn't until she is older that her name bothers her, either. But when 'Little Liza' becomes a cumbersome and embarrassing way to differentiate them, and she is left with just 'Liza Jane,' she begins to wonder, amid the whirl of famous faces, among which her aunt is arguably the most famous, if she is just going to disappear into that other Liza Jane. In junior high she becomes Liddy, and Liza Jane isn't hurt. "So sensible," Bernice says and Liza Jane agrees.

But for now she is Little Liza, and Alec Murray, assessing it later, will be right: it is a charmed life. Mike Rosen reads her English composition assignments. Harry Lanier takes her to the Academy Awards ceremony. Ben Zenovich lets her go to Italy and Alaska on location with Liza Jane. One Christmas in New York, Roberto Vincente takes her to the opera.

She is never quite sure when it is that Ayala begins to drive her crazy. She loves it, and is maddened by it. In Liza Jane's house there is perhaps too bright a light, too much emotion for a time in her life when emotion is a constant upheaval anyway.

Liza Jane thinks college in the east is a good idea. Something small and solid. "A little dull," Liza Jane says to Bernice. "The kind of school Charlie would have sent her to." Liza Jane isn't being critical, has a sense that she casts too large a shadow. Little Liza, Liddy now, wants, like most teenagers, what she doesn't have.

XI
Guilt By Association

1988

Donahue's people had failed to show, but were due tomorrow for sure. Steve Bowman had formed a duumvirate with Margaret Collins: Margaret got celebrities and publicity and Steve got Margaret to hold all the other local dingbats at bay, away from the press. The Pattersons, outflanked by Margaret, bore down on Liddy.

"I fail to see why you have found it appropriate to exclude Liza Jane's friends from your plans."

"What?" Liddy tried to edge away from June and found herself hemmed in by the yellow-and-black police tape that was supposed to keep anyone from being crushed if the Post Office tower fell down. In the street, Margaret's band was playing, and Francie Allen had climbed up on the stage with them. The band leader, in a black leather jacket and a lightning bolt tattoo, looked as if he might faint. He handed Francie the microphone and her trademark howl split the air.

June sniffed, aggrieved. "It must be nice to be able to do anything you feel like, without having to consider other people's feelings."

Liddy tried to focus on June. "Maybe you'd better explain again. It's hard to hear."

"Well, of course that's just the problem. Nobody hears anybody, do they? And we had such wonderful plans." June's lip trembled.

"We want to know," Stu said, taking charge, "what you plan to do about Liza Jane's bequests."

The Ramananda loomed behind him. "Dear Liddy. Our benefactress relies on you."

"How do you know?" Liddy asked, annoyed. She noted that the president of the Humane Society and the headmaster of Apple Valley had converged on her as well. She looked around for Harry or Arlo, but they were nowhere in sight.

"Let's just assume she does," the headmaster said before the Ramananda could tell her how he knew.

Stu Patterson coughed portentously and attempted to gather their attention about him. "We understand that the will has been declared invalid."

Liddy looked over Stu's shoulder at the band. Francie was singing, eyes squeezed shut, wild hair fanned around her head. She held the microphone in one hand; the other's long, reaching fingers massaged the band leader's thigh. Frank was across the street in front of the Arcade, distributing buttons. He looked friendly, but as if he had his mind on something else. Probably his script. Or whether Francie was going to screw the band leader on stage.

"I don't believe any decision has been made," Liddy told Stu. That seemed to sum things up nicely. She could make a list as long as the Arcade of the decisions that hadn't been made. The sun was going down fast, an aggressive display of Ayala's famous pink sunset, rose and robin's egg blue above the tower. "Who told you that anyway?"

"It was in the paper." June sniffled.

"So were plenty of things," Liddy said.

"The point is, we want to know your intentions." The president of the Humane Society fixed her with a firm stare. She had a small spaniel under one arm, as if she might be going to ask Liddy to marry it.

Liddy's hands balled into fists and she painstakingly unclenched them. "I haven't made any decisions, I don't know that the will is invalid, and I hope to hell it's not."

It wasn't any use. They surged around her with the demented persistence of the reporters that Jeff and Alec had been running off the place all day.

"In point of fact—"

"Moral obligation—"

"Dear Liza's memory—"

"I have to find my son," Liddy said. "Talk to Arlo Sheppard. I haven't made any decisions." She ducked under the line of police tape and out again into a row of skipping Deadheads who were cavorting down the street, carrying their own music with them. She emerged into the Arcade, leaving June to patter after her as best she could. Somehow the line scooped up June, too, and bore her in the opposite direction.

The street fair was in full surge. Ayala was a small town, the kind of place where you could organize a street fair in eight hours. Blue Yonder had hand-thrown pots and the Herbalist had a half-price sale. So did the Rexall drug store. The Art Center was doing scenes from *A Midsummer Night's Dream* under an awning in the park, and a folk group with guitars were at the other end of the Arcade competing with the street band and the Deadheads. The police had blocked off the whole of Ayala Avenue from the Arcade up past the old Catholic church and the Ramananda's adobe. Guests from the Inn and the Horsehead Ranch jammed the shops along the Arcade, buying 'Tower Power' buttons and Andean llama-skin jackets. The owner of the expensive spa up the street had her charges out for a walk in their jogging suits, perusing spandex exercise wear and vegetarian sandwiches. Liddy saw Sharon Hamilton graciously taking pledges in front of the Shakespearean troupe, and Ben moodily eating an ice cream cone. Zach was perched on the adobe wall that ran along the front of the park, waving his arms and apparently directing the band. Liddy looked for Jeff, but couldn't find him, or Alec either now. They too had been sucked up by the tide, deposited who knew where. Only Zach, on his wall, seemed to be above the surf.

Liddy sat beside him. He was eating a pretzel dipped in carob and he offered her a bite. "It's weird, but it's good."

"Where did you get it?"

"You gave me three dollars, don't you remember?"

Liddy didn't, but she probably had. Zach held out a carob-smeared hand and exhibited the change. "They have lemonade, too."

"You're going to need it, after that." Liddy chewed her bite, salty and doughy and cut with the strange sweetness of carob.

"Are you going to marry somebody?"

"Who? And why are you asking me?" The tide surged around their feet.

"I like Jeff," Zach said thoughtfully.

"What on earth makes you think I might be going to marry him?"

"Cause he says he used to be your boyfriend."

"That was a long time ago," Liddy said.

"So you married Daddy?"

"Uh huh."

"I can't remember Daddy," Zach said fretfully. "Not very well."

"Oh, sweetheart, I know. It happens."

"I might not like it if you married Jeff," Zach said. "He's nice, but I like it just us."

"You don't get to pick," Liddy said. "And I wouldn't worry. We don't even live here."

"Aren't we going to? Bernice says."

"Would you want to?" Too late, she thought, Why did I ask him that? You should never ask children things like that, they expected you to make good on them.

"Maybe." Zach kicked his feet against the wall, watching the dancers. "Bernice says I could have a horse."

Blast Bernice. Liddy looked down from her vantage point, over the streams of people in the street, so many faces half remembered. She'd grown used to the town being half tourists; to picking the ones she knew out of the crowd. Now they looked as if they might all be strangers, perhaps seen once in the movies. It was the architecture of Ayala itself that was familiar, the stucco wall warm under her hand, the striations of Topa Topa Mountain above the valley, the chaparral hills, dusty and smelling of manzanita and the big white ruffled cups of Matilija poppies.

Liddy saw Jeff finally, perched on top of a mailbox with his sketchbook, recording the passing parade of Deadheads. She swung her feet against the wall like Zach. Will you, won't you, will you, won't you, won't you join the dance?

At dusk the sunset combusted in a carnelian flare that burned its way down behind the Post Office. The wrought-iron lamps in the Arcade's arches came on, and someone began lighting luminarias along the park walkways and the fountain—paper bags weighted with sand and lit with votive candles. In the dusk they were magical.

Theresa was signing autographs with her favorite fountain

pen, pressing the nib gently, exactly the right angle, proof she wasn't dead yet. Which was fortunate because she couldn't afford her own funeral. Theresa sighed. Bernice had told her what was on the film, and now of course what Liza Jane had wanted made sense, in a mad way. Blood sisters or not, Liza Jane had never told her about that.

A woman from the spa tut-tutted over the broken leg. "I do so like Mrs. Talliaferro."

"I don't think a broken leg will trouble Mrs. T," Theresa said. She forced a smile, pushing it past the urge to cry. "She's already in a coma, isn't she?" She handed back an aerobics schedule, her signature slanted elegantly across the corner.

"The poor thing," said the woman.

"Time you put the poor thing out of her misery and get out of that business," Donald Wain said irritably as the woman left. He leaned his hands on the back of Theresa's wheelchair. The Chinese shawl was draped over one arm.

"Those of us who aren't captains of industry haven't your options," Theresa gently. She signed another autograph with a flourish of bright green ink.

"Liza Jane left you her jewelry, didn't she? It's worth a mint," Wain said. "I ought to know."

"You gave her most of it, didn't you?"

"And don't take any moral high ground about being too sentimental to sell it," Wain said.

"Well, no," Theresa admitted. "But the question may not arise. It's all very iffy, and I won't start badgering Liddy like those awful bean sprout people."

"Ridiculous situation," Wain said. "Blasted woman had to have her own way her entire life. Never once thought of bending to anyone else's requirements."

Theresa turned her head up and back to look at him. "She did think about it, dear. More often than you can imagine."

Wain compressed his lips so that they seemed to fold around his resentment. "She never did it."

Sharon watched people in the street lighting candles, shielding them from the twilight breeze in paper cups. They were having some idiotic march, another idea thought up by that Collins woman. Sharon was willing to take pledges, but not to walk around with a candle like something out of the sixties. Sharon knew exactly what she was here for. Her eyes slewed around, looking for Mike. He had finally shown up at Liza Jane's house and shut himself up in the library with Frank. If he thought he was going to evade her that way, he was wrong. Ben was looking for him, too.

Mike had to be told you couldn't just roll over people because you thought you'd had a raw deal thirty years ago. Tear down everything everyone else had built so carefully, with such attention to detail. Couldn't just make up your own version, for Christ's sake, when everyone else had already agreed about it.

Mike leaned against the fence in front of the tennis courts and wished he still smoked. He had a desire for a cigarette as sudden and as vicious as the urge to strangle Sharon—just to go over and put his hands around her throat. Funny, after all these years, that hadn't left him. As long as she hated him, he couldn't grow indifferent. Maybe the script would do it, if it got made. Maybe he could process the experience, as his idiot therapist put it—

transmute it into patterns of light and sound. My wife left me; just a good plot device.

"Sharon's going up in smoke." Ben's shadow fell along the walk beside Mike's.

"She'll implode most likely," Mike said. "Fall in on herself."

"Not surprising. What the hell did you think you were doing?"

"You know," Mike said.

"I bloody well don't know." They eyed each other peripherally, like lizards, talking to the tennis courts. "You're not hurting," Ben said. "Can't you just leave it alone?"

"Define your terms."

"Don't give me the soul's inner anguish." Ben made a quick, dismissive movement, as if Mike were pitching him a story. "Hollywood's done it to people for years. Yours is just the same old whore in a different dress."

"You're lucky you never caught anything from her," Mike said. "Not all of us were so fortunate."

"I got a dose occasionally," Ben said. "Shit, can't you let it lie? You really savaged Sharon."

"You find anything inaccurate in there?"

Ben put his hands in his jacket pockets. His angular profile jutted away from Mike, angrily. "You could get sued."

Mike gave a snort of laughter. "Your old man's studio killed my picture. Go sue yourself."

"A lot more boats could have got sunk, without floating yours. You ever think of that?"

"I thought. I had plenty of time to think. It doesn't take a lot of brain power to write pornography. It leaves you more time than you want."

"Ah, hell." Ben took his hands out of his pockets, examined them. "Are you after Sharon, or me?"

"I'm after myself. I'm interested in finding whatever I've got left that hasn't been screwed by the system. You and Sharon are incidental." Mike looked at Ben, twilight scoring his face, filling in the creases with shadow. "I took some pains with the studio scenes, with characters. No one's going to know you."

"I'm going to know me." Ben flung his hands out, furiously empty. "You're so sorry for yourself you don't know what it was like for anybody else. There was no place you could call your soul your own. If you went to the can there was somebody there to see if you peed like a communist. Did you hire anybody who peed like a communist? Shit!" He brought his hands up against his forehead, rocked on his heels.

Mike leaned back against the chain link fence, crossed his arms. "I know what it was like. It was easier to go along with your old man. Easier not to buck the Committee for Americanism and the Crusade for Freedom and all the witch-finders who might find you next."

"That's not all there was to it."

"Sure. There was money. It wasn't hard to figure out who to save. You saved Liza Jane and let people like me and Bernice Lewis swing in the wind. It was just good accounting."

"Liza Jane went to one meeting!" Ben snapped.

"That's all it takes." Mike smiled. "Once is plenty, like the clap. Once was plenty for a lot of people."

"Mike." Ben looked at him as if he were cajolable. "Isn't there some way to work this through, without—without fucking over the industry? You aren't going to be able to get this made. No one's going to touch it."

"Frank wants it," Mike said.

"Frank's got his own axes to grind. Frank's got PTSD from Vietnam still. I tell you, no one'll touch this."

Mike shrugged. "Studio heads are all bean counters from Tokyo now. They don't have any history to protect. Besides—" The smile reappeared, tight around his teeth. "No one wants to look sensitive about the blacklist." He grabbed an imaginary microphone and shoved it in Ben's face. Ben twisted his head away as if it were real. "If you weren't involved in the blacklist, Mr. Zenovich, why don't you want this picture made?"

Mike watched Ben jerk his chin away. Bastard. "I told Liza Jane I was writing it," Mike said, "and she asked me to go easy on you because it was your old man's company and he would have killed the picture even if you'd had the balls not to. But you aren't going to take this away from me. You aren't going to tell me that my experience doesn't exist." He pushed closer to Ben. "You are not, God damn you, going to make me a non-person again, a desaparecido of the film industry. And if you start working on Frank, you'll dig your own grave. I'll tell Frank. Frank's so politically correct he can't sit down."

"What is this, the oppressed minority of the week?" Ben looked disgusted. "You're on a soapbox. That's what's wrong with the script."

Mike shoved his face into Ben's again, and Ben backed up, coughing. Mike stopped while Ben pounded his chest. Ben took a breath, drawing it in with a whistle. On the tennis courts the lights had come on and a trio of high school boys were playing a pickup game with a pair of limp rackets and a bright orange ball. Behind them the parade was taking shape, floating out of the park and into the street in a stream of candlelight.

"Ah, I can't talk to you," Ben growled. "You'll see. You're going to get your tit in a wringer over this." He stalked away.

The parade moved into the street, a millipede form dotted with lights, drawing Ben with it. Someone handed him a candle in a paper cup. His fingers tightened and the candle flame jerked, ricocheting off the waxed walls. Shit, I was only twenty-four, he thought. But he wasn't like Sharon. He knew what he'd done. In the light of Mike's auto da fe, he couldn't tell if anyone had changed at all, or if you just got good at words like 'growth' and 'potential'; developed 'strategies' for reordering yourself. Ben's father brought his aunt and cousin over in 1939, one jump ahead of the Nazis, and after that a cousin who had survived the camps, but he didn't save Mike Rosen. Jews were automatically suspect anyway, there were too many Jews in Hollywood according to the Committee. You look Jewish to me; we hear that your grandfather was Jewish. We hear your grandmother was a Commie. It had been easier to rewrite, afterward. Take the blacklist out of the third act, it won't play for the focus group.

Ben found Jeff beside him, sketchbook under his arm, his face lit by a cupped candle. "Weirdness seems to be peaking tonight," Jeff observed.

Ben grunted. "It's quite a party."

"Loose in the streets," Jeff said. "Have you seen Francie?"

"What do you want with her? She's made enough trouble for Frank. Don't push it."

"God forbid. I'd sooner put it in a vegomatic. I meant, have you seen Francie? In the sense of, have you seen the Colossus? Or the Tar Pits?"

"Whole damn town's seen her," Ben said, "and every supermarket rag. I can't make her go away."

Jeff chuckled. "Liza Jane could have. Maybe she'll rise up and haunt her. Frank brought her around once right after they were married. Francie didn't even come in second."

The band was packing up its instruments. In the shadow of the Post Office tower, behind the police cordon, they could see Francie's pale hair stand out like a lightning aureole. She wasn't alone.

"I got no patience," Ben said. "She should get herself into a treatment program or she's going to wake up dead. And I will personally cheer the event if it happens. She's given Frank a little tic by the eye he can't stop."

"I doubt a program would cure what ails Francie," Jeff said. "Half those people are just trying to recover from life. Food, sex, shopping, ironing their pillowcases, whatever blows their dress up. They figure if they like it, it must be something they shouldn't be doing."

"Not a problem you've had?" Ben said sourly. He resented like hell the fact that Jeff Austin was twenty-eight and responsibility-free.

"Not till lately," Jeff said. "Oh man, look at the Captain."

The parade flowed past the tree in the middle of the street, opening around it to illuminate Alec and Frank for a moment, caught in the streetlight shadows of its leaves. They were talking, laughing about something, leaning on the trunk. Frank had his back to Francie, but Alec could see her, judging by his expression. She undulated against the band leader, who must have been as stoned as she was by now. Alec's face wore the expression that a man well might while watching a newfound famous acquaintance's wife fuck a stranger on the street. The band leader bent his head, mouth open over Francie's. Alec pulled his eyes away, finished the story he'd been telling. His glance caught Jeff's and Jeff grinned at him.

"Poor bastard," Jeff said. "He doesn't know what hit him."

"A million dollars hit him," Ben said.

"Yeah, in nickels. They dropped it off the roof on him. Along with a dubious pedigree. Poor Captain Midnight."

"What's dubious?" Ben forced his way past a knot of the Ramananda's followers, who seemed to be achieving gridlock around the tree. "I thought he was Carolyn Castellano and Arthur Symes's mamzer. Liza Jane conned me into giving Carolyn six months off, right about the right time."

"I think we're supposed to stop here," Jeff said, touching his arm. "The Ramananda's doing his service." The Ramananda had lifted his arms to the night sky, white robes flowing, his teenage acolytes behind him, ringing the tree. Frank and Alec went on talking, oblivious. A girl in a cerise sari glared at them.

"Why don't you tie them to the tree and we'll sacrifice them," Jeff suggested, and she glared at him, too. The Ramananda folded his hands in prayer and Jeff bowed his head. Ben followed suit irritably.

"Let us converge our thoughts on the need for healing vibrations to bring us back into harmony with the shaken earth." The Ramananda cast his eyes to the ground.

Stu and June Patterson had brought drums and were solemnly beating them in the background. The *thwock* of half-dead tennis balls from the park provided a counterpoint. Ben edged his way past a sari-clad devotee and noted that Jeff, having prayed long enough to be polite, was following him. "That ought to hit the tabloids by morning," Ben said. "If Murray thinks he's embarrassed now, wait until they run a photo of him in attendance on the swami."

"Why not? They've run all the rest of us," Jeff said. "I was gloriously misidentified as Francie Allen's bodyguard. The paparazzi are bugs. I don't see why Bowman can't get them out of here. If Liza Jane went to the trouble to bury something, I won't have them dissecting it in their stupid little rags."

"Shit, what now?" Ben said warily.

Jeff looked uncomfortable. "I guess I can't see any reason not to tell you. It's the worms from the tabloids that get me all protective. But I don't like Bowman either, he's the same worm in a polyester suit. Harry's the one to handle it, probably, and you."

"What the hell are we talking about?" Ben looked

exasperated.

"Liza Jane had an abortion a couple of years before Murray was born," Jeff said moodily. "It screwed her up pretty bad. She had to have a hysterectomy afterwards, her last shot at a kid clean gone. So she got obsessed with Carolyn's baby and gave her own a funeral complete with grave offerings."

Ben stared at him. "How the hell do you think you know all this?"

Jeff shrugged. "Bernice told us. Liza Jane was in the middle of a picture when she had the abortion. She had it on the quick because she was working, and then the studio killed the picture. And then she found out the son of a bitch had botched the abortion and she couldn't have any more kids. So she took the rushes and buried them, out there in the oak grove. She must have carried them around with her for years until she bought the house and decided that was home. The earthquake shook them loose and we found the can. So Bernice told us about it. It gave Murray the creeps."

Ben was silent. The millipede body of the parade, at the Ramananda's urging, began a low chant, like the distant droning of bees.

"Bernice told you," Ben said.

"Liddy and me and Murray. I don't think it was easy. It was bad times for Bernice, too. But it seemed to call for some explanation, beyond the fact that Liza Jane was nuts, which I never bought into. Now we know why she wanted to lie there. It was right where her will said to dig the grave."

The Ramananda's followers intensified their chant. The humming reverberated off the walls of the adobe temple and the Catholic church, a wavering aural mirror like the optical track along a reel of film. It made Ben want to slap at his neck.

A red BMW at the curb was muttering car alarm beeps, punctuated by a voice, mechanical and supercilious: "Please move away from the car." Ben turned from Jeff, stumbled into it, and the alarm shrieked into outraged whooping.

Jeff grinned. "Yuppie toys. I hate those things."

A furious man in a polo shirt ran down the street with his keys in his hand. Liddy and Zach threaded their way through the crowd and Zach ducked between legs to attach himself to Jeff's hand and watch the shrieking car. Ben left them there as the alarm shut off.

Jeff looked at Liddy over Zach's head. "Are you all right?"

"The band gives me a headache."

Zach took Liddy's hand in his free one. He had a candle but it had gone out, and he carried it upside down now. Liddy untangled it from their entwined fingers and stuck it in her purse. "I need to go home. It's time to get Zach in bed."

"It looks like the party's going to go on down here for quite a while."

"Let it," Liddy said. "I'm tired of them. I don't think I can stand any of them another minute. It's like the Barrymores in kindergarten."

"All right." Jeff wriggled a path through the parade, towing them half a block to Liza Jane's old brown Mercedes. He opened the back of the Mercedes for Zach while Liddy got behind the wheel.

"Where's your car?" Liddy asked him.

"I came with Bernice." Jeff slid into the front beside Liddy and tossed his candle on the floor.

"You don't have to come with us."

"Hush. Drive. I've seen enough of the show."

Liddy put the car in gear and eased it out into the street. Revelers were dancing down the center line.

At home, Liddy let the pugs out of the library and they surged around her feet. They looked worried, as if they were still counting each other.

Liddy pointed Zach at the stairs. "Go get ready, I'll be up in a minute." He nodded sleepily. "I talked to Alec a bit," Liddy told Jeff, watching Zach trudge upstairs. "Before we left. He's pretty unnerved but I saw him talking to Frank."

"He was distracting Frank from the Francie show for the public good."

"Poor Frank. Why did he marry that woman?"

"Lost his head. Or his something. Liza Jane didn't exactly tell him not to, but you could see she knew what would happen. Maybe she could have told him not to if they didn't have the history they did."

"Liza Jane had enough history to fill an encyclopedia," Liddy said wearily. "And it's all in my house now. I liked Frank then, though."

"Your house, huh?"

"Slip of the tongue. I'm going to bed. You go to bed. Bernice can let history in when it comes home."

1969

Liza Jane is sixty-one. Her hair is still red and she's still a knockout, but she's cautious about it now. She dresses as if she were forty-five, not twenty. She has a horror of looking like Mae West, undignified and ridiculous.

It's April, when the hills are still green, and Liza Jane, Frank, Bernice, and Little Liza have taken a picnic up to a camp in Rose Valley where there are tables and a mountain stream bubbling over rocks. The pugs are bouncing from rock to rock and any minute one them will fall in. The car always smells like wet dog going home. Liza Jane thinks Little Liza needs family outings.

Little Liza, who is eleven, is on Easter vacation, reading *The Lord of the Rings* while Liza Jane and Frank talk about the premiere of *Commando*. They're all going to L.A. for it tomorrow night.

"They're going to hate it," Frank says. He knows the movie's good, but it's his first big part and he's terrified it will all blow up in his face, that everyone will see him flop.

"They won't hate it," Liza Jane says.

"They may hate it," Bernice says, "but they won't hate it because it's no good." The movie is science fiction, about a future society of professional soldiers whose function is to fight everyone else's wars for them. It's ostensibly an action-adventure film, but the picture has a dark undertow. Given the climate of the times and the Vietnam War, it's going to be controversial. Frank Hill, the picture's star, spent two rebellious years in the Army, including a combat tour in Vietnam. The screenwriter, Mike Rosen, was blacklisted in an earlier political upheaval, an event which has left him residually controversial himself, since now no one wants to admit there was a blacklist; particularly not with Ronald Reagan, one of its chief perpetrators, as governor of California. The producers, who are getting a little nervous about it, want to change the title to *Space Commando*, and have been argued out of that with difficulty by Ben Zenovich, who is the director. Ben owed Mike that much.

Liza Jane looks at Frank, thinks he looks unraveled. If this picture's a hit, his agent's desk will be covered with scripts in a week and he'll be an overnight success. An overnight success is someone who busts their tail for years and finally gets a good role. Then the critics call him "talented newcomer Frank Hill."

"Let's take a walk." She gets up, drags Frank off the bench. If he doesn't do something, he'll go nuts. If this picture's a hit, he'll leave. Liza Jane knows that, but it's probably time.

They walk up the trail by the creek. Around a bend in the path is a waterfall tumbling into the stream in a cold spray of mist. The pugs bound along the bank, racing ahead of them, yapping at it.

Frank stands looking up at the falling water, head tilted back, young and rakish. The spray beads in his brown hair. He grins at Liza Jane with that quick smile she's always liked. He says, "I'm being a pig. I'm sorry." He's grateful to her and he knows he ought to be. He holds an arm out, and she leans against his shoulder, watching that sheet of living water. It's as beautiful and relentless as ice. The creek is snowmelt from the back side of Topa Topa.

"Ben called," Liza Jane says. "While you were in the shower."

"Why didn't you tell me?" Frank's indignant.

"Because he didn't call for you, hotshot." She's working with Ben again, next month. "He wants to know what I think about Algeria." Liza Jane makes a face, squinching her eyes up. Ben loves fancy locations and Liza Jane hates to leave home now.

"Did you melt the phone line?"

"Disintegrated it. But I'm going to Algeria. There's a part for you if you want it, but it's not big."

"Do you want me to take it?"

"Not for me," Liza Jane says.

There's a quick look of relief on his face. He kisses her, wondering for about the millionth time how much of a cad he is. She's old enough to be his grandmother—Frank's very careful not to put it that way to himself, though. There's a fine balance in their affair that comes from admitting that, but not saying it. It's not exactly a business proposition. Liza Jane doesn't look her age, and sure as hell doesn't act it. There are times when she can be absolutely juvenile. Going to bed with her isn't like going to bed with anybody's grandmother. But Hollywood is still conservative. If he stays much longer, if it gets to be too public, they'll both be sorry. Ben's already told him that.

"I don't think I should," Frank says.

"I don't think you should, either," Liza Jane says.

"Are you going to miss me?" Now he's irked that she's taking it so easily. He wonders if there have been any of them that she's missed.

"Dime a dozen." Liza Jane laughs at his outraged expression, looks at him affectionately now. "I will miss you. If I wasn't as old as I am, I would hang onto you. But I can't, and I'm not going to try until we are both ludicrous. There. Do you feel better?"

He feels like a sulky kindergarten child, annoyed because he can't have something he said he didn't want.

"Ben also says reaction to the previews looks good," Liza Jane tells him, and he remembers what it is that he does want, more than anything else. Maybe he's really going to have it. He feels precarious, as if you shouldn't want anything that badly.

The pugs are skipping from rock to rock again. One of them falls in, and Frank, who has boots on, fishes it out. He walks back to the picnic table, one hand holding Liza Jane's and a wet pug in the other. Bernice and Little Liza are packing up the picnic. Liza Jane shakes out the tablecloth, and Frank watches the three of them. The sun is starting to go down, cerise over the mountains, flashy as a poster. In its slanting light, Bernice looks much as she always has and not much different from the way she will later. Little Liza looks like her aunt. Frank thinks Little Liza knows that he's going, too. She's lived with Liza Jane for three years, long enough to know that there's no telling who will turn up in the audience at her school Christmas pageant. She's never tried to make a father of him.

Little Liza takes the wet pug and dries it off with a towel out of the station wagon; the rest of the dogs flow over the tailgate into the luggage space.

Liza Jane puts the tablecloth in the basket. Backlit by the sunset, she looks young, as young as the framed stills on the stairs. Frank thinks she knows that because she turns full to the ruthless light for a moment before she gets in the car.

In Los Angeles the next day, Liza Jane drops Little Liza off with a friend from school who lives in Bel Air, and goes by the studio for a wardrobe fitting. "As long as you're going to be down here," Ben says. He knows Liza Jane hates fittings and traps her when he can. Frank goes along with her, he's too restless to do anything else. Liza Jane puts him on a brown plaid sofa in the corner and gives him a mystery to read.

Liza Jane's prepared to do battle. She wanted Edith Head and she got Dane Endicott. Dane has blond, almost white hair, and a Malibu tan. He likes to 'interpret' costume. Ben must be out of his mind. Dane will take his turn-of-the-century tourists and turn them into visitors from Pluto.

"No shiny stuff," Liza Jane says the minute Dane walks into the room. "No plastic, no aluminum, no gold spray paint. This isn't *Barbarella.*"

"Dear lady," Dane says. He eyes Frank on the sofa. "And gentleman. Wait until you see what I have for you." He sticks his fingers between his teeth and whistles, and two female assistants trot out with a rolling rack full of clothes.

"Just a quick fitting today. And then we'll have you back for bit longer on Friday."

"We're going to Big Bear for the weekend," Liza Jane says repressively.

"I suppose we'll have to make do. You can alter them yourself in Algeria if they're all wrong." Dane whistles to himself, unpinning things, while Liza Jane glares at him.

"We have time before we leave," Frank says, his face still in the mystery. He's reading the end first.

"The studio's sending out a photographer," Dane says, "as

long as you're here. I promised I'd make you ravishing for him."

"A photographer?" Liza Jane is boiling now; Dane looks pleased with the result. Ben didn't say anything about a photographer, but he wouldn't. That's the publicity department. "What photographer?"

"*Modern Screen* maybe." Dane says. "I forget which one. They're all such rags."

But you're glad enough to get the publicity, Liza Jane thinks. She peels down to her underwear, stepping behind a screen for form's sake. One of Dane's girls drops a dress over her head. Liza Jane inspects it suspiciously, peering at the hemline, holding her arms out to look at the sleeves.

"What scene is this for?"

"The hotel dining room."

"Well-bred ladies didn't wear sequins on their luncheon dresses," Liza Jane says acidly.

Dane sucks his front teeth, a noise that Liza Jane hates. "Ben liked it."

"Ben knows as much about turn-of-the-century costume as the Rockettes." Liza Jane looks at Dane's assistants. "Take the sequins off."

"Maybe you should discuss that with me!" Dane snaps.

"I'll take them off in Algeria with my nail scissors," Liza Jane says, "as you suggested." Frank's still reading his book. He's gone back to the beginning now.

Dane rolls his eyes and begins putting pins in the dress. "Goodness," he says waspishly, "you're a bit bigger than your form. I imagine we'd better remeasure you."

"Be my guest," Liza Jane says.

"Lydia, go get her book." Lydia comes back with Liza Jane's size book and the photographer from *Modern Screen*. "We're just going to do a few measurements," Dane says, "and then Miss Sydney will be entirely at your disposal."

"No, we're not." Liza Jane locks eyes with Dane. "You are a pipsqueak and you're not as important a pipsqueak as you think you are."

A snort of amusement from Frank behind his book stiffens Dane's posture into brittle pleasantry. "Liza Jane's such a card," he says.

The photographer takes rolls of film of the costume fittings, eyeing Frank curiously. "How about one with Mr. Hill here?" he suggests.

"Mr. Hill is not in this picture," Liza Jane says.

"Oh, that's a mistake," Dane chirps. "You're so good together."

Liza Jane waits until the photographer leaves. Then she rips the dress she's wearing down the front. The basted seams give way. She hands it to Dane. "You wear it, dear," she says between her teeth. "It suits you better."

"You've been bad," Ben says to her in the limousine on the way to the premiere. *Commando* is opening at Grauman's Chinese, and search lights cut through the sky ahead of them. Little Liza sits beside them in a blue taffeta dress and black pumps with just a little heel, her first.

"I wouldn't wear a shroud made by that idiot. Have you any idea how asinine he'll make me look?"

"Dane's good," Ben says. "His style stands out."

Liza Jane folds her arms across her chest, not going to give an inch. She's too old to look farcical. The memory comes back, in acute clarity, of catching sight of herself in the hotel room mirror, naked, hair tumbled over her shoulders:

She looks fine until Frank steps into the frame behind her, the vitality of his body draining away the illusion of youth from hers. She twists away from the mirror, not wanting to see that, not just now. Frank catches her to him, manic a few hours from the premiere; starts to kiss her, lose himself in sex so he won't think about tonight. His body is so damn beautiful. Liza Jane watches the way his shoulders move, runs her foot down his calf, awed suddenly by so much beauty. When she was young, young men were just men. Now they are things of grace. She holds him as if he were some fleeting work of art.

In the limousine, he takes her hand, distracted from his own nerves by her pouting. "Nobody's going to make you look bad," he whispers. "You give 'em hell."

The driver pulls up in a long line of waiting limousines disgorging people. The press is there, *Variety* and the *Times* as well as the tabloids and movie magazines. They ambush the stars, sticking microphones in their faces, flashbulbs popping with the sound of water in hot oil, leaving blue-green images behind them. Mike Rosen gets out of the car in front of them in a tuxedo, face taut with nerves. But no one recognizes writers, it's Frank's face and Liza Jane's that draw the flashbulbs, leaving them blinded like jacklighted deer.

"If the picture's a success, will you make one together?"

"Is it true that you're married?"

"We are particularly good friends," Liza Jane says acidly. Little Liza grasps her gloved hand as if she is afraid they will ask her something horrible too.

"Frank Hill is going to be a major star," Ben says. "You'll see a lot of him from now on."

"Are the rumors about a wedding true?"

"Certainly." Liza Jane flashes them a big smile. "Ringo Starr and I got married last week."

Then they are through the gantlet of photographers and into

the theater. Ben is chortling, but Frank is too scared to laugh. The rest of his life is up there on the screen. He sits down next to Mike Rosen and they fidget until the lights go down.

Liza Jane feels a hard little knot of fury right under her breastbone. She thinks she knows where the press got the wedding rumor and she thinks about what she will do to Dane. If Ben finds out for sure, Ben will can him, but that isn't satisfactory enough. Dane has made her ridiculous, the only thing she fears in this life. Dane is young, too. It is almost as if there is a conspiracy of young men with their perfect bodies to make fools of older women. She looks at Frank. Frank isn't even thinking about it. He's watching himself on the screen with an anguish that Liza Jane knows well. She watched the premiere of *Anna Manning* that way, when she was young and hungry and didn't care who knew who her lovers were. Ben, on her other side, is intent on the screen, too, and on the murmurings of the sleek, extravagantly dressed crowd around him. Liza Jane feels isolated between them, as if she is the only one really living in her own body right now. It would be nice, she thinks, to be somewhere else and let her body, with its sagging breasts and arthritic knee, sit on the nubbly plush like a mannequin, uncaring.

XII
The Gordian Knot Approach

1988

Outside the kitchen, Jeff could barely stand on the veranda floor where it met the house without getting vertigo. The rest of it sloped precipitously and the tangle of buckled steps looked dangerous. He went out the front door instead and around the side of the house past the pond. The koi cruised in the moonlight like decorated submarines, lumbering and silent.

There was one missing. Jeff swore and set his sketchbook down, searching among the Japanese irises that edged the pool. He found it under the bamboo spout, the one with the Japanese flag on its head, already dried out, eyes milky, mouth agape.

He squatted by the pond, turning the fish over in his hands. "Stupid bastard, you did it yourself, didn't you?" Was that what happened when you got up your nerve to jump—you landed gasping in unbreathable air?

He heard a car pull into the drive, looked up and saw Alec Murray. What the hell, he thought. "Hey, Captain!"

Alec peered dubiously over the lavender border. He closed

his car door and stepped across. "What are you doing?" He looked suspiciously at the fish.

"Contemplating free will," Jeff said.

"Is that another earthquake casualty? I don't think I can handle another one, not even fish."

Jeff tried to imagine it being flung skyward by the tremor in the earth, turning end over end, amazed; scooped up by the deus ex machina. He shook his head. "No, they jump when they get upset. I should've netted the pond. You have to do it every time you put them in a new place, until they get used to it, or if you take them out of their old one to clean it. They can jump clear out. I guess the earthquake spooked them." He laid the fish down on the edge of the irises.

"That's your thought for the night?" Alec said. "Free will for fish?" His voice sounded taut, but not quite as ready to snap as it had been earlier.

"How do you suppose fish make up their minds?" Jeff asked him, contemplating it.

"Probably the same way you do," Alec said. "Allowing for the differences in equipment." He looked at Jeff as if he thought there might not be many.

Jeff forced a smile. "I've got cold feet, Captain. How do I know I won't land in the same place?"

"How do you know you'll get the chance to jump?" Alec crossed his arms.

"Staking out your turf, Captain?" Jeff inquired. "We could run around and see who can piss on the most trees and bark the loudest."

"I'm going in," Alec said. "Go bait someone who wants to fight with you."

"Actually, I thought maybe you did," Jeff said. "I'm sorry, man. Come on down to the cottage and I'll give you a drink."

Alec looked dubious, but Jeff stood up. He tucked the fish

under one arm, sketchbook under the other. "I want to bury this poor bastard anyway."

Alec shrugged and followed him. They took the brick path, skirting the hole where the ground had opened. The coffin had been carried to the back of the house and set decorously on the lower patio.

"This makes three," Jeff said, steering well clear of the gap in the earth. He still felt as if it might reach out and grab his ankles.

"Deaths?" Alec said. "You're counting a fish and a dog?"

"It's all part of the dance." Jeff opened the cottage door and switched on the light. "Funeral first. Drink afterward."

He went into the kitchen and rummaged in a wooden box by the back door while Alec looked around him. The orange cat sat on the lid of the stereo and squinted her eyes at him until Jeff reappeared with the fish and a trowel. She stuck her neck out snakewise, whiskers twitching.

"Ghoul," Jeff said, but she hopped down and followed them. "Put her in the bathroom, will you, man?" Jeff said. "If she sees where I put it, she'll try to dig it up again."

Alec scooped the cat up and looked for the bathroom. The front door banged behind Jeff. Alec edged the bathroom door open, pushed the cat in, and shut it. Beyond the bathroom he could see the studio, Jeff's dancing bronzes set right on their shelf again, cavorting in the moonlight. The sudden fierce wish that he knew how to make something came over him.

He heard the chink of the trowel on a rock and went out to find Jeff burying the koi beneath the Chinese lantern vine. Jeff patted the dirt down, dusted his hands and the trowel on his jeans. He opened the door again. "After you, Captain. If you wouldn't mind letting Madame out of the bathroom, I'll fix you a drink."

The drink proved to be bourbon, neat. Jeff shoved some magazines aside, found a place on the sofa, and sat. He seemed to be waiting for Alec to do the same. The bookcases behind him were still slightly askew, as if their joints had been loosened by the earthquake and their coherence was now achieved by careful balance, and force of will. Alec sank into an old leather armchair that he thought might be Jeff's usual spot. "Nice place," he commented.

"It's had its charm," Jeff said. "The studio is good. And Liza Jane was—" His eyes swam with tears, momentarily, unexpectedly. He wiped the back of his hand across them. "It's been a good place to live. Now—I don't know." He took a swallow out of his glass.

"I thought you had the cottage for life?"

"With Liddy living in the main house," Jeff said. "Christ."

"Maybe she won't move in."

"I'll tell you, Captain, I think I'll make you a bet. She'll move in. She doesn't know what the hell to do either."

"That scare you?"

"Damn straight." Jeff finished his drink and got up. He came back with the bottle.

"Jesus. Here, give me that." Alec poured his own glass full again. "What am I going to do with a million dollars?" He peered at Jeff as if he might be crazy enough to have the answer. "What do I do with the rest of my life now?"

"Fight for truth and justice?" Jeff suggested.

"Fuck you."

"What are you gonna do when they legalize that shit?" Jeff asked. "They'll have to. Right now you're contributing to the biggest boom in organized crime since Prohibition."

"Your political wisdom is a blessing. I'll pass your comments along."

"I'm just jealous," Jeff said. "At least you have a plan."

"It's got some bugs in it."

"Liza Jane used to say to be careful what you want, because you might get it," Jeff said moodily.

"Maybe it's just catching up with you now."

"Maybe so," Jeff said. "I suppose curses don't travel in a straight line."

"You think Liza Jane set you up?"

"Naw. I set myself up. I figured I was who I was, the last of the great hippie romantics, silly little shit. I wasn't cut out to get serious with life." He kicked off his sandals, tucked bare feet under him on the sofa, lotus fashion, cradled the glass between his palms.

"And now you're scared to death you've waited too long to try," Alec said.

"Maybe. I've been sending stuff to galleries. I actually make decent money. I figured that was what I was supposed to want."

"Horseshit," Alec said. He leaned back, an ankle crossed over the other knee. The top of the ankle holster just showed above his boot. Jeff thought he knew it. They contemplated each other for a while. "You want your old girlfriend," Alec said. "But she's got a kid. What about bank accounts and car repairs and Boy Scouts and just generally knocking off the asshole image and being a citizen? Do you want that?"

Jeff laughed suddenly. He threw his head back and pounded on his jeans-clad knee with a fist. "I've got you figured, Captain. You want to hear it? You're in the same boat. You've been racketing around, living out there on some edge because you like it. And saying it's because it's your job. Now you don't have any reason to do it anymore. Now you're going to have to be a citizen too."

"I believe in what I'm doing," Alec said stiffly. He looked as if that sounded pious even to himself.

"I believe in art," Jeff said. "If we didn't think what we were doing was worthwhile, we might as well pack it in. But if you've got the nerve to give me a speech about a drug-free America, I want to tape it. You do what you do because you get off on it.

And you kind of like the fact that women get off on it too. But now your mom wants you to quit and you don't know how to tell her you can't."

Alec's face snapped closed as if someone had put shutters up. "Thank you for sharing. It's been uncommonly nice of everyone to make sure that no matter what I do with my life from now on, it's going to be fucked."

Jeff raised a finger, guru-fashion. "Many of us can say this. Look, damn it, Liza Jane didn't set you up any more than she set me up. She gave a damn what happened to you. Why is it so important to you to ferret out why? She loved you. You don't get to tell her it didn't count because her reasons weren't good enough."

"Mm," Alec said. It was an indeterminate noise that might have meant anything from enlightenment to "Up yours."

The marmalade cat came in and looked at them, apparently weighing their merits. After careful consideration, she bunched her haunches and landed like a rock in Alec's lap. She waited to see what he might be going to do about that. When he didn't move, she curled up with her nose in his belt buckle, from which position she could comfortably knead his stomach.

The three of them sat in introspective silence for a long while, and then Jeff stood up abruptly. "Are you going to come and help?"

"Help what?"

"With the funeral. This has gone far enough when she can't have what the fish gets."

Alec watched with alarm as Jeff pulled on socks and laced up hiking boots. "Are you serious?" he demanded when it dawned on him what Jeff was talking about.

"Damn straight I am. Besides, I put an unembalmed dog in there."

Alec dislodged the cat and got up, taking note of how much

bourbon he'd had. He wondered if Jeff had been drinking until he got his nerve up. He hoped they hadn't had too much, they'd probably fall in the hole. His watch said two a.m.

Jeff switched the light off and Alec followed him out the door. It seemed like a damn fool thing to do, but it wasn't Alec's problem. He'd be glad to help dig. Maybe it would invalidate the will, take the whole thing out of his hands. Jeff headed down the walk toward the darkened house. The orange cat slipped along behind them.

Jeff edged around the hole, heading for the back of the house. "I'm going to take care of you," he told it. Alec fell in behind him.

They slipped up to the basement door, and Jeff beckoned Alec in after him. "You'd better wait here. I expect they're all in bed by now, but Sharon may be up casting a spell or something." He left Alec in the hall outside the screening room and headed for the stairs. The orange cat slid through the crack of the opened door and sat by Alec's feet She looked around her, ears swiveling like dwarf satellite dishes. She seemed to be along for the adventure, whatever it was going to be.

Jeff eased open the door to Liddy's room. Everyone else seemed to be asleep, no lights under anyone's doors in the hallway except the dim light in the bathroom at the far end. Liddy lay on her side, one knee drawn up, her arms in a death grip on her pillow and four pugs at her feet.

Jeff shook her shoulder and she batted at it. "Quit that. Damn it." She pushed at him and discovered that he wasn't a pug.

"It's me," Jeff whispered. "Ssshh."

"What are you doing here?"

"Nothing as crass as you're thinking. Something's got to be done about Liza Jane. Are you going to come with me and do it or do you want to be able to tell the cops you had no idea?"

Liddy looked up at him, trying to make her eyes focus. It was too dark to see more than an outline and the faint flicker of light on his pale hair, a dim aurora borealis above a dark t-shirt. "You'll wake everybody up," she whispered.

"The idea is not to," Jeff whispered back. "I figure we've got a good three hours before it starts to get light."

"You're really talking about burying her." Liddy sat up.

"It's the Gordian Knot approach," Jeff said. "You don't waste time trying to untangle all the legalities. You give 'em a good whack with a cleaver. I've always liked it."

She smelled bourbon, but he didn't seem to be drunk. She got up and put a robe on and a pair of athletic shoes. The pugs all hopped off the bed to follow her. Possible courses of action floated crazily one above the other until they coalesced and only one looked possible, the one that involved digging a grave. Action in its simplest form, straightforward, hands on a shovel, feeling the dry, sandy earth slide along the blade. Digging a hole. Anyone could dig a hole. When she'd been little, in Cincinnati, she'd tried to dig a hole to China.

She followed Jeff down the stairs. "Wait a minute."

She slipped into the kitchen and took Roberto Vincente's wilting roses from their vase. They went down the second flight to the basement, closing the door on the pugs.

"I brought the Captain," Jeff said in warning. "More muscle. Besides, I think he needs the job."

There were shovels in the toolshed. They each took one and went out to the oak grove with the cat, past the downed tree. The ground was soft where the earthquake had split it and they dug cautiously, like Victorian resurrection men, piling unearthed stones in a cairn by the hole. "Six feet deep," Jeff said. "Seven long." He lay down beside the hole and dug his heels into the ground. Upright, he drew a line a foot beyond that.

Liddy dug doggedly, telling herself that it was only a way to China, a passage not a hole, that somewhere Liza Jane would come out on the other side, admiring the scenery and the tile-roofed pagodas. Jeff and Alec were silent, and she looked curiously at the two of them. She suspected them of some weird form of male bonding that left them no longer at each other's throats but oddly allied on ground where she couldn't follow.

They had dug the rectangular dimensions of the grave, sides straight, sheer as a plumb line except for a gaping orifice where a rock that hung half into the grave's geometry had been pried out. The grave was nearly three feet deep now, and they stood in it, lifting the earth out with grunts and sharp exhalations of breath.

Alec's shovel clunked against a stone and they prised it out warily, but nothing else untoward had appeared since the film can that morning.

"What do you want to do with those rushes, man?" Jeff asked him, reminded of their existence. "We could put them back in. This seems to be where she wanted them."

"I don't know." Alec leaned on his shovel. "They're all I've got." He looked stubborn, hands clenched around the shovel handle.

"Of what?" Jeff asked.

"Of her. Of Liza 'Maybe-I'm-Your-Mommy' Jane. Maybe I want them."

"Maybe you do," Jeff said. "Maybe you're going to be a celebrated nut case, holed up in some musty room with horsehair sofas, running them through a projection loop over and over."

Alec glowered at him. He held onto the shovel.

"Jeff, shut up," Liddy said. "If those are anybody's, they're mine, and I don't care what he does with them. I give them to you," she said to Alec. "Liza Jane doesn't need them now, and I certainly don't. Bernice doesn't want them in the house. Take them. Just get them out of here."

"Fine," Jeff said. "Sure."

Liddy put her foot on her shovel and began to dig again. The can of film was an ants' nest. You didn't notice it until you felt them go up your sleeve. The thing had been exploring in the back of her head all night. She didn't want it in a hole in the ground outside her house, she wanted it in Pittsburgh. Liza Jane would have to be content with that. She must have known they'd find it when they dug the grave.

"Are you getting tired, Lid?" Jeff was at her shoulder, solicitous.

"No. Yes, but that's not why I snarled at you. Sorry."

"Sort of a heavy-duty evening," Jeff murmured. "We're nearly done."

"Is the City Council really going to let us get away with this?"

"This is a fine time to ask."

"I wouldn't be out here at three in the morning in my robe, digging my aunt's grave in the backyard if I was entirely sane," Liddy said.

"That may be the City Council's position," Jeff said. "That's why I thought there ought to be three of us. There's nothing shady about anything but the gravesite. We have a perfectly legal death certificate. I'm hoping the publicity attendant on digging her up again is more than Abbott and his cronies can stand. That would really put Ayala on the tabloid map."

"Ayala's a loony bin and always has been."

"There's a big difference between being the world capital of the Aquarian Cosmic Color Society or whatever, and being a place where they dig up dead celebrities."

Liddy eyed Jeff with curiosity. It was hard to see his face under the overhanging oaks. The moon came through them in splinters. Such decisiveness on his part was new to her, although the outrageousness of the idea was like him. She wondered what other metamorphoses had occurred while she wasn't around to watch him.

Jeff stuck his shovel in the ground again and they dug steadily, unearthing more stones as they went until there was a little pile of them and Liddy couldn't lift the dirt out of the grave anymore. They boosted her up and she sat on the edge while they finished, digging in a rhythmic pattern, one bent down while one stood up, then down and up in reverse and down and up like drilling rigs. She wondered how they were going to get the coffin in there.

"They use a winch or something in cemeteries," she said when they clambered out of the grave, using the hole where the rock had been for a foothold.

"Engineering is my department," Jeff said. "I have a secret plan. Yours is figuring out what to say over her. You can have a funeral later, but there ought to be something now."

"What?" Liddy demanded. "You can't just make it up. It's not like writing your own wedding vows."

"Readings from *The Prophet*," Jeff said with a hoot. "Liza Jane would love that."

"No, she wouldn't," Liddy said.

"Do either of you idiots own a prayer book?" Alec demanded.

They turned together to look at him. "Liza Jane had one," Liddy said. "I think. It might be in her room."

Alec went with Jeff toward the house, and Liddy sat on the edge of the open grave, swinging her feet above its depths. Jeff's cat left off lolling in the dry leaves and sat beside her, ears flat, looking at whatever it thought was down there.

After ten minutes Jeff came back with two coils of rope and a cordless drill. He set them down under a tree and disappeared again. He returned with Alec, staggering under the coffin, grunting and swearing. They set it beside the grave and Liddy watched silently while Jeff drilled holes and sank a pair of heavy hooks in the trunk of an oak on the other side. He knotted the rope in the handles at either end of the coffin and threw the opposite ends across a branch that overhung the grave and he and Alec each took one and looped them through the hooks. Liddy got up. The cat scampered into the leaves again. They could hear her faint rustle in the darkness.

"All right," Jeff said. "Pull steady." They hauled on the ropes and the coffin lifted, slowly and heavily like a barge, swaying inward until it hung over the grave.

"Let it down," Jeff said between his teeth. "Slowly."

Liddy bit her lip as they played the rope out again, creaking on the branch. They let it out inch by inch, feet braced against the weight. She couldn't bear it if they dropped it, or the branch broke, tumbling it to the bottom. Popping the latches. She didn't think she could stand that again.

Slowly it settled into the hole. She heard the heavy thump as it met the bottom. Jeff and Alec leaned against their tree, puffing. Jeff held his hand out and Alec smacked it with his.

After a moment Jeff scooted down into the grave and untied the ropes. He boosted himself back out, with one foot on the brass rail that edged the coffin. "We hope you're happy down there. You've been a hell of a nuisance." He knelt on the edge of the grave. "We love you."

Liddy dropped the roses in. "Should we have brought Donald Wain's flowers?"

"Screw Wain," Alec said. "Vincente's the one who sent her roses all those years." He pulled the prayer book out of his jacket pocket. "All quiet up at the house. There was a light in the hall bathroom, but I didn't hear any noises."

"Probably Sharon," Liddy said. "She's blind as a bat in dim light. She always leaves the lights on."

Alec produced a pen-sized flashlight and thumbed through

the prayer book.

"Do you know what you're looking for?" Jeff asked him.

"I went to Catholic school," Alec said. "If there's one thing I learned there, it's that there is a prayer for every conceivable occasion."

"Including burial in the back yard?"

"I don't know about that. This is an Episcopal prayer book. But there'll be something."

They stood silently while he looked for it. A coyote yipped up in the hills, and two more answered. The orange cat came out of the leaves again and sat on Jeff's feet.

"There are some psalms here," Alec said, thumbing through the burial service.

"Go for it," Jeff said.

"Lord, let me know mine end, and the number of my days; that I may be certified how long I have to live."

"My God, who would want to know that?"

"People who want to be forgiven at the last minute," Alec said. "For a man walketh in a vain shadow, and disquieteth himself in vain; he heapeth up riches, and cannot tell who shall gather them."

Liza Jane had been quite adamant about telling, Liddy reflected. But had she disquieted herself in vain? Liddy stared at the enigmatic coffin. And did she know the answer now? Alec had a good reading voice, like a deacon, but the psalm grew more macabrely appropriate by the moment. Alec looked as if that had occurred to him, but he didn't know how to quit in the middle. It ended with, "O spare me a little, that I may recover my strength, before I go hence and be no more seen."

Jeff suppressed a snort.

Alec leapt the intervening psalms with alacrity to light on something familiar. "I will lift up mine eyes unto the hills."

Above them the coyotes began to howl, a canine revival

meeting warbling in concert.

"The choir has arrived," Jeff said.

"The Lord shall preserve thy going out and thy coming in," Alec said, "from this time forevermore."

A faint light was beginning to wash across the sky now.

When he had finished, Alec skipped to the prayers at the end. "Most merciful Father, who hast been pleased to take unto thyself the soul of this thy servant Elizabeth, grant to us who are still in our pilgrimage and who walk as yet by faith…"

That was pretty uncertain footing, Liddy thought.

Alec closed the prayer book and the coyote chorus trailed away as if they had come from its pages, wreathing themselves up out of the old words.

"Fine job, parson." Jeff handed him a shovel. "Let's finish."

They began to pour dirt back into the hole. At first the clumps rattled on the coffin, and then as it filled, each shovelful became a muffled thump, a spatter of quiet rain. The cat stayed close, ears flat, distrusting the silence.

There seemed more dirt to put in than they had taken out, even leaving the stones to one side. A coffin took up room, a room below ground, working its slow way down to China. Liddy was crying quietly as they mounded the extra earth on top, and piled a cairn of stones at the head. Jeff put his arm around her. Whatever war was going on in the house was at peace for the moment. They might have reached a certain peace themselves, or at least a truce.

1971

Jeff is eleven and Liddy is thirteen and they have just met each other at a pottery class at the Art Center. Jeff is already in love with clay, although not yet with Liddy, and she's invited him to watch the Fourth of July parade with them and see the fireworks from the bell tower afterward. He sits in one of Liza Jane's folding chairs to sketch the floats and the costumed riders as they go by: senoritas in flounced red satin skirts spread out like blankets over their horses' white rumps, vaqueros on big silver-mounted saddles, fancy-dress Western riders with fringed chaps and bolo ties. A little boy on a Shetland pony holds an American flag on a pole. On the wall in front of the park the hippies are watching, feet dangling, dressed in their own festival attire, an explosion of long hair, fringe, beads, and feathers. One of them has green peace symbols painted on both feet, and they have draped the wall with a banner that reads: *U.S. OUT OF VIET NAM.* The riders glare at them.

In the evening Jeff and Liddy help Bernice make sandwiches for the people playing low-stakes poker in the kitchen until it's dark enough for fireworks. Jeff recognizes Frank Hill and Theresa Tate, as well as the rector of St. Anne's where his mother drops him off every week for Sunday School. Liddy tells him the beaky-nosed man is Ben Zenovich, who's a director. Roberto Vincente's birthday roses from a few days ago are in a vase on the bar. Liddy tells him about those too. Jeff is impressed by the Old Spanish grandeur of Liza Jane's house and the fact that Liddy has a horse, but what he envies is the fact that Liza Jane and Liddy so clearly belong to each other. Liddy tells him that Liza Jane says if she learns all the rules she'll give her a ten-dollar stake for the next game and she can play.

Adult conversation flows over and around them. For the last half hour Frank Hill and Ben Zenovich have been arguing over politics. Frank is a spokesman for Vietnam Veterans Against the War.

"Already I had the FBI looking for Phil," Ben says. Liddy whispers that Phil is the stepson of a short-lived marriage; no one knows where he is since he got an induction notice from the draft board. "They came to my damn office. I'm allergic to the FBI."

"I'm allergic to this war," Frank says.

"We didn't have enough of this twenty years ago?" Ben asks. "You aren't going to change anything except maybe your box office."

"Deal, dammit," Liza Jane says.

The rector of St. Anne's lays out the cards and the ante. "Stud. The movement needs Frank's visibility."

"Frank's visibility is what I'm worried about."

"Let his agent worry about it," Liza Jane says. "A dollar."

A clatter of chips follows, calling her bet.

"I'm with Frank," Liza Jane says. "You've got to have some principles."

"Define principles," Ben growls. He folds his hand.

Another round of cards. Theresa, with the high hand this time, puts another dollar in the pot. Liddy and Jeff watch the cards, trying to figure out what might be facing downward or still in the pack. That's the secret, Liddy says Frank has told her, to keep an eye on what's missing.

"Raise." Frank puts a five-dollar chip in.

Ben pushes his chair back. He peers out the glass doors to the darkening veranda. "Where are the damn fireworks?"

"It's not dark enough yet," Liza Jane says.

"It's plenty dark." Ben gets another beer from the refrigerator. He looks at Frank and shakes his head. "You'll learn."

XIII
Motion Picture Zombies

1988

The coyotes had started again, but you could hardly hear them behind the bathroom door. Liza Jane's bathrooms were always luxurious, more like goddamn hotel spas, Ben thought. This one had a tub with a Jacuzzi in it, and a professional make-up mirror that would give sunlight or artificial, even fluorescent, so you could compensate for the way fluorescent light always made everyone look like they had food poisoning.

Ben sat down on the emerald green edge of the Jacuzzi and put the gun beside him. If Murray thought taking the clip out and stuffing it in the clothes chest was going to deter anyone who wanted to find it he must be stupid. Funny, its being there when he wanted it. Ben had placed a little bet with himself, the kind you make when you're a kid: if it's there, I'll do it. Maybe Murray hadn't worn it to the street fair, maybe he was planning to get laid and thought it would put her off; if it was Francie Allen, nobody in his right mind would leave a loaded gun around. But it was funny its being there, its belonging to Murray. History had a way of catching up. Same old whore, endlessly giving birth to dead babies. If Mike Rosen thought he could write some life back into his, he was going to find out different. They were all dead, deader than McCarthy, deader than Ben's old man. If you stuck around Hollywood for very long, you ended up dead, night of the fucking motion picture zombies, feeding on the new and clueless. Mike was already dead, he wasn't going to claw his way back out of the ground with a script for a shovel. Frank too. If Frank hadn't been dead when Francie got hold of him, he was now, sucked dry.

Ben was dead too, but he knew it and the others didn't. Once you knew you were dead, you started to rot, and then you couldn't stand the smell. As long as you didn't know, as long as you could keep breathing and tell yourself that your heart was pure, then the zombies wouldn't get you. You were forever young. But once you had that awful knowledge, you looked in the mirror and saw truth. And then it didn't matter whether anyone else knew or not, because all the pieces of yourself were gone, and in their place was something you couldn't look at.

Ben glanced at his watch. It was late, maybe light soon. He'd spent enough time viewing history from the wrong end. Somebody was likely to have to get up and pee, even Murray maybe. He wanted Murray here, Murray would know what to do. But not till afterward. He stood up and stepped into the tub. The gun felt awkward, like a tool he wasn't used to using. It didn't matter, though, he couldn't miss. He put it to his temple and pulled the trigger, spinning himself backward to where the zombies were.

The coyotes stopped again, this time blotted out by the noise of the shot. The bang split the air around them. Jeff and Alec and Liddy stared at each other, caught in terrified recognition, and ran for the house.

"Omigod! Omigod!"

Sharon was screaming. Liddy pushed her way through the people crowding the upstairs hall. Bernice had snatched Zach and was holding him to her, away from the bathroom door.

"I called the ambulance," Harry said as Alec shouldered through. "He's still breathing. Don't move him if you don't know what you're doing."

Alec took in the crumpled form splayed in the bathtub, the spattered blood and worse things. How could someone have blown a hole in his head and still be breathing? The gun was in the tub with him. It had chipped the emerald porcelain as it fell. Alec could hear in his head the noise it had made, the hollow clatter, aftermath to the gunshot. "No, I don't know what I'm doing," he said.

They could hear sirens wailing up Del Norte. Frank turned abruptly and went downstairs to let them in.

Theresa hobbled to Liddy. "Oh, my dear." She put one arm around her, balancing herself on her crutch with the other. "In the bathroom." She sniffled. "So it wouldn't make a mess." She started to cry.

"Out of the way, folks," Jeff said. The paramedics ran up the stairs with a stretcher and canvas bags heavy with equipment, radios crackling. "Christ!" one of them said. "All right, folks, clear back, get back."

Everyone stood dutifully in the hall, staring, or trying not to stare, trying not to hear the sounds coming from the bathroom. Liddy took Zach from Bernice and held him to her.

"What happened, Mama?"

"He had an accident, honey. With a gun." What made a man put a gun to his own head? She stood bewildered between Bernice and Theresa. Sharon had grown quiet and huddled near them too.

The paramedics came out of the bathroom with Ben on a stretcher. One of them carried an IV above her head, the tube leading to his arm. Ben's face was ashen, gray and skeletal as old bones. A gauze pad covered his temple.

"Someone ought to go to the hospital," Frank said. He looked terrified that they would decide it should be him.

"I'm going," Liddy said. "Honey, can you stay with Bernice?"

Zach nodded. It was exciting but not too worrisome. No one had let him in the bathroom.

Liddy went into her own room and pulled on jeans and a shirt.

Alec had come out of the bathroom and was locking the door with the key that always stayed in the lock. He handed it to Bernice. "Give this to the cops when they get here."

"Cops?"

"If you didn't call them, the paramedics did. They'll have to come."

"Of course they will," Bernice said. "I wasn't thinking."

Harry groaned. "I've got to call Steve Bowman. Oh, Christ, what did he do a thing like that for?" He disappeared into his room.

"Come on," Alec said to Liddy. "I'll drive you."

"I'm coming too," Jeff said. He stopped to whisper in Bernice's ear, and then followed them, taking the steps two at a time. He caught up to them at the car. "I told Bernice what we'd been up to. I don't want the cops investigating body-snatching when she notices the coffin's gone."

Liddy was silent, expressionless, tears rolling from blank eyes. As the car was going down the hill, she asked Alec, "Is he going to die? A wound like that. What if he lives?"

"I don't know," Alec said tightly. "Why are you asking me? I'm not a doctor."

"Go straight on through to the highway. I guess I thought maybe you'd—that you'd seen things like that before."

"What the hell would it matter? If I shot someone, I wouldn't know—I wouldn't know what I'd done. I just make the mess," he said furiously. "I don't clean it up."

"Easy, man," Jeff said.

"Jesus, he used my gun!" Alec stopped at the intersection, and asked impatiently, "Where do I go?"

"Turn right," Liddy said. The siren wailed ahead of them. It cut off as the ambulance swung into the hospital's emergency entrance. Ben was already inside when Alec pulled up after them.

They went in and stopped just inside the ER. Someone had yanked a curtain around the cubicle where they had taken Ben. There were a lot of people behind it. In a moment they came out again, wheeling a gurney, fast, through the double doors at the other end. The speakers on the wall squawked requests for doctors whose names Liddy couldn't quite understand. Wineglass, one sounded like, and Lob.

A nurse came toward them. "Can I help you?"

"We're with—" Liddy gestured toward the doors where the gurney had gone. "We came—"

"Are you the family?"

"No, he doesn't— He's staying with us. At my aunt's house, I mean. At my house."

"I see. Well, you better give me what information you can. His name?"

"Ben— Benjamin Zenovich."

"Age?"

"I don't know. Sixty maybe?" She looked for confirmation at Jeff, who shrugged.

"Next of kin?"

"I don't know. There's a cousin, I think."

"You can wait out there if you want to," the nurse said.

They sat in the row of plastic chairs opposite the front desk. The chairs were bolted together and alternated colors, turquoise and faded flamingo. There was no one else around. The Ayala hospital was little and the emergency room didn't see much action.

"Is this place okay?" Alec asked. "I mean is it—?"

"Staffed by rejects from the city?" Jeff asked. "Nah, it's okay. Most of the staff are local folks who've grown up here. It's not fancy. You go to Ventura for CAT scans and things like that."

Alec put his head in his hands. "Jesus, what made him?"

"Who saw him last?" Liddy asked.

"I saw him at the fair," Jeff said. "Just before we came home. He seemed okay. I mean he didn't act like he was going to follow us back and shoot himself."

"What did you talk about?"

"Not much. The topics of the day. Was Francie going to screw the bandleader in the street. Your parentage." He glanced at Alec. "I told him I was worried the paparazzi were going to get hold of that can of film and the abortion story."

Alec lifted his head. "You told him about that?"

"Sure. He loved her like the rest of us. I thought he could help keep the press off."

"Oh, fuck."

Jeff looked at Alec suspiciously. "Spill it, Captain. Why shouldn't I have told him?"

"Because he was the goddamn father."

Comprehension set in, and Jeff slumped in his chair. "Shit."

"How do you know?" Liddy said. "Did he tell you?"

"God, no. But he told me he had been having an affair with Liza Jane when Carolyn got pregnant and she talked him into giving Carolyn leave. And that was while they were shooting *Glory*

Days. Theresa Tate said so too. It had to have been. *Glory Days* came out in early '53, the year I was born."

"Are you sure?" Liddy asked.

"I'm the movie freak, remember?" Alec said bitterly.

"All right, but I still don't follow you."

"*Glory Days* is the movie they put into production right after *Richard Plantagenet* was killed. Right after Ben killed *Richard Plantagenet.* Right after she aborted his kid to finish the movie."

"Oh, my God, poor Ben." Her eyes filled again.

"Poor Liza Jane."

Jeff looked at the floor. "I suppose he was bound to find out. But I wish to hell it hadn't been from me."

The double doors swung open again and a doctor came through them, pulling off his mask. "I'm Dr. Loeb. He's holding on, but we're transferring him to Ventura; they have a neurosurgeon there. Are you the family?"

Liddy explained again. "Is he going to be all right?"

"Nobody with a bullet in their brain is all right. He's not responsive, but there are no abnormal reflexes and his pupils aren't fixed. The neurosurgeon can give you a better picture than I can."

They heard the siren wailing away again into the early morning, too early to be inhabited, the streetlights still on.

"Should we go down there?" Liddy asked him.

"I wouldn't. I'd go home and call his next of kin. I'll give your number to the neurosurgeon and ask him to call you."

Liddy scribbled it down and gave it to him. A faint breath of dawn blew across the room as the outer doors whooshed open in front of a police officer. He was young, probably one of two on the Ayala night shift.

"Ms. Novak?"

Liddy nodded.

"And Mr. Murray?" He looked from Jeff to Alec.

"And Mr. Austin," Jeff said. "Sit down." He pointed to a turquoise chair.

"I need to ask a few questions," the cop said.

The doctor faded backward tactfully. "The desk will page me if you need me."

The cop took out his notebook. "None of you are the folks who found the body?"

They shook their heads.

"That would be Ms. Bernice Lewis," he said, consulting his notes. "But he used your gun." He looked at Alec. "Can you tell me why you were in possession of a weapon?"

Alec handed him his I.D. and waited while the cop read it. "Can you tell me why he knew you had the weapon?" The cop was impressed, but he had his questions to ask.

"I mentioned it to him like a damn fool," Alec muttered.

"Under what circumstances?"

"I don't know exactly. Something to do with just talking to him about my job."

The cop wrote that down. "Did he appear agitated? Or unduly interested in the weapon?"

"Not in the least," Alec said. He was unduly agitated about Mike Rosen's script. No point in mentioning that.

"And when was that exactly?"

"Wednesday morning? Yeah."

"And when was the last time you saw the weapon?"

Jeff and Liddy watched, interested to see how Alec moved into the interchange of evidence-taking. He and the cop established that he had last seen the gun on the previous evening, when he had checked on its presence in the closet, that he hadn't been wearing it because it was too conspicuous in what he called a "social situation." The young cop grinned back at that. Alec knew where he was with this, more comfortable than with the reality of which it was the shorthand shadow. There was distance in the routine, in the familiarity of the exchange. Only when they came to the question of Why? did he falter, slip toward the stumbling answers that regular people gave when questioned by the police.

"I don't know," Alec said. He seemed to be trying hard to keep sounding like a cop. "I saw no evidence of prior intent. No signs of disturbance."

"Hey, man," Jeff said gently, interrupting for the first time, "who knows why people shoot themselves? Who knows what the soul holds?"

The cop ignored him. "What about you, ma'am?"

"No," Liddy said. "I don't know either."

The cop stood up. "Well, thank you for helping, folks. We may be back in touch. I'm afraid we'll have to impound your weapon, sir, but I'll let you know when you can have it back."

Alec nodded. Maybe he would want it by then.

"What I want to know," Jeff said, "is what the hell does 'no abnormal reflexes' mean? Doctors talk in secret doctor code. What's a normal reflex for someone who's got a bullet in his head? And isn't conscious? I'm going down there."

Liddy slumped against him in relief. "Would you? Oh, God, thank you. I have to go home and try to find someone to call. And someone ought to go, no matter what that doctor says; what does he think we are?"

"Befuddled civilians," Jeff said. "Not too far off the mark, but I'm going to go get in their faces."

They went out into the thin gray-pink light, pooling bloodshot over Topa Topa. There was something anatomical in its coloring that was not lost on any of them, but all three suppressed the urge to mention it.

The police had finished at the house by the time they got there. Everyone was in the kitchen drinking coffee and awaiting further news. Bernice met Liddy, Jeff, and Alec at the door.

"Come upstairs." Her iron gray plait bobbed against an old chenille bathrobe. Climbing up behind her, they could see blood on its hem. She popped into her room and popped back out again, clutching the can of film with both hands as if it might leap out of them and roll down the hallway. "Here." She shoved it at Alec. "He had it in the bathroom with him."

"He what?"

"I saw it the minute I went in there," Bernice said. "So I took it out. That's nobody's business."

"That's tampering with evidence," Alec said.

Bernice ignored that. "How did he get hold of it? You weren't so foolish as to give it to him?"

"He found out about it," Jeff said. "From me, I'm afraid."

Alec said, "He took it when he took the gun." He inspected the can, visibly abandoning the notion of handing it over to the cops. "Did you at least clean it?"

"Well, of course I did. Is this going to make trouble?" Bernice demanded. "I've had all the trouble I'm going to stand for. This is Liza Jane's private business."

Liza Jane's, not Ben's. Well, it wouldn't be, not to Bernice.

"I'll take care of it," Alec said. "There's no question what happened, the cops don't need to ferret out why."

"Just get rid of it," Bernice said. "I will not have this splashed all over the media. How could he do a thing like that?"

"Too much knowledge," Jeff said. "He was the father."

"I'm perfectly well aware of that," Bernice snapped. "He has no right to look for absolution with a gun and publicly eviscerate Liza Jane in the process."

"I don't think it was absolution, you know," Jeff said. He laid a hand on Liddy's shoulder. "I'm going on down. See if you can keep the tabs at bay. Make sure Harry called Bowman."

He went downstairs to the kitchen and then out into the morning again, balancing a bagel and a cup of coffee. He coaxed the Triumph into action, decided there was enough gas in it to get there and back, and headed toward the highway. The morning air howling around his head began to wake him up as he neared the coast.

The hospital in Ventura was bigger, the parking lot inhabited even at this hour. Jeff wandered through the lobby, past a family sitting glumly on pale blue couches, and asked a woman at the Information desk for Neuro-Intensive Care.

"Sixth Floor," she said. "But you can't go in there right now. Visiting hours start at ten."

"I want to talk to the doctor," Jeff said. "They brought my uncle in. He shot himself. His name's Zenovich."

"Oh, dear." She consulted her computer. "Dr. Cameron is on call. Go up to the nurses' station and ask. Maybe they'll let you stay until there's some news. But you'll have to follow instructions exactly." She looked at Jeff as if she suspected that aberrant tendencies might run in the family.

Dr. Cameron was with the patient now, the nurses upstairs said. She would speak with him as soon as possible. Was there anything he would like? Some coffee?

"Can I go to sleep?"

"Of course." They showed him to the NICU waiting room, gave him a blanket and a pillow. He sprawled on a couch and passed out. He awoke to find Dr. Cameron bending over him. Or at least it was another person in a mask and a cloth hat like a shower cap. He assumed it was she.

"You're Mr. Zenovich's nephew?" She inspected Jeff with some suspicion. "The paperwork said there was no next of kin available."

"I just got here," Jeff said. "He shot himself in a friend's house," he offered. "His friends need to know how he's doing."

Dr. Cameron pulled off her mask and shower cap, revealing a dark bun and a sympathetic expression. "Well, we usually don't require the family to produce I.D. Is someone trying to locate the rest of the relatives?"

"Absolutely." Jeff hoped Liddy was having some luck, imagined her communing with a hysterical great-aunt who still didn't speak much English.

Dr. Cameron sat down beside him. "What can I tell you?"

"How is he?"

"He's not responsive. But there are some good signs."

"What's a good sign?"

"His pupils are not dilated and fixed. That's a good sign. The bullet appears to have destroyed the bony matter, but not done excessive damage to the brain matter."

"Can you translate that?" Jeff asked. "What's excessive?"

Dr. Cameron cocked her head at him. "Enough to kill you outright. Do you want the details? They're rather graphic."

"He made movies," Jeff said. "He makes movies. We're good at pictures."

"Very well. The muzzle of the gun was aimed at the temple, but pointing considerably upward. Perhaps he flinched at the last moment. They do sometimes. The bullet appears to have slid on the inner surface of the skull and is lodged in the frontal lobe. He managed not to hit any major arteries. He was very lucky."

"Depends on how much he wanted to kill himself, I suppose," Jeff murmured. "What happens now?"

"There is considerable edema caused by the trauma. Swelling. And there isn't any room inside your skull for your brain to swell. We've started him on Decadron to reduce the edema. Another danger is hemorrhage. And of course, infection."

"When do you try to get the bullet out?"

"We don't. Mr. Zenovich is going to have that bullet for the rest of his life, however long that may prove to be. I'm sorry to be so blunt, but you have to understand that the brain is an extremely delicate mechanism and we are much more likely to kill him by trying to get the bullet out than by leaving it there." She looked as if she had made this explanation before, to people who didn't believe it. If there was a bullet stuck somewhere, then you got it out—what kind of doctor left people walking around with slugs in their heads? "Perhaps you could explain that to the rest of the, um, relatives," she said. "Families can find that a difficult idea to deal with."

"I'll try," Jeff said. "Can I see him?"

Dr. Cameron stood up. "I'm afraid 'nephews' don't qualify. Not in the NICU. And in any case," she offered, "he's not conscious." She departed briskly, her flat-soled shoes making a businesslike sound in the empty corridor. She got into an elevator.

Jeff stretched and peered up and down the corridor. The door to the NICU, handily identified and marked NO VISITORS, was to his left. Outside, a motherly nurse with the patient suspicion of a kindergarten teacher peered back at him. Jeff put his hands in his pockets and approached her penitently. "Would it be an awful nuisance if you let me in to see my uncle for just a few minutes? Dr. Cameron said I could if it doesn't disrupt your routine."

"Not at this hour."

"I know," Jeff said. "Could you make an exception? He tried to kill himself, shot himself in the head. My aunt is just crazy, she's at home hysterical, the doctor gave her some sedative, but you can imagine what she's going through. It would help if I could tell her I saw him. Just for a minute."

The nurse sighed but her expression softened. "People don't realize what they do to other people with their foolishness. Just for a minute," she said.

The NICU was eerily like the set of a science fiction movie, circular and filled with unfathomable equipment. At least Liza Jane hadn't had to be here, Jeff thought, tied to a lot of cold blue blinking lights and braindead anyway. What about Ben? Would he stay like this, alive and like this? He hadn't asked the doctor that.

Stupid not to have asked that. Ben's face was still skeletal, as if he had got halfway there, but his color was better. There were tubes in his arms and nose, monitors banked around him, tracing lines Jeff couldn't decipher. The light was dim and the nurse at the inner station in the center of the room moved with a hushed economy, as if each sudden move might create shock waves that could penetrate the patients' stillness. Jeff found himself moving the same way. Too much energy here might do unseen damage, disrupt the fragile electrical fields of the mind.

"Will he wake up?" he whispered to the nurse.

"Sometimes they do," she said. "Honey, what you gotta do is pray. I've seen 'em wake up and walk out of here. But I can't tell you. You go on now and tell his wife you saw him. That's all we can tell you for this morning." She moved quietly through the aquarium-like stillness to the door, motioning him ahead of her.

All we can tell you for this morning. Jeff repeated it like a mantra, going down in the elevator, walking through the salt air to the Triumph. What did it mean? All we will tell you? All we know for certain? The universe is chaotic and we never know anything? Jeff thought he might opt for the latter if he were a doctor. But was it enough to take back with him, enough to take back and give to Liddy? He wanted to give her something solid, the definitive answer, because it might be an answer about them, too. He wasn't quite certain why he thought that, only that the circularity of the universe, spiraling so regularly in its chaos, back but not quite identically to each starting point, was giving him the creeps this morning.

He stopped the Triumph at a Dunkin' Donuts and went in and drank black coffee and ate chocolate glazed donuts, not available in Bernice's kitchen, while he thought.

A meter reader for the city occupied the next stool. "Gonna be hot today," he said when he had finished his paper.

"Yep," Jeff said to his donuts, disinclined to chat.

"I hate when it's hot," the girl behind the counter said. "We don't have air conditioning. Everything feels, like, sticky. I swear it's all this sugar."

"It's the dogs I hate," the meter reader said. "Hot weather and these Santa Ana winds, they get feistier. Some yards, I just won't go in 'em.

"What do you do? When you can't go in?"

"We just guess." The meter reader got up from the stool and picked up his clipboard.

"Can't even trust 'em to read your gas right," the girl said as he left.

"There are no true gauges," Jeff told her solemnly. He paid for a couple more donuts to take in the car and got in again, cheered by happenstance philosophy. No true gauges. And even if the gauges were true, it wouldn't matter because the meter reader wasn't reading them. Which meant there wasn't much point in spending your time trying to measure things. He pulled onto the freeway and hit the gas.

Liza Jane had endless phone books, five-by-eight personal directories, full of crossings-out and interlinings. She hadn't liked rotary files. They had seemed to her impersonal, although she was quick enough to cross names out of the directories. Liddy thought it might be because that way they were only crossed out, never completely gone. Not dead or unforgiven, the way a discarded card from the rotary file was.

Liddy flipped through what looked like the most recent one and wondered how Jeff would do at the hospital. Jeff had never been the type to get in anyone's face, his stated aim this morning.

Go with the flow had been Jeff's credo. But there was that peculiar sense of metamorphosis. She couldn't quite bring herself to think of Jeff as a butterfly. A luna moth, perhaps, unexpected and plastered across her window.

She had taken Zach to camp that morning, refusing to delegate that, wondering what phobias and psychoses he was likely to have as a result of this week. It was hard to tell how much was real to Zach, how much simply an unfolding movie, played inside his head. Liddy's memories of being six had that surreal quality, snatches of adult conversation remembered like lines from a play, circumstances surrounding them forgotten or never understood. Someone's house on a beach somewhere, with sea anemones. Sleeping in her parents' room—to make space for a guest?—hearing her father say in the darkness, "Bob isn't coping with the divorce." Who was Bob? She remembered him no more than where the beach was, but had retained the memory that he couldn't cope with his divorce.

There were no Zenoviches in the Z's but Ben. His cousin (or was it his father's cousin?) might have a different last name. If she had ever heard Ben talk about it, it was gone into the place where the sea anemones lived. She dialed his home telephone and got the housekeeper.

When Jeff came home, she was still on the phone, soothing the housekeeper, trying to impress on her the unwisdom of telling her first-person account to the tabloids. She had got the number of a cousin in Westwood. The names of two ex-wives had seeped into her memory too. They had been short-lived marriages, she recalled, and childless. Liddy remembered going to one of the weddings. Her name had been Dorothy. Would it still be Zenovich? And would Dorothy want to know that Ben had tried to kill himself? Let the cousin decide. Ben saw the cousin regularly, the housekeeper said. Liddy thought regularly might mean Passover and Rosh Hashanah, but that would do.

She hung up the telephone. Jeff knelt down by her chair. "How is he?" she asked him.

"He's still there. He seems to have flubbed it. But I think he could still die of other stuff, infection or bleeding. I scammed that out of a nice doctor. And I saw him for a minute. His color's better. They've been feeding him oxygen. Did you have any luck?"

Liddy looked dispiritedly at her notepad. "Elise Feldman. Some kind of cousin."

"Are you going to call her?"

"I have to." Liddy looked at the phone without moving.

Jeff remembered her aversion to making phone calls to strangers. Elise Feldman would be as strange as you could get. "Here. Get up. Let me do it."

"It ought to be me."

"You ought to be in bed. Anyway, I just told the doctor I was his nephew."

"You haven't had any sleep either." Liddy longed to crawl into bed and leave this to Jeff. "I can't ask you to do this."

She was sitting in a swivel chair. Jeff pulled it back from the desk and turned it around. "You aren't asking me."

"I just don't feel like I ought to impose on you." The stubbornness of sleep deprivation found another hurdle and laid it neatly in the path between her and bed.

"Oh, get up," Jeff said. "Go to bed, I'll break the news to Cousin Elise." He pulled her bodily out of the chair and propelled her toward the door. "Where's Murray?"

"I don't know." Liddy yawned. "He took the film. I'll look for him." She didn't, though. She plodded up the stairs and fell onto the bed.

She woke slowly, clawing her way up through sleep. It didn't feel as if it had been very long, but it must have been. The clock by the bed said noon. Steve Bowman was standing in the doorway, glaring at Jeff, who was standing just inside, glaring back and blocking his way.

"Rick Donald Osborne's here," Steve said. "Donahue's people didn't make it, but Osborne's hot. He's syndicated out of L.A., all over the country."

"Popularly known as Dick Donald," Jeff said. "He fucks anything that will stand still—production assistants, guests of either sex. You might want to lock up the pugs."

"Goddamn it," Steve said. "I don't need this. I got hired to do a job, keep you people in a good light with the media. I get Osborne out here—"

"He's a sleazeball," Jeff said.

"You want him to get hold of what Zenovich did last night and run with it?" Steve snarled. "He will, too, if he thinks he's being jerked around. He's high-powered. We need him to give this the right spin, keep the ball in our court."

Liddy got off the bed. "I'll talk to him. Who else does he want to see?"

"Murray," Steve said. He looked warily over his shoulder. "You might have a chat with Murray first, just to get him prepared. Then see Osborne. And do us all a favor, okay, babe? Make nice. Put on a nice dress."

"Listen—" Jeff said.

"Quit it, Jeff," Liddy said. "I can talk to him. If we give him the funeral, maybe we can outflank the City Council."

"What funeral?" Steve demanded. "I thought we were talking Forest Lawn, maybe a cremation? If you people don't keep me posted, how am I going to strategize for you? Zenovich— Christ!"

"You wanted Ben to notify you first?" Jeff asked.

"I called the paper this morning," Liddy said to Jeff. "And the *L.A. Times*. I put the notice in. I got Noel Ballinger from St. Anne's. Monday at two."

"Good."

"You're going to do it?" Steve said furiously.

"We did it," Liddy said, taking some satisfaction in the statement. "Last night. Now get out of here so I can dress." She pushed them both out the door.

Steve had apparently rallied by the time she came downstairs, after cornering Alec in his room and summoning him to his turn with Rick Donald Osborne. Steve was keeping Osborne entertained in the library, which was even fuller of flowers than before and would probably have killed an asthmatic. Osborne smiled and patted the sofa next to him. His tape crew were set up and ready to roll.

"I understand there's been a further tragedy," he said sympathetically, and Liddy thought he was going to take her hands. She drew them further into her lap. Osborne had the kind of fat, pink, inflated looking face that she had always associated with television evangelists. She thought he was going to offer to pray with her.

"We're agreed that that's not appropriate to discuss this afternoon," Steve said reassuringly. "But Rick Donald likes to have full background."

I'll bet he does, Liddy thought. But there wasn't any way to keep it from the press. The local paper read the police reports. That's all it would take. Steve had probably been fielding calls all morning. So all you could do was feed the sharks a bite or two of what you could spare, and hope they wouldn't go for vital organs. "Well, we're really here to talk about Liza Jane, aren't we?" she said with a smile.

"We are indeed." Osborne faced the camera. "A famous lady is dead. She left behind her a legacy of surprise and drama, a startling request, and, in the case of one player in this amazing story, unexpected wealth. He'll join us in a moment, but right now I'm talking with Elizabeth Novak, namesake of Elizabeth Sidney, and executor of her very unusual will. And how are you this morning?"

"Well, it's been difficult." Liddy gave him her best smile.

"Ugh. I feel like I ought to take you off and wash you," Jeff said. "That was disgusting."

"I thought I did pretty well," Liddy said. "I had him sympathizing over my difficult decision about the funeral, and he thought he'd got it out of me all on his own. I think Steve's still in shock."

"He's got Murray in his clutches now," Jeff said, his eye to the barely open door.

"I don't think it will be a long interview," Liddy said. "He promised not to slug him, but he didn't make any other concessions."

"When does this tripe air?"

"This afternoon. Almost right away."

"I'm worried someone from City Council will see it. You'll piss them off if you don't call them first."

"They'll be pissed no matter what, but I'm going to call Abbott." She peered through the door. Alec seemed to be holding his own, his answers monosyllabic. He was so boring that Osborne probably wouldn't use any more of him than he had to. Steve Bowman kept making excited little gestures at Alec, to which Alec remained oblivious, or appeared to.

Liddy pulled Jeff away from the door. "Why have you got such an attitude about Osborne?"

"He's crass," Jeff said. He managed to look abashed. "And I didn't like the way he looked at you."

"Oh?" Liddy crossed the hall into the living room, mercifully empty for a change, and curled herself into the corner of the sofa, pushing a huge standing arrangement of gladiolas away from her ear. She looked up at Jeff from its spiky shadows.

Jeff sat down next to her. "I'm as capable of being a possessive idiot as the next man," he offered. "I talked to Cousin Elise for you."

Liddy had forgotten Cousin Elise. She remembered her now. "How did she take it?"

"She was pretty horrified. She kept saying, 'Such a shame.'"

"Is there anyone else who should know?"

"A couple more old cousins, I think. She said she'd call them."

"How did she sound?" Liddy felt solicitous, as if she had abandoned Cousin Elise and now must make it up.

"Like a nice old lady whose cousin just shot himself. I told her we didn't have any idea why. She said nobody but God can look in a man's heart. I liked her. We schmoozed a long time. I told her I'd seen him, and he was holding on."

"Is she coming up here?"

"I don't think so. She uses a walker. She said she'd stay in Westwood and pray."

"Thank God. I feel like I ought to tell her to come up, though."

"Why?"

"I feel guilty. As if I'm not doing the right thing. As if I'm not doing enough."

"You're doing plenty," Jeff said. "You've already got enough personnel to fill an asylum up here. You don't need a nice old Jewish lady in a walker, who probably keeps kosher."

"All right, I don't. I just feel like I ought to have her. She's a holocaust survivor. She shouldn't have more horribleness."

"So you're going to subject her to Francie threatening to cut Frank's dick off and the tabloids tricking her into saying God knows what?"

"Oh, God, you're right. I just feel responsible."

"You didn't make Ben shoot himself. That was me if it was anybody, and I refuse to take the blame. Ben had his own agenda."

Liddy pulled a bud off the bottom of a gladiola and picked it open. "I don't know," she said. "Because I didn't stop it?"

"Yeah, right."

"And then I leaned on you," Liddy said to the gladiola. "I let you go to the hospital. I let you talk to Cousin Elise."

"What's wrong with that?"

"I don't have any right to lean on you."

"Why not?"

Liddy stuffed the gladiola bud down between the sofa cushions. Her eyes welled with tears. She had thought it would be effective if she could cry for Rick Donald Osborne, but they wouldn't come. Now they spilled out involuntarily. "Because I went off and left Liza Jane, and left you to pick up everything. Take care of her. Be the kid she wanted. And then I come waltzing back in." She went on crying, sniffling into his shirtfront now. "And there's too much damn history all over the place."

"Everybody's damn history. Museum of emotional baggage." Jeff held her carefully, as if she were an egg. "You want to make something out of it or shall we just go shoot ourselves?"

"Those are our only options?" She could hear his heart

pounding under his shirt, a fast deep rhythm of blood.

"They're the only options I can see," he said.

There was an odd flavor in the air. Theresa thought maybe the bean sprout people were right after all. It was like static electricity. Small clouds of energy passed, spewing sparks, spitting and recoiling from each other, while the miasma of Ben's attempted suicide clung to them like a damp curtain, holding them together. Theresa hobbled into the kitchen on her crutches and set about helping Bernice feed people. Donald Wain called to ask her why the hell she was still staying in that loony bin, and she told him that the funeral was on Monday.

"Damned woman has to inconvenience everyone one more time," he snarled. "I'm taking you home after that. No business gadding about on crutches at your age."

Theresa hung up and called Roberto Vincente and told him, too.

Vincente sniffed mournfully. "She was my girl. Always my girl. Who is this fellow that shot himself in her bathtub?" His voice was thick with suspicion.

"It didn't have anything to do with Liza Jane," Theresa said firmly.

"And I didn't even ask him how he knew about it so soon," she said to Bernice.

"Crook radar," Jeff said. He came into the kitchen with Liddy and stuck his head in the refrigerator. "People bring him things, little bones they think he'll want to know about."

"I called Abbott," Liddy said. "He was practically hysterical, but I told him he could get a court order and come dig her up again if he wants to, but the funeral is going to be on Monday. And on national television."

"Oh, no!" Bernice said.

"It's a trade-off," Liddy said wearily. "Do we want her where she wanted to be? Do we want the rest of the goddamn will valid? I told him if it all went to me, I'd sell the Harding Adobe to that developer, Benshoof. You might call a few other people and tell them that, let them work on Abbott."

"You did fine," Jeff said. He emerged from the refrigerator with an apple. "Give old Abbott the weekend to think things over. Figure out where his bread's buttered."

Liddy looked at the enchiladas Bernice was stuffing. "How many people are going to be here?"

"Nearly all of them, I expect," Bernice said. "They always want to put their heads together, like cows in a blizzard, when something dreadful happens."

"Where's Mike? Has anybody seen him?"

"He's coming over," Bernice said. "I think he's trying to get his nerve up. Frank talked to him early this morning, and said he was pretty distraught."

"Sharon's lying in wait for him," Theresa said.

"And where's Harry?" Liddy demanded. "What are we paying Harry for? Harry can sit on Sharon."

"He went to talk to Arlo Sheppard," Jeff said. "I confessed our midnight grave-digging, and he said, 'Oh, Christ,' and called Arlo."

A door opened and closed in the front of the house. "Here's Mike, I imagine," Bernice said. She went on stuffing enchiladas. "Mike will have to face up to Sharon eventually."

Theresa hobbled to the kitchen door. Furious voices came clearly down the hall, a chorus of snarls and shrieks. "That's not Sharon. Oh, my God, he's brought that harpy with him."

Jeff and Liddy looked at each other and headed for the hall, both with Rick Donald Osborne on their minds.

Mike was there but Francie didn't appear to have come with him. The young leader of last night's band was looking around Liza Jane's house with interest. Dark hair hung lankly around his shoulders and he was dressed in yesterday's black jeans and t-shirt. Francie was shrieking at Mike.

"I want to see him! You go find him or I'll fucking find him myself! So much for his goddamn picture now, his director's a vegetable in the hospital, so what's he going to do about the settlement now?"

"Francie, shut up—" Mike tried to put a hand on her arm.

Jeff bypassed them to turn the dark-haired band leader around toward the door. "You go on home, son. Just figure you spent the night with Circe and got out alive."

"She made me bring her, man." The band leader squinted as he stepped into the sun again. "We got back to the Horsehead, you know, where she's staying, and she like went ballistic." He stumbled on the third step down and seemed to think of something. "Uh— like don't let her drive, man. She's really stoned."

Jeff nodded. He watched while the band leader managed to get his car door open, and winced as the car wove out onto Del Norte. It was like watching his youth drive away with a bad hangover. Still, if the kid had survived a night with Francie Allen, it probably wasn't in his karma to die today. Jeff went back in the house to see what he could do about Francie.

She had found Frank, or rather he had been dragged from his lair by the prospect of her being turned loose on Rick Donald. Sharon came down the stairs behind him, saw Mike, and spat, "I hope you're satisfied now!"

Liddy had closed the door to the library and stood with her back to it, but it was a lost cause.

"Are you gonna get out of here now, Frank?" Francie

screamed. "Your picture's dead because some asshole shot himself and I'm getting phone calls about it, wanting to know if I was involved!" The words came out in a hoarse screech. "I've had it, Frank!"

Frank looked as if he wanted to bolt back upstairs. The library doors opened, despite Liddy's best efforts.

"Francie, sweetheart," Steve Bowman said.

"An unexpected pleasure," Rick Donald said. He surged forward, trailing his camera crew.

"You take any film of me and I'll stuff your camera up your ass," Francie said.

"Rick Donald Osborne." Osborne held his hand out. "It's a thrill to meet you."

Francie said, "Whoever you are, you want a hot news tip? I'll give you a hot news tip. My husband's trying to take every penny I earned, he's trying to take land that's in my name." She spun around, arm extended, and tried to punch Frank. He grabbed her wrist and twisted it.

"Ow! Let me go, you motherfucker! I'll tell you something else. He used to smack me around, that's why I left him. I was a battered wife! The motherfucker gave me a black eye."

"You fell over the coffee table!" Frank pushed her away from him, teeth clenched. He pointed at Rick Donald. "If any of this ends up on your show, I'll see you in hell. You got that?"

"Calm down, sweetheart," Steve Bowman said. "Rick Donald, I don't know what to say. You can see we're in the middle of a little domestic spat here." He edged Rick Donald toward the door. "Let me thank you for coming. I think we got some exciting stuff. Murray was maybe a little stiff, but I think Mrs. Novak gave your fans what they want to see." Murray was still sitting on the sofa in the library, with about the Q-rating of a rock, the way he'd been all through the interview.

Captain Midnight's bowed out, Jeff thought. He couldn't say

he blamed him. "Come on, doll." He got an arm around Francie and smiled at her before she could slug him. "You want to give Frank hell, you got to let everyone calm down for a while. You're going to crash in a minute, I bet you've been up all night, you might as well come on upstairs and find a place to sleep it off."

Francie gave Frank a venomous look. "Take me to your place then," she said to Jeff.

"Nope, no way, you'll scare my cat. Come on and maybe I'll sit with you for a while, you can tell me what a son of a bitch old Frank is." He edged her up the stairs.

"I'll fix him," Francie said. "I don't know why I married him."

"Maybe you should try to figure that out before you fix him," Jeff said.

"What the hell do you know?"

"Not much." He turned her into Liddy's room and dumped her in the four-poster bed.

She looked up at him with marble-blue eyes. "I don't know anything. Just the music. I thought Frank could tell me the rest, but he wouldn't."

"Frank took off," Liddy informed Jeff when he came downstairs. "What did you do with her?"

"Put her in your bed. I sat with her until she passed out."

Liddy groaned.

"You can sleep in mine. I promise I'll keep my hands off you. Come on."

They went out the front and around the house, past where the stone mason was working on the veranda. Bernice and Theresa were still making enchiladas in the kitchen, insulated from things they wanted no part of by a cloud of steam and the heavy smell of chilies. Mike and Sharon were standing by the koi pond, as if the chilies had banished them and their quarrel, away from the domesticity of enchiladas.

"Liza Jane was the one who liked all the upheaval," Liddy said. "I'm almost sorry she's missing this, but it's making Bernice miserable."

Jeff chuckled. "Bernice is a homebody at heart. An old socialist homebody."

The pugs had followed Liddy. Jeff whistled to them and they bounced forward through the dry leaves.

"I have to learn which one's which," Liddy said.

"This is Mu," Jeff said. "And Stu, and Boo, and Phoo the Second."

1976

Phoo the First is watching Liza Jane make coconut cookies, his pop eyes hopeful for anything that might fall. Liza Jane will be sixty-eight tomorrow, and she is still too old to be somebody's mother, particularly an eighteen-year-old with a crazy sixteen-year-old boyfriend. She is making cookies with the vague idea that it's the right thing to do, although possibly a little late, Liddy and Jeff being well past the cookies-and-a-soda stage of courtship and into the deeper waters of a break-up. Liddy is going east to college in six weeks. They might last another year.

Liza Jane checks the oven temperature. A lot of people are coming tomorrow for her birthday and Bernice has Opinions about her clogging up the kitchen when Bernice has cooking to do, so she needs to wind this project up.

She is sorry for Jeff, but she's sorrier for Liddy. Liddy is drowning in Ayala. Liza Jane's house is too full of people who take up too much room. Liddy needs breathing space to find out who she is besides a famous person's niece.

Liza Jane loves Jeff, but Jeff is too young. An accusing voice out of memory tells her she hasn't set much of an example. She can't argue with that, considering Frank. But they were all finite. She knew that. Except for Don. She pictures herself in a cute apron, making cookies, stirring up coq au vin for Don's buddies and their wives, lost in the candy box. Not acting.

By the time she gave him back the ring, the communist-hunters were looking for blood. Donald Wain Sr. was a loud supporter of the blacklist, howling for the head of anyone tainted by suspected lack of patriotism, and he made clear his disapproval of his son's wife continuing to act. That coincided with her picture in *The New York Times* with Roberto Vincente, so it's hard to say which was the last straw for Don.

Liza Jane scrapes the mixing bowl clean, puts the coconut cookies in the oven, and the bowl down for the pugs. She's not sure why she decided to make them. She doesn't like coconut cookies; it was Ben who used to like those.

You could have married Ben and kept acting, memory points out. But I wasn't in love with Ben, Liza Jane thinks mournfully. Ben was too young too anyway and there was too much loss underlying those years. He's coming tomorrow for her birthday with his second wife. She never sees Don, only pictures in *Forbes* or *Fortune,* and sometimes in the newspaper. Don is still worried about the communists getting to Mars before the U.S. does. It's always a shock to see that he's old.

The pugs have worked the mixing bowl under the kitchen table and polished it clean. Liza Jane picks it up to put in the dishwasher. She looks out the kitchen window at the oak grove in the slanted afternoon light. She's supposed to go on location again in a few weeks, but she feels like a dryad now, tethered this bit of forest, growing less and less willing to leave it.

Outside, Liddy and Jeff have settled the argument they were having and are singing along, loudly, with Steeleye Span on a cassette player and dancing around the veranda like maniacs, pretending nothing is wrong.

Still I sing bonny boys, bonny mad boys
Bedlam boys are bonny
For they all go bare and they live by the air
And they want no drink nor money

A florist's van pulls up in the driveway and the pugs hurl themselves at the front door, barking madly. Liddy and Jeff go down the veranda steps to meet the van. Liddy knows what it is, because Liza Jane's birthday is tomorrow. Roberto Vincente always sends roses.

The delivery man hands the bouquet to Liddy, a dozen blood red ones in a vase. She buries her face in their petals and wonders if someone will love her that much, and for that long.

XIV
Recessional

1988

Alec wondered if the hushed atmosphere of the NICU was as much to intimidate visitors into obedience as to signify the importance of its operations. He stood in front of the nurses' station, feeling foolish and clutching a vase of chrysanthemums from the gift shop downstairs. What did you give to somebody who'd tried to kill himself and hadn't managed it? Did flowers signify consolation or congratulations? It didn't matter, because a nurse who reminded him of the sisters at his grammar school looked up and said firmly, "No flowers in the NICU."

"Oh." Alec put them on the counter.

She sighed, as if people were always leaving her flowers.

"I came to ask about Ben Zenovich," he said. "How he's doing."

The nurse smiled at that. "He's awake this morning. You can go in for a few minutes. It will do him good."

"Awake?" Alec had come to make a ritual visit, leave ritual flowers, ask God knew what pardon from the unconscious form. He hadn't counted on Ben being awake.

"Yes, indeed. We're very pleased. And it will do him good to know there are folks who care. That's what they always need the most." The nurse smiled again, encouraging.

"Um." Alec went through the NICU doors and stopped inside to blink in the dim light. Ben's bed was nearest the door, his face recognizable even with the bandage. He was propped up, half sitting, looking at something invisible which apparently inhabited the far wall just above another patient's IV drip.

Alec stood by the bed, waiting for Ben to notice him. He tried to formulate things to say; but when Ben looked at him, what he said was, "Why the hell did you use my gun?"

Ben's face was still gray, his lips cracked. He licked them, waved a hand at a cup of ice.

Alec handed it to him. "I'm sorry. I didn't mean to..." He looked around vaguely for other, better words.

"Sit down," Ben said. It sounded as if it was an effort to talk, barely manageable and fuzzy through the painkillers.

Alec sat in the hard plastic chair by the bed.

"Never tried to...kill myself before," Ben said. "Told me...I may still buy it."

"What did you do it for?"

"Go figure."

"I figured," Alec said. "Austin didn't know he shouldn't have told you that."

"Doesn't matter," Ben said. "There was more. Sorry I used your gun, though." He sounded regretful, as if it had been thoughtless.

"Then why did you do it at the house?"

"You were there," Ben said. "Thought you'd take over...deal with it."

"No, I couldn't," Alec said. They all seemed to think his job made him a person with authority in any circumstance.

Ben smiled. It came out lopsided. "Poor Bernice. She's...hated my...guts for years."

"She took the can of film out of there," Alec said. "Before anyone got there."

"I know. I saw her."

"Saw her?"

"You know...they talk about being...up by the ceiling...looking down? You really do. At least a couple seconds. I saw her take the can. She...grabbed it and said, 'You son of a bitch.'"

Alec tried to decide if this was a genuine near-death experience, or the dope they were giving him. The quote from Bernice sounded accurate.

"She gave it to me," Alec said.

"You give it to the cops?"

"No."

"Crooked Cop Hides Can." Ben lifted the cup of ice to his mouth again. "Liza Jane... Damn woman...never told me. I was there, she never told me."

"What the hell use was it to kill yourself?" Alec asked him.

"Didn't like what I saw in the mirror," Ben said. "Maybe...I'll learn to live with it. If I get bald...scar'll show. Reminder, you know?"

"The funeral's tomorrow," Alec said.

"Tell Frank I said cry over her for me. They won't...let me out till they're sure...not going to have a hemorrhage. Or infection. Bullet's still in there. Damnedest feeling knowing it's there."

The nurse at the central desk glided across the linoleum. "Mr. Zenovich needs to rest now."

Alec stood up. Ben reached a hand toward him. "Where's the film?"

"I have it."

"Tell you anything?"

"Now," the nurse said firmly.

"Wait..." Ben said. "What are you going to do? Go back to cop work?"

Alec looked around him, as if answers might be written on the NICU wall between the patient charts. "I don't know."

"Gonna need a consultant," Ben said. "On...picture I screwed up shooting myself. Someone knows the drug racket. Frank says...background is flat."

Alec was amused. "In Hollywood?"

"Need a cop," Ben said. "You said you're a movie freak. Come see...how they're made...like...laws and sausage. Ought to disillusion you." Ben's voice was fading.

"You're going to sleep, Mr. Zenovich," the nurse said. "We won't have you overstress yourself just when you're doing so nicely." She looked at Alec. "You can come back later."

The NICU door swooshed open, closed again. Ben leaned back against the pillow and closed his eyes. He wondered what was going to happen now that he hadn't died. Maybe Murray would really show up. A million dollars wasn't all that much money these days. Maybe he'd figure out how not to fall through a hole in the ground with it, find a way to keep his vision of himself reliable, not dark with erasures, not like Ben's. Liza Jane would like knowing that. It was all he had to offer her, besides the bullet in his head.

By Monday there wasn't a hotel room to be had in Ayala. Harry said disgustedly that it might as well have been the Tennis Tournament or the Jazz Festival. "You couldn't manage a quiet funeral?"

"After all the histrionics, we'll be lucky if we can bathe without a reporter in the tub," Liddy said. "A couple of them were trying to get at Zach yesterday for an angle—the poor kid can't even go outside to play."

"That when this was taken?" Harry handed her a tabloid. Her face adorned the cover, snarling, teeth bared, a mother warthog defending her young.

Liza Jane's Tragic Niece Despondent
Over Suicide Attempt
Amazing Love Triangle Story

Liddy wondered how much trouble it would be to go back to Charlottesville and explain these things. "Did the people from the City Council come yet?"

"Arlo's wrestling with them," Harry said. "I thought maybe you weren't up to it."

"You thought I'd lose it and scream at them."

"Steve's taking all calls in the office."

"I trust he'll inform us if we should happen to get a personal one."

"If anybody can get through. The only people with an open line around here are the media, and they bounce it off satellites."

The driveway was choked with their trucks, adorned with dish antennas on long, articulated arms. The Ayala cops were trying to keep out anyone with no legitimate business. They had closed the wrought-iron gates across the drive. Beyond them Del Norte was clogged with people on foot, and in bumper-to-bumper cars, kids on bikes and skateboards. If the City Council wanted to dig her up again, they would be notorious forever.

"Have you seen Mr. Benshoof?" Liddy asked Harry.

"Not yet. I think you're crazy."

"He's ammunition. I want Abbott and the City Council to get a look at him."

"And what do you do when Benshoof finds out you're stringing him along? He's got a reputation as a tough."

"He's not tougher than Roberto Vincente." Liddy looked at her watch. The funeral was at two. An hour to go. Vincente and everyone else were here already. Mike looked as if he was under a strain, but holding up. Frank had the blank expression he put on when forced to appear in public with crowds of people he didn't know. Francie was there too, in a short, tight black dress and fishnet stockings, apparently her idea of funeral attire. She was quiet, but she watched Frank with the furious avidity of a cobra on speed.

Rick Donald Osborne was there, outside in his mobile unit, and Will Chapman from the *Times* was in the living room. Liddy wondered in what guise she and the rest would appear tomorrow, or in the case of the television stations, tonight. Beamed up to a satellite, bounced back to L.A., or Charlottesville, or Pittsburgh. What would Alec's mother think of them? Alec had been quiet all weekend, a little distant, as if he were back to being someone she didn't know. Maybe it was because what might have been going to happen between them now so obviously was not. Or it might have been Ben. Liddy couldn't be sure. She felt conceited taking too much on herself. Alec was at the front door now, playing bouncer to anyone who got past the police. Jeff had been in the kitchen all morning, guarding that door, and showing Zach how to roll sushi. Liddy had been afraid to send Zach to camp, plowing through the media and the autograph hounds in the street.

Tony the torpedo was there too, sticking close to his boss. Roberto Vincente had sent another huge vase full of blood-red roses and offered once again to lean on the City Council.

The City Council were bending, Arlo reported. He came out of the library with a look that indicated he might be beginning to have a good time. "They aren't going to say anything definite," he told Liddy. "They just won't file any action, and there may be a very quiet zoning change, affecting this parcel only. They're a little uneasy about it, though. They're afraid you might want to bury somebody else here."

"I might," Liddy said.

"I've assured them that you won't."

Mr. Benshoof appeared, simultaneously with the rector of St. Anne's. Liddy greeted the rector and collected Mr. Benshoof, pointing him at the oak grove.

Benshoof was well known in Ayala, the subject of several court cases between the city and landowners who wanted to sell to him. Margaret Collins looked aghast when she saw him, and held out one hand in what might have been a gesture against the evil eye. Mr. Abbott and two colleagues from the council eyed him with resentful respect, as if he were a missile of some kind, a type of nuclear deterrent. They got in their car and eased it out through the police and the mobile units and the crowd at the gates. They might be going to concede, but they stopped short of giving the proceedings their blessing.

The congregation in the house filed dutifully down the front steps and along the brick path around the garden to the oak grove. Jeff and Zach were escorting Francie Allen. Liddy saw Jeff deposit Francie on the other side of Mr. Benshoof, who liked a pretty girl and had more money than Donald Trump. Benshoof could probably stand up to the experience. Liddy looked around for Alec and found him alone, away from the crowd, on the other side of an oak tree.

"Are you okay?" She felt tentative, apologetic. If you started to make love to a man once, they always assumed you still wanted to.

"I was trying to think of something to give her," Alec said. "Liza Jane. Something to take along." He sounded preoccupied and it dawned on Liddy that he didn't want to make love to her now, either. Maybe telling her the things he had had been the intimacy he had wanted, or needed. How many chances did someone like Alec get?

"To take along?"

"Some prayer. I can't think of the right one. 'Pray for us sinners now and at the hour of our death?'"

"Seems a little late. Unless you mean you."

"Dunno," Alec said. "Zenovich says I should come and see how movies are made. Be a consultant."

"Are you going to?"

"I might. I'd like to see what 'based on a true story' means."

"Why are you hiding over here then?"

"Cowardice, I guess. If one more jackass asks me anything, I may deck him, get in the papers again. I'm not good at this. You people seem to have a handle on it, but—"

"Only with our backs to the wall." It occurred to Liddy that he had said "you people" and that she hadn't denied she was one of them.

"I'm leaving when this is over with," Alec said. "Thin out the crowd in your house a little."

"Right away?"

"I've got a can of old film, I've got Frank Hill's autograph for my mom. I figure it's time. They can send me a check, if and when."

"When," Liddy said.

"When. I guess now I will be upset if I don't get it."

She would bet he'd do it. She would bet he went and hung around movie sets with Ben while they worked out whatever strange kinship a gun and an abortion had given them. Anyone who had handled the underworld should be able to handle Hollywood.

"Don't go without saying goodbye. Please." She put her hand

in his. There was still a faint electricity there. He gave it a squeeze and they walked back to the crowd standing around the cairn of stones. Jeff and Zach were waiting for her.

It didn't look the way graves in cemeteries looked. Not neatly aligned, or springing from emerald turf with the new raw brown dirt sad and barren. There was no turf, just the carpet of oak leaves, and Jeff had raked them over the grave like a blanket, as if she had gone to bed there, burrowing down out of the world. The headstone was ordered and would come, but Liddy was going to leave the cairn of stones. Noel Ballinger, the rector of St. Anne's, stood beside it, prayer book in hand. A little breeze came up and fluttered his purple vestments and black tippet. He looked acutely conscious that his picture was being taken. The legitimate camera crews hovered behind the mourners and the unauthorized lurked in the shrubbery with telephoto lenses. Beyond the police and the gates, the crowd in the streets made a restless, murmuring noise, as if they were all chanting 'Rhubarb.' Most of Hollywood appeared to have made the drive up 101, and the gravel circle in front of the house, and the edges of Del Norte were lined with important black cars. The sightseers were prepared to stay until nightfall, and the celebrities penned in Liza Jane's oak grove would have to be escorted out.

"I am the resurrection and the life," Noel Ballinger said.

Everyone hushed and turned toward him. Liddy felt Jeff's arm slip around her waist. She looked up at him and saw that he was crying. Bernice stood just across the grave from them, her heavy ringed hands twisting the trim that edged the pocket of her skirt. Theresa was in her wheelchair beside Bernice. Donald Wain stood behind Theresa, arranging a filmy shawl around her shoulders, but his eyes were on the grave. His lower lip wobbled and he looked to Liddy appallingly old.

Eventually the congregation was gone, and the media were gone, and the gawkers in the street and the powerful cars; and Alec was gone, with the can of film in his suitcase and the gun that the police had given back to him in its holster under his coat. Harry and Sharon and Theresa were gone, and Frank. Liddy supposed that the others at the Horsehead Ranch were gone, too. The world felt drained, a bottle tipped suddenly on its side. Zach was slouching on a kitchen chair, eating a leftover cream cheese and olive sandwich. He would probably have been able to believe it was a dream if anyone had told him so.

Bernice took off her apron, surveyed a kitchen full of clean dishes, nothing left of the funeral now but the leftovers in the refrigerator, and the flowers in the library and living room. She took the sandwich crust out of Zach's inert hand. "I'll take him upstairs," she said to Liddy. "Turn out the lights when you come up."

Turn out the lights, a householder's duty.

Jeff came through the door from the hall. "The street's clear," he said. "Not a soul to be seen, except for Robaniss next door and he's just mad about the trash in his driveway. I picked most of it up and I took a walk around the grove. Tried to pick up some kind of vibrations. I couldn't tell. I think she's happy down there. Maybe she'll come back as an oak tree."

"I don't think you get to come back as something else," Liddy said. "You have to keep coming back as yourself until you get it right."

Jeff looked at her solemnly. "Life as an endless film loop. Condemned to repeat forever the third grade wet pants, the senior math final, the Las Vegas marriage...into the mists of eternity." He laughed.

"I don't think I could stand it," Liddy said.

Jeff spread his hands out, palms up. "Run it again," he said. "We aren't a movie. It might come out different."

1990

Liza Jane is thirty-five and her nose is thinner and turned up, but that doesn't matter; Frank knows who she is. It doesn't matter that Liza Jane was older than that. The young actress playing Annie, which is what Liza Jane is called in the script, isn't who Frank is seeing anyway. He's seeing Liza Jane as Queen Elizabeth, just the way she looked on the screen when he was fourteen. That was when he knew he wanted to make movies.

Frank has wrapped the picture he was making with Ben. He'll make others with Ben directing, but not this one. Ben's got a funny tilt to his head, but other than that you wouldn't know what happened. The doctors say it may straighten up, or not. Alec Murray is working for him.

Meanwhile the picture is getting a lot of press. The blacklist is part of Hollywood's collective memory, and the industry is suddenly scrambling to demonstrate its newfound accountability in an orgy of self-criticism. Will Chapman has written two columns about it.

Frank looks at the actress playing Annie and tells her that her hair's too red. The script is thick with changes in multicolored inks that Frank wants typed by tomorrow. Frank is directing and starring. It makes him the cog around which the whole project revolves, insulates him from Francie and Sharon and Mike. Mike gets screen credit and a piece of the gross, but the picture belongs to Frank now.

He slips on the character like an overcoat. The set is a

soundstage, a set within a set, movies stacked inside each other like nesting boxes, like a reverberating phrase. This movie needs to be made and Mike's script is good, but he was too close to it. Frank's made small changes to broaden the picture. The nature of art is to tell truth, not necessarily actual facts. Small facts don't matter. Big ones do. Liza Jane told him that once.

AUTHOR'S NOTE

My parents were screenwriters. They were never, so far as they knew, blacklisted. There were times when they just didn't get work. It might have been the usual inconvenience of a freelance career. It might have been something else. Maybe someone had mentioned them, maybe their names were similar to someone's, maybe anything. Then they got work again, and didn't ask, because you couldn't ask.

Michael Wilson, whom Bernice talks about in her explanation of the blacklist to Alec, was a family friend. In 1951 he appeared as an "unfriendly witness" before the House Un-American Activities Committee and was subsequently blacklisted. In 1976 he gave this speech to the Writers Guild of America, West. It seems to me extremely prescient.

> I don't want to dwell on the past, but for a few moments to speak of the future. And I address my remarks particularly to you younger men and women who had perhaps not established yourselves in this industry at the time of the great witch hunt. I feel that unless you remember this dark epoch and understand it, you may be doomed to replay it. Not with the same cast of characters, of course, or on the same issues. But I see a day perhaps coming in your lifetime, if not in mine, when a new crisis of belief will grip this republic; when diversity of opinion will be labelled disloyalty; and when extraordinary pressures will be put on writers in the mass media to conform to administration policy on the key issues of the time, whatever they may be. If this gloomy scenario should come to pass, I trust that you younger men and women will shelter the mavericks and dissenters in your ranks, and protect their right to work. The Guild will have the use and need of rebels if it is to survive as a union of free writers. This nation will have need of them if it is to survive as an open society.

Mike died in 1978. In 1986 he was given posthumous screen credit for *The Bridge on the River Kwai* and other films, and his wife and daughters were presented with his Oscar. I am grateful to the Writers Guild of America, West and the late Zelma Wilson for permission to quote from this speech. I am also grateful to Jeanne Larsen for permission to use the perfect quotation from her novel *Silk Road* as an epigraph.

Thank you also to Lenore Hart and David Poyer of Northampton House Press for agreeing that the subject was uncomfortably timely.

For readers interested in the history and legacy of the Hollywood blacklist, and the lasting damage it did, there are excellent books on the subject, including *Naming Names* by Victor Navasky, *The Inquisition in Hollywood* by Larry Ceplair and Steven Englund, and *Tender Comrades* by Patrick McGilligan and Paul Buhle, among many others.

Amanda Cockrell is the former director of the MFA program in children's and young adult literature at Hollins University. Her previous novels include *Coyote Weather*, *What We Keep Is Not Always What Will Stay*, the *Deer Dancers* trilogy and the *Horse Catchers* trilogy. She has received fellowships in fiction from the National Endowment for the Arts and the Virginia Commission for the Arts. Visit her at www.amandacockrell.com.

READY FOR MORE GOOD READING?

If you enjoyed this novel, you'll also like Amanda Cockrell's *Coyote Weather*, also from Northampton House Press.

Coyote weather is the feral, hungry season, when everything is drought-stricken and ready to catch fire. It's 1967 and the American culture is violently remaking itself while the country is forcibly sending its young men to fight in a deeply unpopular war. Jerry has stubbornly made no plans for the future because he doesn't think that, in the shadow of Vietnam, the Cold War and atomic bomb drills, there is going to be one. Ellen is determined to have a plan, because nothing else seems capable of keeping the world from tilting. And the Ghost, who isn't exactly dead, just wants to go home to a place that won't let him in, the small California town where they all grew up.

Available online or through any independent bookstore.

Northampton House Press

Established in 2011, Northampton House Press publishes selected fiction, nonfiction, memoir, and poetry. Check out our list at www.northampton-house.com, and Like us on Facebook – "Northampton House Press" – as we showcase more innovative works from brilliant new talents.